One Good Thing

ෆ ෨

ONE

GOOD

THING

Patrick McGowan

Polar Bear & Company
An imprint of the
Solon Center for Research and Publishing
Solon & Rockland, Maine

Polar Bear & Company™
Solon Center for Research and Publishing
20 Main Street, Rockland, ME 04841
207.643.2795, polarbearandco.org, soloncenter.org

ISBN: 978-1-882190-81-2
First print edition, first printing March 2018
Library of Congress Control Number: 2018934099

This book is a work of fiction. Names, characters, places, and in-
cidents either are products of the author's imagination or are used
fictitiously. Any resemblance to actual events or locales or persons,
living or dead, is entirely coincidental.

Manufactured on durable, acid-free paper in more than one country.

To my mother, Ann, who taught us to read and write and has written one million words of goodness and light.

Contents

Author's Note

For a million years humankind had not been able to fly through the sky like a bird; it was surely one of our most disappointing shortcomings. Then in a flash we were flying to and from a short hot sand dune, the cold and mighty North Atlantic, from one end of the continent to the other. We were flying and seeing things never seen before, new lands, new peoples, cultures and civilizations. This was the greatest gift in a million years, a gift from God through the science of man. A splendid most beautiful arrival, with men and woman piloting the way.

Because it was a divine gift through homo sapiens, the human touch was all over the history and development of flight. The crashes of early warplanes, covered in butyrate, set afire by weaponry, brought flyers to the ground in exploding carnage and turned the heads of onlookers and survivors. Smooth landings onto water and landing strips caused a nod of appreciation, as one more receiver of the gift mastered the craft. The cough of a weather beast would strike a craft from a cloud-covered world, smashing it into a hill or a mountain, killing all inside the craft and nearby, as it pummeled the earth. My friends who died in flight, I picture you floating above the clouds in peace.

Designers and engineers came forward, as guided by a flyer from another world, drawing lines and curves to make the craft a better avian through the skies. Some may have seen a goddess, a beautiful, naked woman, standing upright with her arms spread at an angle to her body and her toes pointed, her fingers pointed, and her face tilted to the sun. Her body might have turned away from the craftsmen, and she became the inspiration for the paper-drawn design of not just a machine—a ship of the skies, from an angelic image.

Hurtling through the heavens, with a quarter of an inch of aluminum and plastic glass protecting them, ride millions every day around the world with little knowledge of the gift the airplane and pilot are providing them. This is the great advancement that human life has achieved on this planet.

We flew over the mountains and around the pond in the river and found the place of happiness and safe keeping. Others have not arrived; they are still on the beaten human path searching for specks of gold in the trail. From the time I could reflect, I dreamed myself a flyer in the skies. I would listen to a branch against my window at five years of age; it scared me. I would fly myself away in pre-dream consciousness to that place over the mountain and around the pond in the river. The safety place. I am approaching my sixth decade on earth; I still go to that place when I am troubled before sleep. Among the themes of this book are flyers and adventure; please read and enjoy and appreciate all of your gifts, given they are so many, in this short flight of life.

1

The time a man's eyes go their widest happens the instant before he meets a violent death in a fiery crash. It is the moment the human brain works its fastest. Mac McCabe was this wide-eyed man, falling in an uncontrolled spin from hundreds of feet in the air in a fifty-year-old, two-seater aircraft. He was in the front seat. His passenger in the rear seat was an overweight man with incredible pre-death strength, grabbing for anything that he could reach. The passenger did not know how to fly an airplane; all of his moves were counter to the man in the front seat trying to save both their lives. The big man in the back reached for the control stick and extended his legs in a violent jerk to the right rudder pedal of the airplane. The plane was spinning violently to the left. All of the wind had been taken from its wings four hundred feet over the threshold of Runway 35 at the Augusta State Airport in the sweltering heat of a July summer day.

Maria Jacques had just arrived in SUV heaven. She had finally bought the best-looking Chevrolet Suburban on the lot at O'Connor's GMC in Augusta. It was cream-colored and the modern-day equivalent of a land yacht. She drove it around town just to be seen. Her two children, Paul age six and Monique age four, were with her, as ever. She had worked and saved for the down payment for three years, and now she had an eight-year-zero-percent loan that would keep her in debt until GMAC Finance released its ugly clutches. Though that's how she sometimes felt, she cared nothing about any of that now. She was parked at the McDonald's on Western Avenue for the third time this week, buying her kids Happy Meals with two plastic Minion toys from the latest Pixar movie. She had the meals and the toys and her beautiful children in tow. Her job was safe with the State, and she was as free as a bird riding around the capital city. The seats were cooled, the temperature controlled, and the ride was smooth.

She looked left and right around the parking lot to see if any of her friends could see her in this beautiful ride with all the options and Thule rack on the roof. It was a one-thousand-dollar add-on option, and she wanted people to know it was hers. She looked up and froze in shock. A green-and-white airplane was low in the sky, but it was not landing on the runway, as she had seen thousands land in her hometown over the years. The propeller was screaming wide open, and the aircraft was like a shot missile headed directly at her and her children. She snapped back to life, grabbed her children up around her, and became the protective mother bear saving their lives as only she knew how. The airplane was out of control. She could see the face of the pilot with his insanely wide eyes. Death was at her and her children's doors.

Mac McCabe had flown thousands of hours at the controls of small planes. This airplane did not belong to him; it was a friend who owned it, and now it would be demolished in a fiery crash in the McDonald's parking lot in Augusta. He saw the children, he heard the engine turning at full rpms, and he could feel his idiot passenger messing with the controls, while the pilot was trying to pull it out of a fast spin. Mac swung the fist of his free arm backwards as hard as he could, hitting his passenger squarely in the jaw.

"Stop! Don't touch anything! You will kill us!" He yelled as loudly as he could at his friend who, an hour before, was fishing a peaceful stream in the Rangeley Lakes region of Maine, only an hour's flight from their current death spin. The rising trout, the sunshine on his face, were a world away. How quickly things can change.

The big man's foot could not be stopped, but the man unknowingly made a life-saving stomp that countered the spin to the left as the pilot pushed the nose of the airplane down. The size-twelve L.L.Bean boot provided the extra tail control that brought the Piper Super Cub out of the death spin. Mac could feel the control come back to the wings as the wind passed over the top, but he feared it was too late. The right main landing gear came crashing down on top of the Thule rack on top of Maria's new ride. The container split into pieces and the propeller just barely missed the windshield of the Suburban. Maria, shaking, held tighter to her children and crossed herself, shuddering out a "Hail Mary full of Grace, thou art with me."

The airplane's nose came up, under the hand of thirty years of skilled piloting. It limped away like a disorganized kite but slowly gained the composure and speed needed to fly back up to the approach of the high runway above the busy street. Mac's mind was racing. His heart pumping, he slowly eased back on the throttle with his left hand. He would live. His friend would live. Now he needed to land this wounded bird and find the bastard who almost caused the death of himself and his fishing mate.

Back at the airfield, a sixty-million-dollar jet taxied to a stop at the end of the runway. The pilot, a skilled former naval aviator, knew that it was possible, even likely, that he had just killed the passengers in the small plane that had been ahead of him when he overran the Cub with his jet engines and mass of aluminum. He was now under the command of a hedge-fund boss, whose orders were to arrive at the airport on the very second of the clock. This time, the need to be precisely on time had been taken too far, only so this billionaire could schedule in a visit with his kids at a summer camp on Echo Lake in Fayette. This would not be good. The jet pilot knew what a razor-thin buzz job had resulted and that if by some chance anyone else was still alive, revenge would follow.

Mac McCabe *was* alive, and he had an adrenaline cocktail in him that would whip an NFL linebacker. He flew the airplane onto the runway, bumped down on the damaged landing gear, and taxied right up to the nose of the private jet. He got so close that the pilot could see the little plane's propeller spinning fully through the windshield. Mac shut down. He sprang out of the folding door and ran toward the air stair.

The billionaire sat back in his plush, leather seat. He stared at his wife with the phony breasts, the over-stretched face, decked out in paste representing five million dollars worth of jewelry in a safe. She leered at the pilot with lust, when the door dropped down and Mac grabbed him by the shirt, hauling him to the ground outside, fists swinging, as he had been taught in grammar school.

The wife opened her legs and gave her hedge man a quick view of the un-promised land. Despite the scuffle going on below, the only thought that crossed the billionaire's mind was that because of some morons from Maine, that little peek was all he would get from her for the whole damn weekend.

The airport manager and the cops had shown up, and there were the usual coffee-swilling men from the pilots' lounge now pulling Mac off this finely dressed employee. Mac had cut the ex-Navy man's nose with several short jabs to the face and had his own cut behind his ear from the aviator's ring. They were both dragged to their feet and restrained by the police and a small crowd. Everyone had witnessed the near midair collision. Mac felt murderous toward a fellow human being for the first time in his life. He would avenge this deadly action toward him and his friend.

The billionaire passenger stared at his watch, a fifty-thousand-dollar timepiece. Where was his giant black SUV? Where was his driver? What was this nonsense taking up his valuable time outside his new aircraft? Why weren't the police protecting him and his passengers from these maniacs fighting on the grass near the tarmac. His life was being interrupted by these hooligans. He had no idea what was in store for him because of this. These Maine men were going to rise up—the darkness of a threatened soul was headed toward the billionaire with no remorse.

ೞ   ೲ

The American furniture piece called "the recliner" is a piece of wood, cloth, foam padding, and the interim stop between the middle age of a man and the coffin. They don't call the company La-Z-Boy for nothing. This seemingly harmless corporation is as guilty of exploiting man's greed as the others on Wall Street and probably just as successful at enabling the depression and inactivity leading toward the grave. At forty-seven years of age, Kevin Daniel McCabe, known as Mac to his friends and family, was sitting in his favorite La-Z-Boy in the winter of 2014. The first quarter of that year alone, La-Z-Boy had sold thousands of such recliners, and since its founding in 1927, how many millions more? But Mac's near-death, near-midair collision was tucked safely well into the future.

It was the middle of the afternoon; a middle-aged man, if he expected to live a long and healthy life, should not be sleeping the day away in a recliner of any type. Mac McCabe felt a little guilty, for about six seconds, and then returned to dreamland. He thought of this as midway into the deep-dreaming place of his mind. He rested his hand on his dog, an overly energetic golden retriever named Woody, one of a long line Mac had owned for three decades. His other hand, holding the other man's best friend, rested down his pants.

It was a place he had been so many times before, a safe place. He had had dreams about flying from the time he could walk and lusts about women of beauty from the time he felt the softness between the breasts of his baby-sitter at the age of eight. His dream library was a combination of lust and adventure, occasionally mixed with a fish on a fly rod—adventure seemed to be losing out to lust lately in these dreams in the middle of the day.

On this biting-cold winter afternoon on Lovejoy Pond in Fayette, Maine, his dream took place on the tarmac of his home airport of his teen years. It was a warm, September day, with leaves beginning to turn in the bogs. He had just soloed—it was his very first time as a pilot— he was sixteen, and the airplane was a two-seat Cessna 150. His mother was there with a camera. She had raised an adventurer from the start, and now he was flying airplanes before he could drive a car.

She was a beautiful mother in the dream, and still was at age eighty. Back then, he did all he could to win her approval. She beamed with pride, a smile soft and pure on her face. According to his instructor, he was a natural flyer; he had made three perfect landings in a slight crosswind on Runway 28 at the Central Maine Airport. Now, however, the airplane was parked, flightless. The La-Z-Boy squeaked, and he awoke briefly to hear the wind blow through the trees and drop ice near his de Havilland Beaver floatplane frozen into the lake, two hundred feet from the recliner.

His 1983 reverie seemed to ease him deeper into the chair, but 2014 reality caused him to wrap a little tighter in the afghan, as he longed for the past of his dreams.

He tried to go back to sleep, recliner set on the second notch on the back lever; if he could only get this dream back. *Oh, there it is— come back, come back.* Slowly the images reappeared in his mind, and his sixteen-year-old girlfriend was there to congratulate him with a kiss. It was a soft kiss; she had that white silk scarf on. It should have been on him. The dream continued, and now she only had the silk scarf on, and she was offering him herself, both for their first times, in the back of her mother's station wagon. Abruptly, the dream ended, and he found he was excited to get up and move. Mac loaded more wood into the stove and shook his head, as if he were shaking off a dream hangover. He had to move, get moving, move forward, straight ahead.

It was a winter of misery. Climate change? The snow came early and deep and way too soon. The fuel bills in northern New England were the highest ever, and the big pinch was on—the money pinch so harshly felt and so easily dealt out by the utilities and big oil. The costs to the poor, cold Mainers occurred because of the oil speculator rats, running unchecked through the American economy—and Mac's mind.

To top off all this chill and hardship, there had been a temperature inversion during the week of Christmas 2013 in Maine, resulting in an ice storm that had laden the wires and transmission poles so badly that thousands were without electricity when they wanted it most. The band of land between Rumford and Camden became a sheet of ice, putting you on your back, kicking your sorry Downeast ass. Hundreds of people lying on their backs, impoverished, falling on the ice, with no electricity in their homes. This was a sorry start to another Maine winter.

The local utility management, who sent all their profits to their offshore parent company, had not done their jobs for many years in clearing wires of newly growing branches. Maine is the Pine Tree State, with nineteen million of it's twenty million acres heavily forested. The power company's linemen were again the heroes of the ice and warriors of winter. These clearers of downed trees would move tons of branches and logs out of the way and miss their family Christmas because of the greed of management and the power of the northwest wind.

Nowadays whenever Mac fell back into Dreamland, nestled down in the warm Caribbean sun, government piggies would gather for their holiday festivities and crowd him out. Senators and Congress people with billionaire hedge-fund pimps, would hustle him to be paid off in the best way that anyone could: food, sex, booze, and cash. Most of the payola would be in the sewers of the islands the following day, but the cold cash would last forever, at least until their cold dead hands finally released their clutch on his dreams.

The folks elected to Congress in this fevered America were the best in the world—the best money could buy. Eighty-four-degree heat and blue endless surf with an expense account that saw no limit and never found the address of the people who were sucking it all in, was the order of this winter in the islands. The earth-burrowing worms all expected it. Like taking a daily shower, this was owed to them, and their fleshy little paws without calluses needed the grease from the nasty money machine. The machine that had created the greatest concentration of wealth in the history of the free world ran unchecked at breakneck speeds like a cocaine-fueled Casey Jones on a downhill, runaway train—until he woke up in the dead of winter.

But they were still in Saint Bart's. The billionaires driving the millionaires out with treasure exchanged by the mighty—the jet riders, the real estate buyers, the corrupters of governments at every level, in every country. You could identify them by the smell, the extra-white teeth and the fake boobs, the hair implants: the tacky artificial.

In an instant, the mobile device would buzz, the Falcon jet would be fueled, and another group of people in another place would need to be impressed or paid off. They could go coast to coast without refueling and stay in the most luxurious accommodations known to humans. The food flowed, the booze was the world's best, and the sex was any way they wanted it.

They needed to accumulate more or die like the addicts they were. This class of people had rigged the system so that they could perpetuate this style of life for the generations of their bloodlines. There was no religion except the demon of greed. No one would touch them—not the IRS, not Congress, not any legislative body in the world. If governments tried to gain even a small portion of their wealth for the public good, there was always offshore and further offshore, the little vault that held so much on the little island so far away. The song kept ringing in his head: "you can see them out for dinner with their piggy wives, clutching forks and knives, eating their bacon . . . Have you seen the little piggies?"

Mac McCabe was in front of his woodstove on this Christmas morning. Again, his family was without power. He burned wood and hoped that the pile he had split and stacked would make it through to May Day. He knew that the beech wood would burn hot and overnight; the oak would do as well, but the big pile of maple and ash were giving him pause. He wondered if the local logger he had used for a decade would allow him credit for a couple of cords of ash wood—only until ice-out, when he could get his business ramped up again for another year.

Mac stared out the window at the water on Lovejoy Pond in Fayette, at his aging, neglected and sorry-looking 1956 Havilland Beaver, still on floats and frozen into the shallow icy waters of the thirty-mile watershed in west central Maine. His business, Allagash Air, was in its twentieth year of operations, but business had declined. The Beaver, a majestic marvel of air travel, was the ultimate bush-flying machine with its nine-cylinder 450 horsepower Pratt and Whitney radial engine and seating for four passengers and all of their gear and supplies.

Mac had started the business with a dream of providing the best possible adventure into the northern reaches of Maine and its ten million acres of unorganized territory. Maine was carved by glaciers, with thousands of lakes, rivers, and ponds. Mac was a trout fisherman's magic carpet driver, a wilderness camper's wet dream, providing rides to backwoods hikers. He had made a thousand dreams come true; he was a pilot extraordinaire with thirty-two years of flying and three thousand hours at the controls of the Beaver, as well as other high-performance bush planes. If it had floats or skis, wings, a prop, and a motor, Mac could fly it and fly it well. The reflexes he developed as a pilot at sixteen were still sharp in his forty-eighth year of life.

Today, seven days after the winter solstice, when the light changed and the days lengthened, he would start working his way out of this depressed state. The plane would fly again; not for four months yet, not without some risk to the fuselage from ice falling off the trees, and not without some risk of an animal burrowing into the firewall and chewing avionics wires and other chewy items on their winter menu. On this scenic little pond, Mac shot every squirrel and every chipmunk within two hundred yards of his home for just that reason.

He shot the little bastards with a twenty gauge over-and-under shotgun, a model that never failed to decommission the gnawing little furry rodents. If the top barrel didn't work, or if they twitched in the slightest, he gave them the second barrel underneath just to clinch the deal. The flea-carrying pests were a threat to his livelihood—the same reason man has fought with animal for as long as anyone can remember. They also made a mess of his western spruce rafters inside the family home, when they burrowed inside the walls. Squirrels were vermin to Mac McCabe, almost as much as his corporate kings of greed who were destroying America.

Fayette was a beautiful little town of 1,200 souls, nestled in amongst five fine lakes and the thirty-mile watershed connecting people to water, winding north to south in western Kennebec County. Mac had arrived there in exile from a bad first marriage. He arrived in Fayette with a fifth-generation local girl named Kelley Gunther, who had pulled him up off the bottom, married him, and given him a bright-eyed child with love. Kelly was a beauty of local legend—"smart and sassy," he would say. It was the perfect location for a "float flyer" and his airship to begin an enterprise.

Sometimes he would cut the tails off the squirrels for a fly-tying client or fishing friend. Most of the time he just cast them onto his neighbor's lawn to draw the crows and the turkey vultures to the abutting land owner, the retired financial planner who never stopped complaining about airplane noise to anybody who would listen. He had moved in from New Jersey, and no one had ever told him that floatplanes were here on Lovejoy years before motorboats and jet-skis.

On one long winter the neighboring malcontent went to the local planning board to have a "no floatplane" ordinance enacted in the town of Fayette. The proposal would ban all floatplane operations from any of the five lakes in Fayette forever. Mac had placed five consecutive days of dog shit in his complaining neighbor's mailbox, an old Maine expression of dislike and disdain. There was nothing like a neighborly stool sample from your golden retriever to go with your *Time* magazine's weekly arrival.

Mac eventually agreed to fly the planning board chairman's son to summer camp on Sebago Lake for the next five years. The neighbor's proposal disappeared in the night, never to be seen again. Mac continued to deliver the best of his golden retriever, Butch, every Saint Patrick's Day until Butch got hit by a dump truck, chasing a squirrel in the middle of Lovejoy Pond Road.

Mac had ended up grieving for a month when his jerk of a neighbor keeled over after a massive stroke and died. Out came the bottle of Paddy's Irish whiskey to raise a toast every evening for a week to the man's demise. Paddy's was hidden in the back of McCabe's fishing tackle. It did not sit front and center with the Jameson's or the Bushmills; it was only brought out to celebrate a well-lived life, the death of an adversary, or the joy of the birth of another McCabe.

Mac McCabe felt he was a good man, a quality man, a stand-up guy, who worked hard at all he did and usually mastered it through practice and determination. His natural gifts in a mental and physical capacity were above average. He knew men he thought were perfect in many ways: flying abilities, lovers, craftsmen, bullshit artists, and finish carpentry. He envied them, but only a little—in a melancholy, two-shots-of-whiskey kind of way. When it came down to it, their faults were far worse than most, he figured; the perfect ones usually were not so perfect.

He had never suffered from jealousy the way so many other men had over women, possessions, money, good looks, or youth. He was handsome, well spoken, and a good businessman. He had been satisfied with his lot in life, but he was convinced that he had to change in a big way in the coming year of 2014. He had to focus on the last half of his life and what he could get done—just human actions of good work with good intent. To the core, he was a good man often fraught with swirling, bee-stinging-type demons abuzz in his head. This was the hand that he was dealt, as it was to so many others. He thought, *when the demons come you must fight back and cast them off, or at least try.* Unfortunately, the demons had won him over a few times already in his life.

He gazed out the window of his home and frowned at the icicles dangling off the wings of the aging de Havilland floatplane. He knew that the compression was low in two of the cylinders and his aircraft mechanic would definitely make him replace them before spring flight operations began for Allagash Air. Where would he get that money? Always the winter question—except the question bubbled up a little earlier this year. It usually started working its way into his mind around Saint Valentine's Day, when the taxes were due and the firewood pile diminished. It seemed appropriate that it would be on his mind at that time of year; the true passion in his life, besides his family, was the gift of flight. No flight was happening this spring without two new cylinders and an annual inspection that was costing more and more every year.

His mechanic, a one-eyed Vietnam War veteran, was the only reason he could keep flying and stay within the means and cash flow of his company. Mac praised the man as the savior of general aviation in central Maine. His hourly rate on antique aircraft was less than the local Ford dealer selling plastic cars and trucks. Forty dollars an hour and all the right-wing bullshit you could put up with in a single day.

Periodically, before long flights or in marginal weather, McCabe would remove his Saint Christopher's medal from its hiding place in the Beaver, give it a little rub, and pray for the smooth and safe operations of his aircraft, his own performance, and the annual gift of a man, mechanic Bud Barry—Barry, whose health had been in steady decline for twenty years, who chain-smoked unfiltered Camel cigarettes. But he was a round-radial-engine expert of a man. Bud loved the round airplane engines that were fewer and fewer in service each year.

When Bud would finish the annual inspection on the de Havilland, he would leave a pack of the Camels in McCabe's survival bag, knowing that if the Beaver went down in the woods in Northern Québec or remote Maine, McCabe would want to light up. He would smoke to keep the bugs away, ease his tension, provide some clarity. Bud Barry knew that true clarity in thoughts of direction or airplane mechanics began on the lit end of a Camel unfiltered smoke.

Mac hadn't smoked for twenty years but loved the smell of a burning "straight pipe," as he would refer to the vintage Camel cigarettes. He had lit a couple on a fishing trip the year before after catching a twenty-seven inch salmon on the Hart Jaune River in Northern Québec and felt his head swirl and dizziness overcame him. It was a nice melancholy buzz in the Canadian woods. He never lit another, but there was always hope.

Bud Barry was one in a string of friendships that Mac had developed, who had come to civilian aviation through military and war flying. They kept their hand and heart in it for the love of aircraft and the motors that took them skyward. Barry had been a gunship mechanic on Huey helicopters in Vietnam. He had learned the hard way, discovering the internal mechanisms of the workhorse war choppers. At nineteen, he scrubbed the blood and human hair off the panels protecting the internal shafts of the *wop wop* turbine engines and their wide rotor blades. He often washed blood from the floors of the choppers to begin the maintenance. He hated the war and the Democratic President Lyndon Johnson who sent him there—and all Democrats from then on.

Fishing and hunting friends were Mac's core, his trusted Maine people. People had drifted in and out of his orbit for decades, and he was always welcoming to the new people and always happy to see a few go. Many were after his camps and his trout pond lists; sometimes it took him longer than others to see through their phony smiles and half-empty bottles of Jameson's. It was a costly education, but he had come to master the art of dealing with these "phony fucking friends." He would still drink their whiskey; it would soften his edge.

The Saint Christopher medal, Mac's top karma creator, came straight from the Vatican trinket store just outside Saint Peter's Cathedral. It was gold, and McCabe bought it with his eldest daughter from his first marriage while on a trip to Rome. That and the four-leaf clover given to him by his friend Mikey "Dart" McMahon from Clare Castle, County Clare, Ireland, seemed to have provided good luck for his flight operations now going on three decades.

He was superstitious, and yes, he was a Catholic. Half of his forty-eight cousins were as well and sinned with the best of mankind. He sometimes thought he should have been a better Catholic. His aunt Bridget told him every Christmas, "I pray for you to come back to the church for daily mass, Mac." She attended mass almost every day of her life. She could not understand those who didn't. The patron saint of travelers, Saint Christopher, was always in the aircraft that McCabe flew, from the time he soloed on his sixteenth birthday to nearly four decades of flight later, without any personal injury to McCabe. There had been a couple of crashes, a couple of bruises, busted aluminum and tubing, but no injuries. The saint had gone from nickel to seventeen-carat gold, but he was always there, guiding and protecting. Flying along the treetops Mac would sing aloud, "very superstitious, writings on the wall."

McCabe had crash landed three times during his flying career. He believed that any pilot who's had thousands of hours of bush flying is going to go down. The skill part was to do it without killing yourself or anyone with you. McCabe had perfected that little trick after three engine failures and subsequent landings "off airport," as the FAA would come to call them.

He remembered his former flight instructor yelling in his ear. The muscular ex-Marine pilot would say, "Fly this aircraft right until the moment it stops moving, whether or not there is a runway in front of you—or not. Whether or not the prop is turning or the engine is running, or not—do not ever lose control of this or any aircraft, you long-haired son of a whore!"

McCabe could hear the words blasting him from out of the 1970s as if yesterday. His instructor liked him but hated hippies, long hair, and drugs. He brought a pair of scissors to Mac's solo flight, where it is customary to cut off a piece of the new pilot's shirt. After he had cut the shirt, he said, "Now let's trim that hair up above your ears, you little bastard!" Mac escaped out the hangar door.

It was now the fifth day without electric power at Mac's family's lakeside home, and he could see the tears in his daughter's eyes when he told her that the lights on the Christmas tree were going to be out another night. Jacqueline Ann McCabe, his six-year-old, was depending on the lights to guide of Santa's sleigh, as she had for all of the years of her life. She was a gift, a late-life gift. He called her Jackie after Jackie Cochran, one the great aviatrixes from the 1920s and 30s. He also believed Jacqueline Kennedy was one of the most beautiful women that ever lived. Cochran was an air racer, Kennedy was all culture and beauty, and he wanted that for his Jackie, who made his heart skip.

Jackie ran off to clothe one of her sixty-two Barbie dolls. She skipped when she ran, as if she were on the yellow brick road with the tin man, the scarecrow and the lion. Mac smiled and vowed that he would do one good thing before he died. He'd do it for her. He had to do it while he had the physical strength and the mental capacity to accomplish it. Time was passing too fast, he thought.

He now knew, more than ever, after the death of three of his closest fishing friends the previous year in a crash with a Cessna 185 above the 52nd parallel in Northern Canada, that life is finite. The end of life could come at any time; no one knew what day it was going to show up on the calendar. He just didn't know on this date in late December of 2013 what that "one good thing" that he would do could be.

He was a man of plans—flight plans, work plans, building plans, plans for love, plans for deceit, getting-back-at-others plans, and plans for survival. He had made thousands of flight plans that had been executed precisely and in full. The new "good-thing" plan had not surfaced yet, but he knew it was coming.

2

The chip on the shoulders of many Irish Americans was as big as the Blarney Stone itself and rightly placed on most accounts. For over a century, the Irish in America were looked at as cheap labor and dimwitted. Many signs were placed in windows in Boston and beyond by the Anglican gentry, saying in bold letters, when jobs needed to be filled: "No Irish Need Apply!" No matter how the lot in life of an Irish American improved, there was always some Pilgrim to disparage their success or tout it as the result of a theft or other crime. Joe Kennedy's "bootlegging crime" was the most common finger pointed by Yankee Boston brahmins.

The Civil War in America became the blood pool of newly drafted or conscripted Irishmen on both sides, North and South, accounting for a large percentage of the six hundred thousand war dead. These old, bad feelings ran deep in most Irishmen, even in the new millennium. America was the land of opportunity for millions, but for early Irish settlers it was one step above an Englishman's starvation village in the land of Eire. The Irish had come a long way in America; they had had two American presidents and hundreds of captains of industry and commerce, but the sting continued in so many places.

The first banker to turn Mac down for a business loan for his flying guide service was Mr. Morris Lancey, who had a family history in New England dating back to the Mayflower. McCabe had the mental condition known as Irish amnesia, which is when a person of Irish descent only remembers the bad things that ever happened to him. Mac had it bad for Mr. Lancey and all his relatives.

Mac had written the business plan with the help of a friend with an MBA from Harvard. The plan had no holes in it, and he had the required twenty-five percent in cash to put down for startup money. He was turned down flat by Lancey. He slammed his fist on Lancey's desk as he got the rejection.

Morris Lancey was a Yankee blueblood, who pissed Yankee Doodle syrup and farted salty New England sea air. He was not going to put his name on a loan to a low-class Irish, at least not one from the McCabe family, where they bred like rabbits, drank like sailors, yelled at football games, and cursed at the wind. These were loud people who always threw the last punch in a fight and never backed down from anyone. He never had to fight them—all he had to do was look over his half-rimmed glasses and say with a smile of the ruling class itself, "I'm so sorry, but this loan just doesn't meet the bank's lending criteria at this time."

McCabe got the loan for Allagash Air with the guaranty of a local contractor and pilot who had given Mac his first airplane ride and just liked Mac's smile, as he would say out loud to whomever would listen. Mac always made a good first impression. "You don't get a second chance to make a first impression," McCabe's father would say to him as a boy. "Keep your head up and don't slouch, and smile as if you have all of your teeth."

Morris Lancey's name was not spoken again in the McCabe family; with a bold red line drawn through it, it was written with bold black letters in Mac's journal, along with a few other names that were cursed and spat when spoken, names with a trip to hell ahead of them. He might in fact meet them there, no one knew.

Allagash Air was up and running in 1998 with a Cessna 185, a Piper Super Cub, and $50,000 in operating funds. The Bank of Boston was writing the loan with a small-business guaranty. Lancey's grandfather was spinning in his grave, which just happened to be the grave next to Owen Brewster, a former Maine governor and senator, who was the secretive leader of the Maine branch of the Ku Klux Klan in 1937, with membership topping forty-five thousand, all fighting proud— proud to hate, proud to suppress the human spirit until their dying day—and steeped in superstition.

Pilots are a superstitious lot as a group. Many of Mac's friends had died flying into mountains in bad weather. Some of them had thousands of flight hours in their log books. McCabe came from good Catholic Christian stock that prayed at the altar of their Lord and Master throughout the year. Many of his relatives went to the big Catholic church in Skowhegan, at least once a month. They didn't want to be too far away when the big bell tolled for them. As a matter of fact, to a couple of his aunts and uncles, the preference would be to just drop dead on Good Friday, while doing the Stations of the Cross. Straight ticket, no stops, divine arrival at the pearly gates. If they weren't betting on ponies at the racetrack, a church was always in sight of the McCabe clan of County Caven, Ireland, now living in America for 151 years.

Mac did not understand why good, decent, by-the-book pilots would fly into a mountain, crash and die, while carefree, callous, risk-taking aviators would go on for decades without a scratch or dent in the aluminum. He knew that it was a matter of skill, luck, and consistency; start doing things out of routine, and you are headed for trouble, as far as flying techniques are concerned.

Kevin Daniel McCabe was a full-fledged member in good standing of the church of the Great Blue Dome. There were too few beautiful Sunday mornings that needed a fly presentation to a native brook trout to keep Mac cooped up in a sanctuary built with stone and concrete. His mother would constantly remind him about her attendance at Mass and his lack of. Mac would grab her and hug her and say, "Pray for me, Ma!"

He believed in God and accepted the Father, Son, and the Holy Ghost. The great outdoors and the waters of Maine and Northern Québec were his places of worship. He knew Saint Peter was a fisherman who needed more men like Mac himself to conserve the land and waters, allowing the mass of men to carry out their godly duties and their destiny. Recently, he interpreted the new pope in Rome had validated his activity and missing Mass over these past few decades. Worshiping in nature was quite all right with this new top man in Rome. He was an environmentalist and a lover of nature. This new pope was awesome. Mac had been waiting for him for forty-eight years.

Catching and releasing beautiful, God-made North American brook trout was truly a divine action. Every now and then, Mac would keep a trout, cook one, or bring one to his wife or mother. They were the two most heavenly women breathing air on this round earth, and certainly worthy of this gift from God.

Mac knew the State of Maine as well as the best of its pilots; you could not get him lost anywhere in its twenty million acres. He had a sense that few pilots had. An old wartime pilot had singled him out: "Cats eyes with all of the lives—seeing in the clouds and avoiding the mountains." He was lucky and smooth as a pilot, like a cat stalking its prey.

His passengers, his sportsmen, and all of his customers experienced the best that the state had to offer while spending a day with Mac and Allagash Air. The tail number of the Beaver, N410KE, or "Four Ten Kilo Echo," as he would announce to the controllers in the Bangor or Portland towers, became known statewide as it flew over with the radial roar. He loved the small mirror he had placed to the upper right of the pilot's door to look at the rear of the floats. This would let him know if the load needed to be shifted and if the rear spreader bar of his airplane's floats were close to being under water.

You could load the Beaver with almost anything, but you needed to balance the load precisely—fat people in the front, light baggage in the rear. Center of gravity was your best friend in trimming for speed or landing in a tricky current on a river or lake. McCabe had violated the loading rules only a few times and almost paid dearly in the lands above the 52nd parallel, where aircraft mechanics were few and far between and making mistakes was not allowed if you wanted to live. The other benefit that the mirror provided was to see the smiles and the shining eyes of a child or first-time passenger taking a flight over the most beautiful state in America.

Mac developed his Canadian trip for his customers after the logging roads allowed total unchecked access to the lakes and ponds of northern Maine. He had not seen a client catch a brook trout over four pounds in Maine waters for almost a decade. He knew his clientele would want bigger fish and bigger adventures. He hated the thought of dealing with customs and passports as a pilot, but you do what you have to do to survive in business. Mac had made the commitment to flying to Canada in 1997. The trips were longer, and they meant more time away from home, but the smiles were wider, and the results were bigger and stronger fish. Both trout and salmon in the northern waters above 52 were worth the work and the reward.

The brook trout in Northern Québec and Labrador were very special; they were the result of very cold water and severe conditions. They fought off the northern pike, a spiny, toothed bastard, that would tear the stomach out of them and then eat them piece by piece. When these trout were caught they would fight to the end with every bit of strength that they could muster. A small twelve-inch fish would fight like a twenty-inch hatchery-raised trout in Maine. McCabe had traveled thousands of miles into the bush with sports to catch brook trout, and his success rates were good. He knew when to go and how to catch them. He had thousands of fly patterns at all times, and he wasn't afraid to try every one of them to see if they would work. He had his special flies tied for himself, plus his odd favorites. A well-tied fly was better than a lure or a worm any day in Mac's opinion. He was a fish-hooking master; all that knew him knew that.

One day in 1987, on the Broadback River in western Québec, McCabe had been fishing with his friend and fellow guide, Johnny Norton. Johnny was six-foot-three and could throw a fly fifty yards to the rise of a trout. His walk was one of a gangly, uncoordinated man, out of sorts with the size of his body. When you put a fly rod in his hand, though, he had the moves of Rudolf Nureyev. He was poetry on the river; he had deadly accuracy to the sight and movement of trout in water, with his floating line, leader, and fly. Mac would fly him for free, just to watch him fish and catch and fish and catch all the day long.

Johnny was fishing the pool opposite Mac on the famous Canadian river, when Mac stopped to watch Johnny catch a fish on every cast. Mac was doing well, but maybe one fish every fifteen minutes, and small fish at that. They were small for the Broadback River, everything below a pound. Johnny Norton, however, was catching two- and three-pound fish and playing it on almost every cast. They both had the same fly on and were fishing pools within a few yards of each other.

"OK Grand Monarch of the River Broadback," Mac shouted with a French Canadian twist on the accent. "What am I doing wrong?"

"Fish the Muddler fly subsurface. The river will provide a whizzing noise to the deer hair of the fly, and the fish will strike at it. They aren't hungry but they will get mad. These trout have no hunger now—they're moving upriver and being territorial. You're fishing the fly top-water and only getting the small, slower fish," Johnny yelled back at Mac across the roaring river.

How does he know this? McCabe thought to himself, as he tipped his hat to the fish catcher across the river. "Sonofabitch thinks like a fish," he muttered underneath his breath.

Ten minutes had passed; Mac had changed his technique and was having no luck at all. He could see the trout, he had great eyes. And he could see them moving up through the rapids, and the dorsal fins appeared now and again. He knew that some, because of the distance between the fin and the tail, were very large trout. He knew they were over six pounds; he had seen them on the wall and in the photos at the Broadback River fish camps. Now he could see them live, in front of his fly today. But he wasn't catching any. Maybe Norton had told him wrong on purpose. No matter how good the friends, the rules were different when you were on the river. It was a competition that Johnny Norton rarely lost.

Across from each other on that hot July afternoon, each with a spot of river that was heaven on earth, they toasted each other when they pulled the Labatt's from the river and ate the sandwiches prepared at the main lodge. McCabe pulled the second Labatt's out of the bag with an early afternoon beer buzz in mind. He stood up and grabbed his favorite L.L.Bean Double L, 7 Wt., nine-foot fly rod that had been with him at every stop on every river he had fished in the past twenty years. *Come on, sweet Judy Blue Eyes, catch me a trophy on this gorgeous Canadian afternoon.* He had a buzz and a motive.

He put a new Muddler on the line and weighted the end of the tippet with just a fine touch of weight. He started his false casts to gain line length and then remembered his guide Richard Legere, who at the breakfast table had said in broken English, "You dumb American fishermen practice all year on your manicured lawns to throw a fly a hundred feet across the big Broadback River. Sometimes you dumb bastards—" he paused, "the big trout lay on the banks two feet from the shore. But you keep impressing yourselves with those long flowing casts. Ha ha!"

Richard was a miserable host for a fishing camp; he would steal your booze while you were out fishing and take your smokes right out of your pocket at the dinner table. What was yours was his. Mac caught him stealing precious avgas out of his Piper Super Cub one day, and Richard told him it was a surcharge for staying at the camps. Avgas was like liquid gold in Canada, twice the price of the U.S. fuel, and every ounce was needed for the long ride home.

Mac thought he was truly blessed as he looked at the big blue sky above him. He stopped his false cast in mid flight, grabbed at the line, and pulled it back through the guides. He stood four feet back from the banks of the river and above the big rapid and hand-fed the line out to the river. It wasn't even a cast. This was not normal, and he knew that his chances were reduced by his abnormal actions. The rod tip snapped down like a hand from the river had purposely given it a big false tug. It wasn't false, though. The reel zipped and sang with the sound only a big fish taking a run can make. The trout was on the run, and the tip of the rod had never seen this type of jerking action. It was a four-piece, so that it would fit in any floatplane easily. The eyelets were twisting in an unusual way that Mac had never seen. He knew this was the fish, his trophy, the one chance given to a fisherman on every trip.

The fish made a run for the opposite bank with the reel zinging with departing line off as fast as Mac had ever seen or heard it. He kept watching the rod tip and the line move around the rocks in the rapids, quickly heading downriver. The leader was new and strong, and Mac had complete confidence in his line knots. He had learned the bad-knot lesson many times over the years. The concern was the wearing of the leader on the rocks or in the corner of this big fish's mouth. He kept the rod tip high and reset the drag.

The fish stopped and held in a small pool thirty feet downriver. Mac eyed the bank to make sure he could walk down, keeping pace with the fish and trying to move him into a pool, where he could be played honestly and fairly.

Johnny Norton, without the current and rocks to deal with, watching with intensity, yelled, "It's at least a six-pounder, McCabe! Don't screw this up, buddy!"

McCabe thought to himself, *Yeah, right. You want me to screw this up so you can talk about it for ten years on the ponds in northern Maine.* The potential "one that got away" was on his line. Only, he was going to change the end to that story—right now. The tip of his rod moved up and down in two-foot jerking motions.

Trout don't jump when fighting a fisherman—salmon do, and with great beauty and motion. Trout take their energy deep in the water and build it up to break away at the best time: when the current increases, when they can turn that fly in their mouth, when the angler screws up, drops his tip or hauls too hard or lets too much slack on the line. Mac raced down the river with the rod tip high and an eye on the riverbank. To trip into the fast-moving river, lose the fish and break the rod would be as bad a thing as could happen to him at this point.

The trout was tired and wearing out, and Mac could feel it. But they always had one good last run in them, so he was preparing for that and looking the water over for break-off hazards. The fish kept tiring, and Mac was on solid footing; he had moved seventy-five feet downriver following this fish. Norton was on the other bank staying right with him, as he watched the battle.

McCabe was reeling his line in with his left hand and using the right to keep the rod tip high. He tightened the drag a little more. He stayed back from the water, so as not to spook the fish into another run. The leader had been tested, and upriver a branch was working its way down between him and the fish. A branch on this path through the river's water would definitely break this fish off. This could be tragic, just tragic, to lose this fish on this most beautiful day.

The Canadian rivers are different. They are big, fast moving, thick with current, power, and swiftness. Mac had fallen into the Broadback once and had been swept sixty feet downriver in just a few seconds. He had clawed at the rocks, breaking his fingernails trying to get a grip. Finally, physically exhausted, he had caught a rock that would allow him to swing a leg up and over, and he pulled himself to shore. The incident had scared him to the point of shaking nonstop for a half-hour on the river's bank. His friends had helplessly witnessed it from the opposite shore. It was a reminder from the nature gods that he was a speck of matter on this large planet and could be dead and gone in the blink of an eye under its power.

Mac loved these rivers, but like flying in the big wild country of Québec, Labrador, and northern Maine, letting your guard down for a moment could endanger your life. Love them, fish them, respect them, experience them—few people ever would. The beauty was like nothing else to be seen in North American nature, with rivers twisting and turning through mountains and flowing into large lakes with untouched shorelines for hundreds of miles. A fisherman might always have a good stand on rocks in the water, casting for trout, but when the trout hit and you changed your stand, the water could sweep your feet from under you in seconds.

The fisherman spotted a pool just below the big line-cutting rock between him and the fish and let out some line by hand. He turned the rod on its side, maintaining the tension. The trout followed directions like he was taking a highway exit, and Mac grabbed behind his hat for the net that hung down his back. This fish would overfill this little net designed for two-pound trout in northern Maine. He could feel the tightness of the line and knew it was the last run for this trout. He held it firm and in place; the pool looked safe, no hazards. He started to steer the nose of the fish toward the bank; the fish was played out and all but caught. Slowly, Mac bent down and guided the nose into the net and turned the net with the skill of a fly-fisher, as half of the trout's body entered the cherry-wood-rimmed webbing.

McCabe moved up the bank quickly with his catch and knew that this fish would be killed, boned, and eaten by his mother two days later in Maine and later mounted for display at home. The fish was a spectacular male trout that had grown to be just less than seven pounds. It was twenty-six inches long and fat like a football. It was colored with the markings of the Québec reds that brighten up these rivers like swimming rubies with emerald spots. It might as well have been real jewels to Mac—this fish, this moment, this day, was priceless. A day of angling like no other, a fish like no other, not the biggest, not the strongest, but the best of this time in this special place, on the Broadback River. Mac felt complete as a fisherman. How could it get any better?

3

The winter of 2013 passed with a great deal of trouble for many people in Maine. Fuel bills were sky high, and there was the added expenses of snow-plowing bills, food bills, and medical bills—all overpriced in a system evermore unchecked by watchdogs, let run wild by the people. Who was responsible? Who to blame? McCabe stormed in his La-Z-Boy dreams. The administration in Washington and Congress all without purpose, without direction! The hardship hit the elderly and the poor folks the worst; the working poor were hanging by a financial thread. The winter thaw ice-out let loose the Kennebec and the Penobscot Rivers, and they flooded their banks along hundreds of miles of riverfront, just reminding the good folks that Maine was a harsh and beautiful home. The people had taken it on the chin again, again, and again—but from whom? Mac's cat eyes searched in a fog of emotion in a world red in tooth and claw.

And if the spring came with a late green-up, when the trees brighten again with budding leaves, customers were still few and far between for Allagash Air. Annual maintenance costs had put the McCabes behind, and aviation fuel spiked another seventy-five cents per gallon. It was not looking good for the twenty-year-old business. He tried new marketing strategies on the internet and called his sister-in-law, a web designer, to ask for help with his online presence. Hannah Gunther—married to Kelly's brother Jackson—was a former corporate programmer and web designer. She had gone into business for herself and was doing well in the world of web design and business software maintenance. McCabe called her the Geek Goddess, much to Jackson Gunther's chagrin.

Jackson was a former Army Ranger and Afghanistan War veteran, now working at the local mill. Paul Bunyan Paper employed 1,200 people in the town of Jay and was the center of the economic universe in west central Maine. Keeping the juice running to the big beast known as Number 5 Paper Machine, Jackson worked as a union boilermaker in the bowels of the seventy-five-year-old mill.

Hannah was five-foot-ten with long brown hair and blue eyes; she had the walk of a runway model but without the unhealthy figure to go along with it. She showed no sign of aging or change after delivering two beautiful blond children. They were eighteen months apart. She was getting it done as fast as she could. Give birth, develop websites, run marathons; every box checked off. She liked the country life, loved her husband and children, and could shoot and fly-fish with the best of any of them who visited her home during the sporting months.

If there was a family who could live off the land, from garden-fresh food to smoked fish and cured venison, it was the Gunthers. They would be living fine, when the breadlines started in the cities of America; they would survive, when so many others were burning their furniture for heat. If America was three generations removed from the Great Depression and just one holy warrior away from a dirty nuclear bomb blast, the Gunthers smiled and sat quietly at the school plays and community outings. They were a family expecting the worst of America's future. Jackson had seen "a look" on the faces of thousands of Taliban soldiers—they wanted to take this American way of life from him and his family. He was in no doubt that by 2025 there would be three billion Muslims in the world, and not one of them of any age would like anything about Americans anywhere. If Jackson generalized in politics, he specialized in being a survivalist and a very well provisioned one, in both bullets and food. And at five-foot-eleven with 205 pounds of swizzling grizzle, he was nothing any able-bodied man would want to grab onto. He had done two tours in Afghanistan as Ranger and scout and had come home to Fayette with a seemingly keen motivation to get all of that behind him and fast. He had been ordered to do things that should have been asked of no one. He knew how to kill fast, without hesitation, and he knew how to kill slowly, with every cut nerve sending a pain to the front of the brain. He wanted no more to do with any of it and regretted most of it. Like all good soldiers, he hated war, but with so much passion that, unlike many veterans who eschewed any more guns and killing, he could not let go of his weapons. They spoke for him. His gun collection easily matched any U.S. civilian's.

He saw beauty in the eyes of his children, felt the love in their embraces, and shared their happiness in the snow angels they'd make with every first flakes of the season. This world had kicked him in the balls more than once; there would be no more of it, he thought, again and again.

In the endless war Jackson Alexander Gunther fought around the blood-red poppy fields, he kept a small bit of his firepower locked in a gun-safe three feet from his night stand. There he had an AR-15 rifle that had been modified at the paper mill by a machinist to be a fully firing automatic weapon, two Glock 9 mm pistols with 15-shot clips, a 270 Ruger bolt-action rifle with a bull barrel and a 5–15 variable-power scope, his own personal sniper rifle. There were two twelve-gauge shotguns, one an automatic, the other an old pump that his grandfather had left him, two thousand rounds for the AR, one thousand rounds for the Glocks, and five hundred rounds for the 270. All of the ammo courtesy of Uncle Sam, who never saw the boxes of ammunition enclosed with the packages sent home during the two tours Jackson had served protecting the poppy fields of Afghanistan. Hannah had stored them religiously.

The FedEx driver always questioned the weight of the packages coming to Jackson's wife from Afghanistan, but the sight of her bending over to tear off the shipping tag made him want to drive those deliveries as often as possible. Especially when her husband was so far away and the home so deep in the country. No neighbors on either side or across the road. If he timed his run a little closer to lunch, maybe the conversation could go a little deeper than the weather. He was yet another man so sadly mistaken by her friendly smile and careless reveal of cleavage or brightly colored bras. She seemed clueless to a man's ill intent.

Jackson did not believe in unlimited gun and ammunition ownership, but the laws of the state and the country allowed it. At no time when the gun crazies were loose with their Saturday night specials and street-sweeper shotguns would he be outgunned. He figured that at any time during an invasion to his home, he and Hannah could deliver five hundred rounds per minute to an unwanted intruder. It was a small arsenal, but it was deadly. He always thought of contingency plans for him and his family, like so many other Americans.

He had spoken to Mac about an evacuation drill, if the country were under attack, like when September 11 happened. "How fast can you get us to your cabin in Northern Québec?"

"Four hours with all of you, all of us, and limited gear and fuel," Mac responded. "It's a one-way trip, though; no shuttle service for that little journey."

Mac had thought about it, but not too much. He remembered the civil-aircraft grounding across the nation during the 9/11 attack. This was done by the U.S. Government, as the bin Laden family left the United States in their Gulfstream luxury jet. He would never be grounded again—by anyone. He had devised a low-level flight plan to Lac Barbel, above the 52nd parallel in Northern Québec, where he would never be an object on anyone's radar. He would fly right to his well-provisioned cabin. Low level and high speed, as fast as the Beaver would go, anyway—120 knots at 2,300 rpms. He had burned the midnight oil for two weeks straight, thinking and mapping, devising this escape flight to Canada for himself and his family.

The plan was downloaded onto his GPS unit, titled the Osprey Flight, as the Beaver would never be higher than an Osprey hunting from a tree along the rivers. He would fly up the Kennebec from Augusta, sneaking north along the west branch of the Penobscot, across to Chesuncook Lake, around the top of Gero Island, east to the lakes of the Allagash Waterway, a northerly swing up the Allagash River, over the hill near the Saint John Valley, to the spit of land connecting Maine to Québec and the Saint Lawrence Seaway. Then wild Canada and the flight north through the five large dams along the watercourse north of Baie-Comeau. The plane would never stop for fuel or weather; the flight plan was already programmed. He dreamed about this flight, knew that he would somehow make it someday, and he was a planner. It was ready when he needed it. The thought of this escape to freedom did not occupy his mind at all times, unlike his in-laws who lived it with drills, provisions, and plenty of bullets.

Mac thought most of the talk about the survivalist's agenda was foolish, but he had not seen what Jackson had seen. Sometimes when he watched ISIS on the morning news, they looked like vermin, and he thought of his flight plan to evacuate some of his loved ones in his little airplane on the pond. He would need to use the long, straight lake above Lovejoy, called Echo Lake, to take off loaded with supplies and his family. Echo Lake was where the rich folks sent their kids to summer camp after they got done sending them to boarding school each year. He would need to have full tanks of fuel to reach his destination—his beloved fishing cabin nestled into the backcountry of the Canadian wilderness.

He would need to bring the things that could keep a family alive and sustained for a fair amount of time. Mac had some guns, but not many. A 308 rifle, a 45 handgun, and a 20-gauge over-and-under. He bought his ammo on sale at Dick's Sporting Goods and had enough to survive a month in the North Woods. He had a lot more fishing gear than any normal person. It was his weakness, like Imelda Marcos and her shoes—he had many fly-fishing rods, waders, and reels. He was a sucker for a new fly rod at L.L.Bean's flagship store in Freeport. He, like thousands of others, was pulled relentlessly into the vortex known as L.L.Bean—all drawn to the boot.

Mac based his evaluations of his fellow earth dwellers by first asking the question, after meeting them—can you fly? what do you fly? how much have you flown? why don't you fly? Did they fly floatplanes? ski-planes? or tail-draggers? If they didn't fly, did their fathers fly?—the older planes, the classics flown by true stick-and-rudder pilots, with the wheel for directional control under the tail surfaces. The other judged values came from his own people—are they good to children and dogs? Do they call their mother often? Do they stay true to themselves? Are they living a life of quiet desperation as Henry David Thoreau said of the mass of mankind? Will their life at the end be happy? Or will they still be searching for money and power? Are they phony?

Mac was a believer in being the "captain of his own fate" and "delivering his own destiny, one day at a time." But humans had been flying for less than a century, when Mac began his flight training. For a million years, they had watched with other ground animals, while the birds went over the ponds and around the bend near the mountains, and they wondered at what they saw. What did those birds experience on the other side? He had been there, over the mountain and to the other side and taken thousands of family members and customers there. He was meant to fly—pressured and impatient on the ground, he felt destined to be born at this time and this place with this de Havilland. Astral alignments in a network of dreams connected him to his astrology chart and guided him along at 115 knots, 2,500 feet above ground level. Motoring in the skies like an aimless eagle of lost flight,

Mac had been above the clouds and along the river valleys. The lyrics of Judy Collins sang to him in his La-Z-Boy,

> I've looked at clouds from both sides now
> From up and down and still somehow
> It's cloud's illusions I recall
> I really don't know clouds at all.

4

Mac's wife Kelley was a strawberry blonde with green eyes and shoulder-length hair. She worked as an X-ray technician at MaineGeneral Medical Center in Augusta. She had high cheek bones and an almond complexion. She was a sweet and loving mother to Jackie, but could be what Mac called the "hockey referee" when she wanted to. *Keep the games moving, no fighting or high-sticking; don't slow down, things to do, people to see, work to get done.* She was a beautiful woman to most observers, until you crossed her. At that point it was "keep your distance and watch your head." She was in the middle of her life and had had a bad relationship before Mac. Despite her failed relationship, she thought McCabe was worth the chance, and she was right. He turned out to be more than she could have hoped for, even with all his baggage dragging along the ground. He was devoted to her and their beautiful daughter, Jacqueline, the princess of Lovejoy Pond.

Kelley had found Mac drunk in a bar, with kind eyes and a sad story to share. He had been thrown out of his home by his first wife for being unfaithful, and his twenty-year marriage was over. His kids wouldn't speak to him, and he was running with a bad crowd in some fast-moving nightlife. The Old Port section of Portland after hours was where every bar offered a new experience—not always leading to a good place with the right partner, which gave credence to that old line spoken to Mac by his uncle, "There's no fool like an old fool." But Mac found his way through it, married Kelley, and had a child. He was like most men who discovered their mortality as a result of sudden stupidity. *If you can work through it, you'll come out the other side stronger.*

For many years there had been several flying services in Maine that offered flights in a de Havilland Beaver. Most had either sold them or gone out of business. Two flying charter services were running 206 Cessnas on composite floats or 185 Cessnas with amphibious floats. They were both workhorses, but none offered the attraction and nostalgic romance, room, and power of the de Havilland. The other flying services had held on to their airplanes right to the end, finally selling to outfitters in Labrador or Alaska and ending their special ownership. McCabe swore he would never do that, although 2014 looked like it might be the year that they just couldn't write the checks any longer for the big bird.

Kelley highlighted the shortfalls on the ledger on a weekly basis now, her voice seeming to be louder and more pronounced this year, or and maybe she was just making a louder presentation because Mac was losing his hearing. Then again, maybe she wasn't. She was the keeper of the books and payer of the bills. She was the person who wrote the creditors' letters in the fall and winter asking for a payment plan for fuel, maintenance, and insurance. She was the contact person for all of it, and didn't like it much—didn't like it much at all. Mac always seemed to make it up the next flying season, but it was a perpetual struggle toward that break-even point every year that passed.

May and June were steady, but not a banner opening. Despite Mac's assurances that it would get better, Kelley wondered when. The days became longer, and the thoughts of heating bills, high snow banks, and diminished wood piles were thoughts gone by. The fish were biting. The Maine Forest Service asked Mac to fly a patrol twice a week during fire season, and a little extra dough was coming in the door. He borrowed a Piper Super Cub from his friend Jack Weston to do the job, and it helped save him about $40 an hour in operating costs from the gas-guzzling Beaver.

The spring trips to the woods and waters were almost always the same for Mac, his company, and his Beaver. He did them over and over again every year. He often tried to spice it up with a different menu or added beverage. He bought different liquors and different food, as suggested by Kelley. Most of the dinners for his sporting customers were precooked, gourmet meals that she had made at night and frozen for the trips. Mac would make breakfast and lunch and did a fair job at both. He carried a Martin camper's guitar for evening sing-alongs and had a fine tenor voice to bring the half-drunken sports to life in the middle of the evening.

The flight to Katahdin Lake was as magnificent as you could imagine. Mac would always fly his scenic route up through Greenville, up across Mount Kineo, around the Big Spencer Mountain, across Rainbow Lake, and in front of the great Mt. Katahdin. And there, hidden on the backside of the big mountain with a drop in the landscape, was a beautiful little lake just called Katahdin, where Teddy Roosevelt had hiked and camped, and the artist Marsden Hartley had painted from its beaches. This place was in permanent conservation. Never would it be developed with lake homes and subdivisions.

Mac liked this flight, and he liked the people now with him; they cared about the fish, the lake, the mountain, and their state. Mark Curtis Warren had convinced other corporate leaders in Maine to participate in conservation projects, and Mac had taken groups of potential donors for over-flights on lakes and lands that were to be conserved. He liked that work. It was work that he had discounted in price because it had meaning. The work of conservation was permanent, forever to be enjoyed by those he thought of as "normal everyday average Americans." They never felt entitled to conservation land, just fulfilled and appreciative of its existence and perpetuity.

Teddy Roosevelt had gotten the start of his lifelong wonderment and love of the natural world right here in northern Maine. Mac thought President Roosevelt was the greatest conservationist in the history of America and that the president had learned his ethics in Maine. An asthmatic kid from New York City, he had felt the energy from the clear clean air pumping in his lungs. With wild rivers and majestic mountains, he took his love of the land westward and made forty million acres of national parks and wild lands, along with John Muir and the Sierra Club. Maine was a part of this national legacy. McCabe knew that and wanted to do his share. The National Park system has been called America's greatest idea, and T. R. was America's greatest citizen, in McCabe's eyes. He busted up the trusts of J. P. Morgan, Standard Oil, and the railroads; he kicked the rich bastards in the balls and smiled all the while. It was enough to let the president's imperialist warmongering well off the hook. When Mac read of his hero exulting after the charge up San Juan Hill that he had shot a Spaniard in the stomach and crumpled him "like a rabbit," it reminded him of Jackson's nightmares, and he bounced from the Lay-Z-Boy to change the subject and take to the skies.

During this latest trip, Mark Warren, the check writer, wanted a new dimension added. He wanted over-flights of some of the mountain peaks within the parks and a special overnight with his new fishing friend. This new twist caused a few eyes to roll with the other bankers on the trip. Could it be that she was moving up the corporate ladder within the bank, while working directly under the boss? Or could it be that this woman from New Jersey had found a new love of fly fishing and the outdoors, and the best teacher just happened to be her boss and the CEO of the bank?

If you wanted to catch fish at the best time of the year in Maine or Québec, you had to fight off bugs, mosquitoes, no-seeums, black flies, and maybe a few moose flies that took small chunks of your flesh with them after they bit. Mac had a lifelong war going on with the flies that fish feed on, and he was losing the war a little bit more every year. No matter how hard he tried to explain the "you need to fight flies in order to fight fish" rule, his paying customers hated the little bastards but couldn't find the wherewithal to focus. Warren wanted to take Felicia, his top commercial lender, to a spot either in or near the park, where there were "no bugs" and the fish were biting. He had given Mac a heads-up in an email before the group arrived, so Mac scouted a spot near Webster Lake on the west side of the park, and plans were set in motion.

The eventual night was like no other for President Warren of Cumberland Savings and Loan. The cries of the loons matched the sounds Felicia made while having her fourth orgasm in the two-person tent on the high bank near Webster Stream in the north Maine woods.

So the 2014 banker's trip was a success. Mac's tip bought a new fly rod and paid off the cylinder replacements on the Beaver. It was a great way to start the season. The cash flow had kicked in for Allagash Air. The forest-fire patrols and successful fishing parties could help the struggling business break even for the first time in eight years.

He was sure that the shareholders and the board of directors of the bank wouldn't mind, as the bank was about to have a newly energetic and positive voice at the helm. Warren a brand new man, made whole by a woman at the base of the natural wonder of Maine, Mount Katahdin.

When Mac dropped another satisfied party off at Sebago Lake, he returned home with a smile on his face and full tanks of gas in the de Havilland. The plane had never performed so well during his ownership. He walked into his home on Lovejoy Pond with the swagger of Errol Flynn. Kelley met him at the door, just returning from her job at the hospital. "There is a phone message from Rocky Wilson. He wants you to call him right back." Kelley had a lift in her voice, like she knew something special.

Mac hit the play button on the machine. "Hey, Mac, this is Rocky in Greenville. I have a buyer for your Beaver. You had said last fall to keep an eye out for a potential buyer, and I have a live one. Call me soon, buddy!" The message made him a little nervous and uneasy. Rocky had a buyer for his airplane, and judging by the happiness in his voice, Rocky had figured out how to make a lot of money on Mac's baby. He decided not to return the call, not yet.

5

On Friday, July 18th, Mac invited his friend Liam Patrick Mitchell to ride with him on a three-hour, fire-patrol flight up through the Rangeley Lakes in northwestern Maine. They called them the Rangeleys, as they were world renowned. The area was famous for fishing and backwoods adventure. The mountains and lakes were spectacular. Liam and Mac brought fly rods to test their skills on the river near the woods. It was one of Mac's secret fishing spots that few knew about. There was a backwoods airstrip near a pool filled with trout and salmon—a short walk from the airstrip to the river and paradise.

No matter how much Mac McCabe wanted to promote his business, he would never give away the most special fishing spots to anyone—anyone except his close friends and maybe one relative. They were the secret gifts that once let out were lost forever. Special fishing holes were the prime real estate of fly-fishing priests and their disciples; it was a limited group that had this knowledge, and it passed from generation to generation. If you broke the silence, you were doomed to years of no strikes and fishless days. The internet and social media had caused the ruin of many wilderness ponds and streams—these special areas would never give trout to Facebook fishermen. Mac believed in the silence and the sanctity of secret trout holes.

He had caught another bush pilot and outfitter trying to get the data card out of the GPS device in his airplane, and Mac had threatened to sink his Cessna 185 to the bottom of Togus Pond. He had told Mac he just wanted a look at the new Garmin avionics in the Beaver. The liar wanted the secret fishing spots; he wanted to violate the trust. Mac had the GPS password-protected after the failed larceny attempt. He shunned the pilot from then on.

There are only so many secrets that one man can keep in his life; past lovers, financial failings, indiscretions of the wallet and the heart, secret fishing spots. You could only hold them so long until, like overfilling a funnel, they would just seep out over the top through the years. Mac had them all bundled up, only confessing his many secrets to Kelley in their years together.

Liam Mitchell was a big man, six foot two and just over 230 pounds. He was a big load to haul in the two-person Super Cub. The airplane could carry the load and perform fine; it was a just little tight for his shoulders, but they made it work. Both fly rods were neatly packed down the fish pole tube extending down the fuselage inside the tail of the airplane. Liam knew where they were going, and even though they wouldn't be at their spot early morning or late evening, the prime river fishing hours in Maine, a sinking fly line with a streamer fly and a bead-headed nymph for a dropper could very well do the trick. Fresh brook trout for him and his wife for dinner, he thought with a smile; he was a happy man.

The two friends took the small airplane out to Runway 35 at Augusta State Airport, with Mac doing a faster-than-normal taxi. He began the preflight checklist, checking carburetor, the heat, magnetos, and fuel, as he worked his feet on the rudder pedals. He was steering between the big jet aircraft arriving on the tarmac, bringing rich folks to see their kids at the summer camps on the beautiful lakes of Maine. It was Parents' Weekend, and the jet fuel was flowing fast at the airports in Westchester County, NY, and Teterboro, NJ. The boys and girls with their billions were headed to the Northeast, and it felt to this small-craft pilot that they were always in a hurry. Mac had to keep a close watch as he moved amongst the twenty- and thirty-million-dollar jets newly arriving at the normally quiet little airport. He was flying Jack Weston's Cub, and he had to be extra careful not to put a scratch on it, although he really didn't care much about dinging up the jets.

McCabe had used the same standard checklist before taking off the entire time he had been flying. For over thirty years, he used the word, CIGARR, with a double R, prior to any takeoff, no matter the airplane he was flying. The letter C was for controls being free and clear in the airplane. I was for a scan of the instruments, making sure the altimeter was set, there was oil pressure, oil temperature, revolutions per minute, and manifold pressure. *G* was for the gas; make sure you have some and make sure the selector for the proper feed tank is in the correct position. *A* was for altimeter and avionics, to be checked and turned on. The first *R* was for the run-up of the engine and propeller, making sure the magnetos and carburetor heat were checked for operations and that there was smoothness in the change of rpms. The last *R* was for turning the radio on and communicating.

On this day, with all of the jet jockeys in the air, talking on the radio was very important. Many of these pilots never looked outside the windows of the costly jets they were flying for seemingly carefree owners.

The Super Cub used about 250 feet of runway out of the 5,200 feet at Augusta and started climbing out at 1,500 feet per minute. Even with the two big boys in the cabin, the Piper wing was made to climb and it did. The two men with the light hearts of boys flew off to the northwest in search of smoke from possible forest fires—officially. Unofficially, they were looking to catch a large brook trout on secret water in the woods, near the pond that had no name.

Their airplane leveled off at 2,500 feet above the ground and proceeded toward the western mountains, where they would fly the fire grid for the forest service for three hours. Mac used the landmarks to the west for this trip that he knew by heart. The smoke from the mill at Paul Bunyan Paper in Jay was billowing out with full-mill production underway for all nine paper machines.

At the mill, the sweat pouring off of him, Jackson Gunther pried the panel off a breaker box for one of the paper machines that was giving him trouble. *Too hot, too old, too much corrosion on these old wires*, he thought. He needed to make it safe and reliable, and the mill owners did not want to spend too much money on maintenance.

At the airport in Westchester County, the line boys were scrambling to fill jets with Jet A fuel, complete food orders, and get the rich on their way—all with the goal of keeping complaints magnified by wealth to a minimum. They were sweating profusely and the smell of jet fuel was so thick that many had hidden replacement oxygen tanks with masks in the rear of the main hangar so they wouldn't pass out. A little shot of O_2 every half hour kept them in the game. Each plane had a tail number and a departure time assigned to it. It was the pilot's job to make sure the air conditioner was on and the engine was running, so none of the passengers would be too hot when they reached their magic carpet.

The performance between the critical times of 2:30 p.m. and 6:30 p.m. was a unique, valued part of the fixed-base operator's performance each weekend. Mac figured the fuel being used to cool down the cabins of the jets this day would have heated the entire town of Fayette from October to May. Every one of the more than a thousand inhabitants, in their little homes, double-wides and year-round lake homes, needed just this much energy, now turning to exhaust. Each jet held ten people but would usually have no more than two passengers, sometimes four and one little dog made to sit in the gold-trimmed seat. The little dogs each pooped little diamond dog-shit nuggets on the fence line of the airport's tarmac and in Mac's turbulent daydreams. It seemed no one ever questioned this canine behavior, the waste of energy, or people's work. Everything was owned, and if more was needed, it would be bought. These flyers were wasteful souls, too preoccupied even to walk their own dogs.

Running the engine and cooling the cab for the arrival of the passengers, Falcon Jet N7REK sat with the others at Westchester County Airport. Pilot Terrance Dowd thought, as he awaited his passengers—the owner and wife—that he had just used enough fuel in one engine to heat his eighty-eight-year-old grandmother's home in Buffalo for an entire season.

Terry was a skilled pilot with over twelve thousand hours of logged flight time, almost all of it in jets. Military jets for the first three thousand hours and the rest in private corporate jets owned and chartered by the rich and famous. He had picked Romeo Echo Kilo up at the Dassault factory, brand new for its owner, Roscoe Edward King, and been flying it since. King was financially worth over $6.75 billion and, as a *Times* op-ed once said, was "one of America's baddest billionaires," as he had shut down yet another factory and sent the jobs overseas. King liked the tag. A framed copy of the headline hung above his Manhattan office desk. Andrew Carnegie and J. P. Morgan were his heroes. Especially Carnegie, who had built a railroad across America with Irish and Chinese labor that were paid pennies per day. As they dropped and died from exhaustion and famine, he had them buried along the tracks. King revered the ruthless determination.

Chainsaw Al Dunlap, the corporate raider and fraudster, was another of his heroes. King got a charge out of any exercise of the philosophy that it's all about money and power. His romantic hero had chopped up several paper mills around the country and Canada, sold off the machines, and sent the production to South America and China. He then used the world-renowned brand name to keep Americans blowing their noses and wiping their asses with what they thought was a product made in the good old U.S.A. King figured people were born to be played, just as animals were put on earth by the Creator to be shot for sport. It said so in the Bible, according to Roscoe King. Dunlap had chopped up Scott Paper, killing thousands of American jobs, and made a personal fortune while doing it. He sold off the woodlands to clear-cutting land developers; as one union leader said during the labor protest, "What government in the world would let this happen to their workers and then issue press releases congratulating themselves for expanding international trade? Only the government of the United States of America!" King loved the quote as demonstrating that even Uncle Sam knew the score. Ol' Chainsaw Al was misunderstood; King figured he had learned from fallen giants and would carry on the fight.

When the Federal Department of Labor explained to Mr. King that he would have to pay health insurance and wages for years accumulated by the workers in the mills that he was closing, he called his K Street lobbyist in Washington. "I don't care what it costs me! I want the law changed." King was proud to dream big. Laws lay in market baskets in quaint Medieval streets floating in the clouds out his jet-seat window, while the lyrics of the union organizer played over the speakers,

> I dreamed I saw Joe Hill last night,
> Alive as you and me.
> Says I, "But Joe, you're ten years dead."
> "I never died," says he.

Jackson Gunther and all of the other 1,100 sweating workers in the Jay mill that day working for Paul Bunyan Paper Company had no idea that the man who was about to buy their mill was in fact the devil himself. All he needed was a horn and tail.

He was going to visit the mill on this trip to Maine. No one knew this except his pilot, Terry, who would double as his driver, and the mill manager working for the investment fund doing the selling. If the union president or the workers had known King was sniffing anywhere in the neighborhood, they would have welcomed him with pitchforks.

Every bit of fuel, maintenance and labor to run this beautiful jet, a flying monument to greed, had to be written off as a business expense every year. This trip was to visit Tower's daughter Naomi, who was attending Camp Abenaki on Echo Lake in Fayette. The business end was seventeen miles from his daughter's summer camp.

King had gone to summer camp on Echo Lake, and Naomi was there for ten weeks. She was swimming in the cold clarity of one of Maine's finest bodies of water. Her parents visited her for one three-day weekend—she was twelve years old, and it was her fourth such summer in Maine.

On approach, Roscoe King thought he was challenging his pilot to keep sharp. Dowd thought he was a "mighty large pain in the arse," as his Irish aunt Mary Kate would say. The Irish loved the word, "mighty." After all, the flight computations were done by the onboard computer in the jet's flight systems. But the paychecks to Dowd always cleared the bank. He was on his third wife and his second alimony schedule—he could take a little shit. The pay was good, and the alimony was steep.

This trip was a fifty-six-minute flight from Westchester County to Augusta State Airport, according to the computer in the Falcon. It would always allow for busy air traffic getting out of the New York controlled airspace and some time for light traffic landing into the Augusta Airport. It was a nice ride, Dowd thought, with no anticipated weather problems—Interstate 95 on the left and the Atlantic Ocean on the right. This was one of those perfectly clear days that pilots dream about, and King could not screw this up for him. His right-seat pilot was a kid named Richardson with 1,100 hours of copilot jet time and no threat to Dowd, the pilot in command (PIC). He had seen that happen before——younger, lower-time pilots would befriend owners and slowly communicate that they could do the job cheaper and better. They were nothing but low-time, job-stealing jet jockeys.

Gloria Jean King had been named for the '70s feminist Gloria Steinem. She knew it from an early age and resented it. She was forty-two and did not have a six-inch section of her body that had not been altered, tucked, lifted, or enhanced by a plastic surgeon. Gloria King was ever so often referred to as a "bitch on wheels," in her social milieu. She could dress down a maître d'hôtel or a bellboy like a knife as sharp as a deer skinner in the wild counties of northern Maine.

They had been married for twenty years. Twenty was the magic number in New York State to guarantee her a full half of what he owned, should they divorce. Gloria was grateful to her mother Gracie, a Long Island socialite, who had mastered the art of divorce all the way to the bank.

Gloria always sat in the right front seat of the Falcon, where she could make direct eye contact with Terry. The seat was custom made for King at the factory. She sat in it on every trip. This trip the song circled in her head,

> Baby you're a rich man, too,
> You keep all your money in a big brown bag
> Inside a zoo . . ."

They had been cruising through the sub-stratosphere just below the speed of sound, all systems performing at peak levels, with a fifty-six-knot tailwind at an altitude of twenty-five thousand feet.

At the same time, Mac and his friend Liam had flown along the Rangeley's with a slow, gentle turning motion, as if the airplane were performing a giant slalom ski race through the clouds. They had flown near Saddleback Mountain on the Appalachian Trail. These clear, clean lakes are some of the most beautiful in America— Rangeley, Richardson, Cupsuptic, Umbagog, Mooselookmeguntic, the Pond in the River, the Rapid River—where great trout lie. Mac had completed his fire observation run along the New Hampshire border, where he joked to Liam Mitchell over the headsets, "Down on the right is the New Hampshire border; no taxes, you know. Live, freeze and die."

The lakes had shone like jewels in the afternoon summer sun. Mac tapped the fuel indicator above his left shoulder. "We will set down on a little dirt runway and walk through the woods to a pool along the Rapid River." As if his arm were a fish pole, Mac made a slight upward jerking motion with his hand and arm to indicate a fish being hooked. Liam smiled a big smile with a gleam in his eye. The wind was calm, with a slight breeze out of the northwest. He pulled the power and turned the Super Cub downwind to land on a 1,500-foot dirt airstrip carved out of the middle of the woods.

The airplane landed and was stopped and shut down in less than five minutes. Mac and Liam wasted no time running the fly lines through the guides on their rods and selecting flies from their fishing vests. A small trail that had been used for fifty years broke out on a slice of river. The river called the Rapid had been known as a trophy-fish river for decades. The fisheries biologists in Maine had targeted the river for restoration and designation and had been working it for a long time. The strain of brook trout was a true, hearty, pure strain that could survive in the cold water and reproduce with a Darwinian drive.

Mac and Liam had fished the river before, but this was the first visit by Liam to this pool. He cast a small floating caddis fly upriver and watched it drift by with a little tension applied to the six-weight line. Two fish rose at the fly but no takers. He cast and worked the water and the pools with no success for another thirty minutes. Mac had walked downriver to another pool. Liam wondered if Mac had intentionally put him at the slower pool. It was just a fishermen's suspicion—they all had it, Liam was certain, even about best friends and relatives.

Mac had made a number of back casts ending in trees behind him twenty feet off the river. He finally dropped into the pool, filling his Bean boots with water, and started to roll cast towards what he believed was a fish swirling and feeding above a large rock in the river.

Splash! The trout took Mac's muddler right off of the surface. The rod tip went down and the fight was on. *A fat, lazy trout feeding in the afternoon sun—not likely*, Mac thought. The trout moved through the current in a very deliberate manner. It was hooked and would be caught soon. The fish was now visible; it was a three-pound trout, for sure, and he was playing it to the shore. He now realized that the net for his fishing vest was in the back seat of his truck, back at the Augusta airport. That was not good. This big trout needed a net.

As he stepped back away from the bank of the river, Mac laid his rod sideways and extended his arm toward the woods. The fish came slowly to the bank, all played out and slowly giving in. Mac reached down to turn the fly and release it without touching the fish. The trout, a beauty in the sun, even with its summer colors, saw his hand and made a flop with all of its remaining strength and was gone down the rapid. Mac turned toward the path to leave, and he caught Liam staring at him from behind a cedar tree.

"You bastard," Liam said. "You put me on that, no-fish fucking pool, and you're down here hooking three-pound trout."

Mac smiled at him and made a motion to walk back up the riverside trail. "I am sorry, Liam. Didn't I leave you my instruction manual when I dropped you at that pool?" Mac smiled slyly to lighten the jab.

They walked together, talking about nature's beauty, fish, women, and good whiskey. Mac walked toward the pool that Liam had been fishing and said, "Do you want me to catch a couple and show you how it's done?"

"Yeah, go ahead, you prick. Throw that worn-out, frayed muddler fly of yours in there and see what happens." Liam was feeling a little indignant now. No one in Maine had studied more about fly fishing than he had, and even though he grew up in Chappaqua, New York, he had done his time in the Maine woods. He had written columns in sporting magazines for three decades and was thought to be one of the finer sports writers in New England.

Mac made four false casts and put the fly just above a rapid moving quickly away from the bank. The fly started to eddy out, and just before Mac retrieved it a trout hit the fly and swallowed it firm. Mac played the small twelve-inch trout to the bank and let it go. Liam put his rod down and made a motion towards his friend's throat with both hands as if to be strangling him.

"Don't do it, don't do it! Unless you can fly your fat ass out of here, you better not choke me. I know you want to, but you have been out-fished on this fine summer day. But if you let me live, you will be brought back again to this spot. Brought back by a fly-fishing god!"

Liam gave him a shot in the arm with his big fist, and Mac thought, *OK, fair enough. Another fine moment. Friendship, fishing, and flying—all things good this fine summer day. It's a beautiful day, don't let it slip away.*

CB   BD

The Cub had blasted out of the small dirt strip with ease. "This is what a Super Cub was made for," Mac shouted into the headsets. "We'll fly back over the mountains and get a decent view of a conservation parcel that I worked on back a few years ago."

Liam had hiked into Tumbledown Mountain many times as a younger man, and this day he would see it from a hawk's view, flying a hundred feet above the little pond on the top of the mountain, where hikers cooled themselves in the hot summer days. This particular day was a nice eighty-four degrees, with a slight breeze—and it was apparently a good day to remove all hiking gear and clothes and skinny dip in the high mountain pond. It must have been a college summer outing or one of the camps letting their guests go into the Maine woods alone. But there they were for all the world to see—or at least for Mac and Liam to see. There were over twenty naked young people jumping off the rocks and frolicking in the mountain pond.

There was no talk on the headsets in the Cub, just one smile to another from two love-lacking, middle-aged men who had just seen a dozen naked young women in the water below them. There were no Snidely Whiplash looks of perversion, just an *aha!* sigh of men who had witnessed the art and beauty of the female form, all of these miles out into the wilderness. Liam thought to himself, *this must be a reward for me from God; Mac is my angel of transport.* They circled twice and started back, and the plane dipped again and made a third pass over the naked swimmers as they all jumped up and down and waved at the airplane.

The flight home had gone quickly, too quickly for both of the men. "Augusta Unicom Super Cub November Two Nine One Eight Alpha is five miles northwest for landing on Runway Three Five." McCabe keyed the mike and made his intentions known.

Aircraft radios were a nuisance to McCabe. He had spent a quarter of a century flying back country in northern Maine and Canada. There were no airports or pilots or controllers to speak with where he flew his passengers. He certainly wasn't going to announce on an aircraft frequency the places where he was taking his sports. It was a very bad idea for a pilot to reveal the destination lake. Today was different, indeed; there were all of these jet jockeys flying around the state capital's airport, and many of them were not familiar with local flight customs. Mac announced his next move, "Super Cub One Eight Alpha turning base to land three five at Augusta." Mac's voice was clear—his intention was to land the airplane on the main runway at the airport below him.

A quiet, low voice came over the Unicom frequency on 123.0. "Falcon Jet, Bravo Juliet Romeo ten miles to the south for landing on Runway Three Five, local traffic please advise. We are on a ten-mile final."

It was Terry Dowd piloting the billionaire to Parents' Weekend on the lakes in central Maine. Dowd was now feeling the pressure cooker of working for Mr. King, who had told his pilot that he wanted to be on the ground in fifty-three minutes' flight time and not one minute later. Terry had the three General Electric jet engines screaming at 320 knots over the ground—way too fast at this low level; he would be over the airport in less than a minute.

The jet was over Merrymeeting Bay below the Kennebec River, and Dowd turned to King and said, "We will be on the ground in three minutes, sir, right on time."

King looked at his Breitling Chronograph and said, "You have three minutes and sixteen seconds exactly to have these wheels stopped on that runway." He had now moved out of his seat behind his wife and was crouching between the two pilots, demanding performance both mechanical and human. He was paying for it.

The GPS told Mac the little Cub would be on a three-quarter-mile final for the runway threshold in thirty seconds, a short, final touchdown and taxiing to clear the runway. Ten minutes max for the whole thing to happen. Mac spoke through the internal intercom to tell Liam that there was a jet on their ass, and they would have to expedite the landing. *These jet assholes never fly the pattern like a normal aircraft. Ten-mile final, what pilot crap!* he thought.

Dowd turned to his boss and said that there was an airplane in front of them going to land, and it would delay their arrival by a few minutes. They both knew the Cub had the right of way. And there was no deadline, just a black GMC SUV awaiting his arrival to take him to Fayette and his daughter's summer camp, but still he leaned into Dowd, "Land the fucking airplane, Terry, I mean it!"

Wake turbulence is compared to when a large ski boat zooms by your little canoe on a lake at 45 mph, and you end up dropping your paddle and hanging on for dear life upon the sides of your little boat. With airplanes it's a little different, however. It can kill instantly, lowering you to the ground and slamming you into a runway with great force. It would be the vortex of the high-powered jet acting as the hand of God smacking you down like a bug.

Jets create a lot of wake turbulence. The little propeller-driven Cub was on a straight-in final for Runway Three Five, when Liam saw out of the corner of his eye the wings of the Falcon go twenty-five feet under the Piper Cub. The next thing the airplane experienced was all of the wind beneath the wings of the disappearing and a dropping sensation like no other.

They had lost two hundred feet in a second and they were only seven hundred feet above the ground. The airplane nosed to the right and went into a spin. Mac could see the canopy of the Dunkin Donuts on Western Avenue right beneath him, and the airplane was dropping in an uncontrolled diving spin. He put his left hand on the throttle and firewalled the engine, pushed forward on the control stick and kicked the opposite control rudder of the airplane. He thought about control and direction—when you are in a dive and spin the natural thing is to want to pull up. The life-saving move, though, close to the ground, was to do what Mac was doing. Push the nose down toward the ground.

The airspeed indicator on the two-seat airplane was approaching the red line of *never exceed speed* and the tachometer had already gone to red-line. The instrument panel appearing in front of McCabe was throwing out every terror warning it could send to the eyes, ears and brain of the pilot. The speed, too fast; the rate of descent, moments from impact to the ground; the rpms, way over engine specs; the turn and bank indicator, way out of conformity. Mac, as many pilots who have crashed, had no time for last thoughts and prayers. He had never been put in this death spiral so close to the ground. The windshield was full of the earth and cars, and as it spun lower, there were people as well.

Liam had grabbed for something to hang onto before the crash happened. He touched the control stick. Mac could feel it. "No!" he screamed into the headset microphone.

Liam let go immediately and reached under the seat. He grabbed the cushion with both hands and pulled up. He had written front page headlines about violent small-plane crashes, and now he would be one himself. At least he would die with a friend nearby, he thought. Tragic, but with a friend. They would probably need dental records to identify the bodies. His brain had gone into a death spiral along with the Cub.

The jet had taken all of the flying air from their wings, and the Cub was reacting accordingly. It was an out-of-control, earthbound mass of metal, engine, propeller, and wings flopping through the sky. The control stick between Mac's legs could be the last thing he would hold in his life. But it was the one thing that could save him and his friend, and now this family getting into their car, from a terrible violent death.

He had both hands on the stick—there was no need to grab the throttle or the flaps. The throttle was wide open and turning the engines faster than it had ever done before. He could feel the flight controls come back, and the airspeed indicator was responding. *Maneuvering speed*, he thought. Seconds from impact, Marie crossed herself and held her children tightly. The whining of the propeller and motor was deafening to all standing on Western Avenue that day.

Mac pulled back on the stick in a smooth motion, adding a firm press to the left rudder pedal. He needed directional control in addition to climbing speed. Suddenly there was a thud followed by a cracking and crunching sound. The tire of the airplane had hit the Thule ski-and-storage carrier on top of Marie's SUV, causing it to be inverted like a deflated football. The plastic smashed into the parking lot, and the aircraft kept its flying speed, flying off like a wounded goose trying to gather the strength to live.

Mac looked out the left window to see the tire and wheel undamaged. What he could not see was that a gear spar had been bent by the impact with Marie's new Yukon. The motor was still wide open to the firewall; he reached to his left and eased the throttle back, bringing the plane to seventy-five knots on the airspeed indicator. They would definitely live if there was no other structural damage to the aircraft. Left turn, right turn, left aileron, right aileron, back and forth on the elevator—the airplane was flying straight and correct. The controls were solid.

Mac looked for the Saint Christopher medal to give it a touch. It wasn't there; it was in the de Havilland Beaver back on Lovejoy Pond. "No wonder," Mac chided himself under his breath. *What's wrong with you, you dumb Mick bastard?*

The eight-foot-long Thule storage unit Marie had installed on top of her new vehicle had acted as a very short ski jump for the oversized wheel on the Super Cub's left landing gear. Mac had started the recovery from the spin, but if not for the slick black plastic of the Thule storage container, the Cub would have settled the final eight feet to the ground, pancaking into the parking lot. The Yukon was parked in the most perfect spot. A smaller wheel on the plane would have punctured through and caused a crash and fire. A shorter storage bin would not have given the aircraft enough momentum to skid off.

The manager of McDonald's, his belly jiggling, ran to Marie and her children, offering his comfort. "What happened, what is going on out here?" He had never had this type of incident taught to him in manager training. He had his book of coupons in his back pocket and offered Marie the entire thirty free Happy Meals in the booklet. Marie just brushed the tears away from her cheek and squeezed her children tighter. The black plastic from the destroyed Thule container atop her Yukon was still flapping from the impact.

6

Pilots have envy, often jealous of other pilots and the aircraft they fly. More power, better comfort, cool avionic systems, twin engines; it's a progression that many subscribe to. And then there are jets—you have arrived at a pilot's perfection and nirvana. Not to Mac.

He had arrived on his twenty-second birthday, when he purchased his first Cessna 180 Sky Wagon. The Sky Wagon was a 230 horsepower bush plane that flew as a "tail dragger" and floatplane. It was a kickass performer of a bush plane that Mac had loved from the fist throttle advance. The first power climb out with the 180 signaled his arrival as a true aviator. It was his magic carpet, his ticket to ride.

To Mac's thinking, there were pilots, and then there were pilots. Real pilots were stick-and-rudder men and women like himself and his pilot friends. They flew Cubs, Cessna 180s and 185s, Beavers, Huskies, Decathlons, Aeroncas, Maules, and other aircraft that had a tail and wheels to steer it across the runways and airfields of the world. They flew into the bush with skis and floats and did not have to ask permission from some controller on a radio to fly places—they just went.

These folks were the closest thing to modern-day adventurers. They were unique in this world of composite aircraft with glass-screen navigation systems and controllers that regulated every movement through the sky. McCabe loved flying and flyers, but if you flew in the bush in North America, whether it was in Alaska or Labrador, Mac had a special place for you as a brother or sister in flight. Bush pilots were dying off from old age; they were the greatest generation of flight.

Maneuvering low to the ground was bad; it was dangerous and

often fatal. The end of Runway 35 dropped off onto Western Avenue. On any other runway, in any other city, in any other place, this incident would have resulted in a double fatality, the plane smacking the ground in a low-level, uncontrollable spin caused by the wake turbulence of an overpowering jet. McCabe had trained in aerobatics and knew spin recovery and mountain turbulence maneuvers very well. That training saved his life this day.

The last thing the airport manager needed was an incident on this particular weekend, the busiest of the year at the airport. An unfortunate incident showing up in the *Kennebec Journal* was not good for business—what if all of these jets decided to land in Brunswick instead? The manager cringed at the thought.

Both McCabe and Dowd were cuffed and stuffed into the back of the city police cruiser and taken to the main hangar of Maine Instrument Flight.

"Hey, man, I did not see the airplane on final," Dowd lied to the manager, a man he had purchased thousands of dollars worth of jet fuel from over the years.

"You saw me, you heard me, and like you jet-flying assholes have been doing for years, you ignored me and my airplane! No one does twenty-mile finals to this runway or any non-controlled runway. We enter the pattern, fly downwind, cross wind, base, and then final to land. Just like they teach you in school, asshole." Mac screamed at the man—a foot from his ear. He was still steaming.

The cops were writing in a pad with great speed, but they weren't getting any of it. There were no skid marks, no bodies, no crushed fenders, or deployed air bags. This was as foreign as a vacation to Québec for them; the language just wasn't matching up to their report forms. The local police removed both sets of handcuffs, threw their hands in the air, and drove off.

The airport manager, who knew Mac locally and had known of his flying business for years, encouraged the two to shake hands and move on.

Liam said to his friend, "Hey man, we are all in one piece, we fished the Rapid today, no one is hurt, no dents in the plane. Let's get the hell out of here and have a couple of shots."

McCabe looked at Dowd and said, "You didn't kill us . . . but you're going to wish you had. This isn't over. We won't forget your little stunt here today."

Dowd nodded slowly. He could see that Mac and most likely Liam were both in the "we-ain't-fuckin'-around club," as Mac liked to call it.

After the cops left, Mac and Liam tied the Super Cub down on the low-rent side of the airfield. Dowd texted the driver of King's Escalade to pick him up at the airport—he was, quite literally, a bloody mess.

Liam followed Mac home, out Route 202 then on to Route 17. He knew he had to spend some mind time with his friend. Kelley would not be home for a couple of hours, and Mac had plenty of time to clean up and get his story straight. She might hear about it from the folks at work at the hospital or in town. He would not be explaining the near miss; she just didn't want to hear about that sort of thing. She had bad feelings about flying in general. She couldn't rid herself of the bad thoughts—the darkness of it all—no matter how hard she tried.

The Escalade raced past Mac's F-150 4x4 truck, in the opposite direction, as it sped back to pick up the pilot and drop him at the Senator Inn and Restaurant. Dowd would spend the next two nights drinking and trying to get laid. Roscoe and Gloria King were in a rented camp on Echo Lake. It was provided by the owners of Camp Abenaki for the most affluent parent visitors. The camp had a small boat and a canoe to paddle across the lake and visit the awaiting summer-camp kids. King was looking at a balance sheet for the Paul Bunyan Paper Company. He was about to put a knife through the heart of this entire region of Maine. Without a second thought, he would buy the mill and cut the workforce to zero.

Mac pulled into the Weathervane parking lot on 17, the local watering hole on Maranacook Lake. He walked in, with Liam wheeling the Toyota Tundra right up to within inches of his bumper. They sat down and ordered two shots of Jameson's and two black coffees—it was the middle of the afternoon. In perfect sync, they dumped the shots into the coffee.

Mac looked at Liam and said, "They have bought America, the politicians, our assets, our souls, our hope. These billionaires of the new millennium are the worst barbarians we have had on this earth since the cavemen ran in hordes clubbing and slaughtering their fellow man in efforts of greed to gain all things on earth."

Liam responded, "We could file charges, contact the FAA. We could line up witnesses; we could really get this guy."

"Which guy? The pilot? He ain't the guy. It's the man that he is flying around, the one that controls the world as we know it. America's oligarchy, the new enemy within, and we were within inches of him." Mac stirred the hot coffee with his pinky finger. He threw the mug back with the whiskey rushing to his stomach and head. Black coffee with a dark whiskey filling a black stomach next to a quickly blackening heart, McCabe was going Irish dark, and Liam liked it when he got like this—he appreciated the determination and vengeance.

Liam, a trained journalist, quickly Googled the tail numbers of the Falcon jet on the FAA registry site and showed his friend the results. The aircraft was registered to an offshore LLC controlled by a hedge-fund manager named Roscoe Edward King of New York City.

Mac sat quietly for a long moment, then finally looked up and said, "That's our boy, Liam. We need to go to school on this prick of a man."

Mac was motivated now. They would both spend a lot of time in the next few months learning about what made this man so special he almost killed them with his jet.

In his Lay-Z-Boy, Mac had opined that he just lived from song lyric to song lyric, all jumbled the way memories unfold in daydreams. Songs remind us of times and places; for Mac the memories could be so strikingly vivid as to divert his sense of direction in life, his moral compass. He would take hold of these lyrics like lifelines. Now all he could think of was: "He built a fire on main street and shot it full of holes," until Bob Dylan's voice tapered off in his head, leaving him strangely grounded.

Liam Mitchell was a master at research. He had worked at one of New York's largest daily newspapers and had mastered the art of finding things out. The most common question asked about Liam, from politicians, criminals, and businessmen was, "How the hell did he find out about that?" The data grab on Roscoe King had just begun. Everything that Liam learned gave him insight into a human being bent on power. He knew that the world was filled with people like King, but this was up close and personal.

7

On payday of Friday, February 13th, 2015, Jackson Gunther opened his paycheck. In it was a note from the mill manager that read, "Due to the pending purchase of our mill by Midas, LLC of New York, we will have to downsize our workforce substantially. Today will be your last day of work and your security card will no longer work at any entrance point on the mill property. We thank you for your ___ years of service. If we have an opening in your job classification, we will be more than pleased to rehire you. Otherwise, consider this your first and final notification of termination." It was signed by Gerald Joseph, mill manager.

A temporary clerk in the front office at Bunyan Paper had failed to fill the blank with an *8* for numbers of years of service. Jackson had been there for every shift in that paper mill for eight years without missing a single day of work. He had carried his department as a mill-wright and pipe-fitter. He could do anything on the floor. The shop steward told him to slow down. "Don't work so fast, my man. This pile of work will be here in forty years when you retire; just do your part."

That was not the way Jackson was built. He did it and did it fast. He was the closest thing to a human machine anyone in this mill had seen. Now, because he was the last man to come into his department, he would be the first one to lose his job. He was union to the core, born and bred. How would he explain this to Hannah? The union must have signed off on his termination, right? *They must have*, he thought. Why him? What about his kids?

He had a fifteen-minute commute and hunted for a month every year filling his freezer with deer meat, partridge, pheasant, and rabbits. He could hold one hundred days of winter meals for his family wrapped and frozen on the last day of hunting season of the year. This year was a bonus, as his name had been drawn in the Maine moose hunt lottery, and he had 250 pounds of additional meat in his father's and his sister Kelley McCabe's freezer.

He shot animals on the fly and always thought they should get a little head start—he was a game hunter, big and small, with fair chase in mind. He had never given the enemy in Afghanistan that courtesy. Most of the time the Taliban leaders never knew they were in his gun's high-powered scope sight when their heads exploded from his fifty-caliber sniper rifle. He had requested Army sniper school on a whim after he had made his fourteenth low-level airborne jump. He was good at all of it.

He didn't understand this layoff. He had heard about layoffs from boys in the papermakers' local who had been through the Rumford strike in the 1980s. He had seen downturns in paper orders, but his job was to keep this behemoth running and trouble free. The work would never end, he had thought, had hoped. Now it had ended. It said so right on this paper with the Bunyan/Midas letterhead. Nowhere was the name of Mr. Roscoe King to be found on Jackson's termination notice. His name was running circles in Jackson's head, though.

One hundred and sixteen other letters were dropped in the paychecks of Bunyan's employees. It was known locally as the Valentine's Eve Massacre. It was the first of a dozen more days in store for the Jay mill workers. Jackson left the mill bewildered. He was angry, but knew he needed to find a way to focus his anger. Good, bad, or otherwise, he had to make a plan for himself and his family—like his brother-in-law with the airplane, he needed to be a planner.

He opened the freezer when he arrived home and thawed a package of tenderloin venison that had come from a deer he had shot the past November. He would thaw it and cook it in a red wine sauté and serve his wife and two children this meal with sides of asparagus and wild rice. It would taste delicious, it was all organic, and he smiled when he served it.

Jackson would not tell Hannah until the next morning. He needed to sleep on it. He needed to make a new plan for himself and his family. He was head-weary from thinking too much, but he was never body weary—he was an unstoppable, physical specimen of man.

He was five foot ten and solid muscle from toe to ears. He had light-blond hair and steel-blue eyes from the gene pool of German, Swedish, Scottish, and American Indian ancestry. He wore his hair tightly cropped with a set of clippers Hannah used every two weeks. He had a compressed goatee, like the character Michael played by Robert De Niro in *The Deer Hunter*. Mac's line for Jackson: "Abe said, 'Where you want this killin' done.' God said, 'Out on Highway 61.'"

Gunther had been a fighter from his very first days in school—whether as a young boy or an older one, any kid who gave him a hard time usually got a pop in the nose. He was told to do so by his grandfather, who took great part and pride in his upbringing. "If you get that part settled right away with potential enemies, you will always instill fear and respect for life in those that meet you. You will, however, take a beating every once in a while." He remembered those words from his grandfather like a ringing bell. He loved his grandfather very much.

He never studied much but always aced the tests he took. He had a photographic memory—from maps to textbooks and from math problems to other people's notes, Gunther could recall it all. He had the gifts of physical strength, stamina, and mental capacity. In his youth, Jackson would beeline to the scene of a crime or an accident, especially if there was an explosion involved. He could disassemble a cherry bomb or two and blow up the mailbox of his bus driver—just to show that if folks did not mind their manners, Gunther would do as he pleased—he would sit anywhere on the bus at any time. He was eleven years old, liked gunfire, hot flaming brush fires, fast cars and motorcycles, and pretty, bright-eyed schoolgirls.

The teachers could not find a way to focus his energy or his stamina; the high school football coaches were finally able to capture the youngster as a teen, only to find he had tremendous speed and would run straight into a brick wall for the right cause. A championship would be the right cause. In his final season, he had played both sides of the ball—offense and defense—as a senior starter and co-captain. He averaged ten tackles a game and rushed for over 1,600 yards as a tailback. He was 160 pounds soaking wet but had a drive from his muscular legs that would mow over 250-pound linemen with little effort.

He was scouted by Division II and Division III schools for football, but once the high school principal had a word with the scouts, many of them just walked away. It was 2001—both the state championship and the homecoming game were on the line for the good folks of Livermore High School. "Do you have a bomb shelter at your college?" the principal would ask them seriously when talking about Jackson Gunther.

"Why do you ask? What's the joke, the story?" a recruiter asked.

"Well, three weeks ago we had a homecoming game with our rivals over in Rumford. The Rumford mascot is a ram, and they had a nice, life-size, wooden sculpture of a ram at the entrance to the athletic field." He continued the story with a finger in the air moving in circles. "Someone bored a hole into the animal with a portable, large-bit electrician's drill and packed it full of gunpowder. Just prior to the game, three spectators wearing hoodies cleared everyone within a twenty-five yard radius away from the sculpture, and through a remote electronic detonator the ram exploded in a thousand pieces."

The home field advantage for Rumford diminished to a whimper. The Livermore team won 42 to 17, even as the police bomb squad delayed the start of the game by an hour. Gunther had 160 yards rushing and 18 tackles. The case would never be solved. It was legend—the game and the boom.

The police had not been able to find out who had done the terrible deed, but two of the assistant coaches at Livermore, where Jackson played, had seen an old-style flip phone cell on the dash of his Ford Ranger 4x4 the night before the game. The cops questioned Jackson—both the State Police and the local Sheriff's Office. The sheriff had bet a thousand dollars at the Legion Hall on the Livermore team—this boy wasn't going anywhere with the State bomb cops. He may have done it or he may not have; the sheriff loved Jackson and the way he ran the ball.

Jackson was as cool as they come while being questioned. When one cop squeezed his shoulder tightly to make his point, Jackson looked up at him and said, "Is that as hard as you can squeeze?"

The police would not have thought twice about Jackson as the perpetrator of the crime, except the old-style phone was suspect. Gunther was a techno redneck who had all of the latest smart phones and apps, stolen electronically by his then-girlfriend, Hannah Cook. He hadn't had a flip phone for five years, but those old phones still had the ability to detonate from afar.

"He would be a great addition to your college," Principal Bailey said. "He could even be a star collegiate athlete, but if you have the potential for something to blow up on your campus, he would be your guy—he could blow it up or set it on fire, literally."

Bailey loved to watch Gunther play football, but he never knew what would happen next at the school. Several cars had been burned, off the school grounds, belonging to young men attempting to win Hannah's love or maybe a one-night stand with the tall beauty.

Around the time hunting season started during his junior year, Gunther was accused of losing a game so that he would not miss a day hunting with his father and uncles. It wasn't true, but his football head got lost in the woods when the guns of November barked in Fayette.

Sometimes he would disappear for days at a time, spending nights in the woods alone. He would text Hannah a GPS location to meet him before sunrise. There would be two buck deer dragged to the end of a back-woods dirt road—one for his family and one for her family; the legal limit was one deer per hunter. Her family was poor by most standards; her father drank away most of the Friday paycheck by Monday morning most weeks. The local game warden would have to get up a lot earlier in the day to catch Jackson Gunther. But no meat or fish were ever wasted by him. He had his own food bank in operation—a business that operated on the end of a .30-06 Winchester bolt action. Gunther was a good man to the people he loved.

But there would be no college campuses for young Mr. Gunther. The day he walked into the Army recruiter's office in Lewiston, the young sergeant looked up and thought to himself, *Praise the Lord! Here walks in my monthly bonus check for recruiting. With this young Turk, I will reel him in slow.* He prepared the bait for the new recruit. Jackson smiled. He wanted to serve his country and kill terrorists.

Jackson had seen the recruiting video of this new Army-of-One and knew that he was that One. America was still in Iraq and in its third year of the war against terror in Afghanistan. He read everything online that he could and knew that there were no weapons of mass destruction in Iraq. He felt young Bush had to avenge the attempt on his daddy's life, and he had no problem with that at all. He also figured that most every person in every powerful position in this government of America was a liar.

Jackson had presented an oral report on President Clinton in his junior year of high school and had done a wonderful job of explaining Clinton's economic policies and the twenty million new jobs in the new economy. He had presented a brief NAFTA explanation with good clarity to the class. Just as he was wrapping up, he held up a finger and put a crook in it and said to everyone including the teacher, "I did not have sex with that woman, Miss Lewinsky."

The entire class broke out laughing—you could hear them all the way into the gym. For his irreverence, Jackson got a week of detention—he had spent a lot of his high school years in the detention hall. He very rarely believed anyone talking to him was a truth-teller. Whether it be the school principal, the president of the United States on TV, the governor, a U.S. senator, a state senator, the local town manager or selectmen, he always began with the notion that they were lying to him. He was rarely wrong, but the nuances escaped this marksman. They seemed like distractions that only made it worse.

With all of his cynicism based on history and experience, it did not cause him much concern or restrain him from joining the United States Army. He wasn't that crazy about taking orders or listening to someone yell at him, but he knew that in that big arsenal of Army weaponry and explosives, they had a lot to offer. He could not wait for the birthday presents that the United States government was about to lay at his feet. He was nineteen and headed for basic training at Fort Bragg in North Carolina. Airborne school would be the first place they would send him after basic training. And soon after, weapons and bullets and more weapons. It would be like Christmas to him every month. And he loved the physical training.

Gunther was told by his Uncle Walter to not raise his hand when they asked who knew how to shoot a rifle. He knew that Jackson was a crack shot, but figured the Army would never send him to sniper school if they thought he had brought any skills with him to the firing range. Ego dictated that the military needed to think that they had trained him. He wanted that school, jump school, Ranger school, advanced weaponry, scout school, tanks, and anything that could blow up something else; *artillery and rocket-propelled grenade training would be nice*, Jackson thought. But his uncle was right—he had to appear humble at first.

He remembered his father saying to him, "Just look straight ahead and say, 'Sir, yes sir!' for the first eight months and beat them all at the physical training and on the range. Things will go your way. Don't eye-fuck 'em or talk back. Take the shit. They will see your potential."

They did. The training officers knew he would be a natural leader, a soldier, and as importantly, an efficient killer. They knew there was some killing to do in the mountains of Afghanistan, and this boy was one who would get it done.

In Afghanistan there was a brand of Taliban leaders who brewed a special kind of hatred and death; they moved with groups of about twenty men, mostly in their early twenties and late teens. They drove Toyota Tundras and Land Cruisers and the like, mostly new with low miles, with automatic weapons mounted on the trucks and an AK fighter standing up through the sunroof.

One of their specialties was to instill terror in peaceful villages that seemed to take no side in the never-ending war. They would demand to know who owned Western items. When no one would speak up, they would start searching the homes, committing atrocities before the assembled villagers.

They moved about the country trying to stay one step ahead of the drones and patrols, recruiting more desperately poor young men along the way. Like all terrorist organizations, including Mac's beloved IRA during "the troubles," they recruited with threats, religion and bravado. They were told their next life would be a paradise filled with earthly pleasures and delights, one version of an old universal story. They decapitated slowly and murdered with swiftness. In Jackson's mind, they were evil beasts in human form, and they needed to die without any due process. His job was to hunt them down, gather information, engage and execute them.

Intelligence was gathered to determine who these men were, what their backgrounds were and, more importantly, what their war crimes were. They had to have multiple war crimes. The crimes had to be corroborated by documented eye witnesses; there had to be a file with photos of the crimes, and names of victims and the families. There had to be chronologies, timelines to all of this activity detailed daily. This was a special version of delivered military justice. There would be no accusations of My Lai or slaughtering of innocent civilians displayed in front of Congressional committees and hearings.

Gitmo was no longer a destination for these Taliban leaders and other branded terrorists. They would be going to hell—many sent directly by the man from Fayette, Maine.

Jackson did not make friends easily—he never had. His father and his grandfather were his best friends, his hunting buddies, his go-to guys. They would cover for him for anything, and he would do the same for them. Anything. He wasn't looking for friends like that. He did find and serve with men that wanted to be near him, wanted to hear and laugh at his Maine accent. Mostly, they were men from the South, men that could skin a buck and run a trout line.

They were a group of men that had refined their war trades and could be counted on to have your back in a firefight with the enemy, whatever enemy presented itself in whatever spot in the world. Jackson had those types of friends now; it had taken a while, but he had them now. They would load each other's clips, answer each other's questions, and finish each other's sentences. After a few months, these men from different corners of America became a band of brothers in these hills of Afghanistan.

"I'd like to spit some beechnut in that dude's eye and shoot him with my old 45," Mac meanwhile sang in the skies.

⊗ ⊗

It was winter 2004 in Afghanistan, when Jackson's team was activated earlier than usual one morning. He was trained to do the same job with the same efficiency every day, but this day had a little more sparkle to it. A full-bird colonel had pulled in the night before to brief his lieutenant; they would know soon enough. *Don't get too excited,* he thought to himself.

They had grabbed Korazied in the fall of 2004 on a bright September morning—Korazied had been in the original deck of fifty-two terrorist cards. He had aged and slowed a little by the time Jackson and his buddy, Master Sergeant Linwood "Buckshot" Peller from Savannah, Georgia, got him near a major heroin processing facility forty miles north of Kabul. The team had a brief firefight and killed three insurgents.

Buckshot got his nickname from a sawed-off, twelve-gauge Remington automatic shotgun that had been modified to hold eight shells—a shotgun never left his side. He was a freak about no one touching it—it was "bad karma" and "bad luck"—and he always had a small condom over the full-choke barrel to keep the sand out of the automation.

Buckshot was Jackson's friend—he liked the killing a lot more than Jackson, but he was precise and seemed to have grown up along a similar path to Jackson, south of the Mason-Dixon line. He was brought up with hunting and fishing, football, loving parents, national pride, and an absolute disdain for politicians, liars, and cheats. He had been in some bar fights and won a few. He circled around Jackson like a wolf in a pack at first; soon he figured out this wolf—this Yankee wolf—would hunt with him in this pack, together.

Sometimes Jackson shook uncontrollably after these grab-and-go missions. If he could just hold Hannah for one night—he dreamt about her every night. Maybe he could lose these shakes.

America was a weapons factory for the world—one-time friend, one-time foe. A great general of American history had warned us— General Dwight D. Eisenhower. If he could see the state of things now, what would he think? Jackson had a short list of heroes, and Eisenhower was on top.

Jackson loved to tell the story of General Eisenhower's note, written just before the D-Day invasion of Nazi-occupied France: it said, if the invasion failed, he was entirely at fault—an exemplary act of responsibility and courage in American war history, a stand-up guy, like no other in Jackson's pantheon. Today a group of underfed, undertrained, underequipped terrorists, numbering no more than a hundred thousand worldwide, had tied up the U.S. military for over fourteen years. Where was the leadership? Where was the courage? Jackson thought most of it had been buried in Eisenhower's tomb.

Korazied was the man all the teams wanted to capture, and Jackson and Buckshot had grabbed him. He would be buried in a hole in the desert no one would ever visit.

This man was not a child rapist or killer of women; he had cut off many men's heads and had demonstrated the art finely to his trainees throughout the countryside. He was a warrior against the West and had organized terrorist bombings and helped to fund them. He would now spend the last twenty-four hours of his life with Americans who had watched the 9/11 videos continually and seen photos of his trainees' handiwork throughout the villages of this troubled place. He was thinking of a paradise beyond now and wondering how he could cause himself to die immediately, saving himself from the torture and the questions. It had come to this with the American soldiers, like so many of his comrades over the years. He was tired—tired of running, tired of hating so much and so many for so long a time.

The Americans would leave soon, he thought, just like the Russians who had killed his father. The Americans' new black president had said so; they too would be gone, and now, so would he. He closed his eyes while upright on his knees, hoped he was facing to the east, and began to pray to Allah. He thought of days in his youth tending goats in the meadow below the mountains, before the Russians, before the Americans. It was a peaceful thought.

Jackson would not be questioning this man, who was a high priority; a couple of senior officers in his special unit had been flown in along with the questioner. There were ten Taliban fighters tied together and alive today. They were broken up to find out who was the next in line behind Korazied—there was a pecking order to this band of misfit militia men. Jackson and Buckshot were tasked to find this out.

A drone picked up a large movement of Taliban into the area. They were at least four hours away at their current speed. If the U.S. troops called in an airstrike, it would draw unwanted attention. They needed to move the high-value prisoner out of there, Jackson thought, band up the rest, and load them into a troop transport for imprisonment and questioning in Kabul.

Jackson did not want any more exposure to this terrorist; he wanted him flown out and to get back to business as usual. He was now afraid this was not going to end well, and he did not want to be a part of it. The colonel he had seen the night before was inbound, and things were heating up. Buckshot volunteered to end the captive right there. "He's never gonna tell you anything anyway," he told the captain while smoking a camel. "You could pull all of his fingernails out and cut open his stomach and move his bowels onto his chest. He won't talk. The guys at this level like to die for the cause, with sealed lips."

Ten minutes later a chopper took off, followed by a gunship. Fifteen minutes later the chopper came back around—this time Korazied was tethered off with a yellow static line swinging wildly, as the helo moved side to side. He was hanging by his feet, and the chopper buzzed the convoy carrying the prisoners. He never talked, never confessed or revealed a word; they cut him loose eight hundred feet over an al-Qaida-friendly village that was into the heroin trade, the very place where he had originally been apprehended.

His last thoughts were herding the goats near the streams as a boy at the base of the mountains of Afghanistan. You could hear his bones crunch, as his body crashed in the middle of the town square. He had just started to hit terminal velocity, the maximum speed a human body reaches in freefall, 120 mph. The colonel put his long knife back into it's sheath and signaled the pilot to return to base. The interrogator gave the colonel a high five. They had photographed and taken a DNA sample of Korazied—one more dead terrorist.

Jackson's thoughts took him home as he drove down the mountain road with the new prisoners. He thought about trout fishing in Maine, hunting with his dad, and how things were really starting to suck in this war, in this place so far from home. He knew that this bad free-faller had done horrible things to the people here and to some of his fellow American soldiers. He also knew that in the village where the martyr made his unannounced arrival from the sky, ten more boys would take up the jihad and be facing another soldier from another small town in Maine soon. It was endless—*these Afghans were born to fight the infidels, the invaders to their homes and villages, and they had no sense of country, no flag to wave. Their country was their religion, Mohammed was their leader, and Western infidels were their enemy for life.* Even though Jackson had thoroughly researched the history of the region, these and other generalizations overwhelmed him here.

In the two months between his deployments, Jackson married Hannah in a ceremony on the lake at Echo. A small picnic boat-launch area near "the big chimney" was the setting for the wedding. Their friends and relatives had all helped to make the place as special as possible. Jackson's uncle, along with the local sawmill, helped build fifteen eight-person picnic tables and place them at the boat-launch site. The Gunthers took the site over and made it the best it could be for this loving couple in the fall in Maine, getting married for life. All hundred and one feet of the Chimney—august landmark and remnant of a tannery built in the late 1800s—stood witness.

Jackson liked his new brother-in-law, his sister Kelley's new husband, Mac McCabe—he liked the fact he was a sportsman and a bush pilot. He could see himself landing on northern lakes with the man. Jackson could see that working out for him, later on, with his unborn son and future fly fisherman. He'd had other ideas for the betrothal of his sister that did not work out. This guy would do for now, he thought; she could do a lot worse than Mac McCabe.

8

At twelve years old Liam Mitchell had read Jack London's short story, *To Build a Fire*, ten times; he wanted to feel the cold and the forlorn desperation of the character trying to stay alive. Trying to light his final match as the trees released the snow putting out the last hope for fire and warmth. The man in the story freezes to death.

He would pretend this tragedy in his back yard in January of 1979. He wanted the loss of feeling in his fingers and the frozen tears to show him this man's misery. He would take two matches and try to light the fire under his father's clump of white birches. He would fail and begin to freeze. He would go inside, and Allison would fix him a hot cocoa and a fluffernutter sandwich—his best friend, his mother, always came through.

He called his mother Allison. It was not a "mommy" type of relationship. She was a hard, cold woman who worked two jobs and liked to drink vodka martinis. He was five foot eleven in the fifth grade. He had grown too fast to have the agility for basketball. He was awkward and uncoordinated. He was a book nerd, but no one made fun of him.

The first thing his uncles taught him in third grade was to hit a man in the nose. Not the shoulder, you could shrug that off in minutes. Not the stomach, it was a cheap shot. They taught him to stand toe to toe and hit a man straight in the nose with his right hand, left hand up in defense, awaiting a return punch. His older cousin Brendon, who would become a cop, took a sharpie and put a big nose on a punching bag. "Hit that. Hit that till it hurts your arm. Hit that spot on the bag."

He took the instructions correctly. No one made fun of the overgrown book nerd in Chappaqua, not this lad.

"A punch in the nose will make a man remember you, Liam." Brendon had given and received many in his life. "It is a soft and sensitive piece of flesh that swells and stings and breaks when you hit it at just the right speed and force."

The Mitchells were fine people. If you fought one of them you fought all of them. If you were friend to one you were friend to all.

Liam was an English/Journalism major and was writing for the college newspaper. He loved to expose the executives of the college for excessiveness and opulence. Sneaking into the president's functions with a notepad and camera, he would investigate the endowments and the sources. Troubled alumni with financial means would pay for a building with funds swindled from a bank or a sketchy government contract. He knew the weaknesses of mankind—money, sex, power, deceit, and despair. He had been told continually about it by his grandmother from the time he was five. "Men are born to sin, they'll sin until they die."

He tried to develop an open mind and a fairness in judgment of others, especially of people in power, such as deans, faculty, and department heads. However, he could not help himself. He was so jaded, so tainted, he could barely like himself. Father Murphy had fondled his best friend's private parts and other lads serving mass as altar boys; his father had cheated on his lovely mother; his uncles all drank themselves silly and fell on top of him as a young man. He had carried almost all of them from the bar to the car and driven them home. Even at the age of thirteen, he would drive his uncle's Buick Electra up the street, smoking a cigar, like he owned it. He was the driver for his alcoholic uncles and their friends three years before he had a license. They called him the "wheel man," and he enjoyed the designation. He liked the way he could rest his wrist over the steering wheel of the giant Buick and drive with one hand. They wouldn't let him do it in driver's education three years later, though. He already knew how to steer like a bank robber's getaway driver.

His years in the Ivy League in Connecticut were productive, and he learned a great deal about the world and those that would rule it—they had been running it forever. Unlike his fellow students, he did not want to be one of the world rulers. He thought the Wilson Doctrine was a tip of the hat to the status quo of monarchs, dictators and thieves.

His grandmother had told him there was only one true leader in American history and that it was the man gunned down in Dallas. A Roman Catholic son of a bootlegger with a bad back who just happened to be of Irish descent, John Fitzgerald Kennedy. The Kennedy family was from Roscommon, which was two villages over from Bridget Kathleen Mitchell. "I knew his cousins," she would say. "All good people, supporters of the IRA and the fight for Irish freedom against the British."

Liam graduated with honors and submitted job applications throughout the Tri-State Area, but jobs were scarce with papers in trouble. He had a friend who worked at the *New York Post* and knew some editors and some folks with an inside line to the publisher. It was a tabloid, a subway mat for wet feet, but it was a people's newspaper and had a tremendous readership throughout the city. People loved the trash, yellow journalism, and the way they took on the elite and powerful. He would do it. He may be stuck for life in that rag, but he would do it.

One day, a senior editor walked by Liam's desk and threw a *Daily News* front-page story of a newly released mob boss on his desk. "We are not getting this story—this man is back and he is in control. Mitchell, get your 'learn on' about the mob and this family."

Liam looked up at his editor, one of the world's original ball busters. "I love the City Hall beat, I love the boxing coverage, I love my little court stories, I hate the mob. They don't like press, if you haven't figured that out. They especially don't like the writers from the press who write about them. I don't want to live in fear." He pleaded with the editor.

It didn't matter. He was the low man on the totem pole, and he was now going to cover New York's most violent mob family for the *New York Post*. He was headed for Little Italy, and he really wasn't welcome. He was Irish, and everyone knew the Micks and the Wops didn't mix well.

Liam had fallen in love with a lovely, intelligent woman from Brooklyn. Sara Lewinsky was the brightest light he had ever had in his life. She was an anthropologist and worked deep down in of the Museum of Natural History; she catalogued and opened boxes from an expedition that had taken place a hundred years ago. She loved the challenges, discovery, and intrigue that came with her work. She fell for Liam at the annual sojourn to the White Horse Tavern, where

Dylan Thomas had drunk himself to death. The Welsh poet and many other writers would gather there to drink. Thomas would drink until he could not walk, the famous words being "Twenty-three shots . . . I think that is a record." Then it was off to Bellevue Hospital where he died a few days later of alcohol poisoning.

The fine end to Dylan Thomas would befit half of them before their lives were over, while Liam might live on as a cynic. Still, in the vomit-stained corner of the White Horse, Sara spotted him with his thick, reddish head of hair brushed over like a young Van Morrison, singing at the top of his lungs lyrics by Harry Nilsson. "You're breaking my heart, you're tearing it apart, so fuck you." She was in from that moment; he was her man.

They married in a ceremony that was elegant and simple, with a rock-and-roll band and one of the first chocolate fountains to ever appear in America. His grandmother, who had poked her nose into every minute of Liam's upbringing, whispered to her son Brendon, "Is she a Jew?" with a nasty emphasis on the word *Jew*.

"No Ma, she was adopted by a nice Jewish family in Brooklyn; her people were from Galway." It was a lie; Sara was a fine, beautiful, intelligent, Jewish woman, from a fine, Jewish family. There was a mixed marriage happening right before Bridget's eyes, and she did not have a clue.

"All saints be thanked," Bridget Kathleen Mitchell said and proceeded to cross herself, twice.

His new beat took him up and down Mott Street and around the neighborhoods of Little Italy and Chinatown. He loved the smells, the bakeries, the game, ducks and chickens hanging in the window, the noodles, the myriad of faces, the overwhelming daily attack to the senses. He soaked in the chaos of people hustling, cooking, baking rolls, rolling cannoli, dealing dope, and holding tightly onto children crossing the streets. He gawked at old Saint Patrick's Cathedral, lived with the streets and appreciated the value of the differences in America. He walked the melting pot. It was his beat.

New York City was the center of the universe and Liam Mitchell was riding at the crest of the highest wave. Man, this was the kind of life he could be a part of forever. His editor liked his copy; they cut and edited, and cursed and threw his stories on the floor. But they did it to all their writers, especially the new guys. However, there was something that they liked about this man from Yale via Chappaqua; he was not the hardscrabble beat-street pounder they were used to, but he was going to work out. He had an easy smile and an added edge of height and weight.

The first mobster Liam encountered was sitting outside the bakery known as Bennie's in the middle of Mott Street. He was sitting in an '98 Oldsmobile, all shined up with wire wheels and a chrome grille. Liam simply walked up to him and asked him if he knew where the boss was.

Suddenly, a hand appeared on Liam's shoulder and he turned quickly to see a face familiar to every person in New York and much of the United States. "I'm John, you are Liam. We know all about you. Check your facts with Vincent here before you print, and we will have a good working relationship.

"The way all of this works in our lives and in most of this city, as we know it, Mr. Mitchell, is like this. We like you, we love you, we use you, we drop you, and we fuck you."

Liam was standing eye to eye with the man. "We never want to get to the point where we fuck you, capiche?"

Liam nodded in agreement; he felt the boss's breath on his neck. A famous quote popped into his head at that moment, "Leave the gun. Take the cannoli." Liam knew every line in *The Godfather*, every line.

He was taken completely by surprise. This man in front of him was much shorter and had a good face. Not a kind face and not a phony face like other criminals he had seen, but a good face that began with a good head of hair and eyes that bore right into you. His chin could have belonged to Tony Curtis or Rock Hudson. On the surface, this was a handsome, well-dressed man of the city.

Liam told his editors about the encounter. They were amused and talked openly about Liam's new best friend in Little Italy. It was a new day; he loved the excitement, the wonderment, the not knowing.

New York City had three thousand black Lincoln Town Cars moving people to and fro. Every time he saw one, he wondered if he was being watched. If he saw one in the Village he would think, *What are they doing down here?* Paranoia came with this assignment— long-term, everlasting paranoia. This was a new sensation for him. He had felt something akin to it when his grandmother Bridget would visit his mother's home when he was a boy. Now he felt it in a different and bigger way. He took to carrying a flask to help calm his nerves a little—everyone in the newsroom had one.

Liam was becoming a man on a mission. He knew that his paper did not win Pulitzers. He also knew that many of the nation's top news sources were within ten blocks of each other in Midtown Manhattan. People would read his byline and see his stories; he could be the go-to guy on organized crime on the talk shows and radio programs of America. That would be a good goal for him to strive for. He shared his thoughts with Sara—his heart, his muse, his lover, his friend.

The first time he spoke by phone to a radio talk show about his new favorite headline subject, the radio host nicknamed the mob boss. *Why didn't I think of that?* Liam wondered. The nickname went viral in the days before viral was even a thing. It fit perfectly, and showed up in the subways wherever you looked.

The phone on Liam's desk rang. He rarely answered this phone but was glad he decided to pick up when he heard the gruff, heavily New York accented voice on the other end of the line. "Hey, this is Vincent. Is this you, Mr. Mitchell?"

"Yeah, this is Liam Mitchell." *Well, this is a new development in our relationship*, Liam thought.

"Liam, I hope you are having a good day there at the paper. I am outside with our friend, and we were wondering if you could come outside for a minute?" The voice was firm, and Vincent was clearly not actually asking but telling Liam he would be coming outside. Liam said that he would be right out and enquired what he should be looking for.

"Don't worry, Mr. Mitchell, we will find you. Use the 53rd Street entrance of your building."

Liam let his editor know, as he walked swiftly past him, that if he did not return within half an hour he had been either shot or kidnapped by a mobster named Vincent.

"Bring me a coffee when you return, Mitchell. Black, two sugars!" he yelled as dashed out the door. He really was not concerned about Liam's safety; he had three more new guys who would step in and do his job on Monday morning. He needed coffee.

Liam knew there was a nice newspaper somewhere, surrounded by peace and tranquility, that would welcome this smart Ivy League man with big-city experience. He remembered his uncles taking him to Moosehead Lake in Maine as a boy. He wondered if there was a *Moosehead Daily* that he could work for. Maybe he would check this out tomorrow, or even tonight.

When he got home, he had made it back earlier than Sara and

stopped along the way to grab a bottle of Jameson's Irish whiskey. He was two drinks deep when Sara walked through the door. He told her everything—the ride, the faces, the fear, the implications, the nerves, the chills—that had happened all in one little ride around the block. He knew he would have to complete the "assignment" and was worried that it might never end. He had seen reporters who had these never-ending assignments. Even the society writers were boozers, drinking bottomless martinis in uptown bars and swanky restaurants. He knew that he could catch this little affliction quite easily. He was now drinking whiskey neat, no ice or water to lessen the bite. Neat was not neat; it was a problem.

He decided the time was now. It was at this moment that he would pull the ripcord on his parachute and land somewhere in the great state of Maine. It didn't matter that it was a place he had visited only once and knew almost nothing about. For some reason it represented safety. Sara knew even less. She loved New York City and wanted to spend the rest of her life there as three generations of Lewinsky's before her had. But Liam knew what had to be done.

Would Sara come? Would she agree to leave the island of Manhattan for a place in the sticks, with below-zero winters and mosquitoes? He was afraid this was not in the cards for her. Where would she find a Bloomingdales?

Sara had a friend from Brooklyn whose landlord had ties to Maine. She would call him and ask to meet with the woman. She could see her man was coming undone and this would not end well, if something didn't change. He was buying yellow liquor by the half-gallon instead of the fifth now and going through them at the same pace. She started looking at towns in Maine for places to live and what she might do for work.

Liam was intrigued by the thought of ten million acres of unorganized territory, where recreation was unlimited on private and public land. He would make this an adventure. He would write a book like Jack London or maybe Ernest Hemingway. He would learn to hunt, learn to fish, learn to become an expert with firearms and sporting equipment. He and Sara would pitch tents and cook wild game on Coleman stoves and campfires. By God, he would do it. Especially the firearms part. He would learn to shoot with the quickness and accuracy of Clint Eastwood in *Dirty Harry*. There was not a chance in hell that Vincent or anyone would be able to harm him or Sara. This little journey and change in life was the closest thing to the witness protection program that they could impose upon themselves. Now where would he live?

Maranacook Lake was in the departure corridor for the de Havilland Beaver plane belonging to Allagash Air and its owner/pilot Mac McCabe. Mac seldom varied from his course in departing or landing. Most of his flights were to the north, and most of his landings were either north or south on the compass heading on Lovejoy Pond. Ice-out in spring 2002 found Mac flying directly over Liam Mitchell's rented lake house.

At first Liam thought it was a wonderful novelty to see the old floatplane with the unique engine noise go over his home. But after the tenth morning of 5:00 a.m. departures in June waking him and Sara up, he sought to find out where all the racket was coming from. It did not take his curious mind long to find the base of operations of Allagash Air on Lovejoy Pond. There it was, a hand-carved wooden sign on Lovejoy Pond Road. He whipped the Tundra into the driveway with his best New York attitude in tow.

He was met by a chocolate Lab with a wagging tail and looking for some kind of treat. Kelley McCabe was in the doorway two minutes after the dog had barked. The vehicle still had New York plates on it, and she thought she might have missed a reservation somehow.

This lakefront home had no neighbors. It was remote and secluded, with a driveway that said there was only one reason to enter; either you were a customer or you lived here. There would be no joy-riders in this driveway—Mac had designed it that way. "Can I help you?" Kelley asked.

"Is this the place where the loud, noisy airplane is from that flies over my home early in the morning and wakes my wife and me up?" His question was full of accusation.

Kelley could fall into an attitude in a split second and had met non-Mainers like this a hundred times before. They wanted to stir things up and make Maine like whatever place they had left. She stared just another second and took a breath. *Maybe I will handle this pecker-head a little different—why not?*

She called the dog and bent over to clip the leash on. As she bent, her Lucky jeans revealed just a hint of a purple thong to the visitor. Unknown to her, it disarmed him immediately. He thought she could fill out a pair of Lucky jeans as well as anyone on Fifth Avenue. It seemed as though she was alone here. Who the hell was he to give this beauty of the woods a difficult time?

"My name is Kelley McCabe, our family runs a guide service and floatplane business here on Lovejoy Pond. What is your name and where do you live?"

"Liam Mitchell, nice to meet you." He shook her hand. "My wife and I rent a home over on Maranacook Lake near Tallwood. I have been working at the *Kennebec Journal* for the past six months." All of the defensive body language was disappearing from the conversation.

"You folks from Livermore Falls?" Kelley joked, picking up the New York accent immediately.

Liam had to think for a minute, where was Livermore Falls? He smiled and the ice was broken. He returned to the purpose of his mission from the neighboring lake. "What about the noise?"

Kelley was a fifth generation Fayette resident and had known all of the town's history from the time she could walk and talk with her Nana, the former postmaster—a knowledge she was determined to pass on to their daughter, Jackie. She motioned for Liam to come into the little office that she had with the Allagash Air sign over the doorway. She had set up the coffee pot to encourage all that entered to pour a cup. She motioned to the pot for Liam to help himself. He did.

"Floatplanes have been on this lake since the '30s, almost before outboard motors. We try to get along with our neighbors and folks on the other lakes around here. Show me on the map where you are staying, and I will ask the pilot to stay clear of your area." She purposely did not say the pilot was her husband. Mac had enough people bad-mouthing him and did not need a man at the *Kennebec Journal* writing some nasty smack.

Liam pointed to the cove in the point near Tallwood Estates on Maranacook and said the floatplane goes directly over his home. The map was Mac's secret list of fishing locations. "Why all the colored pin markings?" he asked Kelley.

"They are markings for fishing locations and camping areas where our business has boats and campsites set up." Kelley knew if she had revealed to a newspaper man the location of the best fishing spots in the state of Maine, someone would be skun alive, namely her. This was religion to her husband and his small group of fly-fishermen buddies.

"The map is peppered with colored pins. Maybe that would make a good story for our outdoor writers." Liam was treading on turf he had no awareness of.

"I don't think so, Mr. Mitchell," she said as she bent over the desk to grab a brochure of the business and again flashed just a blur of purple thong. "Please stop by again, and I will speak to our pilot about his route and the noise."

Liam thanked her, patted the dog's head, and left the office. Kelley thought the man was pleasant and cordial, even though he looked as though he might have a bad temper with that orange flash of bushy sideburns. She double-checked—the can of pepper spray was still hanging from a nail behind the door. Maybe they'd get some business, maybe a favorable news story, who knows? She put Liam out of her head and went about her day. She was so proud of herself for not copping an attitude with this stranger, who could potentially cause a lot of trouble for her and Mac.

9

Mac had a notion that a connection to nature made people better, that it brought out the best in them. It brought about a purity of the soul that was an opportunity for transformation of even the worst human being. He had seen it happen with his own eyes. He had flown them, some of them bad men. He had heard their evil schemes over the Dave Clark headsets in the de Havilland. Plant closings, subprime mortgages for the masses, pollution of the environment, cutting of roads through his wilderness, destroying thousands of acres of habitat and nature. He had seen the ill will and greed in men for most of his adult life. He was doing his part to change that; the Beaver was his enabler to end bad intentions. Sometimes it even worked.

Mac could see a co-conspirator in Liam as he started to hang with him and trust him. They had a fondness for Irish whiskey and the songs of Neil Young. They would sit on the shores of Maranacook and plot a little treason for the powers that be in the state of Maine. Liam would tip Mac about stories that were breaking at the Statehouse, and Mac would tell of a trout spot giving up two-pounders. It was a friendship working its way out, as they do. They spoke of love and the poetry of W. B. Yeats, the writing of Fitzgerald and Pound.

They understood each other. Mac had been an elected legislator for a short time and had run for U.S. Congress on the theme of single-payer health care. He had almost won, which was a complete surprise to him, as he'd had no intention of winning. He just wanted to make a statement, and he did.

Twenty years later it seemed nothing had improved; it had only gotten worse and he more cynical. Liam was right there with him riding on the Cynic's Whiskey Train every Saturday afternoon from 6:00 to 8:00 p.m., either on Lovejoy Pond or Maranacook Lake. It was said that whiskey was the reason the Irish did not control the world. These two Celtic clowns were living proof, in living color, on the lakes of lovely Maine. They were drinking it on ice twelve months a year.

They fished in the spring and hunted in the fall and drank and ate together year-round. They had become friends with a purpose. The only thing left was to figure out which purpose to take on. They had both discussed doing one good thing in their lives before they pushed on through to the other side.

There was a lot of sadness in the schools; the store was selling a lot of booze. The country store couldn't keep Pabst Blue Ribbon or Bud Light stocked and cold. There were divorces in the works and men taking jobs in other states. Women who had been driving the new SUVs were hiding them behind the garage as the payments to the banks and credit unions went sixty days out of cycle. The credit cards had been maxed, home equity was tapped, and this was an honest to goodness economic crisis in Kennebec, Franklin, and Androscoggin counties.

The governor, who was a Right-wing nut job, held his hands in the air and yelled at the cameras, "My hands are tied. I can't help people find jobs. Pull yourselves up by the bootstraps and get going!" His security detail of state troopers had been doubled after the infamous Jay press conference. Many people in the impacted area had great stashes of guns and ammo; almost all of them had conceal/carry weapons permits.

The irony of the governor's statements was that Herbert Hoover had said the exact same thing at the beginning of the Great Depression. "My hands are tied," was a statement endorsing greed and corruption, low tax rates to the richest people, and market failures unmatched under a free-market economy.

Liam lost his job at the newspaper in a sellout to another hedge-fund chop-shop and was writing outdoor columns for the monthly sporting magazines of Maine. He could tell a sharp story. Sara was the curator at the Maine State Museum and brought home most of the couple's income.

Mac had taken the Beaver out of the water this year. It was still covered with snow but needing far less work than the year before. Its aluminum was shining in the late-day sunset. He loved this aircraft. Was it wrong to love something so inanimate, made of so much metal? Should he be so materialistic? He loved certain people much more, he mused, the thought lightening his guilt.

Then it came to him, the notion he had had on the day the power was out at his home the year before. He could do one good thing in his life, and he knew what it was. It would take one bad thing, maybe two, to do the one good thing, but he knew just what it was. He started making notes on white lined paper. It was a different type of flight plan, but Mac was a planner.

He wrote down time columns, travel dates, getting the specifics together for this mission. Did he have the guts to pull this off? Could he do it alone? It was an idea that would take perfect execution to succeed. Would the end be worth it? What if he was caught and went to jail for the rest of his life? Could he spend a long time incarcerated without the love of his wife and daughter?

He knew men who had done time from his hometown. It was the worst; they had been screwed in the ass by multiple men at different times during their incarceration. He would not stand for that. He was still going to do the deed; he just needed a partner that he could trust beyond all others. His first thought was that Kelley was it. She would be the one to stand by him through anything. But the thought of depriving her of her daughter and the closeness to her family for the rest of her life was heartbreaking. She was ten years younger than Mac. The embarrassment doing the time would kill her. No, he would never tell her about his plan. He would have to disguise it as new business venture.

Then it came to him—Jackson was the man. He already had a hate on for the billionaire King. Jackson was a man of a million secrets, and he would be buried with all of them.

Jackson had been home two years from the war in Afghanistan, and there were two children now. Hannah's business designing and maintaining websites was a success. They had doubled down on the mortgage principle payments and had their home almost paid for. They were active parents in the community and were always involved in local charity. Now who would help *them*, with Jackson out of a job and most of the town in destitution?

Could they go to their local lender and get some home equity to pay some of the bills? Some of the laid-off workers had used the credit unions for their mortgages, and they were being helpful. The large banks with the better rates and one-day decisions on thirty-year mortgages, not so much. Many people had tried and failed. No one wanted a home in this area of the county now. The realtors were organizing a fire sale for the mill workers and their families. They were the first set of vultures to begin the orbit around the dying community. There would of course be others looking to make deals for pennies on the dollar.

Mac would speak with his brother-in-law and of course his newfound rebel friend, Liam Mitchell. He invited them to the Chimney boat launch on Echo Lake for a day of ice fishing. They would talk it over; they would devise a scheme, and they would see it through. He would lead them to do the one good thing in all of their lives for so many people. And like all good things it would start with something bad, and this was going to be really bad. This would be a crime against criminals and nothing less than what the bad guys deserved.

10

It was a cloudy, snowy morning on the Sunday after Valentine's Day. Mac rolled over in the king-size bed and ran his finger up and down on Kelley's back. It was 6:30 a.m. and she was still sleeping. Mac, in his depressed state of no flying and no money, had gone a little overboard on the Valentine's holiday. He had brought home two small filet steaks and a bottle of Kelley's favorite Pinot Noir. He had made a special dinner with roasted asparagus with hollandaise sauce, garlic potatoes, and a Caesar salad. He bought large strawberries and a chocolate sauce to dip them in. To top it off, he bought her a dozen of her favorite pink-and-white long-stem roses. There was a good chance of a lovemaking extravaganza on the lake that night.

They had stayed up late and opened an extra bottle of the Pinot that Kelley had hidden away. Jackie was away at her grandmother's for the night. The two were alone and in love on Lovejoy Pond. Mac tickled her a little more and after five minutes of jerking away in a "leave me alone" motion, Kelley rolled over and faced him. "Do you want to make love to me, McCabe?"

"I know I drank a lot of wine last night and had a beautiful Valentine's Day celebration, but I think I may have to check into the sex addiction therapy group on Monday." Mac smiled at her with begging, puppy-dog eyes and she grabbed his head, pulling it between her breasts. They made love again with the sun slowly peaking into their bedroom window.

Mac was going to fully lay the plan out today. He had told his brother-in-law and friend to both meet him at the boat launch at the

Chimney on Echo at 8:30 a.m. They would set up their fishing traps and drink some peppermint schnapps and discuss the plan that Mac had running through his head.

As far as Liam and Jackson knew, they were just meeting to set up the traps, do some fishing, and drink some schnapps. The rest was a surprise, and Mac worried the others would not agree to join him on his mission. Liam had done extensive research on Roscoe King and had almost two hundred and fifty pages on the man who ruined so many lives. Early in the process, the name William Pierce surfaced in connection with King and the teardown and ruination of Paul Bunyan paper. Liam was going to be tasked with an even bigger research project as of 10:30 this morning.

Mac always thought of ice fishing as not actually fishing but something more like bait dangling. He loved to do it, especially with friends in the winter, when his business was slow and he could snowshoe and enjoy time in the out-of-doors. His brother-in-law was an ice-fishing fanatic and owned the shack, the snowmobile, the dogsled, and the auger to bore through the ice. He did it at night for smelts and on every day he had off in the winter. Mac knew that Liam just liked the camaraderie of being with friends in the cold and outdoors and appreciated the connection created through a hole in the ice between him and thousands of fish swimming in a big circle looking for his bait.

The three were brought together that day to conspire to commit a crime in order to do something good—do something good for a great number of people in a country that had forgotten about the masses who had been the focus of Washington, Jefferson, and Lincoln. Were the planners of the American Revolution criminals? American commerce and government had largely forgotten the masses, in favor of the few check writers. Those in charge had brought about an historic windfall to greed. This talk, this plan, would either be each man's greatest challenge and accomplishment or the biggest failure three fuckups could muster.

The auger started with a *putt putt putt* and a kick of the single cylinder, puffing exhaust into the ten-below-zero air. Jackson insisted on being the hole driller. Five traps were allowed per person by law, and he would have all fifteen drilled in twenty minutes. He had to have the traps and the holes in perfect symmetry to the island and the lake shore. The holes had to be free from all ice particles and clear for his

line and leader to sit exactly in the center of the hole. Mac thought
he was a little obsessive-compulsive about the entire business, but he
supposed there was still a lot to like about his brother-in-law.

Echo Lake was different in that it was a very desirable game-fish
lake in central Maine. There were not a lot of lakes like this that had
consistent, healthy populations of brook trout, salmon, and togue.
Early in the season a smelt dangled on a hook just below the ice, the
length of a five-foot monofilament leader, could bring several nice
landlocked salmon in no time at all. Mac loved a fresh meal of salmon
or trout caught through the ice and a fine bottle of white wine. He
would cook it on the grill for his wife with a little lemon and butter. He
knew that Jackson would be catching fish—he always did. It would be
a part of his freezer stash, gathered with other wild game throughout
the year in anticipation of the apocalypse.

Jackson moved with a specific drive this clear, cold morning. Maybe
it was his desire to catch a lot of fish. Maybe it was that he was mad
about losing his job so close to home and with men he liked—all of
whom had also lost their jobs—with nothing more than an impersonal
note from a time clerk who'd stamped the mill manager's name on the
farewell. Jackson was not smiling much, and he was not making a lot
of eye contact. He was moving quickly and mechanically, as if he were
on a mission and just getting it all done—like he had done this before.
Done it before in another country, in another existence, with other
men, desperate to survive and prosper. Men who had another man's
boot on their neck who needed to jump up and strike back and yell,
"Enough is enough, enough is enough, enough!"

Mac could see this was a doable deed with Jackson, but Liam was
a concern. But he thought Liam was in need of a little treason against
the Man. He had also lost his job to a hedge-fund Ponzi scheme.

Jackson flipped a picnic table upside down and hauled it behind the
snowmobile to the spot where the men would drink, fish and—plan a
crime. Jackson had fished with his brother-in-law many times and had
read Liam's sporting columns for the past few years. But Jackson had
never fished with Liam.

Men who hunted and fished with Jackson were sized up within
the first half hour. What did a man bring to the table for any of these
outdoor sporting activities? His brother-in-law had the keys to the
great North Woods and Canada with that old floatplane. There was
never a question of his contribution. The magic carpet of a floatplane

was like a treasure to Jackson that he only tapped a couple of times a year with great gratitude. Mac understood all people's gratitude, or lack thereof, with great perception. He knew that Jackson was grateful for his flights, grateful for his sister's choice in a man.

The three were all fans of fine whiskey, but there was no whiskey today. The traps had all been baited and set. The men sat with excitement around the table that had a big heart carved in it. It was done with an Army Ranger's knife and said, "Jackson and Hannah 4ever." Jackson had neatly scratched it in on the wedding day of the soldier from Fayette and his beautiful bride. The wood carving was as fair and fine as if done the week before. Even local vandals would not mess with Jackson Gunther's wedding-day table.

Liam twisted the top of the schnapps and yelled "Flag!" as the trap furthest from the table went up, indicating a fish had latched onto the bait and was taking the line out.

Liam took off running after the flag and the possible fish on the end of the line. Jackson looked at Mac and said, "If he touches that line on my trap, I will have to square the fat fuck from New York away early today." Sometimes inexperienced ice fishermen thought that all set traps belonged to the group rather than an individual, but most ice fishermen did not think that way. Jackson's traps were Jackson's traps; keep your hands off the Jactraps, unless you want your lines cut. A different kind of line went through Mac's head, courtesy of Hank Williams Jr., "And we can skin a buck, we can run a trout line, and a country boy can survive."

Liam did not touch the line, but did get to the hole first to watch the reel spin as if it were part of a winding machine at a factory. A fine fish was moving this hook and bait at a rapid speed away from the ice hole as fast as it could. Jackson arrived at the hole fifteen seconds after Liam. Liam looked at him and nodded with a grin, "That reel is churning the water in that hole. Nice fish on that line, I'll bet!" Liam was very excited about the first fish of the year.

"We'll see," Jackson responded with a cautious eye and a slight smile as he bent over the hole and got down on one knee. He grabbed the trap and slowly removed it from the water, as he had done hundreds of times. He pulled the ice away with his bare hands. Liam thought it must be zero degrees in that water.

Jackson slowly provided resistance to the running line by squeezing his fingers together, slowing the fish's running speed by half. Then with a short smooth stroke to the left, he set the hook in the escaping fish's mouth, and the battle began between man and fish.

The battle lasted no more than three minutes, and a nice eighteen-inch landlocked salmon was on the ice. There was no catch and release for Jackson. He had lost his job, and his family would eat the bounty this land and water provided. The fish was gutted in forty-five seconds and stored away in the pack basket inside a Ziploc bag. He would go on to catch three more before the day was over. Technically it was two over his legal limit, but he was catching his brother-in-law's limit, as well. Mac did not care; he had a different mission today.

They returned to the picnic table and gave fist bumps to each other for "blood on the ice" and the first fish of the day and year. After all was said and done, Jackson was the only successful ice fishermen that day. He hooked the smelt through the lips instead of behind the back fin. He used a translucent monofilament line that was longer than others typically used. He always out-fished others on the lake. All technique, he thought, taught by his grandfather. His grandfather, dead now, was a good man who had lost his job due to a strike at a large paper mill started by greedy men in greedy corporations in the greedy place where all the greed is born and bred for generations.

As they sat and sipped, Mac simply started talking, as if a meeting coordinator had given him the floor to speak on the record. He laid out the plan as the fire in their eyes kindled on the ice. Then he cut it short with, "This is what I am proposing to you guys, if you want to do this. If you don't, we will never speak of it again, ever."

Mac could see that simple righteous vengeance, Justice League cartoon-style, was almost enough, having vilified the marks, King and Pierce, along with their social network and family. It was time to bring out the moral compass.

Mac was on his feet again with arms moving in sync. "I will set up a company to do a single-payer health-care system for the five New England states. It won't be government run, but it will have to be government endorsed. I know a man who has had this model in the works for almost a decade. He can do it for less than $10 billion, but we want him to succeed. So we will give him $11 billion. I will make sure the money comes to him in a not-for-profit 501(c)3 company."

Liam pounded the wooden table and said, smiling, "I always knew you were a socialist, McCabe!"

Jackson, a strong union man, had heard corporate leaders talk for years about the competitive advantage in countries that had single-payer systems, where employers and employees were not burdened with the extra costs of paying for the nation's health care, augmented by the exorbitantly private health-care industry, including the opulence of Big Pharma. All three men had family members who had either died or taken ill and been underinsured or not at all. There were millions of people across America in the same situation—uninsured or underinsured, and shit-out-of-luck dead underground. The American health-care system was eternally broken, and the capitalist money wanted it that way.

"I like it. Something good comes from robbing these pricks. There are a lot of what-ifs, though, Mac. Everyone in Maine knows the sound of that Beaver. How are you going to pull that off without tracing the airplane and the kidnapping to you?" Jackson had already started thinking in details, not concepts. He was on board.

"I don't plan to use the Beaver, Jackson. I am going to have to sell it and get a different airplane. A 185 can do the job with long-range tanks and a performance boost." Jackson knew from his sister that Allagash Air had been having cash-flow problems for years; he also knew what a heartbreaker this must be to Mac to have to sell it.

Jackson took another hit from the peppermint schnapps. "You bastards will have to get into shape, and we will have to practice this to the second, with no screw ups." Jackson realized he liked the plan and wished that his old buddy, Buckshot, still had both legs and lived on the lake they were now fishing. The two men sitting with him looked old and slow, but the airplane and Canadian component made it a true adventure. He liked motivating men and taking part in adventures. This would be an adventure of his lifetime—one for the ages.

Liam looked at Mac; he knew this was coming; it had been in the works for some time. It had been coming since the time he saw Mac poking at the ribs of King's pilot on the grass off the tarmac in Augusta. Mac McCabe had that clarity of recall that remembered the bad things that had happened to him and especially remembering the people behind the deeds. It was the worst case of Irish amnesia that Liam Mitchell had ever seen. He was pretty sure he had it as well. "I'm in!" Liam said, putting his fist down on the table with force.

Jackson thought for a short moment that he might be getting played by these two but decided it was the real deal. He said to his brother-in-law, "If we are caught we will spend the rest of our lives in jail. We will never see our wives or our children again, our families. There are a hundred things that can go wrong with this caper. Let me give it some thought, and we'll meet again in a week at the same spot with some research and details. I want details, Mac. Right down to the vehicles, flight time, contingencies, weapons, technology. No one says a word or writes a word about this at any time. I will create a code for us all to use."

Jackson was in, but he wasn't saying outright. His mind had started to return to Afghanistan and the grabbing of Taliban leaders and the thrill of pulling those well-planned kidnappings off. He had to call Buckshot—he hadn't spoken to him in six months. He missed his Army Ranger friend who had lost his leg on just such a mission. Maybe if Jackson had done something different, Buckshot would still have his leg. One of the many cycles of guilt unshared by the numb civilian world that would vote without paying attention to the next war.

Buckshot had taken his settlement money and opened a gun shop in Georgia with an SBA veterans loan. "Buckshot's One-Legged Gun Shop—Weapons Sold, Traded and Repaired" was written on the sign. Business was great, every gun nut in South Carolina and Georgia thought Barack Obama and Nancy Pelosi were going to show up on their doorsteps and take their firearms, so they were buying in bulk. Buckshot liked to promote these fears. His cash register was ringing, and he loved to promote hate and discontent toward any Democrat.

They day went on, the booze bottles were emptied, the fish was in the pack basket, and the three men's brains were swirling like tornados. When they finally parted, heading for their separate homes, they agreed to meet back in one week.

Jackson laid the four plump salmon into the kitchen sink, and Hannah smiled and gave him a big squeeze. "You smell like cheap booze and fish guts, Jackie Jack." She only called him that when she wanted something done. Something like cleaning the stink of cheap cigars, fish guts, or cheap booze off his breath, body, and clothes. She cut the heads off the four fish and double wrapped them for the freezer that was still filled to the top with deer and moose meat.

This man she loved was a provider in all the ways that a husband could bring to a marriage. He was a lover, a worker, a hunter, a gatherer, a gardener, and a father that loved her and her children absolutely. She could never entertain the thought of being without him; he was back from that wasted war started by worthless men. He was hers for life;

they would get over this little bump of a job loss and move on. He was a union worker with a trade, and the local would find him work. She had no idea that the thoughts in Jackson's head today could keep him from her for the rest of their lives. He never let on that there was anything different about today, just turned on the news.

Liam returned home to Sara with a spring in his step and a slight buzz in his head. He had smoked a couple of joints on the ice. He loved marijuana and how it left him feeling. Mac would sometimes take a hit, but not Jackson today. He had a piss test for a job interview on Monday and did not need anything showing up in the lab. He thought marijuana should be legalized, but didn't everybody?

Liam was excited about the plan, but he questioned whether or not he could do his part and go through with it. He looked at his big gut hanging over his pants and wondered if he could even get into shape again. Back in college, he had been a solid tight end for the football team, could bench three hundred pounds and run a six-second fifty yard at Yale. He was so far from those days, now living in the backwoods of Maine, half broke and all the way fat. He would study these two men, King and Pierce, right down to the exact point of their daily existence. He would know why they did things, when they took a shit, when and where they ate. He'd learn the name of their pets, their boats, and the places they kept their money. Damn, he loved Google.

Mac came home stinking just as bad as the other two. Kelley walked by him as he came in the door. She plugged her nose with two fingers and held out a towel just out of the dryer.

Man, did he love this woman; he would tell her that the Beaver would be sold this spring, when he got out of the shower. That would make her entire weekend a big hit. He trotted into the shower and got a good steam going. He was just about to wash his hair when the shower curtain pulled back and there stood Kelley, naked. *She could easily be a Victoria's Secret model*, he thought. This day was one fine day in the life of Mac McCabe.

Mac had never kept anything from her since the day they met. In truth, he had told her too much on that first day in an effort to derail the deception that had permeated the final years of his first marriage. She was honest as well, telling all of her secrets and dark times in her own history. Now Mac was going to keep the biggest secret of all time from her. He did not feel good about that. He could not tell her what he was about to do. He would sell the Beaver and hide some of the money to pull off this crime. He couldn't tell her, because he needed to protect her; she needed to be with their daughter and her mother, who was frail and dying of cancer.

He would never say a word until two years later, when they would take their share of the money from the robbery. He could live in prison for a while, he thought. The crime would take place in Indian country, basically in another country, above the 52nd parallel. Who would arrest me, and who would try me and convict me? Not a jury made up of the disparaged men and women in this county of Kennebec, he was sure of that. He did not want to think about it.

11

Mac started an online list of asking prices for de Havilland Beavers on floats. He recorded prices and engine and airframe times with modifications and special equipment. When he started to deal with Rocky he wanted all of the facts about the current airplane market. He did not want to be hoodwinked by this airplane dealer who was good at what he did. Rocky needed to be watched.

All indicators were that the airplane would sell for between $350,000 and $375,000. Mac had done a lot of work on the airplane and had purchased it with all of the Kenmore Air modifications done in Seattle. The airplane had a few dents, nicks, and scratches, but the floats didn't leak, it had an upgraded engine, and the three-bladed prop was low time. Mac would fly to Rocky's business in Greenville in Weston's Super Cub on floats and start the deal. He would target an early May sale. He would also start looking for a 185 Cessna in the meantime to take the Beaver's place at Allagash Air. It had taken Mac years to accept the eventual sale of his beloved airplane. He could not imagine being without it. People identified him and the business with the old radial engine noise and the flying service. He had now turned the page and was ready to move on.

Kelley had an idea what the plane was worth, and she had counted on the windfall to pay off the home, buy a new SUV, and put a large deposit into Jackie's college fund. She would get all of that in partial form, at least. Mac would create a stash for his criminal escapade, which would also contain a rather large retainer for a criminal attorney, should they be caught. Mac had flown with one of the best criminal attorneys in America. He had talked about murderous clients and premeditated crimes. His mind was fully involved in the premeditation of a specific crime now. He would go about his business, make the deal on the Beaver, get ramped up for spring, and never take his mind off what he was going to do on the Friday of the third week in July, 2015.

The next Sunday, the three men gathered again after setting up their fishing traps and the picnic table. This time Jackson had a map of the area and two sheets of graph paper. He had measured the distance from the Augusta State Airport to both the boys' camp on the west side of the lake, called Camp Awenouch, and the girls' camp on the east side of the lake, called Camp Wabanaki. He had calculated the whole plan at three different speeds.

One camp was on Echo Pond Road and the other camp was on Pond Road between Kent's Hill and Mount Vernon. He had scouted five locations on each road to create a diversion and make the billionaire grab. The diversion would be a car with a flat tire in the middle of the road for both grabs. He called it the "Bonnie-and-Clyde move."

Mac had told Jackson that he would have money available by Memorial Weekend to buy, guns, ammo, and gasoline. They would need two diversion and transportation vehicles, falsified documents, and drugs. A special body bag, and other high-tech equipment— laptops, satellite internet systems, travel money to get to New York City and the Cayman Islands. He had told Jackson that he had $25,000, but he really had $60,000. He knew that Jackson would spend it all if he knew the total. He could see him arriving at a training session with a rocket-propelled grenade launcher or an automatic machinegun. You can get anything with the right budget.

Liam had started his homework and had photos of the two men, their wives, and their children. King's daughter would be at the girls' camp. FAA records indicate that every year for the past six years the Falcon jet had arrived at the Augusta State Airport between 11:00 a.m. and 1:00 p.m., never any earlier and never any later. Pierce had a son from his second marriage, who would be attending the boys' camp for his third summer. King had apparently talked Pierce into the camps, the lake, and the location, after he had done the Bunyan deal.

Pierce flew in a Cessna Citation jet that was his own, but also part of the Net Jet fleet. His arrival time historically could not be tracked, as he may have used another Net Jet airplane. He always rented a Mercedes 350 GL with a driver from Portland, and the driver does not provide security, just transportation. King rented from the same firm and had an Escalade with a trained security driver for him and his wife all weekend. Rumor in the Portland office was that he had asked for an ex-Navy Seal to be his detail for the weekend. Most likely he would be armed. Jackson piped up, "Wonder why he doesn't go for an Army Ranger?" He grinned and winked at both men.

"There will be a lot of rented Mercedes and other SUVs out here on the road for the weekend," Mac stated. "We will need tag numbers and exact descriptions for these vehicles, just knowing it's a black escalade won't be good enough. I don't want my brother-in-law coming out of that bathroom with just his dick in his hand." Mac was imitating the line in *The Godfather* where Michael kills the crooked cop and the mobster.

Jackson laughed; the line from Sonny Corleone was often used in his group of hunting buddies in Fayettenam, discussing the possibility of a deer crossing their paths. "We can put a magnetized locator on them if we can get close to the vehicles at the airport. Remember, both vehicles will have the emergency locator with the North Star system that can be activated in a second." Quickness was success in this endeavor.

"This is where the training that you two are going to get in the next four months will make the difference between our success and our failure." Jackson looked them up and down. "I hope you have both started a weight-loss and strength-training ritual. You will need to be able to run an eight-minute mile nonstop, swim a half-mile, shoot with accuracy with both hand guns and rifles, and we will train in the gravel pit in Jay fifteen times until we are all perfect for this mission. One man screws up their job—we are all in prison for life. We will never get out of the state of Maine. We have to work in parts, becoming a whole." Jackson's teaching days were coming back—teaching men to survive, succeed, and to live. He could only hope these two were up to the task. He had faith in Mac, but the other guy, Liam, was an ongoing concern to him.

All day long, the middle-aged men on Echo Lake would race each other to the flags that had gone up on the traps. They each had a successful fishing day—Jackson had changed the leaders on both Mac's and Liam's traps without them knowing about it. He had changed the way the bait was hooked. He had started the care and feeding of these two already; he knew that they would need it. They scheduled the following weekend to be in the same spot to discuss transportation and technology, these being the two main components of this kidnapping and robbery—and they had one hundred and forty-three days to get it all figured out.

Jackson started hanging around the house a lot more than usual; he had a lot of questions for Hannah. Questions about the internet and satellites and passwords and alarms and electronic transfer of funds. Hannah looked at him after an afternoon of constant questioning. "What are you up to, Jackie Jack?" She looked at him while grabbing his two cheeks with both hands. "What is racing through that skull of yours at high-speed internet connection speed?"

"Nothing baby, nothing at all." He had been found out. "Sometimes I wish that I knew as much as you do about the cyber world. I should learn this stuff from you; maybe I can do a tech job in my new career."

Hannah had worked with the tech nerds in the computer world for more than a decade and knew that this man she married would never be one of those dudes. "You do have all my knowledge, Jackson," she said. "Because you have me, and I come with the hard drive of information that you need—whatever, whenever, baby.

"The lucky thing about all of that is with all of that tech knowledge you also get this!" She pushed her ass out towards him and made a circular motion. He gave her a quick smack and went to check his wood furnace in the basement. A thought crossed his mind as the went down the stairs. *What if after we grab the two billionaires Hannah goes with me to meet the boys in Québec?* It could be disguised as a husband-and-wife fishing trip, and she could do all of the technical work flawlessly, while they were committing the kidnapping part of the crime.

He placed two logs onto the smoldering ashes of the wood furnace in the basement. Then his thoughts made an abrupt one-eighty. She would be involved in the crime; she could go to jail with him. His children would be without parents. Their lives would be ruined. He had second thoughts about his brother-in-law's idea. But he really hated these two men, King and Pierce, who had screwed so many people. So many families and friends and small businesses, like loggers and trucking companies, were now desperate. These men needed to pay. There had been times, even before Mac revealed his idea, when he could see himself ending these two just like he had the enemy in Afghanistan. They were low-life pond scum. He could do it, kill them both in cold blood and not lose a minute of sleep. He could hear the brain matter smattering beneath his 9 mm.

Hannah was a woman with a great sense of individualism and self-accomplishment. She had a fierce sense of loyalty to her man and her family. Jackson suspected that if it came to it, she could easily be programmed to function as a robot. If it had to do with her family, she could use deadly force to protect them from harm. She and Jackson had discussed this more than once. She knew about King and Pierce. She had sent a virus into their personal computers and company mainframes. She had also hacked into King's personal email and had copies saved of some incriminating communications with a New York prostitution and escort service.

She was already a supporter of the cause, he figured, because it was Jackson's cause—she just didn't know how far things were going to go. He had taken the pledge at the Chimney launch on Echo Lake to not tell a living soul of this plan. Hannah was different though; they were one unit. They were joined for life to support, love, and cherish each other. They had written their own vows. One vow was that Hannah would agree to help reload Jackson's spent shells, and he would agree to hand wash and wax her SUV once a month. The wedding guests got a big laugh out of the vows joining these two together.

Early the next day, Jackson went to his quiet place on the backside of his garden with his cell phone. He dialed up Buckshot in Georgia; he was living just outside Plains. Buckshot saw the call coming in with the 207 area code on it and knew who it was immediately. His heart sprang.

"Got any Billy beer down there, Rebel boy?" It was the man from Maine. The shooter, his friend, his brother-in-arms, he missed him every day of his life.

"All we got down here, boy, is moonshine. And I know your Yankee ass can't handle that." Buckshot was drinking quite a bit now. A lot of idle time in the gun shop makes a man take a drink now and again.

"I am going to need your help, man. I can't tell you everything now, but I will need some weapons and some ammunition sent separately by UPS to my home." Jackson was speaking quietly now, as the moon came up over Lovejoy Pond. He knew what the response from Buckshot would be.

"What are we talking, brother? You looking for an arsenal? You need any smoke canisters, communication gear, intel? Say the word and you'll have whatever I have and can put my hands on."

"I will need all of that and more. To start with, three AR-15s with five hundred rounds of ammo, three PPK 9 mm autos with five hundred rounds, and three shoulder holsters and harnesses, two large, one extra large. Three radios with two scrambled channels, headsets, and shoulder push to talk mikes for each. I am outfitting three men. I will need it all sent; I can't buy anything local. I don't want any receipts or any tracking system."

Buckshot was beginning to get very curious on the other end. "Do you need me, man? I can be there in fourteen hours. My old man and brother can run the shop. I can be in that God-forsaken country you live in before the sun sets tomorrow night. I hope you know that, Jackson—"

Jackson did know that, and he badly wanted to say, "Get your ass up here, we have a mission to do." He would much rather have his one-legged friend from Georgia than the two men who were in on it now. He let this thought slide and held his tongue. "You are the best friend that I have ever had, Buckshot. You will know in due time. But I don't need you now. Copy?"

"Roger that, amigo—call me the first of the week, and we'll talk shipping. I have almost all you need now in stock. And you won't be paying for this." The phones went dead. They had each picked up where they had left off, and there was no need for salutations, small talk, or happy goodbyes. They used to finish each other's sentences, and it seemed that nothing had changed. They were reconnected, and it was a solid Maine-to-Georgia thing; it was an Army Ranger thing, it was a brother-in-arms thing.

Oh beautiful for spacious skies,
For amber waves of grain,
For purple mountain majesties—

12

The day had come for Mac to work a deal out on the Beaver, and he was dreading it. He was on his way to Greenville in Weston's Super Cub. It was the end of February and he had to get this airplane deal underway. Rocky was expecting him. The green-and-white Cub touched down on the ice-covered lake in front of Rocky's hangar. He waved him to taxi up to the gas pumps and signaled to kill the engine. Mac turned it into the sun hoping to get a little solar boost in restarting the airplane on this twenty-degree, sunny winter day. Every little trick helps a bush pilot in the north.

"Did you bring the log books, the 337 repairs, and the new cylinder paperwork?" One thing about Rocky was that he was thorough, and Mac liked that about him very much. He just hoped that he would not get a thorough screwing from the man with the giant grin standing in front of him now. Rocky knew that Mac needed the dough, and he knew that his old lady had been pushing him for years to dump the old de Havilland Beaver. They trudged through the snow that had now totaled a record 104 inches in Greenville, Maine. There would be a mighty runoff in the spring of 2015, Mac thought distractedly. And it would be followed by a mighty robbery in July. The thought of this adventure made him smile at Rocky, like holding four aces. The Grateful Dead played in the distance, "Sometimes the light's all shining on me. Other times I can barely see. Lately it occurs to me, what a long strange trip it's been."

"I think that I can move the Beaver in about two months for you; my commission is ten percent. You got a problem with that, McCabe?"

He wanted to put Mac on the defensive from the get-go. They had a lot of history together in aviation—almost three decades worth. It wasn't all pleasant or conciliatory from either party's perspective. Rocky had carried Mac through the winter on a very expensive engine overhaul on the Pratt and Whitney motor. The nine-cylinder, 450 hp radial engine was hard to work on and tough to find parts for. Mac had paid him with interest the summer after the overhaul, but there was still a little bad blood, and Rocky had figured he would take a little premium on this deal for having to put up with Mac's historically late payments. They were mutually distrustful. Mac also had the thought that with the right internet marketing, he could sell the rare airplane himself.

"Let's sit down, Rocky, and work the whole plan out. You know I'm not going to give you ten percent for selling this airplane. But you also know I am going to need another floatplane to be customized and prepared for the spring and summer business." Mac was looking at him like they were long-lost friends.

"So, if you take five percent for the Beaver sale, I will pay you a two and a half percent finder's fee for a 185 Cessna or something like that. You know with the internet and a good web person, I could do all of this myself. But I'd rather not screw around with all of it. You know it will be hard to let the Beaver go, and I want to pay lower than the market value for the 185 replacement airplane."

"Yeah, that works—when you actually pay."

Rocky had stuck a jab into Mac. Still smarting from the six-month wait to be paid for the engine overhaul, he was really getting under Mac's skin.

"Okay," Rocky continued, "let's start with that idea of yours, and we'll get it going. I have two 185s going to Sweden this spring that I will have to modify and retrofit. I'll sell your Beaver for 375k and find you a Cessna 185 for under 200k, and plan on doing around 20k worth of upgrades and modifications to the engine prop, floats, and airframe."

Both men satisfied, they shook hands and walked out the door together toward the Super Cub parked in the snow near the gas pumps. "Fill up the Cub for me, will ya Rocky?" Mac asked him nicely.

"Cash, right?—" Rocky was still speaking with a little edge about money.

"No, I want to put the avgas on Weston's tab." There was no tab, and Mac knew it. Rocky had screwed Weston on a repair bill twenty years ago, and when he would not pay the overcharge Rocky added two hundred dollars to his fuel bill three years later. Weston, who watched money like a hawk, picked it up and had never done a penny's worth of business with Rocky in over twenty years.

Mac flashed two one-hundred-dollar bills and motioned to top off the tanks.

While he was at it, Rocky shouted, "Tell Weston I can get him top dollar for the Super Cub today; I know he paid forty grand for it, and I can double it today for him."

Mac opened the doors on the Cub and climbed in to start the airplane. He rocked the tail with the stick back and forth, freeing up the skis in the snow. He was airborne, three hundred feet climbing out, as only a Super Cub can. *I don't think Weston will be making the call to sell the airplane, especially to Rocky*, he thought.

As much as Mac had dreaded this day, it was done, and the Beaver would be listed for sale in the trade papers in the morning. It was a new day for him and Allagash Air. He was headed to the gym after he put the Cub away in the hangar in Augusta. He needed to lose thirty pounds to be at his college fighting weight and ready to pull off one of the biggest crime capers in the history of American robbery. He had lost five pounds in less than two weeks by changing his diet. With all the changes, he was feeling a new excitement, drive, and direction.

Mac thought about the two 185 Cessnas headed for Sweden. He could work the deal with Rocky to make the Beaver trade and the 185 acquisition happen with just a short lease of maybe a weekend in July for one of the Swedish-bound aircraft. If things worked out, the aircraft used to commit the crime, to transport the billionaires to Northern Québec, could be three thousand miles away in a fjord in Scandinavia before anyone got wind of the kidnapping being pulled off. He had to make it work. It was all about timing. Timing for your life, your lover, your family, your work years, your retirement, your investments, your actions—timing was everything in life. McCabe had blown a couple of key timing events in his life; he was hopeful that this plan of his was not one of the missed opportunities. He turned up the speakers in the air.

There's a chink of light, there's a burning wick
There's a lantern in the tower . . .

13

Joe Dieter was a believer; he had been in for the long haul. His entire life's work was to convince state and congressional leaders of the need for a single-payer universal health-care plan for all Americans. He had proven the economic model as a value to the U.S. economy since 1990. There were no doubts as to the value of the system and the long-term results for the country.

He had a small office on a second-floor Congress Street address in Portland, Maine. The office space was shabby, the heating pipes rattled, it smelled of cheap coffee and looked as if someone had spilled cocaine all over the floor—it was actually coffee creamer. Joe dreamed of success for his plan, but he feared it would never go through Congress. The health-insurance companies and their politicians had won every round they had fought against Dieter and his colleagues around the country.

The enemy and their propagandists had convinced Americans that between the doctors, hospitals, and pharmaceutical companies, insurers were saving American business and consumers. The truth was just about the complete opposite. People were in fact needlessly dying from carelessness and greed.

Over twenty years the industry's product had gone up 250 percent. Autos went up just 33 percent, energy 85 percent, food 110 percent, and consumer goods 96 percent. No commodity had screwed the American public more than the increase in health insurance. Not including the cost in human suffering and death from lack of care. Medical costs had gone up 200 percent, and college tuition had gone up 175 percent. It had all gone up way beyond the tracking of middle-class American wages and salaries—which had stagnated. Health care, medical, and pharmaceuticals, were 20 percent of the United States gross domestic product.

Over the same time period, in countries that America competed with, it had gone up only ten percent in Germany, Japan, England, Canada, all of the Scandinavian countries. France and Spain had them all beat, increasing less than ten percent. Mac liked to rant on about how Americans had allowed their Congress and the past thirty presidential administrations to screw them to the wall and appreciate it at the same time. Teddy Roosevelt had proposed a universal health program for Americans, as did Ted Kennedy in 1970. Now the cost increases seemed unstoppable. Obamacare, based on an anti-single-payer Heritage Foundation plan to feed the industry giants, was a life-saving stop-gap for millions, but itself barely surviving the capitalist-crazed hatchet men and women empowered by international money. Schemes abounded, not least in the Kremlin, to ratchet up the United States from a plutocracy into yet another kleptocracy—a multifaceted partially coordinated heist beyond Mac's wildest dreams, with all the appearance of legality.

Joe was feeling that he'd never see change in his lifetime. He drank three pots of coffee a day. His own health was in question. Boxes of Dunkin Donut munchkins lay crushed and empty in the large, full trashcans in his dingy office in Maine's largest city.

Mac stood, leaning up against the office building on Congress Street—with an empty cup of coffee. It was the end of February, 2015. He had his aging L.L.Bean leather flight jacket on with the collar turned up. He had been wearing this jacket for twenty years, and he thought it was the coolest he would ever own. But its days were in the past. There were oil stains, and rips in the stitching, with dark stains from grease and dirt on the tan shearling collar. One of his feet, clad in his beat-up Bean boots, rested against the building and the other on the ground. Two attorneys approached him, bound for their fifth-floor offices. One of them reached into his pocket and dropped a dollar into Mac's empty coffee cup.

"What the hell?" Mac said to one of the finely dressed men.

They both suddenly realized that the man leaning against the building was not actually homeless; he just looked that way. "Sorry, dude," the young attorney said, as he walked away swiftly, hoping not to get hit.

They both began to laugh looking back at Mac who yelled out, "Hey!" They turned back towards him, and he flipped them his middle finger.

At the same moment, Joe Dieter came around the corner. He stopped and said to the not-homeless man, "You OK? Everything cool here, man?" Then he looked closer. "Mac, is that you? What the hell, man? What are you doing here? Come in, man, let's have a coffee."

"I have been waiting for you, Joe. I need to speak with you. I have an idea that might make a difference for a lot of people."

Joe listened on the way into the building. He had not seen Mac for almost twenty years, but Mac wasted no time in getting right to the point. Joe noted he had aged. He had thinning hair and graying sideburns. Was he poor? He looked a little destitute, loitering on the streets of Portland. He had heard he had been divorced, and he wondered if he was a beaten man—he certainly looked that way. "Are you OK, Mac?" Joe looked truly concerned as he questioned his old friend.

"Yeah man, I'm great." Maybe he should have dressed up a little more to come in to Portland, he thought. Kelley had told him to wear a sport coat and dress shirt—hell, she was always right. Jesus, those asshole lawyers had thought he was homeless. Kelley thought he was going to meet with a financial planner concerning investments to be made pending the sale of the Beaver. But Mac had other things in mind this morning, as they sat down in the office. "I read an article you had in *Down East* magazine last summer about a privately run single-payer system that might be modeled in New England."

Joe's first pot of cheap coffee was coming down through the filter. *Privately run?* Joe decided to let him talk on.

Mac continued, leaving aside pleasantries of old times, which did nothing to dispel Joe's accumulating concern. "We could do all of New England as a startup, with enabling legislation passed in all states for around nine billion dollars. That's figuring annual costs per person, in aging states like Maine, where the folks are much older and the costs are higher. The important part is the involvement of the public plans like teachers, state workers, universities, defense workers, high tech, and large retail—like food and L.L.Bean types. The higher the ages, the worse the health, the higher the costs to the network. We would actively dissuade all health-style customers like obesity and diabetes groups as not desired in the plan, smokers too. They'll all usually be dead in a decade, anyway, and we will be up and running by then. We could not discriminate but would have to tag the survivor's premiums with an extra cost." Mac could feel his brain fog over as he reeled off numbers and plans of going public on Wall Street, recycling bad money for something good.

Joe's look of intensity deepened trying to follow the dream. He knew that all single-payer systems were government run, financed by progressively spreading the cost to all taxpayers. There was simply no viable private health-care model. That was the problem for the free marketeers. Markets don't work like that. Or did Mac want to compete with the giant nonprofits already in the U.S. market? Joe listened for clarification.

"No wonder the American people won't have this health-care discussion!" his unexpected friend suddenly exclaimed. "It's people talking over their heads! It needs to be explained simply: These are the people screwing you; these are the people who are not screwing you. People need absolutes." Mac's eyes darted round the room while Joe carefully poured the coffee.

"The rest of the world has managed to figure this out." Joe offered a fresh start to the conversation. "When Americans finally figure this out, they will put the savings in their pockets and buy that new car, go on vacation, or save for a college education for their kids. In the meantime, and for the past sixty years in the U.S., bend over America! The insurance companies are the people who are giving it to you in the ass every day of your life."

"Keep the message simple, and stop confusing the masses with nonsense—" Mac reaffirmed, but cut himself short, much to Joe's relief. Then he addressed the man he had not seen in two decades with this: "Joe, what I am going to say to you right now is confidential and can never be repeated to anyone else in the world. Can I trust you?" Mac stood up and closed the office door to ensure privacy.

What now? Joe wondered.

Mac continued in even tones, getting a grip on himself, "What if I brought you eleven billion dollars in the next six months to start your dream program in New England? I know that you have a ton of work to do in each state, but you have a lot of it done already. Drafting legislation, lobbying lawmakers—hell, we could pay off half of New England's entire legislature and still get the program up and running."

Joe did not like that kind of talk at all. He always knew that McCabe could be a little rough around the edges, but his heart and head had been in the right place. "Are you serious, man? Where the hell are you going to get that kind of money? Did you hit some worldwide lottery? What the hell, Mac, tell me what you know and what is going on here?"

"The truth is, Joe, I absolutely cannot tell you, and you have to accept that. If you are interested, you'll have to take it all at face value. If not, forget I ever darkened your doorstep in my shabby flight jacket and oil-stained boots." Mac was playing his sincerity card now with Dieter.

"You will launch this as if you have had some private philanthropist give you a long-overdue money bump. I am that philanthropist; I need to remain anonymous. Forever. This is not bullshit, and this is not negotiable. You will need to have the not-for-profit in place. I'll need to see your plan and hold you to it for implementation. I figure even with your expertise, Joe, you have a fifty-fifty chance of success, and I am aware of it. As I'm sure you can well imagine, it is not my money, but I will be controlling it. You will need the best tax lawyers and lobbyists in New England or America working for you. Make those deals now in anticipation of the money coming to you in August. I will set up an email and internet receiving site for you to send information to me. I will have people reviewing it from my end as well. It will be double password protected." Mac came up for breath, looked at his friend for a long moment, and asked simply, "Are you in, Joe?"

Joe shook his head and leaned back in his leather chair with the worn-out armrests. "Eleven billion dollars, Mac. Eleven billion dollars?" He planned to retire in four years and spend the cold months in Winter Haven, Florida, at his parents' home. He had not saved any money, and he was damn near broke. Now this guy was walking into his office, looking like a bum, offering to change his life forever with eleven billion dollars for a health-care program. *This is a dream*, he thought, *or a nightmare*. This was not happening. He was a practical guy, a realist; these things just don't happen.

Or maybe—just maybe—they do. Was he getting that desperate, too? "Mac, I have no reason to believe you other than you have always had a reputation as an honest man. I'm going to trust that that's enough. I will give you a memo tomorrow outlining a plan should this money come in during the month of August. I will have the paperwork done, some of it already is. Strange, huh?"

Joe sat silent for just a moment, then came to a decision. If it was real, fine; if not, then he'd humor his long-lost friend. Either way okay, what's to lose? Also, though he felt a twinge of guilt, he would be more comfortable with Mac back out on the street. "I'm in. I cannot accept money that has come from the illegal drug trade, and you know that, right?" Maybe Mac had made some money hauling drugs in his airplane and needed to launder it with a clean U.S. entity. But eleven billion? That would be a lot of cocaine. That couldn't be it.

Joe had moved here to Maine to be a hippy after graduating from Yale. The health-care quest had hit him after losing two friends, one to cancer and one to a tractor accident. His friends would be alive today if they had had good health-care coverage or any at all. Was his life's work finally being fulfilled by this wild Maine boy? Or had Mac broken down and finally decided to cash in with the capitalists—if you can't beat 'em join 'em.

"I have never dealt drugs, Joe. I never bought or sold as much as a loose joint," he joked, but he was being honest. Mac jumped up, guzzled the awful coffee, and left the building. Just like that, he was gone. Joe was left staring at the open door.

Mac McCabe left the city of Portland that morning thinking that he had a deal with his old friend Joe Dieter. It would take a lot of work to put all of this together, but he needed to stop thinking about it for now. He had to put all of the other to-do items together with all of the moving parts. He needed to get in shape. He needed to sell the Beaver, work with his friend Liam, and keep his brother-in-law focused—as if he weren't. He needed to put trips together to the Cayman Islands and to New York City. The days were getting longer, the time to the event was getting shorter. There were 168 days until Parents' Weekend on Echo Lake in Fayette, and they had just one more day on the ice to discuss the work ahead of them.

14

Mac had purchased two round-trip tickets for himself and Jackson to go to the Cayman Islands. He needed to come face to face with a banker who had a reputation and who may have had similar conversations with other men involved in similar deeds. He needed Jackson to assure the banker that this was in fact the "we-ain't-fuckin'-around club," that the men were serious players in a world of offshore money.

Liam had researched and personally interviewed one of his classmates from Yale who had been caught laundering money offshore in the Caymans. Liam had told him he was writing a book. The man, Wilmot Dixon, had been convicted by the Department of Justice and had gone to comfort prison, serving just two years of his ten-year stretch. He was out, and he was tanned, and he was spending the other half of the two hundred million in Martha's Vineyard, Antigua, and Vail. Life was good for "Willie Boy," as he was called at Yale.

He said the prison time was the easiest two years of his life. He lost thirty pounds, gathered a great deal of criminal expertise, and was set with a solid twenty percent of his investment laundered for life. His wife had divorced him after thinking that he was a criminal who had lost his entire fortune. He passed a series of emails off to Liam while they sat in his living room at the Bluff. They were from his ex-wife wanting to reconcile and get back together.

"Look at this one, Liam: 'We never really understood each other, I want to get back together and have a child with you, Will, remember our first years of marriage and the commitments to building a life and a family? Love Olivia.' She wants to get back together and have a life and a child. Liam, she was so fast to dump me, wanting her name back and wanting no association with me. I guess I must have forgotten to tell her about the extra hundred million that I had in Zurich. God, sometimes this shit just slips my mind. I think it's from getting older. She didn't want a penny of alimony, a car, or piece of property. Whatever happened to sickness and health, good and bad, and all that other shit?"

The idiot is laughing at his ex-wife and smiling to himself. Liam listened to his old friend, the whole time wondering when he could get the name of a banker and a bank in the Caymans that he could contact on behalf of the new LLC being formed in Delaware. Mac's high school sweetheart, an attorney in Wilmington, was putting the finishing touches on the limited liability corporation, Loose LIPs, LLC, post office boxes in Delaware, Zurich and New York City.

"The guy that I used threw me under the bus with the Feds. Some new Obama-wanting-to-fuck-the-rich-guys agreement between the governments. I will give him credit for transferring the half that I have now and instructing me exactly how to get it back in the U.S. without a trace. He is a banker, Liam. You know they have no morals and no compass, just cash and more cash and more cash and better returns. Not that I or anyone I have ever worked with has character or morals, but you should know this going in. As you develop your characters for this book, I mean." He winked at Liam—he was suspicious for sure.

"How much we talking here, Liam? I mean how much we talking here for the safe-haven part of the money you are sending offshore? In your book, you know?" He chuckled.

Liam did not take the bait. He wanted to say "ten billion, asshole," but just smiled and kept looking down at his writing tablet. This idiot had cheated his way through Yale and now had three twenty-five-year-old former *Sports Illustrated* swimsuit models keeping house for him next to Jackie Kennedy's old Martha's Vineyard home near Oaks Bluff. He and Liam were never that close in college; they had smoked some weed together and slept with some of the same coeds. Liam thought of him as nothing more than a pompous fool with a checkbook.

"Here are the business cards of three bankers that will talk with you in the islands. Do you want me to make you a hotel reservation? I can hook you up," Willie offered. Liam declined with a dismissive wave of the hand.

"Suit yourself. The first guy, Jean-Pierre Mitterrand, is the grand-nephew of the former prime minister of France and has great international banking connections. He will never screw you other than jacking your fees and knifing your interest rates. If you have over a billion, see Claude Chirac. He will take personal care of what you have and need, very discreet, Liam. But if you are over a billion dollars then you should be talking to me right now. Seriously, there are no bugs in this house. They were all removed when I helped take down Eliot Spies." He laughed long and loud.

"The third guy is black, and his name is Ricardo Ortiz—yeah, like the Red Sox slugger. He is from the Dominican Republic, and he is the best banker in this business, in the world. He is costly, but he provides four or five levels of insulation from all governments and money thugs. They are everywhere in the islands. He has been doing this for almost thirty years and is totally a self-made man. He may have punched out by now, Liam; he was making a great deal of money every year and had a good group of people around him. He deals with the richest of the rich; you would never be able to call him directly. I could call him, if this was for something more than a book." He winked at Liam and smiled again. "If it's any less than a billion, call either of the other two; they will treat you well."

Willie walked to the door and out past his new Bentley. Liam opened the door to his own Toyota Tundra with 150,000 miles on it and some muddy Maine road dirt covering the fenders. He gave his old college friend a handshake, got in and rolled the window down.

"Nice ride, Mitchell." Willie Boy had to give his lower-middle-class friend a final jab. Liam mentally gave Willie the finger and headed for the ferry to the mainland.

Liam had all that he needed; he would make the calls for Mac and Jackson and set up the appointments in the islands. He did not know why they had not asked him to go with them on the trip to the Caymans, but his next job was to set the trip up to New York City, so they could check out the targets on home turf. He knew the city, and he would have the best itinerary set up. He could really prove himself in this part of the planning. He hoped that he could successfully complete the rest of his part for this adventure. He was not totally sure of himself, and he noticed his hands shaking a lot. He was smoking a lot of pot early in the morning—really most of the day. They must have known. They must have been able to smell it on him. He thought maybe he would get airsick on the ride up to Canada with the prisoners. He was doubtful quite often now, coming up with every way he could screw this whole thing up.

He was to devise a text to hand to the billionaire's wives when the kidnapping occurred. It would be a minute-by-minute description of what they were to do for the entire time the men were in the Canadian wilderness being robbed by the three conspirators. He was also charged with the internet observation of the wives when the victims were taken to Canada. They had to stick to their instructions to the minute or the caper would be compromised. The installation of cameras and monitoring devices into the women's purses and the restaurants and bookstores they would be sent to during the weekend had to happen in a matter of seconds. Liam had made the schedule in advance and had included driving instructions. He was paying attention to detail and trying to anticipate all problems that would arise.

It had to be exact it and had to be precise. Liam doubted his technical abilities and whether he could pull this off. Maybe he could speak to Sara about this. She was good with technology. No. He could not speak with anybody. He almost spilled it all to Willie Boy—what was he thinking? Did he want Willie to know that soon he would be as financially successful as he was? He hated that Ivy League rat-race to the top. Ninety percent of the graduating class he was in had that attitude to screw the world. He would never be that man—maybe a new Toyota Tundra, but surely not the Bentley.

15

Jackson didn't know what to do for one of the few times in his life. He had doubted this mission—not his role, not really Mac's role. He doubted quite a bit of Liam's part in the whole thing. He had broken and told Hannah the entire plan.

She had caught him looking up hotels in the Cayman Islands and traced a reservation two weeks from the date. She waited for the right moment to confront him about it. She had never trusted anyone, especially men, before she met Jackson. All of a sudden every doubt a woman could have about a lover, a husband, and a man came into play. What was this? She knew he was going on a four-day, end-of-season, ice-fishing trip in the Allagash, as he had done for fifteen years. This reservation was right in the middle of that week. He would never miss this trip. She would get to the bottom of this. She suddenly worried that Jackson had gotten the PTSD thing.

She was totally beside herself and on the verge of a mental breakdown. This man, who had never even uttered the words "Cayman Islands" in his life, had a two-night reservation, and in the spot marked "number of guests" on the internet form it said "two." This was just unbelievable to her—did he not love her anymore? She knew that he was upset about losing his job and being out of work for the first time in his life. He didn't put it on a family credit card; maybe he had a stash of cash somewhere? She had so many questions, and she wanted so much to love and trust him unconditionally. But this sent a red flag way up in the sky. She printed out the reservation and wrote in a heavy, black sharpie across the top, "WTF Jackson?"

She always made herself and Jackson a little treat before bed and after the kids were down for the night. She left a bowl of Ben and Jerry's Grateful Dead ice cream on top of the printed paper and waited for a reaction from the man she loved.

"Oh Hannah, what you must be thinking?" Jackson's face went flush white. "This is not what you must think, I can explain." Or could he explain? To any straight-thinking person, which Hannah was, this idea reeked of total craziness. He grabbed her with both hands, straining his muscular arms, but she pulled away with equal force.

"Talk to me about Cayman Islands, boy," Hannah hissed through gritted teeth. "Keep your hands off me—let's hear what you have to say about this little printout."

He thought he would need a drink and started to move towards the liquor cabinet. "Need a little liquid courage on this one, island boy?" She was not letting up.

He stopped and turned to her. He kneeled down in front of her as if she were a queen about to behead a traitorous knight returning from battle. He could not bring himself to speak; he just hung his head and shook it slowly. This was the worst moment in his marriage. He knew that all evidence indicated a betrayal of his most important and precious relationship. There was nowhere for him to go but to the truth. He would tell her all of it, as he had wanted to do three weeks prior. He would ask her for her help and expertise. He knew that this was their *Romeo and Juliet* moment—if things went bad, they would go down together. This beautiful angel of a mother and wife, how could he even think of including her in this scheme?

He picked his head up and looked her in the eyes. "Baby, this is awful. I know what you are thinking, but please let me explain what I am doing. I love you more than anything."

He reminded her of the near miss with the billionaire at the airport in Augusta. She had known about the connection with the sale and ruination of Paul Bunyan Paper Company in Jay. She knew Roscoe King's name, and it made her angry just to hear the mention of the man.

There was a moment as Jackson was speaking that he finally saw it all clearly—the key to moving forward and being successful was not the three buckets of testosterone but this wonderful, feminine woman, who could unlock all of the technical challenges facing them, in order to move the private capital of billionaires into the pockets of friends and family. She was the answer. Jackson looked into her eyes and began to describe the entire plan with dates and details.

"First off—if you are making this up because you are having a romantic affair with a woman in the Cayman Islands in two weeks, you should forget this and go straight for an academy award," Hannah responded. "No, really, Jackson. This is the most farfetched, idiotic thing that has ever come out of your head."

She began to smile and Jackson knew that he had her. She looked at him with a sad face and tear-filled eyes. "There are thousands of men in prison for selling an ounce of weed and breaking into camps on Lovejoy Pond and stealing lamps and chainsaws. If we are caught, we will do no more time than those idiots, and we are going to steal billions. Who would have thought that I was married to a criminal mastermind?"

His head fell forward between her breasts, his second favorite place to be. He knew that her involvement in robbing these two men would make the difference in Mac's plan. How would he tell his brother-in-law that he had violated his trust? He suddenly felt guilty. He felt that he had betrayed his team, like when Buckshot had been hurt and lost his leg. He was still feeling guilty about the men he'd been unable to protect in that phony war. He had to call his brother-in-law now.

"And another thing," Hannah called after him as he headed toward the door, "you better make those reservations for three in the Cayman Islands. You two fools are not going there alone to set this money transfer up from a satellite feed in Northern Québec."

Jackson smiled. He was so relieved, he felt like the Apache gunships had just rounded the corner and were saving his ass from failure and the enemy. She gave him a new confidence and a spring in his step; she had done it since seventh grade. He would drive to Lovejoy and tell Mac that they had been busted by the geek goddess. He knew Mac liked that reference to Hannah—it would be explained so much better that way.

ය   ∞

"You *what!*" Mac exploded. He was sitting in his office; Kelley was in the home with Jackie cutting out snowflakes. "The reason that we didn't tell our loved ones is that they need plausible deniability if we get caught. Haven't you heard of prosecutors threatening the incarceration of one family member to save the other from doing time? It's the oldest trick in the book." He just shook his head at his brother-in-law and stared into his eyes. You could cut the tension with a knife. Mac was wondering if they should just shelve the whole thing right now. Jackson hung his head; he knew that he had betrayed a trust, and that was something he just didn't do.

"Think of it this way, Mac," Jackson stammered and looked again, deep into his sister's husband's eyes. "Kelley wouldn't stand for me being locked up; she'd be scraping up the codes of the lockup procedures to try and liberate me and any other sad sack behind bars. You must know this, Mac. She'd be right there beside me, helping. Can you say that about Liam?"

Now Jackson was cutting close to the bone. Liam was Mac's friend, and by God would do his part. Yes, Liam would come through. But Mac would be lying if he said he didn't wonder about Liam's abilities—Jackson flat out doubted them.

"Liam will be fine. He is training and losing weight and doing the research and the outreach. He is putting our New York trip together now." Mac looked straight at Jackson and his Irish was coming into blossom. "Don't sidestep this screw-up of yours with doubts about Mitchell. What the hell were you thinking? Hannah will go to prison with the rest of us, and your kids might as well be orphans. Think of contingencies, backups. Jackson, hell, you're the master of that kind of shit. Picture her in a women's federal prison with some group of women hovered over her, and not in a good way." He wanted to paint a picture without being too direct.

Jackson was ready to defend his wife's abilities. "We will need her in the early research, the FAA tracking, the location of all of the assets, and what funds and investments they are in. We will need her for logins; she already has her own program underway to find people's passwords that is ninety percent effective. She has already been on King's email and copied some very incriminating messages from him to hookers and a coke dealer. She is the fourth member that can make this all happen, and we either need to bring her in or just end this whole damn thing."

Jackson was finally painting the entire picture for Mac. Mac could see her working the deal with the bank in the islands; she was a very convincing woman. At five foot ten, with three buttons undone on a Ralph Lauren shirt, her leaning in to draw a man's consciousness could be very convincing. She was trustworthy, she could shoot, she could fish, she could survive in the Canadian wilderness for a year without anyone finding her. She was a woman in full, with a command of technology, the internet, and Jackson—the latter being the most important in Mac's mind.

"OK, what's done is done," Mac declared. Jackson let out a breath he didn't know he'd been holding. Mac reached into his pocket and pulled out ten one-hundred-dollar bills. He put them in Jackson's hand. He had sold the hydraulic skis to the Beaver and had $25,000 cash in his pocket that Kelley had no knowledge of.

"Take Hannah to Freeport and go to J.Crew and Ralph Lauren outlets and put her into the sexiest top-shelf business outfits that you can find. You go to L.L.Bean, pick up a blue shirt, a white shirt, and a blue blazer—the travel one with the pockets. Buy new shoes and a couple of ties."

As he spoke, he reached into another inside pocket of his shabby flight jacket and handed him another thousand dollars. "Looking good, Jackson, Hannah will know what I mean. Business travel. We are going for the big Kahuna banker; we need to look like we deserve his attention."

Jackson waved the money back at Mac like he did not want or need it. He was almost insulted that his brother-in-law had offered him any cash.

"This is what I am doing, the money thing, Jackson. This plan already has a budget. If I lose enough weight, hell, I will fit into the clothes, and you can give them back to me in six months. I might need them for the trial."

A big smile came across his face, and his brother-in-law smiled back as they shook hands in a right-on fist grip, holding each other's shoulder.

They would need to meet with Hannah soon, all together, and explain to Liam the change. The technology was Liam's thing, and he was having trouble with it and almost wanted to bring Sara in on the plan. He would not do it; Liam was solid. He was working it through and gaining confidence, one day at a time. He was only smoking weed every other day now, though he knew he had to stop completely in June. It was his own, self-imposed deadline to lose the weed.

ভ৩ ৪০

The fourth meeting of the group followed the first three in structure, but this one had a little twist in that there was no booze to be found. It was in Mac's office at the air service with a fourth chair brought in from the garage. The beat-up, wooden round-back that was brought out for Thanksgiving dinners and birthday parties looked out of place with the metal folding chairs around the small table.

The meeting was supposed to begin at two o'clock on a Sunday, and Mac was usually quite punctual, but it was after two now. Liam tapped the table; he was totally straight and very serious. He had his Yale football game day face on. It was ten minutes past when the door finally opened. Hannah walked in brushing the cold off her Carhartt winter coat, turned and smiled at the group. She took up the room like royalty. Jackson could smell a little more perfume than usual; he loved the J'Adore that Hannah wore on special occasions. He was wondering why the extra dose of perfume today? Then he realized her motives— it was all about disarming Liam. *Yes*, he thought, *the legs and the smell— that might do it indeed.*

"You boys are planning a little party, I guess?" She took her seat in the odd wooden chair. She winked at Jackson as she spoke. She had three pieces of paper with her. One was a small sheet of over fifty emails that looked as though they had come off of some kind of inscription printer. The emails belonged to Mr. Roscoe King and they were to an escort service and an Upper West Side cocaine dealer. One of the other pages was a web program of aircraft monitoring from the Federal Aviation Administration that she had easily hacked into detailing flight plans, souls on board, and flight times *en route* to a particular destination. The final piece was a complete breakdown of the $6.85 billion that King was worth—what investments he had, where the money was, the names and contact info of his portfolio managers, and the account numbers for everything.

Liam was disarmed and relieved. He wondered what the hell had happened, but this was OK—if the boys were cool with it, so was he. She brought a great deal to the table, maybe more than he did.

She looked across the table at Liam and reached for his hand, "We are all going to spend a lot of time together in the next five months. I think we will be a great team. I know these two bozos," she nodded at Mac and Jackson. "I don't know you, Liam, but I have read your columns in the sporting magazines for the past couple of years. I know you love to shoot and so do I. I also know that two weeks ago I did not have a job in this operation, but I do now. We can make this all work. As far as the cut goes, I am in with Jackson. We share his piece of this."

In that moment, she had disarmed all nonbelievers, which had even included her husband to a small extent. Everyone seated around the table was in total synch. They would move separately together now, as one unit aligned and joined. The line from Robert Frost's *The Tuft of Flowers*, "together from the heart, whether working together or apart," drifted though Mac's mind like a dream. It was a turning point in this journey that would not be forgotten by any of them.

16

The plane was delayed onto the Cayman Islands' main landing strip. Liam had connected the three on the trip with one they all figured for the island's top banker and most skeptical man. He had sent a car for the them to the airport. Ricardo Jesús Ortiz was one of the most famous, and infamous, men in low-profile banking. The driver of the Rolls Royce Silver Shadow was a tall blonde, Hannah's height, with a full tuxedo and driver's cap on. She looked the part, with chiseled cheek bones and brown, tanned skin, salt-swept hair straight to the middle of her back.

She was Ortiz's driver and lover. Svetlana would relax the visitors with a glass of champagne or two on the way to the hotel and pick up any conversations that might reveal something for her man. The new arrivals, of course, did not know this.

Banking to Ortiz was not a study of numbers or margins, points or yields. It was fully a study of the human character; he believed the eyes could tell him the story of any soul and reveal all motives. Facial expressions, hair lines, furrowed brows, age lines, and body language could also tell a story no one would find in the financial pages or the journals. Not one good customer had escaped Ricardo in his three decades of international banking.

He liked Americans, but he had met the most ruthless and untrustworthy among them. Many were Texans, and a few were New Yorkers, but the crowd from California was the best for him. He had watched them make their money unknowingly and accumulate great piles of it in what he called "the Silicon Valley." Many were young and personally grew the finest marijuana he had ever smoked. When these customers deemed they had paid their share and more in state and federal taxes, they drew the line, and Mr. Ortiz in the Caymans put a stop to all of that needless taxation so bothersome to their fortunes.

Hannah had mapped out the banking strategy with Liam's approval. She had it in a finely tuned PDF that she would go over in great detail, face to face with the man, Ortiz.

Ortiz had never been to Maine. Svetlana was from Saint Petersburg, Russia. She had a cousin who was a translator in the Bangor area. She had called her to see if she had any knowledge of McCabe, Mitchell, or the Gunther family. She had heard some things about McCabe—he was known for his flying service—but nothing about the rest. Svetlana knew from her cousin Anya that living in Maine was a lot like Siberia for five months out of the year.

She watched and listened for voices in the back of the twenty-five-year-old Rolls—there was no talk, no noise. They had all refilled the champagne glasses twice. If that didn't loosen their tongues, then they were either very secretive or very scared to meet her lover. It was the latter, she concluded. They were scared to be here and be in this car and on the way to meet this man.

Lana was the nickname Ricardo had given her; together they represented a visual uncommon in most of the world. Svetlana looked like Lana Turner to Ortiz. He was a movie buff, and she was his best connection to the beauties of ancient Hollywood. They were a team of financial genius rolled into one. She dropped the three at the hotel and said that she would be returning to pick them up for dinner—at Mr. Ortiz's home at 7:30 p.m. that evening. She advised them that it would be a late night, and that jackets were required.

Hannah changed the rooms to have adjoining suites. Jackson was very much out of his element, and she told him to stop looking like a kid at Disney World. Mac had been in this element before, not driving a Rolls but flying the well-heeled to their destinations and dealing with their schedules and "piss-ass little wants and needs." He might get used to this life, he thought, and immediately dismissed it. It would be hard wearing Armani and a Panama hat in the Shawshank known as the Supermax State Prison back in Maine.

Hannah had the two men sitting around the table on the porch. "We'll have to just be honest with him. He's already researched us back and forward, anyway, and is basically taking this meeting for folly." She had their attention. "We'll tell him everything except how we'll get the money and from what source."

Hannah had a new game going, and she was good at it. For some reason Ortiz had picked up the entire tab for them during their stay, without ever meeting them. There was no wealth search engine that would ever make Ortiz believe that he should be sitting with these paupers from America's Siberia, other than possibly an entertaining evening with some new Americans in the islands.

At 7:15 the phone rang in Mac's suite. "Mr. McCabe, the automobile has arrived to drive you to the Ortiz home." The front desk knew where they were going. Everyone on this island knew the man that they were here to see. Maybe their new hats should be pulled a little lower over one eye, as there were cameras everywhere all the time. Hannah had a newfound paranoia, and it was well placed.

It was a palatial coastal home built with contemporary architectural style and a portion of the front deck directly over a one-hundred-foot drop into the ocean. The infinity swimming pool made the bather feel as if he or she were swimming off the end of the world. It was a stark, white home with robin's egg blue trim; it looked like the home of a Middle Eastern oil monarch.

The double doors were opened simultaneously, and there stood the driver who had picked the trio up at the airport. "Good evening! You are most welcome at our home." It was Svetlana dressed in evening wear from head to toe—from earrings to shoes, an ivory print on an Italian base fabric of coral.

She was overwhelming to look at and to hear her accented speech, *Not Russian at all, nor French, maybe a little Hungarian*, Mac thought. Was Hungarian considered European? Buda or Pesht—where was the break on the Danube? He let his mind wander in bedazzlement.

Hannah and Jackson stood clueless, taken aback by her commending presence in front of the estate. Then she moved as if she were a breeze coming off the bay, swirling with elegance about the room.

Hannah felt underdressed as well as outclassed. She had on her back the most expensive dress that she had ever owned. It had cost $800 at the Ralph Lauren outlet in Freeport, and she had seriously considered taping the sales tag inside the dress and returning it to the store when she was back in Maine. She could buy the children two big LEGO sets and put $500 into their college funds with that kind of money. She was this woman's size, she noticed, and wondered for the first time in her life, how she would look from head to toe in Chanel.

Ortiz came through the grand opening of the outer foyer. He was in a blue suit with a two-toned shirt and collar. It looked a little like a banker's uniform to Mac. It was surely cut to meet his frame. He was the same height as Mac, around five foot ten and in excellent physical shape. He was very dark, to the tone of an African not light-shaded by generations in America. He had engaging, darting eyes that seemed not to miss the smallest detail of a man or a woman. His eyes quickly came back to a full view of Hannah, head to toe. This was a very fine-looking woman in his home tonight.

Mac had his L.L.Bean blazer on with a light-blue shirt and printed Lauren tie. It was the best from his closet, and he too felt underdressed. His brother-in-law looked much better than he, with his frame cut out of *Esquire* magazine, his aqua-blue eyes and short-cropped hair. Mac sucked in his gut a little more—at least until they got to the table for dinner.

The women quickly hit it off with talk of mutual admiration. They had eyeballed each other several times on the ride from the airport, as Lana changed the rearview mirror from the traffic to Hannah's face. It had also given her a view of the two men, but she was focused on this tall woman with presence and grace.

"Do you know Willie?" Ortiz was breaking the ice with a common question about the person who had brought them together. Still overwhelmed, the two men looked at each other like they didn't know what he was talking about. Mac spoke up, trying to save face. "Oh yes, Mr. Ortiz, Willie is a friend of our partner, Liam Mitchell, and he graciously made the introduction to you. None of us have ever met him, I'm afraid."

"Does not matter, and please call me Ricardo. Willie is an ass, and worse than that, he is a dumb ass. I believe he just was released from prison." He spoke with an island accent, almost Jamaican in the Bob Marley vein, only very refined. *Refined reggae*, thought Mac. Mac could tell Ortiz was the real deal. They could have been in front of a campfire on Chamberlain Lake in the Allagash, and Mac could still tell the difference. He had seen a thousand phonies and could peg them in about a second. He could spot the scared, insecure ones immediately in the rearview mirror he had on the Beaver. The backstory to this man must be fascinating. He would try to find that out before the night was through.

The men all had crystal tumblers of bourbon in their hands. It was on ice and tasted sharp and fine. The women had a white wine in stemless glasses. The early evening talk was light and full of energy. The trio had no idea that this would be their business meeting here and now, not the one that was scheduled for tomorrow at 10:00 a.m. at the bank. The women roamed the home and visited many of the rooms on a grand tour of the sprawling estate. Svetlana was not married to Ortiz, though they had two children together who were away in Switzerland at boarding school. Ortiz's Gulfstream jet would fly them to visit the children the following weekend. His jet, one of America's finest craft, would cross continents without refueling, Mac thought ruefully.

Ortiz was a man of developed business acumen and curiosity. He would not be talking anything about money or business until the third hour of the evening, when the liquor had flowed some more, and the friendships had started to bud. If their camaraderie had not started, he would have had one more fine meal prepared by his French-trained chef and the added joy of viewing a spectacular beauty of a woman. There were no wasted moments on this earth for him. He had scrambled for scraps of food in the dumpsters of the Dominican Republic. He had held his starving baby sister as she died from malnutrition and disease. Few knew and few would ever know.

He had arrived in this place after starting life in a family of ten, in the worst slum his home country had to offer. Only Svetlana, who had all his passwords and access to his fortune, knew this and the deepest of his darkest secrets. As far as anyone who mattered was concerned, Ortiz was the adopted son of a British banker, who had taught him the trade until he had refined it to an artistry unmatched in his field. He had been courted by every bank in the world; he stayed with the Royal Albert Bank in Saint George, where he had started working many years before. He had promised the man who took him in—clothed and fed him, raised him from the age of seven—to stay with this bank for life. He never considered a change, even after the man's death. He had given his word, and his word was good. A solid, good word was so uncommon on this island, in this world of finance and deceit.

The meal was served in stages—a true seven-course meal of fish and lamb. The conversation never stopped concerning children, sports, fishing, and American baseball. Jackson was a true Red Sox fan, and so was Ricardo. He was not related to David Ortiz but had met him several times and was a fan. He had three bats that had belonged to him in his own opulent version of a man cave, which also happened to have a Monet and a Picasso on the walls opposite the bats. He stated that the art of the baseball bat and the slugger Ortiz from his home country surpassed all of his wall hangings.

Hannah had photos of their children and their home and the lifestyle in Maine. Svetlana demanded that they be plugged into their screening room to view on a wall-size movie viewer that she and Ricardo watched more than any other device in the home. With the best view on the high cliff in the island, the two cuddled constantly in the movie room with Casablanca in a never-ending loop. Bogart was the favorite. Ortiz had several clients in Hollywood and was an avid autograph and memorabilia collector.

"Mr. Gunther, may I call you Jackson?" They had crossed that bridge hours before, but the banker wanted to turn the evening towards the formality of the purpose for which all had arrived at this place tonight.

Jackson nodded and smiled. He had a Fayette whiskey buzz underway that occurred no matter where he was sitting or who he was with. The buzz was the same warm feeling anywhere in the world.

"I have taken liberties, I must confess," Ortiz continued. "I know of your military service and your heroic work in the country of Afghanistan on behalf of the American people. You are a true hero. I sense that you are here looking for a banking service as a result of something you have done or are about to do. It is not my business as of yet."

He nodded toward Mac. "Mr. McCabe, there is nothing in your history to make me sense that you desire wealth or ever worked to achieve wealth in your chosen vocations. I reviewed many of your speeches as a congressional candidate in the nineties and admired your passion greatly. But money? It never appealed to you. To any of the three of you, including this lovely person named Hannah, who appears to have an expertise with the internet and computers. I have learned she is quite the aspiring blackhat, and covers it with a web-design company. She is truly talented, but again, never appeared as a gatherer of gold." Hannah was blushing; she had been found out and in the most flattering manner.

"I truly do not know what you can bring to me and what I can deliver for you. But my keeper of inner flames," he glanced at Lana and smiled a full and loving smile, "has given me the approval that she so often withholds from our guests. Whatever you are up to, I am sure it is of the most noble of intentions. There is nothing to tell me otherwise. Recently your country's *60 Minutes* show has revealed what

I have known for a very long time about a breach of banking client lists from HSBC. The offshore banking community is devastated." He mimed wiping tears in a comical way.

"Now they all want to speak with the black banker. You have a large country music man in America who sings 'How you like me now?' I would not know this, other than that Lana is a fan of all of that country music, Mr. Chesney and all. I will take your money into my bank whether it is ten cents or ten billion. I will protect you from taxes, and I swear I will expect nothing but a fair rate of a holding fee."

Jackson had had a little too much to drink. "What is a holding fee, Ricardo?"

Ortiz set his apéritif down and looked at the three in his living room. He raised both arms and asked, "Does it really matter? Hannah, I will expect you to come to this island to visit Svetlana three times between now and July, which is when I believe you all plan to do your large-scale banking. I would like to use you as a consultant for our bank to take some liberties with our friends in the Swiss banking community." To assure there were no ill intentions planned, he nodded at Jackson and said, "You must accompany your lovely wife, and bring your children, if you so desire."

"One more toast to our futures together." Ricardo smiled and stood, brandy glass in hand. "Mr. McCabe, you have been to Ireland as many as twenty times, I believe. It would be in the order of the house this evening to all say, *Sláinte!*" The Irish toast ended the evening. The glasses were raised on high. Ricardo knew it all, everything about all of them, Mac thought. *Have I really been to Ireland twenty times?*

They had a deal with Ortiz now. They did not know what the deal was, but they were under his wing. So far, they had nothing to lose, and he had nothing to gain. The three believed that they had made a friend in the offshore banking world, and they had. It was the finest evening any of them had experienced, and they pinched each other as siblings might, while on the ride back to the hotel. Did this just happen to us? The query was universal across the back seat of the Silver Shadow. They were all buzzed as they gathered in Mac's room after being dropped off at the hotel.

"I have a good feeling about him," Mac said. "I came to business with a severe distrust and dislike for bankers. I always thought a banker was someone who would give you an umbrella when it was not raining and want it back when the rain started." It was a quote from Mark

Twain, who had made and lost fortunes. Mac had used it undiscovered for so long he almost thought it was his. "We don't have a lot of time, but if he wants Hannah here, I think that she should come and help the man out. I don't think he has any improper ideas about you, Hannah. I think he is sincere."

"He loves that woman, Svetlana," Hannah piped up.

Jackson nodded his head in agreement. "They're uniquely a couple, very much entwined," he concurred with his wife.

Mac said, "I bet he could have anything that comes in this rich fifty-shades kind of lifestyle, but this isn't the guy for that. Hell, he loves the Red Sox! We need to play ball with this guy; he's the top in his business. He leaned toward me during dinner, and he said, 'All of you together don't have a net worth of two million dollars combined, including Mr. Mitchell. That is a rounding error during the day in our bank. It does not matter your worth or your dollar amount combined. You three are good people, including the writer, Mr. Mitchell. I will help you with whatever you have up your sleeve; you will be my project for 2015.'"

"He said that to you, Mac?" Jackson asked. There had been tiny bits of conversations throughout the night that allowed the group to conclude that both Ricardo and Lana were on a specific fact-finding mission in a very discreet manner. They had carefully targeted all three people visiting. They looked at each other with a sense of awakening. Hannah grabbed her laptop and asked them both to remember the questions that were asked throughout the evening. She would record them to a new file named "Slugger," both for their new banker friend and their common admiration for David Ortiz, the greatest hitter ever to play in Fenway Park—except of course Ted Williams.

They all woke up with a bit of a hangover the next morning. Mac thought for the first time in a long while that not all of the one-percenters in the world were evil. He did hedge his thoughts with the idea that he had spent little more than four hours with the man who would be handling his future in a few months—122 days, to be exact, he calculated.

They were dressing for the 10:00 a.m. business meeting when the phone rang; it was Lana. She said that there would be no need for a meeting today. She would pick them up in forty-five minutes and to have beachwear and a change of clothes: jeans and t-shirts would be fine.

Mac wondered if they had been had—was it all a big joke the night before? Jackson looked at him with the same question in his eyes.

Hannah spoke up, "You two, I cannot believe you two. There was never going to be a meeting today at the bank. He spoke with all of us for about ten minutes and knew whether or not he would be doing our banking for us. Hell, maybe Svetlana had called him after she dropped us off from the airport and given us the OK. This is all a mystery to us, but I bet he knew shortly after seeing us and doing his research whether we were in or out. You two need to wake up—and fast."

Svetlana pulled up in front of the hotel in a Land Rover, the back end full of snorkel gear and towels. She was smiling, looked fresh, and was completely in charge of the itinerary. "Sometimes when I pick up a client or a wannabe client, I call Ricardo on the drive in and tell him that these people are no longer potentials for the bank. He never second guesses me. I have dropped people off back at the airport within an hour of their arrival, who were some of the wealthiest people in the world. You folks from Siberia, Maine, have a new friend in the Caymans. Well, two actually. Now relax and let's have some fun today!"

Hannah jabbed her husband in the ribs and winked at her brother-in-law. This was a bonus day for the laid-off millworker and his broke-ass brother-in-law pilot, she thought. They swam and snorkeled in the clear, blue Caribbean and the dangerous waters of the world's most secretive banking system.

Ricardo's lover and partner was showing them her private beach spot, where only a few were welcome. At 1:00, a Bell 407 executive helicopter flew around the corner of the cove. Jackson's hands started to shake, and Mac wondered if this were some sort of bust or something. The chopper hovered in place about thirty feet off the water, and the door opened on the pilot's side. A man stepped onto the skids and let go into the water with mask and fins on. It was a very dark man with an athletic body. Ricardo splashed into the waves with vigor.

"I checked the weather in Bangor, Maine," he yelled as he surfaced and the helicopter roared off. "It is twenty degrees and snowing with a wind chill of minus five Fahrenheit." The trio nodded in unison. "Sounds about right," Mac chuckled.

Ricardo cocked his head. "You must tell me—what is a wind chill?" He laughed as he cleared his mask and dove again into the liquid turquoise of the shoreline.

17

They arrived in Portland, and Liam picked them up in his aging Tundra with dog hair and joint burns all over the seats. The three looked refreshed and enthused. Mac had a cherry burn on his Irish skin, and both Hannah and Jackson had earned a bit of color. All three had this calm demeanor, as if to imply it would all be OK, everyone just needed to do their jobs.

That motto, "Do your job," had been the motto of the world champion New England Patriots. Liam had that bumper sticker on his dashboard, and the group had adopted it for their work as well. Jackson tapped on the sticker with his finger and for the first time smiled at Liam and gave him a thumbs-up. Liam had been waiting for that sign, and he felt a part of the team again. He was glad he hadn't quit and glad that his connection had paid off for the four of them. Mac didn't tell him of the snorkeling, the meal and the hospitality, the free rooms, or the Rolls Royce. Liam loved to snorkel—Mac would wait to share that news.

The men did not stop talking the entire trip home from the Portland Jetport. They were like first-graders returning from the Christmas holiday with a list of their new presents and gadgets. Hannah had her laptop open and was quickly creating accounts for her work for Ortiz. She and Lana had exchanged five emails since the time she had landed in Maine. Ricardo had a plan for her, for sure; she wondered why he could not trust his IT people in the bank. She would be glad to help, of course. This was connecting and networking like she'd never done. She liked Lana and Ortiz, but she still hadn't figured out what she could do to help them out. She already had job one in front of her, and that was a bigger challenge than she had ever faced. July was coming fast.

The New York trip was set. Mac and Liam were going, and now Hannah wanted to go as well. She had only been to New York City once, and she wanted to get the lay of the land in King&Pierce-ville. Mac told Liam to go cheap, make a reservation at the Leo House on Eighth Avenue. It was a clean little place to stay, run by nuns, with shared bathrooms and costing $90 per night. It was down the street from the Chelsea Hotel, where Liam wanted to stay, where Brendan Behan had lived, as well as Henry Miller, Sid Vicious, Bob Dylan, and many other writers and artists. Jackson stayed at home and was doing his best to potty train his son.

Little Linwood Mark Gunther was named after Jackson's best friend Buckshot. Jackson called him Li'l Buck; his mother called him Poopsie. Hannah had never met a child who was so hard to potty train and who thought that the changing of a diaper meant that it was time for an immediate bowel movement. Just how much poop could one baby make? She was beside herself and threw the training task to her supercommando husband. She had trained the kid's older sister single-handedly, and now it was his turn.

She yelled at Jackson on the way out the door. "Do your job!" She was smiling and looking very cosmopolitan for a girl from Fayette. Jackson held the fourth dirty diaper of the day in his hand and scowled. It was only ten o'clock as he watched his wife drive off, burning a short patch of rubber on her way.

Maybe it was just that Maine people spent too much time looking up at the skyscrapers and wonders of concrete and steel on the island of Manhattan, but the horns seemed to blow a lot louder and more frequently when the Vacationland license plates crossed the Brooklyn Bridge. One wise-ass cabby leaned out the window and yelled at Mac, "Did you lose your lobster, asshole? Drive it like you own it, and keep moving!" Liam chuckled in the front seat, giving the big yellow Ford a wave. Hannah stretched her long legs across the back seat and flipped the cab driver her single digit salute.

"Welcome to New York City, just like I pictured it," she smiled. "Skyscrapers and everything with all the pricks in the world gathered up in this one little island."

Svetlana had texted her that morning to come back to the Caymans in two weeks, if possible. Maybe a side deal could be struck with her two new friends in the international banking world. Hannah would think about this and talk to Jackson about it. Maybe they would not have to pull this kidnapping and robbery off. Maybe they could make a great living with her new friends Ricardo and Svetlana.

Reconnaissance accomplished, they thankfully took the West Side highway out of the city to the Triborough Bridge, zipped up to I-95 through Connecticut, back through Massachusetts and coastal New Hampshire. Mac drove the entire distance without any help. He was a pilot and a transporter of people, he couldn't let it go, even in the four-cylinder Ford. He laughed out loud while the others slept, as he passed by the Seacoast signs for New Hampshire exits. *Twenty miles of coastline and they call it the Seacoast. Hell,* he grinned to himself, *Maine has enough coastline to stretch to Oregon and back when you added in the island shores.*

He would be home with his wife and daughter and a glowing fire and a home-cooked meal in three hours. He idly wondered if he would be able to do that a year from now, wondered how the food was in prison. He heard Liam begin to snore and Hannah was talking in her sleep. It was all totally inaudible gibberish, but she seemed to be troubled in dreamland.

The words sailed from the CD player, "Cathy, I'm lost, I said, though I knew she was sleeping. I'm empty and aching and I don't know why . . ."

18

Jackson cut open the box sent by Buckshot from the One Legged Gun Shop in Georgia up to his buddy in Fayettenam. He mixed some double-grounds camp mud coffee with the childlike curiosity of Christmas morning. The box had three levels of Styrofoam; each layer held the pieces of AR 15 assault-style rifles. It looked like a toy puzzle to Jackson. He could almost do it blindfolded, as they had many of the characteristics of the M16, a weapon he knew well.

He pulled out the first, the action piece. There was a note directly underneath the plastic-wrapped gun part. "This weapon has been modified to be fully automatic and can shoot twenty rounds in four seconds. This is the only weapon that has this modification, as I would not want the two dumb Yankee pricks handling the other weapons to blow their toes off. Just because I have a leg and a half doesn't mean I can't help you, brother." And with a hand-drawn smiley face at the bottom of the note: "P.S. Eat me after reading."

Jackson smiled and longed for the friend he had not seen in several years. He performed the assembly of all the weapons and placed them in a wooden box, padlocked it and stuffed it above the rafters in the garage. He was completing his equipment list and was successfully training his fellow partners in crime.

Jackson's son Buck finally did a number two in the potty and yelled to his father to come look at the prize in the little plastic child's toilet. Jackson was so happy he did three jump-up-and-turnarounds in the living room. This was a great day! Hannah would be so proud!

Li'l Buck jumped up pointing at his father and said, "Hokey Pokey,

Daddy, Hokey Pokey!" Jackson did the Hokey Pokey for half an hour and would have gone for another hour if the toddler hadn't fallen over and gone to sleep on a floor pillow.

⊰ ⊱

Hannah had a steady stream of emails going with Svetlana about another visit to the Cayman Islands and some technical work for the bank. Svetlana had asked her to call her Lana from now on, which she preferred, as she did not like the name association with her former homeland. Vladimir Putin was becoming a very naughty boy, steadily going from bad to worse.

Lana had said she would send the jet to Portland to pick her up. Hannah declined the jet ride but accepted a first-class ticket out of Boston, to be in the islands March 5th through the 7th. Hannah would have two full and different agendas on this trip.

⊰ ⊱

Mac found himself in the doldrums of winter. The snowfall was over eighty-two inches total at the end of February, and he could not stay ahead of the work. The temperature was never above ten degrees Fahrenheit, and the wind never stopped blowing through January and most of February. Like all winters in a seasonal business, there was no money coming in on his side of the ledger.

Kelley was doing it all—utilities, groceries, insurance, gasoline, and car repair. She was wondering in a new and curious way how Mac had come up with the money for the Cayman Islands trip and the three days in New York City. Did he have a secret stash? Was he doing some secret banking that she did not know about? Had he run up one of those damn credit card offers? What really started to get to her was that he seemed not to have the usual winter no-cash blues that followed him down the road yearly.

The Valentine's holiday had passed. It was the first of March, and Saint Patrick's Day marked the start the work clock for Allagash Air. Mac had usually taken his old Ski Doo Tundra on a hundred-mile backcountry snowmobile trip, up through Chesuncook Lake and the Allagash Waterway lakes to go ice fishing just before his work season started. This year there was no talk of it at all. Weston had not called and bothered him to get ready. Mac had not started packing up his gear. He had not missed the trip for twenty-five years. Over their years together, Kelley had become an expert on the psychology of one Kevin Daniel McCabe. She had studied him from the moment the two caught each other's eye in the barroom in Hallowell, almost eleven years before. Something about this Mac was different.

She now wondered continually about him. She knew that he was very pensive of late; she had caught him at least once a day sitting in silence with a far-off stare. What the hell was on his mind? Would he get a real job with pay and benefits as all her friends' husbands had? Would he get out of this business and stop her constant worrying about plane crashes and money? Would he write the fishing book that he always wanted? What the hell was with him lately? She had never had so many questions about the future of this man that she loved so much. Maybe the selling of the de Havilland was a tipping point. She did not know whether to be hopeful or afraid.

And as we wind on down the road
Our shadows taller than our soul

Mac turned down Led Zeppelin and answered his cell phone. Liam sounded ecstatic. "I have just crossed the twenty-pound mark in my weight loss. How are you doing, you fat bastard?" Mac had not been so fortunate, but he had lost ten pounds, and his goal was a lot less than Liam's.

"We'll start a weight watchers group at the supermax next winter." Mac was still hanging in the negative about being caught and going to prison. "Come over, Mitchell. Let's throw the cap away on this twelve-year-old bottle of Jameson's that I got for Christmas." Mac was looking for some mental distraction.

"I am on my way, Mr. McCabe." Liam stopped to pick up three lobsters and a bottle of white wine for himself and Mr. and Mrs. McCabe. Jackie would rather have a peanut butter and jelly sandwich.

It was hard for anyone in on this plan not to discuss it or allude to it when together in one place. Liam was like a kid awaiting Santa Claus. He hugged Kelley like it was her wedding day when he walked through the door on Lovejoy Pond. His face was aglow, and Kelley thought that he might be stoned. It usually took a few drinks get him to the place where he was when he walked through the door that day.

She stood in the kitchen as the two started on their first drinks out of the special bottle distilled in Dublin. She scratched her head and wondered just what the hell these clowns were up to. Maybe she would just confront them in about three drinks. Maybe she just would.

"All right boys, what the hell have you two got going on?" They both were speaking in some code that she could not quite understand. She was standing there in front of both of them with her hands on her hips and an edge in her voice.

"What in Christ are you talking about, Kelley?" Mac was talking like he had been caught with his hand in the cookie jar. "What?—" He held his arms wide like he was ready for handcuffs.

Sometimes she would just like to handcuff him to a post and take a broom to his bare ass. "Jimmy the dunce, huh? You don't know anything, do you? Well you have never pulled anything over on me in all of the time I have known you, and now is not the time to start, Mackie boy."

She smiled as she walked away, but Mac knew that it was not a smile that was sincere or friendly. How would he ever do this without telling her? She was his most trusted confidante. The lobster pot was boiling over, and Kelley was taking care of it. He talked to Liam, but kept his eyes on his wife's perfectly rounded butt in its pair of very tight jeans.

They went on to finish the twelve-year-old bottle. After the first two drinks it tasted like the same old Jameson's. The two delinquent Celtic wanderers raised the final glass and yelled *"Sláinte!"* After they said their goodbyes, Liam drove the back way to his home on Maranacook Lake. He was all over the road, and the last thing he needed was a DUI this close to grab day.

They had all agreed to continue to practice and work out and lose weight and keep their mouths shut. It became a quartet that was playing in tune. Jackson had designed practice grab routes on surrounding lakes with similar roads and geographic features. Liam started to develop psychological profiles of the men and women who would be accompanying them. He knew that these alpha male men liked to stay physically strong and sharp. They probably all had the best trainers and diet and could run a ten-k easily. He was right about that—Hannah had verified it through the schedules and emails. The wives, meanwhile, had the best bodies money can buy.

☙ ❧

March came in like a lamb. It had left a lion of a winter behind with wood piles depleted and fuel tanks drained and emptied. The Beaver was sitting on the banks of Lovejoy Pond, protected from the ice cracking and buckling in the cove. It looked so lonely to Mac, so abandoned now, and for the first time in over two decades this airplane would not finish the season at Allagash Air.

Mac looked at the airplane, his old friend, and wondered if they would ever fly together again after she was sold. He had two thousand hours of flight time behind her control yoke and knew every move the beautiful aluminum airplane could make. He likened her in his mind to the women on the frescoes by Michelangelo on the ceiling at Saint Peter's in the Vatican—shapely, full-figured women. This airplane was a lover that protected you from adverse weather and cold. It was curvy and shaped like a large bosom protecting and suckling its pilot.

He saw his work as a bush pilot and guide as more art than science, more poetry than prose. He knew that the smiles of the men and women who engaged his business were life changing and could not be reversed. Flight was beautiful, and it was dangerous and edgy, especially in a bush plane in the wilderness. The men who were scowling from not catching fish or wiping bile from their chins for not having a stomach for turbulence would rarely return. He actually didn't want them to return. Mac remembered his banker friend with his new companion from last season and the light step and joy that they had while packing their gear to leave Lovejoy Pond.

His trips, his guiding service, and his knowledge of geography in Maine and Canada made people's lives different. There were destinations on the sides of mountains and stream beds where people made decisions to change their lives. He was a transformer of the human direction and destination. It had nothing to do with nature and fish—it had everything to do with soul, spirit, and inner strength. In Mac's mind, nature and soul were separate. If strength of character might control nature, Mac was happy to provide it. He was convinced that he did this for his customers every day that he got out of bed and cranked up that 450 horsepower radial engine. His wonderment— the stare that Kelley now caught him with daily—was more about the awareness of his own mortality, the loss of life of his friends. Where were they now? Were they waiting for him?

This caper that he had hatched was the death-defying scream of a middle-aged man finding his way through the darkness of the human journey and existence. There was no turning back now. He regretted Hannah's involvement—she was so smart, so talented. Her children, his niece and nephew, were so beautiful. It was too late now; it couldn't be done without her. She had brought so much to the table. He needed to speak with her about the wisdom of becoming involved with Ricardo and Svetlana. He would do that soon.

CB   BD

Hannah called Kelley and asked if she would go shopping with her in Freeport. Lana had sent her two five-thousand-dollar gift cards to the outlets stores. She was going to buy some new outfits. Hannah, older and worldlier, loved her brother's wife. She would take her to Cole Haan and Banana Republic.

There was a note from Lana that came with the gift cards, and Hannah really did not know how it was meant: "All business, dressing all business this trip." It had a little heart smiley face under the signature.

So as to deflect any possible insult from the gift, Hannah was taking her sister-in-law on a little spree and intended to spend it all in one afternoon. Jackson and Mac did not need to know about this. She would be leaving for the Caymans for a two-day trip in a week, anyway.

Kelley was taken by surprise. Her sister-in-law had called her at work and asked if she had any personal leave time to go shopping with her in Freeport. Kelley knew what clothing looked best on Hannah and was not shy about giving her opinion. She was a local fashion maven, if there was such a thing in Kennebec County. She had all of the newest handbags and sunglasses from Coach and sweaters from Ralph Lauren. Her wedding band was from Tiffany's, and her boots were from Cole Haan. She owned five pairs of shoes from Manolo Blahnik and four Jimmy Choos. People she passed on the street did not have a clue that she was completely styling most of the time, as she left her home in the woods in Fayette. Kelley often teased her sister-in-law about looking like she had just fallen off the turnip wagon in Wayne.

The two had a loving and loyal—if sometimes tumultuous—relationship. Hannah had kept Kelley's brother from blowing things up. Hannah had given Kelley's mother two beautiful grandchildren, her a niece and nephew with her maiden name, Gunther. The two always had a slight edge between them, and both worked to keep that edge from becoming an all-out catfight in the family. Kelley was particularly interested in why Hannah had gone to the Cayman Islands with her husband and brother. Maybe she could get some answers. She decided to take the afternoon off and hit the ATM for a couple hundred dollars for a purchase of a new Coach bag she had seen online.

Hannah's SUV had pulled up, and the two were on the road looking for some retail therapy. "What is going on, Hannah? I feel like someone is planning a surprise party for me, and I'm completely out of the loop. You know me, I need to know what's going on."

Her grandfather had told Kelley when she was a nosey little girl that curiosity killed the cat. She decided not to heed the folksy old man's advice and had been that feline ever since the age of five. "I mean, what is up with the three of you just breezing on down to the tropics without me? What was that all about?"

Hannah was quick on her feet. "Your husband is thinking about a winter floatplane operation in the islands. He wanted to surprise you and thought that if Jackson and I went we could get away from our kids, and you wouldn't be suspicious of his trip. We had fun. I picked up a web client in a bar in Georgetown. As a matter of fact, they sent me a gift card that you and I are going to totally devour this afternoon."

Hannah had disarmed her sister-in-law for the time being, especially with the retail offering she'd placed on the dashboard, with as yet no sign of its value.

Kelley smiled at her tall traveling companion, "Mac has never mentioned a word about flying in the Caribbean, never. He has been acting a little weird since he decided to sell the Beaver, which could explain it."

Hannah knew very little flying lingo but quickly responded, "He seemed to be all jacked up on Obama opening up Cuba and the opportunity for a floatplane. He mentioned something about a Maule airplane with wheel floats or something?" She smacked the steering wheel with a hell-if-I-know body gesture. She had Kelley nodding her head and thought herself very good at this deception thing.

They walked into Cole Haan, and Hannah told the clerk that she would need a large shopping basket. It really did not need to be that large; you could burn five grand in Cole Haan in minutes. Kelley kept an eye on Hannah and everything she tried on and pulled off the racks. She had practiced that Anna Wintour look many times after reading *Vogue* for thirty years. There was no way that this woman was getting out of this store without something "classy and elegant" while she was on watch. She would let her get a little crazy at Banana Republic, but not here. Cole Haan Freeport was Kelley's favorite store in the state of Maine.

Hannah picked out two dresses, sandals, two pairs of high heels, two blouses, and a handbag. She had spent half the gift card and was now stopping herself. "This is my treat, Kelley. Buy whatever you'd like. I have $2,500 left on the card, and it's yours." Kelley was shocked. What was up? This was all upside-down.

"This is a gift card from my new client in the Cayman Islands, sistah; spend till it's gone. *Mi dinero es tu dinero.* We are not leaving this town with a penny left on these cards."

What kind of client sends someone a five-thousand-dollar gift card? Kelley was looking like she had been hit with a mallet. Pennies from heaven? Hannah had never spent more than fifty dollars on her in the fifteen years she had been with Jackson. Even on her birthday, Christmas, and her wedding to Mac. *What the hell,* she thought. She was a retail piranha. She pulled a leather jacket, a pair of shoes in her size she had been eyeing for months, some new high-heeled boots, and a blouse made by a Maine designer named Jill McGowan. The thing was made from imported fabrics and cost $600. She did it all in less than twenty minutes. "That's done! Did I tell you that I'm loving my brother's wife quite a bit today?" She smiled and hugged Hannah. They were two very good-looking women feeling free in Freeport with generous gift cards.

Kelley was much more engaged at the Banana Republic store, pulling four and five outfits at a time off the rack. "What's the temperature there now?" she asked Hannah. "I wish I was going with you." Hannah was pretty sure that she did not want her sister-in-law on this trip and remained awkwardly quiet to this remark.

The two finished their shopping and started the one-hour trip back to Augusta to pick up Kelley's car. They did not stop talking the entire time about life in the islands and building a business and other exciting things—about a change to come.

03   80

There was nothing like a good shot of retail at the end of a miserable winter in Maine to lift the spirits. Kelley walked into her home on

Lovejoy Pond with a smile on her face and a skip in her step. She had found out the big secret, and she told Hannah that she would not let on. She enjoyed having the higher knowledge in this game of hide the peanut under the shell. Mac was sitting at his computer working out the spring and summer flying and guiding service. He had the third weekend in July marked DNS, which meant to Kelley, who would be taking emails and phone calls, "Do not schedule."

He had two Canadian trips scheduled, one for the end of June and the other the weekend after the Fourth of July. The calendar looked normal to anyone's eyes but his. He had blocked the second week in July for Beaver maintenance, which appeared to be an unusual entry for the busy time of year. In actuality, he hoped to have the Beaver sold and delivered way before that date. Rocky had told him that it would sell fast, and he had calls coming in already after two weeks on the market. He needed that cash soon; they had to get the electronics for the border crossing, the flight monitoring, the GPS receiver—

He had perfected an undetectable route of flight over the waters of Maine, New Brunswick, the Saint Lawrence Seaway, and the rivers and lakes of Canada. It started at mile zero and ended at mile 743 on Lac Barbel, Québec, above the 52nd parallel where his Canadian fishing lodge stood deep in the wilderness. The flight had been done with every obstacle, from wind towers to electrical generation towers, all within a ten-foot variation in obstacle altitude.

The technology existed that would allow him fly the entire 743 miles without ever looking out the cockpit window. He could take off and land without ever making ground reference. It was true Star-Wars-age technology that had escaped Mac and his bush flying for over a decade. He had been sneaking into Maine Instrument Flight School in Augusta and taking lessons in a glass-cockpit simulator for two months. When he plugged a flight plan into their data input system, it showed the average speed of the Beaver, winds aloft, and turbulence. It was incredible to Mac—you actually could teach an old dog new tricks.

He had every system backed up, except the pilot. That was him, he was his backup, and he had sat for the four-hour and twenty-seven-minute flight with the simulator six times. Three times up into Canada and three times back from Canada, all simulated exactly to terrain and water bodies. He could now fly this very special route in his sleep. In all of his trips to Canada, he had never taken a flight on the deck, low to the ground at top speed with such risk. A cough or sputter in the engine, forgetting to change tanks, anything that would cause the propeller to stop turning, could put the plane down in twenty seconds at that low altitude.

They would have to fly that low in order to avoid radar and the international border securities. His airplane would look like a fast-moving flock of geese to anything that might pick them up. He thought about bird strikes and the Sully Sullenberger landing of a passenger jet on the Hudson in New York City. Sully was the best pilot in modern-day aviation, if you asked Mac—a true hero.

McCabe had managed to learn all of the technology. He had it down pat and well understood. He had back-up power systems, in case the airplane lost electrical power. He had gone high-tech in a matter of months and was ready to make the flight of his life. He had surprised himself and hoped that he was able to teach Liam how to make an emergency landing in a 185 Cessna before the third week in July. He'd had no notion of teaching him to fly, but since the incident with the jet at the airport, Liam had become more interested in the art. He had always asked a lot of questions, but lately he was asking a lot more, and the questions were on point. Mac was pleased and impressed.

19

Today Hannah Gunther was turning heads of both women and men with a light ivory business suit easily fitting her frame as if tailored in Paris or London. She boarded first-class on Jet Blue for an early morning flight out of the Portland Jetport. Jackson had dropped her off. He was so proud of the mother of his children, his wife and collaborator. This morning he wondered if she looked just a little too pretty and most definitely too stylish. After all, she was a girl from Fayette, and she was married to a redneck war veteran, who imagined he'd taught her to shoot and clean trout.

She had enough money in clothing on her back to feed their family for three months. He was out of work and about to commit a kidnapping and a robbery.

Kelley had fixed her hair and had given her a new makeup kit that was stocked to the brim with the best Freeport had to offer. She sat in first class as if she belonged there. The regular travelers that morning wondered who this new woman was, traveling to JFK. Who was she going to meet? Jackson drove off with the gas gauge reading below quarter tank, hoping to make it back to the Fayette country store, where he could charge fuel for the next month without pressure to pay. The little store had carried him and his family with a credit account through five generations. It was always paid, just sometimes a little late.

She looked around the first-class cabin and settled into her seat. When she opened her laptop computer, she entered a new world very few minds could follow. She had a gift. She was learning a lot about Ricardo Ortiz. When she came online, it felt as if she owned that world completely. The flight was smooth as her strokes across the keys. She sent photos of the Manhattan skyline to Kelley and thanked her for the beauty aids and the fashion consult. Kelley loved Hannah's brother, and there would never be a doubt about that. The plane was delayed out of JFK into Georgetown International Airport, but the Rolls Royce was awaiting her when she stepped onto the curb.

Lana was waiting in a business suit; they would go directly to Ricardo's office at the bank.

When they entered the finely finished interior, tellers and desk occupants stopped their work and looked up briefly. They knew when Svetlana walked through the door they should have their game faces on, because something was in the wind. She was the connection that brought so many of them new clients from around the world and some six-figure holiday bonuses from the man on the fourth floor. She got their attention, and of course a pleasant banker's smile—slightly turned up, not too happy, not too excited.

There was a slight wait, while Ricardo dealt with a customer in Hong Kong. The translator was having trouble explaining a margin that amounted to several hundred million dollars. Ricardo softly requested a second opinion to make certain of exact clarity between the Asian customer hiding a fortune from his government and his overseers in Beijing. There had to be no doubt.

Lana remarked in a catty Russian accent, "You have spent your gift cards very well, Hannah. Did you shop on your own?"

Hannah immediately attempted to beguile her in the only manner a jealous woman could understand. "My sister-in-law was with me. She has read *Vogue* every month from her sixteenth birthday. Oh, and she's Mac's wife. Do I look OK? I was not quite sure what to buy."

"You look fabulous, my darling. We are both so glad you are here. There is much to be done."

Ricardo's office was a spectacle of success and opulence. He had more paintings on the wall from Cezanne, Picasso, and Van Gogh, millions of dollars worth of originals that few people in the art world knew were hanging in a banker's office on Grand Cayman Island. The world's most secure banking address must be the place to hang some of the world's most sought-after works of art. Hannah spotted a few that she had seen in an art class she had taken at the University of Southern Maine. Electives that slightly piqued her interest made for the opening of a conversation.

These paintings would never hang in his home. That space was for artists he supported in the Dominican Republic, where he went four times a year for special, secret projects. The art brought clients and customers to his home who wanted these paintings because Ricardo owned them. The result was that artists from his home country made excellent profits from the sale of their art, lifting hundreds of families and artisans out of poverty. The extreme poverty that Ricardo had known as a boy lingered quietly in the back of his mind, shards of a past that pricked only in dreams gone foul and the occasional nightmare.

The three sat in a triangle of comfortable furniture amongst the art and the photos of world leaders taken in Davos, Zurich, and other places where people meet to move wealth around the world. Ricardo sat back with an astonished look of admiration. "Dear Hannah, my lovely Lana said that you may be arriving in couture, and I think that you have outdone yourself. Exquisite, madam!"

Hannah blushed through both layers of foundation she had applied that morning in the woods in Maine, before her husband took her to the tarmac. "Thank you, Ricardo. You are so kind to help me, and I am so looking forward to working with you and Lana on this special project."

"Hannah, it is not one special project, it is several projects that you will be working on for many years, we hope. We do not know what you and your husband and brother-in-law are up to, but I believe that it is a very big project that may not be entirely above the law. It is not our desire to know, as long as it does not impact me, Lana, the bank, or our customers. We wish only to give you support and assistance."

"Support and assistance" were welcome words. Hannah did not know exactly how to handle all the transactions demanded by the crime. Mac had alluded to an investment back in America of a large amount. Other parts were being clarified, as she found more information about King and Pierce and where the actual funds were. Mac had not disclosed the entire plan to her. Most likely, Mac himself didn't have everything formulated—she feared it was still a fermenting brew.

Ortiz leaned in. Svetlana knew he would get directly to his purpose for Hannah's visit. She had seen him do this a thousand times, and it was what he did best. He could close the deal, and he would do it with a charm, grace, and finality so often left out of the mysterious world of international banking.

"There are people I deal with, Hannah, who are customers in this bank and other banks in the Caymans and Switzerland. They move their money at opportune times, not so often as to draw attention for taxation or to the criminal nature of its involvement, but in time to take advantage of certain opportunities."

Hannah wondered if these two were onto the little scheme that Jackson and Mac had cooked up. She had a terrible poker face, and she looked straight at her shoes. Svetlana nodded to Ricardo, noticing Hannah's body language.

"I am not talking about what you and your boys have in mind, Hannah." He touched her arm in reassurance. "As I have said, we will help you with whatever services you need, and I believe that you will need many of my services. I will do it gratis. I want many of these men—mostly men, very few women—evil men, to feel a pinch. A pinch that does not kill them but wounds them financially for life, the way bad people would normally be treated in proper societies. Unfortunately, in today's world, Hannah, the societies are all but proper. And your America is no exception."

Hannah did not like a foreigner to say bad things about the good ol' U.S.A. and her knee-jerk patriotism spurred a flash of indignation towards her hosts to ripple across her downturned face.

"Don't misunderstand me; the United States is still the best example of a free society in the world. But if I put a list of my clients in front of you, who are hiding money from taxation and killing your jobs, it would shock you. The list goes to the very top."

Hannah thought about King and Pierce and knew that if she was aware of these two, there must be many more out there. Her edge softened, and she was back in eye contact with both of them.

"I want you to work for me through an independent corporation that I have formed. You can work out of your home and will need the best available technology and secure high-speed internet, along with my financial software, which I am asking you to enhance. I will give you information that you will study and work from. You will have to develop deep informational databases on all of the people I give you, and I will help feed the databases. At a certain point, when they are vulnerable—due to world markets, political climates, exposed personal indiscretions—we will take action regarding their finances." Ricardo paused and tried to get a quick read on how Hannah was taking this in.

Seeing that they were still on the same page, he continued, "I will not say to you at any time what to do; you will know what to do and when. We are on a five-year trajectory with this project. I will pay you very well, more than you have ever dreamed of. I know that you have a project that you are working on now, and I believe that it involves some of the skills that you will provide to us. I will never ask you what you are doing now or compromise your integrity in regards to your husband and brother-in-law. Some of the people I am working with have been involved in your husband's past. I know of his heroism." He sat back in his chair and opened his arms as if he had unfolded the witch's crystal ball in the *Wizard of Oz*. He nodded towards Hannah and smiled at Svetlana, a soft loving smile as if his part of the task were complete.

Hannah responded, "What will make a difference to me in my life and in my world are my husband and my children. I want a life for them that will never have to depend on the people that you have just described. I never want my husband to go through what he has been and seen in the war again. Twenty-five years ago I was given an Apple laptop in school by a Maine governor, who thought that we should join the twentieth century. All the fifth graders in our state received them. The work that I've done over those years since has sharpened my skills to a point where I'm at my professional peak. I'll work for you six months from today, for a six-month period of time and a contract. At that point we three will sit and discuss how we will go forward. I need to learn more, but I am interested in what we are discussing from many different points."

The atmosphere in the room became more exciting as the minds began to meet. Hannah looked Ricardo squarely in the eyes. "I will give you my complete confidence. I'm aware of your status and how hard you both have worked in your lives. I, like others, like the thought of making a lot of money, but I don't work for money so much as I work because I like what I do and I feel accomplished at the end of most days." She smiled at them as if she knew a secret. "I believe I can accomplish what you would like to have done for this banking project of yours."

Svetlana began to speak with a bit of the queen's English, "We will pay you in an account set up in our bank. We believe that you will need other accounts for other sources of money. No money will be sent to you until we have made sure you are okay with the source. You must understand the project of the U.S. Treasury Department: our bank is on a watch list—you should know that. We will give you a retainer in four months, just before you start, of $150,000 and discuss additional compensation as we proceed."

Hannah knew that four months would be just after Parents' Weekend on Echo Lake. She wondered if she would need the money for a legal team. *Curious timing*, she thought. Maybe she could go totally legitimate with these good people in the Cayman Islands. What they were asking was not technically legal. She would check the cyber-crime laws here and evaluate what she might be violating.

"That's fine. I will make one trip here between now and August. I'll text you, Lana, and you can make arrangements prior to my arrival. I like the outline that you have given me, but I always speak with my husband about these things. The first test that we both use in our lives is we have to like the people that we are working with, and we both like you."

Ricardo agreed, "Your husband will be an excellent counsel for your decision-making process, Hannah. We hope that this is the beginning of a long and fruitful relationship. He is a real hero and a wise man." He stood and clapped his hands together once. "Now let's have ourselves a fine dinner, and will you be spending the night with us?"

Hannah found the question a little disconcerting and said that she would be staying in town. "Of course," Lana responded. "We have a reservation at the Ritz-Carlton for you in my name." Hannah suddenly realized that she did not know Svetlana's last name. She was glad that she would be staying in town. She needed some alone time to process everything they had discussed.

She spent the first half of the next day in Ricardo's private computer headquarters located a block from the main branch of the Cayman Island Trust Company. She spent two hours learning the Cayman's own special code. She was a quick study.

That afternoon she relaxed on a private beach on the west side of Grand Cayman. She and Svetlana went there together and talked about the future and a business partnership. Svetlana had told her that she wanted more children with Ricardo. She seemed to want a friend and a bond that she could share secrets with. She had secrets to share from her past—secrets from her childhood in the Soviet Union, a father who served in the politburo and disappeared in the night forever and left her family in poverty.

Hannah slipped out of Georgetown quietly the next morning with just a small bag, dressed in jeans and a t-shirt, carrying her laptop—a laptop loaded with a new set of secrets and lies. No Rolls Royce, this time she took an island cab. She had officially signed up with Mr. Ortiz. She was running with the big dogs. She had to speak with Jackson about abandoning this plan that he had. She could not lose him to a prison, a crime, a dangerous escapade fraught with risk. This kidnapping and robbery was a serious personal risk that she did not have to take, now that she had connected with Ricardo Ortiz and his partner in offshore crime.

She smiled to herself, ensconced again in first-class above the clouds, as some old lyrics came over the headset, "As I pulled away slowly, feeling so holy, God knows I was feeling alive."

20

Liam's files on the King and Pierce families and friends were over four hundred pages long now. Liam knew almost everything about them, and what he did not know Hannah did. They had a life of misery, deceit, and privilege. Liam knew so many people like them that he had grown up with and attended school with. He really did not dislike these men because of the wealth issue—that issue seemed to fire up Mac and Jackson. Liam was a free-market conservative and believed if you split all the wealth up in the world equally, in five years it would all be back in the hands of the same people. He was involved because he could finally see passion in others that had been missing from his entire life. This newfound passion to do something beyond his previous human capacity stirred him like religion. He would do this, become rich, and move away—and dream of doing it again for the rest of his life. He idly hoped it would not bond him with the marks he had so thoroughly investigated.

The team of four was now, trained, skilled, close to being ready to execute their plan. Liam had completed the booklets that would direct Gloria King, Alexis Pierce and Terrance Dowd in every movement while they were in Maine and the husbands were in captivity. There were instructions on places to eat, visit, shop. They were given items and product numbers to purchase at stores, selfies to take, where to send them. The notes told them that if they followed every instruction explicitly, their lives would return to normal on Monday morning. If they called the authorities or handed the booklets over to the police, their lives would never be the same and nothing could prevent them and their closest relatives from a terrible, violent death. The notes also said the organization that had taken the husbands was international with members on all continents. A digital file showed surveillance of their husbands in places the wives knew about throughout the country. There would be no doubt about how serious and prepared the people were who had just grabbed their men.

Hannah's greatest fear after hacking King's email for months was that his wife would want her husband dead, and she and the pilot would run off together. She could not find one person in his universe who really seemed to care whether the man was alive or not. Sometimes Naomi would sprinkle a kind remark to her father in an email from boarding school regarding care for the earth and the environment.

Kelley was increasingly concerned about all that was swirling around her—Hannah's trips to the island, Mac becoming more distant and tossing so much in his sleep. Why was her husband spending so much time with her brother? They had a few things in common, but what was all of this new buddy-buddy bromance going on? She thought of herself as perceptive; there was something in the air, nothing ever slipped by her. She was always on high alert for changes in the people she loved, people that needed to keep it steady and copacetic. She needed to get to the bottom of all of this weirdness soon.

ᴄʒ   ꙮ

"Mac, this is Rocky, I've got a live one!" It was the message that Mac did not want to hear. The Beaver had been on the market for less than two months and Rocky had a buyer. Mac, who could procrastinate with the best of them, did not procrastinate this time. He knew he needed that money and that timing was everything. It was the end for him and the flying machine he had loved so long and put so much sweat and cash into for so many years. Mac McCabe without a de Havilland Beaver—it would be the talk of the aviation crowd all across the state. They would think that Allagash Air was going under. *Screw 'em!* he thought. Someone was going to own a great airplane. His airplane, not Kelley's or the bank's, his airplane, it would be truly a sad day for him.

Mac called him back within the hour and asked if it was a real offer. "Yeah Mac, it's a flying service from B.C. Some young guy has been running 206 and 185 Cessnas for five years in a flying service and wants to upgrade. He seems like a great young man who appreciates the Beaver like you do." Mac knew Rocky was trying to play him a little now.

"What's the offer?" Mac cut right through the bullshit.

"He will give you 355k, and you need to fly it out to him with a new annual. He will do the pre-inspection. He's an engineer in Canada. He wants all new batteries and a certified avionics system."

The phone was silent for ten seconds, "How much for you, Rocky?" Mac didn't mind being the prick that always asked the tough questions early.

"Just my straight ten percent, Mackie." Mac hated it when he called him Mackie; that was for his wife and mother, and a few friends. Rocky was surely not on that list.

"Let me sleep on this, Rocky. You double-check to see if the guy is prequalified to purchase; we don't need any of that Canadian bullshit that happened with my 180 back in the nineties. I'll talk with Kelley and call you back in the morning, promise." Mac would not actually be speaking with Kelley. This sale had already played out; the overnight would just allow him to beat Rocky down to a five percent sales commission.

Back in 1997, he sold his 180 Cessna to someone in Canada. Mac had to fly to New Brunswick and steal it back from the buyer, who had said the prop was damaged and canceled his check. The Canadian dollar had taken a bad bounce and the buyer had got cold feet. There was nothing wrong with the propeller. Mac and Jack Weston flew up in the Super Cub and landed on a beach next to where the buyer had parked the plane. Mac snuck through the woods with a duplicate ignition key and waded out to the front of the airplane, cut the ropes, unlocked it, started it, and blasted off the dock while the owner was still cuddled up in bed next to his wife. It was 6:00 a.m., and Mac and Weston were headed for the U.S. border just as the Royal Canadian Mounted Police pulled into the lakeside driveway in New Brunswick. Rocky was the broker on that little fiasco.

Mac called Rocky back first thing the next morning. "Here is the deal, Mr. Rocky. I'll accept 375k in a U.S. bank check only. I will give you 25k only, and you will have to include the annual and whatever work he needs. I will pay for parts and labor to install, if we both agree it is needed. I will deliver it with you around June 1st. Not a word of this to anyone, especially Kelley. You will have to open up an account at the Greenville branch of Bangor Savings with both of our signatures needed to move any money. I will need a fully modified 185 to go into service immediately, so you can start that search now. Don't mess around with him. Make this deal today and get a 50k deposit."

Rocky knew that Mac did not like to haggle, and he could go south with that famous Irish temper any minute, so he agreed because he knew in the back of his mind that he could get ten thousand dollars worth of parts and labor into that old Beaver easily.

The phone went silent, the deal was done. Mac was feeling very emotional—was he going to cry? He only got these feelings at funerals or when Jackie squeezed his neck and said, "I love you, Daddy, more than the moon and the stars." Was he getting soft? Did he really care for that old hunk of aluminum that much? Maybe he could buy it back in a couple of years with the grab money? He needed to pull himself together.

It was a long day for Mac. He wondered what to say to Kelley when she returned from work. He had rarely lied to her before the hatching of the plan, but now he was, and it was complicated by the timing of what to let her know when. He was not a good liar. He had been busted by her for just the little white lies that leaked out of him from time to time. He would have to really stone-face her. Maybe he would just say that a guy was in negotiations between him and Rocky. She wouldn't call Rocky, would she? She had caught Rocky looking at her lustfully many times over the years and reported it to Mac. No, Rocky would never tell her, and she would never ask him about Mac's business. Then again, she was asking a lot of questions these days.

A few days went by, and there was no chatter about the sale or calls from British Columbia. Mac did not know what to make of the silence. He assumed that the man hadn't accepted his counteroffer, and it made him a little nervous. He had started to spend money that he did not have yet. His father had always told him never do that, it was very bad luck to spend money on a deal that had not been consummated. He waved his left hand across his face as if to cast out all those thoughts and crossed himself. He had to stop that crossing business, as well— never cross yourself for money matters, material gain, or possessions. His aunt would have slapped him in public for that exercise, he thought. She was the president of the Daughters of Isabella at the church in Skowhegan. She went to mass every Sunday of her life and always told Mac she was praying for him daily. He believed her and feared he may need her prayers sooner than later.

It was a long week before Rocky finally called and said that he had made the deal with Andy MacLean, the operator of the flying service in British Columbia. He had agreed to all of Mac's terms and was very excited about owning the de Havilland. They would like to speed up the sale by a month and wanted it out there by the middle of May. Rocky was holding a check for the deposit and would keep it until the final sale went through. Mac was slowly moving on from being the owner of the airplane he had flown for over two decades. He was turning the page and wrapping his mind around a newly conditioned Cessna 185 with wheels, skis, and floats.

He would never be without an airplane. Even if he was crippled in a wheelchair and ninety years old, he would have an airplane that he could look out the window and see. He would have that airplane fueled and ready to fly him to his next adventure and destination. There would always be Kelley to meet him at his destination, she would smile at him, hold him warmly, and make love to him into the evening in front of a fireplace with good beech-wood sparking the atmosphere with heat and passion. Good dreams were starting to return to him now. His life was positive, February was gone, and thank God that month of misery had left. He reached out of his La-Z-Boy and turned up the music: "I can hear her heartbeat for a thousand miles, and the heavens open every time she smiles."

ରୁ ଚ

Jihadi John had just been identified on television screens across America, and Jackson was beginning to get some of those old familiar feelings. He had found men like him hiding and running from his guns across Afghanistan. This man who, had cut the heads off decent, innocent people, including Americans, just for attention and religious extremism, was causing an itch Jackson wanted to scratch. His phone rang, and it was a Georgia area code, coming from the warmth of the south to the chill of the north.

Buckshot was on the line: "I've been waiting for you to call me, you son-of-a-bitch, so I've stopped waiting and am now volunteering for whatever mission you're planning. I won't take no—you know I'm as good with one leg as any of those Yankee bastards you've hooked up with."

Jackson laughed a soft laugh that only told the caller he was glad to hear his voice. Jackson never understood what he called "the gay thing"—the physicality of it, the cuddling, public displays of affection. He knew that he loved his father, his son, and this man on the phone.

"I know you've been thinking about the same thing I have, Gunther. Let's go git that bastard. I know several former Rangers and Seals that have hooked up with this Dark Sky Security outfit. They have put a price on the asshole's head of twenty-five million dollars. Hell! we would take fifteen hundred plus combat pay a month and grab men twice as dangerous as this cat. I'm having a private label made for some Winchester buckshot with this guy's face on the box. I've sold a thousand cases, preordered, and they're not even in my store yet."

Jackson smiled and thought about his crazy rebel friend with one leg—one leg because of him. How could he possibly be pulling off this most important mission without his friend being involved? "Your namesake just took his first crap on the toilet, Peller. You would be so proud of those two little turds staring up at you from the potty. You need to see 'im before he gets big enough to kick your ass." Jackson was hoping he would not be coming too soon.

The next sounds from the other end of the phone were his fears coming true. "I'm coming up for Easter, to see my boy and catch up. I have found a woman, and I'm in love. No, she's not a stripper, and yes, she has all of her teeth. Sometimes I wish that she didn't, though." They both laughed, and Jackson knew that he wasn't going to change Buckshot's mind.

"We'll be there on Thursday the 2nd and leave on the 5th. Can you handle me for four days, amigo? I'll need a bed that doesn't squeak. We are in the early stages of love, you know."

Jackson was happy for his friend. He hoped that he had a good woman. He knew that he had been lucky in that regard, himself, while so many of his fellow soldiers had not. A good woman for a man like Buckshot would be hard to come by. He was lugging some ugly baggage, and only a few women could put up with it for a lifetime of marriage and partnership. He was grateful for Hannah every day of his life. She was sent to him by angels, as far as Jackson was concerned.

ᑲ ᑐ

The inventory for the grab was starting to pile up now. Jackson had complete control over every bullet, stun gun, pepper spray can, and strap tie. They had handcuffs, buck knives, and bug nets. He had a special communications system that Buckshot had set up for him. He needed some medical supplies for the trip, anything that he could put in his short pack—pain pills, cold meds, allergy pills, EpiPen, air splints, sponges, syringes. He needed to get his hands on some sleep juice—he needed to make sure his two special passengers slept for the entire trip to Canada without killing or crippling them. He had a friend who was a wildlife biologist and knew a tranquilizer used on a 150-pound black bear that should do the job for these two, up and back. How would he do that?

He wondered about the "Karate Kid," Mr. Pierce. Jackson wondered if the dojo had had that ever-so-important conversation with the student. The conversation went like this: "Never ever raise your hands for defense or offense when you are staring down the barrel of a gun."

Early demonstrations of strength proved to work in almost all of the grabs Jackson had done in the military. He had said more than once of his victims, "They don't fear the bullet half as much as the fist up close. The fist has to be hard and swift, targeted at tissue with a lot of nerve endings, like noses and ears and frontal lobes."

Ↄ   ⁊

Kelley's Saint Patrick's dinner was an extra-special event this year. Jackie was learning about the country of Ireland in her Girl Scout troop. As per usual, when Jackie went for the big learn, Kelley went all out. All of the relatives were coming on both sides of the family. Charlie was bringing his shillelagh, cousin Michael was going to wear his kilt, and Kelley's mother, who was as Yankee as Doodle Dandy, was wearing a leprechaun's outfit. Corned beef and cabbage and Guinness stew would be served promptly at seven, and the home would have the Irish tricolor hanging outside. Liam Mitchell would read poems from William Butler Yeats. Mac's friend Emmet McMurphy would sing *Bold Robert Emmet*, of the Irish patriot hung drawn and quartered, as the parting glass would be filled with the twelve-year-old Jameson's that Mac had walked in the door with just before dinner. He brought an entire case of the "tears of the baby Jesus," as his uncle had called it. Kelley looked at him strangely, wondering where he got the money to buy this little gift. This was really strange. Mac giving away bottles of twelve-year-old Jameson's, even on Saint Patrick's Day. This was very strange indeed.

It was Kelley's finest hour. She loved to entertain and especially have her family around her. The placemats were doilies in Irish linen, and green carnations were placed around the quaint lakeside home. Mac looked about his house and was so proud of his wife and daughter. He wondered if it would be his last Paddy's Day meal here, on the lake, at Lovejoy Pond. The thought gave him chills.

He was completing the tasks of a doomed man; one by one, he checked them off the list and put them in a file folder above his office in a cubby hole connected to the garage. He would leave a note in a place where he knew Kelley would eventually find it. A note with account numbers and names of bankers and phone numbers, all in one small half-sheet of paper inside an envelope with the name "Kelley" and a heart smile hand-drawn on the outside. He also placed an affidavit stating that the actions that he had taken over the weekend of July 17–20, 2015, were totally of his own volition and motivation.

He knew that his father would guide Kelley through a prearranged financial maze, organized without telling of the crime. Mac smiled when he thought of his father. He had been a taskmaster when Mac was a boy, and he had become his best friend and coconspirator in the last two and a half decades. But he too would be deceived.

21

J oe Dieter emailed, "Anything happening, Mac? Should I prepare
for something? How's your plan going?" Mac was furious and
wondered if he had made the right choice with Dieter.

He responded with one word: "Call!"

Mac's cell rang, and it was Joe on the other end. Mac had told him
no contact until he reached out to him. "Joe, no emails, no contact,
meet me at Byrne's Irish Pub under the bridge in Bath in two hours."

The phone was quiet on the other end. Mac knew that Joe had
gotten the message. The call ended.

Byrne's Pub was a real Irish pub in downtown Bath, Maine—the
shipbuilding capitol of New England. The founder of the pub was
a retired Navy master chief. He and his family had retired to Bath, a
sailors' town, to build his dream of a pub like those found in Dublin
and Galway and on the coast road in Dingle. In Mac's opinion, he had
built the best Irish pub in Maine and had all the characters to go along
with it. When Mac was in his twenties, he vowed to visit every Irish
pub in the world; he was now in his late forties and had only been to
767. Byrne's was top shelf.

Joe Dieter was a stranger to pubs, booze, loud singers, bar-top
dancers, and bagpipes. He would be much more at home in a medical
library or in the halls of Congress with the single-payer people he
had hung out with for over thirty years. He would often have a small
glass of Liebfraumilch with his special diet of fish and fresh organic
vegetables.

Dieter walked into Byrne's looking around, bemused, at the strange posters of a toucan with a glass of Guinness on its beak. Mac was sitting at a table in the corner of the bar. It was one in the afternoon, and he had a twenty-ounce glass of the dark brew with a white foam top. Joe sat down across from him, and Mac did not offer him a drink. "My friend from Castle Clare, County Clare, Ireland, calls Guinness in a tall glass 'A Blonde in a Black Skirt.' I call it a dose of health food." Mac raised the jar, as if to toast his seated friend, and took a long haul off the stout. Joe smiled so very slightly, he was clearly uncomfortable.

It was Friday the 20th of March, and Mac put the glass back on the table. "In 122 days you will get a call from a cell phone that you do not recognize. It will be in the middle of the morning. The only thing that you will hear on the other end is the name of a bank and an account number. You will be the authorized signer on the account. I will need you to sign a blank paper before you leave here this morning."

Joe wondered what he had gotten himself into and if this was all for real. Was McCabe losing it? Was he involved in some terrible scheme that would drag them down? Dieter had built a reputation over the decades—even the hard-right governor of Maine had called him a "very respectable kook."

"This will happen, Joe. In one year you will have ten billion dollars to formally announce with a Request for Proposal document in all five New England states that funding is available to deliver a single-payer health-care system. You need to put the enabling legislation through in every state.

"One year—" Joe interjected, but Mac was on a roll.

"Start with the teachers' unions, state employee unions, trade unions, universities, legal associations, municipal employees, postal workers, and any place where they use their brains. They will love it. Charge thirty-five percent more for a family that has a smoker, twenty percent more if they have family members who are obese. We will make this about lifestyle as much as insurance; initially offer it as discounts rather than penalties; in five years, we will shut the tobacco companies out of Maine entirely."

Mac continued undaunted, "Stay away from the retirees, loggers, fishermen—any place where they have high injuries and costly hospital bills. They are sicker and needier."

Joe's heavy eyebrows darted up.

"We can pick them up in the third and fourth year of operations. You will need the best lobbyists on both Democrat and Republican sides; set three hundred million aside for outreach and the PR side of this. This will be a privately held corporation that will have half of the operation costs of private insurance. We'll need exemptions from Obamacare, which should not be hard to get—everyone hates it."

"They do?—what about people with preexisting conditions covered by Obamacare?"

"Fuck 'em—we are bringing single-payer health care to the people."

"To some—"

"It has to begin somewhere. Joe, are you really going to turn down this ten-billion-dollar opportunity?"

There was a long silence, and Joe went to the bar for a glass of red wine. When he returned he began to engage. "I see, Mac. We'll treat New England like a country all on its own. We currently spend twenty percent of the five states' GDP on health care, not counting pharmaceuticals. My numbers, which have all been verified, will show that we can drop the GDP costs for New England by a full ten percent per year within five years. We will have to go for some liability reform for the docs and real tight hospital costs controls. One procedure, one payment, Providence to Caribou, right Mac?"

Figuring his long-lost friend had lost his doubts, Mac had settled back into the corner sipping his Guinness. "It hasn't changed Brother Joe; every country in the industrialized world has proven this model, the single payer model! We are going to build a system that is free of all of their warts, take it private, and nationalize it with an IPO on Wall Street."

"Shareholders, Mac? You want me to build you a monopoly powerful enough to muscle out the oligarchs in an industry worth over twenty percent of GDP—with just ten billion, Mac—seriously?"

"In less than a year you need to find the biggest prick that you can dig up to run the business side of this. Someone that has been removed from a national corporation for making them money and fucking the stockholders. That's your guy, or woman, for that matter. Start looking now, Joe."

"You will need a business plan—find a couple of UMaine economists and business professors and have them play a what-if game with you, promising them an endowment. You will sprinkle this money all over New England, Joe. Go to Harvard, for Christ's sake; they will sell their own mothers for a million-dollar pledge, and maybe ten, I'm not sure. Never went there." Mac ordered another Guinness.

Joe thought the man might be getting a little drunk and wondered how many he had consumed before his arrival. "I really should not question the source of this money, Mac?" He was backtracking now, covering his ass.

Mac leaned across the small table and put his nose about an inch from Joe's rimless round John Lennon glasses and looked straight into his brown eyes. "Every penny of this will be from a legitimate source, Joe. If you want out and don't think that this is your cup of tea, tell me now. I will find someone else that will accept ten billion fucking dollars to do a good thing. Don't you want to do one good thing before you die, Joe? Do you want to be laying on that deathbed from eating too much kale and organic chicken shit and wishing you had done this deal with me? Come on, man! This is your life's work laying on a platter in front of you."

Joe figured he could find some use for the money, if any, and he could probably handle Mac. And if not, then the risk might at least give him something to lose. He cared about his old friend and understood the stress of failure all too well. "I'm in, Mac. I just have my doubts, it's my nature. I've been getting whipped around, beaten up, and rejected for all of my life. I've been called a whacko and spit on by Tea Party rednecks. Part of all this—from me to you—is I just don't believe that it's happening."

"This has an eighty-twenty chance of happening, Joe." He was quoting his brother-in-law, Jackson, who between him and his wife had now commandeered almost all of the operation. "Those are good odds, and we—" he paused, collecting his thoughts. When Mac spoke again, he was deadpan. "I am not doubting the money coming to you in full and you setting this all up. When we are ready, I will explain the ownership and the board of directors and your role and compensation. This shit is for real."

"Can I get you a drink?" Mac suddenly asked, realizing he had been rude to his companion in the pub but without registering that Joe was still sipping the wine.

"Do they have Irish whiskey in this place? If they do, will you order me a shot of the finest in the bar?"

Mac fired off a request to Master Chief Byrne working the pulls. "Can you find me two shots of twelve-year-old Jameson's behind that mess you call a bar?"

"Only the finest for you and your good friend there," was the chief's response. The publican and his grandson had been in Mac's Beaver on a fishing trip and was quite proud of his friendship with the bush pilot from Lovejoy Pond. The fact that he was Irish and loved the pub didn't hurt, either.

The two talked about dates and lobbying contracts and state legislatures and labor leaders in New England. They finished their whiskeys and departed. Mac pulled Joe by his coat into the corner of the alley to the left of the pub. "Don't call me or email me, Joe. If you need to speak with me drive to Fayette and look for me. I do not expect to see you for a long time—122 days to be exact. You have plenty of work to do in the meantime. Much of it you have already done. We will both do this one good thing before we die. I promise." He looked straight at the academic-looking fellow he had pinned into the corner. He idly wondered if Joe would visit him in prison. He almost slapped himself, thinking he'd better rid himself of these bad thoughts altogether.

Mac walked away with a Guinness-whiskey buzz and wondered about Joe Dieter's dependability. *Another egg-headed think-wonk—dealt with 'em in the Legislature. If they, these "intelligentsia," were ever in a bar fight, should you be able to engage their logic, they would be thinking about what angle they should strike their opponent's jaw. In the meantime, the opponent would be swinging a haymaker from downtown, and they would be knocked out,* he reasoned.

Mac thought the solid science of the progressive movement was dead in the water because these people had no fight in them. They did not know how to conduct a good ol' American street-fight. Their lives were an endless postmodern walk in the desert, without purpose or direction. Their intelligence and logic were burdens around their necks; they needed their ideals and purpose to be weaponized with a killer instinct, the ability to organize their supporters and dispatch their opponents and detractors. Anytime Mac saw them on TV trying to explain something that would never connect with anybody, he shook his head, zapped the remote, and despaired back into the La-Z-Boy.

22

There was no morning this day for Mac. It was a night blended into a day, and it would be his longest day by the time the sun set after 8:30 that evening across the western Québec skyline.

It was Friday the 17th. He had a good horoscope, and he was hoping Norah would be wearing blue, maybe even green, on the morning news, which in recent months he had begun to imagine told something of his fortune in addition to the news. He definitely hoped she would not be wearing red. This day was a green light. He and his friends were ready—never more ready—for anything. Jackson had been talking about "good karma" and auspicious signs as well and was very mellow these past few weeks.

The airplane was ready, completely filled to the top of the wing tanks. He had enough fuel for a flight to Canada along his special low-altitude route. A twenty-mile-an-hour headwind would cause him to run out of fuel fifty miles from his cabin. The forecast called for light winds and variable with a chance of thunderstorms building in the afternoon along his flight route. Jackson had a sixty-five-gallon storage tank in the back of the Toyota that would refuel Mac at the cabin in Québec. It had 100 octane aviation fuel, colored blue, weighing down the back of the rented SUV. It weighed 455 pounds, and it caused the vehicle to squat over the tires.

The sun came up at 5:15 a.m. over the trees at the eastern end of Lovejoy Pond. This day was a gift of fifteen hours of daylight. This was the day they had been planning for so long, and it would change their lives forever. Mac was convinced that the good would surpass the bad that he would do this day in July, in Maine, in the bright sun, in broad daylight. The Hard Sun lyrics of Eddie Vedder wouldn't leave him alone today, round and round in his head.

> There's a big,
> A big hard sun,
> Beatin' on the big people,
> In the big hard world.

Mac was nervous, apprehensive, and giddy, all at the same time. He was like a high school player preparing for a state championship game. His breath quickened and his step lightened. He had lost twenty-five pounds. He could bench press 200 pounds and over 550 pounds with his legs. God had given him two fine sturdy legs; he would need it all today, mind, body, and soul.

He walked to the dock and heard the hollow wood between his steps and the water echo like drum beats. He thought of the song, *The Streets of Laredo*. Why couldn't he shake these crazy bad thoughts.

The airplane was rough in its initial appearance. It was red and white and probably still had the original 1978 paint job. Rocky had taken it in on trade; he was going to paint it on Tuesday and put a new interior and headliner in it. The airplane already had a new Continental 300 horsepower engine with a brand-new three-blade McCauley propeller. Mechanically the airplane was solid—it flew straight. When Mac returned the borrowed craft on Tuesday it would be prepared and shipped to Sweden to its new owner, an executive at Milicosky Paper Company.

Little did Rocky know the work that this little four-seat, high-performance bush plane would have in store for it this weekend in July. Mac had a decal made with the tail numbers forged. He took the last wrecked 185 recorded in the NTSB report system and reproduced it with a local decal company's handiwork. It just happened the number was N715SP. It was a lucky number that would translate to November Seven One Five Sierra Papa to anyone in the airplane world. It coincided with July—the seventh month—of 2015, and the SP? Well, that could stand for Single Payer.

Mac had been practicing starting the aircraft with the fuel pump and the fuel injection; he was a carburetor man from way back, and these new fuel-injected planes were tricky. The plane had a new battery and a backup that was in the Toyota, should something happen in the woods of Canada. Could you ever be overly prepared? Not for Jackson or Mac, not on this day.

A pilot with years of safe flying, Mac had used checklists from the age of sixteen. Today he had checklists laminated in his cargo pants pocket, a list for every portion of the trip, from the grab to the drop-off. He felt the small PPK automatic pistol under his shirt. This was a different sensation; he had never worn a concealed weapon in his life. He had carried a .357 and a .45 outside his hunting jacket while hunting in the North Woods, but this wasn't the same. He would wear it until the return trip and the drop-off on Echo Monday morning. This was a day he needed to remember every minute of. He hoped it would not go so fast that it would block his memory. He seemed to be experiencing that more often these days.

Kelley knew he had a North Country trip and some business with Rocky over the next few days, but she did not know he would be in Canada. As far as she was concerned, it was business as usual for Allagash Air.

Mac was up earlier than usual. She had frozen meals for two days and three men. Mac would pick up the booze, burgers and breakfast supplies for his small cooler. She did not want to ask too many questions of her husband; he was still a bit down, now the Beaver was gone.

For her, this was the end of an era in their lives. She had never looked toward the lake at the end of the dock and seen any airplane other than the tan-and-brown de Havilland Beaver. Now there was a strange looking 185 Cessna, pretty ratty to her eyes. She hoped this was not the Beaver's replacement for Allagash Air. She was as much a part of the business as Mac was. She knew they could not sustain the big airplane any longer. *Goodbye and good riddance*, she thought. She had $150,000 in a bank account and knew that there was some more somewhere that she had not gotten her hands on yet. She hated to see a sad face on her husband; it had taken her a long time to work Mac to this place.

The sunshine had appeared on the logo of *CBS This Morning*, and Mac had stood in front of the TV for a full minute. The three anchors appeared, and there was beautiful Norah in the deep Kelley green sleeveless dress. Mac pumped his fist and yelled, "Yes!" He clicked the big screen off and headed out the door for Jackson's home two miles down Route 17.

Kelley rolled her eyes, turned the TV back on, and continued brushing out Jackie's hair for vacation Bible school. Apparently, all Mac needed to start his day was Norah in a green dress. Kelley hoped that her husband would be OK selling his most beloved airplane; some men did not handle these big life changes well. He really had been acting weird lately.

CB   BO

A strange truck showed up in Jackson's driveway, with Georgia plates on. It was a large Ford three-quarter-ton, four-wheel-drive crew cab. It was all tricked out with a lift kit and custom wheels and exhaust. It was brand new. Mac wondered who would be driving this rig. The doors remained closed. As it made a slow turn, the bumper sticker on the back said, "I sell ammo so Obama can't grab it." Mac wasn't a fan of the sticker; he had been a loyal Democrat his entire life.

Mac had arrived to find Hannah with three twenty-five-inch computer screens in front of her. One monitor showed FAA flight planning software. Another had a photo of the driver for Pierce's rented Escalade and the rental contract for King's Mercedes SUV. Her own to-do list was posted on the third, with computer code taking up half the screen. "Both of these vehicles for King and Pierce have the North Star panic button installed," she called out as he entered the room. "The Mercedes has a different brand but the same type of service."

Mac and Jackson would be approaching the vehicles immediately after Hannah had distracted them with a broken-down Volvo she had borrowed from a friend and muddied up the license plates. Go for the hands immediately. If one of the occupants is on the phone grab it, hit the cancel button, and throw it back toward the transport vehicle. Watch their hands, especially the driver. Jackson would come in with a sawed-off, twelve-gauge automatic shotgun and Mac with the PPK.

Mac heard the shower running upstairs in Jackson's bedroom area. He heard the water shut off and feet coming awkwardly down the stairs. "Mac, this is my best friend in the whole world, Buckshot Peller."

Mac stared at the prosthesis, the beard, and towel-dried hair. Buckshot had Georgia Bull Dog athletic shorts on.

Mac, feeling all kinds of emotions today, wanted to yell at his brother-in-law. Instead he looked straight at Jackson's friend, put his hand on his shoulder and said, "I guess I have been expecting you. Do you speak the king's English? I can't understand that Southern mumbo-jumbo shit. Oh, and your namesake took a crap on my front steps last week." All three started laughing at once. Mac had managed to defuse a potentially difficult situation.

Buckshot would be on the high ridge near the point of the grabs for both King and Pierce. He would be camoed out and carrying a Winchester .223 caliber bolt-action varmint rifle with a silencer on it. If either driver or billionaire made the wrong move, flinched, or tried to be a hero, there would be a dead body to deal with. Mac had just joined the we-ain't-fuckin'-around club, for real, that Jackson and Buckshot had started long ago in the hills of Afghanistan. Buckshot had just hit the head of a ten-penny nail at five hundred yards with the same rifle the week before to win the state championship.

Mac felt as though he should have been consulted, but he had left his hot-headed Irish pride at the doorstep. This was all about being smooth and functioning at a much higher level, beyond even murder, he had convinced himself—"beyond good and evil"—for now. But Liam would never know about Buckshot; Liam was the wheelman and the muscle.

The transport vehicle was a ten-year-old Chevy Suburban that Mac had bought at a car auction in Gardner for three thousand dollars. It had 250,000 miles on it and ran like a top. He had gutted the inside and the windows were already smoked. It was the closest thing to a rolling war wagon you could find.

Mac had a cousin who hauled junk cars to the largest automotive crushing service in New England. On Wednesday morning the transport vehicle would be headed for the port of Boston, completely crushed and loaded on a ship to be sent to Taiwan, to be recycled into new General Motors steel. It would never be seen again on the roads of Fayette.

It was 9:00 a.m. and the flight plans for both of the jets had been entered into the FAA computer. King's jet was coming out of Teterboro, and Pierce's jet was out of Westchester County Airport. If they flew on schedule, they would be into Augusta State Airport within an hour and a half of each other. The men would be with their wives and pilots, and one with a driver. They had a weekend of family face time set aside for this Parents' Weekend at the summer camps in Maine. The men were relaxed; neither of them had a major deal pending, and neither of them had one person in mind to put the screws to in the coming week.

Jackson Gunther would be awaiting them both with a team trained for a kidnapping and robbery that would be the largest theft on record in the United States of America. There would barely be an outdoor moment this three-day weekend that Buckshot Peller, through his high-powered scope, wouldn't be able to eliminate them and all those with them in a matter of seconds, fold up his tripod, put his guns behind the seat of his Ford F-150 4x4, and be back on the road to Georgia to be with his new girlfriend.

Jackson had a different set of backup plans. He had a backhoe fueled and tuned up, ready to dig its sixteen-foot maximum. He would bury everybody else associated with this caper in a matter of thirty minutes—he had timed himself. He would sink the rented SUV vehicles off the 340-foot-deep granite quarry in Hallowell, and this would be on the unsolved mystery channel for the next two decades. He would be learning a new trade at the Union Hall and teaching his children to swim in Echo Lake like his grandfather had done before. He wasn't going to jail and neither was his wife or family. He was a planner, and he swore he would make all of this work one way or the other.

These targeted men were bad men; he had concluded that many months ago. Whatever became of them and their traveling mates on Monday morning, it would not lose Jackson Gunther ten minutes of sleep for the remainder of his life. He did not want to kill them, neither did Buckshot, but they were the targets for this mission, and it was his job. He had accepted it when his brother-in-law almost got killed by King's jet and Pierce had sold the mill to King to be chopped up and sold to the Chinese. The fates of King, Pierce and their parties would be determined by them and only them over the next seventy-two hours. He and his team would just respond accordingly, with collateral damage including Liam Mitchell in the backup plan. It was war, he reflected.

But at the end of the time allotted, he assured himself, the two marks would both would be robbed of over ten billion dollars; he and his wife would have a hundred million in a bank in the Cayman Islands, and he would not have to worry about anyone not letting his children into the colleges that they would desire to attend. Money was power and Jackson was in, same as his targets.

Liam had put all of his affairs in order for this day as well. He had made out a new will and left a note for his wife in the gun safe that only she had the key to. It was taped on the metal wall of the case behind his prized trap-shooting shotgun. The Italian-made weapon had brought him hours of enjoyment and even a few trophies.

He had put his all into this training and coordination these past months. He was ready, but he didn't know if he could kill a human being. But he figured that Jackson had already answered that question for him.

Liam was completely competent with both the PPK and the AR-15. He could shoot fast and pull and replace the clips on the weapons in consistent time trials. His AR was semiautomatic and would only shoot when the trigger was pulled. This was the same for Mac's rifle. Jackson had the fully automatic AR that could shoot twenty rounds in four seconds and reload with an additional clip and have forty to sixty rounds out of the barrel in less than a minute. All of the bullets would arrive on target until the barrel was so hot it would not fire.

Kelley and Jackie passed Liam on the road. Jackie waved to their big friend in the Tundra. "I like big Liam," Jackie said to her mother as they turned onto the highway. "His pants are really loose, Mommy—he needs 'spenders to hold them up now." Kelley laughed and wondered where Liam was going today.

Buckshot had moved his truck behind Jackson's house. It was out of sight and out of mind to any passers-by. The truck was always fueled and ready for a road trip. Buckshot had not felt this much excitement for a long time. He knew that Jackson had control of all aspects of the operation. He did not understand the flight to Canada and why they just didn't do these guys in some shotgun shack here in the woods in Maine. These scum suckers were not worth all of the fuel that they were burning to get this job done.

Buckshot had no problem greasing either one of them after Jackson had told him what they were doing to the hard-working families in west central Maine. He knew that if something bad was going to go down regarding killing these men, it would happen in Northern Canada. Jackson had told him about the great north of Québec and the Caribou herds, wolves and bear. He wanted in on that part, too. It just was not going to happen for him this trip. He would be changing Li'l Buck's clothes and putting him to bed on Saturday night, when his mother and father were doing their business in a place far away and out of reach. Buckshot would not hesitate to lay down his life for anyone in Jackson's immediate family. He could never stay in Georgia when his friend was on the line up in Maine—that would never happen. He loaded the green-tipped bullets into the clip of the .223.

Hannah had her eye-scanning and palm-and-handprint devices packed in her laptop case. She had passwords to the accounts of both men's stock portfolios and other offshore banking. She had spent over five hundred hours finding birth dates of the children, parents, pets, college graduation dates, and dorm-room numbers. She had perfected the software that had an eighty-five percent chance of finding passwords and access codes to any person's accounts and files. She had done the work for Ricardo Ortiz and Lana. She was field testing it this weekend, and she was quite confident that it would work. It was a key-type device that would electronically give the owner a new password to a variety of accounts and files every eight hours. It was fairly foolproof, and she had a notion that King had both that device and a personal locator implant on his body.

Everything was fueled: aircraft, rented Toyota Sequoia, transport vehicle, propane cylinders in the cabin, and outboard motor tanks at the camp in Québec. There would be a boat ride and a faux murder on Saturday afternoon. The mannequin of a body would be weighted, shot through the head, and dumped into two hundred feet of the cleanest Canadian lake water in the northern hemisphere. Liam Mitchell would perform the act, and Jackson and Mac would remove the black hoods so that the two billionaires could watch their fate should they not cooperate with Hannah on Saturday evening. What was one dead, fake billionaire at the bottom of a Canadian lake in the middle of the wildest place in the Canadian outback? Mac called it "motivation" and the "key to cooperation."

"A Dassault Falcon 7X jet has just departed Teterboro Airport with the tail numbers of King's aircraft registration," Hannah announced with official intonation. "It will be on the ground at KAUG in fifty-seven minutes, no delays. Flight plan says Captain M. Dowd filed the plan, and there are two souls on board." She turned to her three comrades, and Jackson made a swirling finger gesture in the air—it had all begun.

"Liam, remember the intercept point is at Great Northern Motor Works on Route 17. You pull out right behind them, look for the black SUV Cadillac Escalade. There will be many of these on the road today." Liam had been through this many times before; he nodded at

Jackson and gave Mac a thumbs-up. "We will be in the bushes across from the Volvo Hannah will be driving. She will have the hatchback up and a spare tire in the road."

"Falcon November One Five Romeo Echo Kilo, twenty-mile final for Runway Three Five at Augusta State Airport; local traffic please advise." Mac recognized the voice on the handheld aviation receiver that he had in his shirt pocket. It was his sparring partner, Mr. Dowd, talking on the radio from Mr. King's jet. He laughed now about the incident and felt no hard feelings for Dowd anymore. He knew that Buckshot was in the bushes on the high ground above Echo Lake and would put a bullet in his ear if he got the right sign from Jackson. He hoped that Dowd would be mellow today. After all these years of screwing Gloria, maybe he didn't feel so inclined to protect the boss. Otherwise, Mac felt indifferent toward Dowd living or dying, and he now felt the same about King.

Liam was not to leave the vehicle and definitely not the driver's seat. The grab was to last no more than three minutes total from the time the doors popped on the Mercedes SUV. If it went to five or six, they doubled the odds of encountering another vehicle on the camp road.

23

Hannah had the dusty old Volvo station wagon parked on the side of the Echo Lake road. She was sitting in the front monitoring the flight of Pierce, who had just left Westchester County. The controllers had cleared him to flight level twenty-five, and he was one hour and two minutes into his route, his Gulfstream G650 was a little slower than the three-engine Falcon that King owned.

She shut down the laptop, put all of her hair in a do-rag, and pulled her Daisy Duke-style blue-jean shorts down just above her pubic hair line. She was going to give the two front occupants of the Escalade the best thong shot they had ever had. She had a tube-top on, and her body was tanned brown. They would pull over, she was sure of it. They were men, and they could not help themselves. Buckshot would glance over towards Hannah with his scope set up on his tripod; he was totally camouflaged in the woods of Fayette. *What a lucky bastard*, he thought of his friend Jackson. Hannah was a goddess to Buckshot.

Roscoe King's Escalade had slowed by the Kent's Hill School. Gloria was telling him loudly that Naomi should consider this prep school. It had glowing reviews and a strong section in environmental studies. He nodded and said to his wife, "She can go wherever she wants. I think that she likes this area." He had no clue that a child of his attending this school, where he was inflicting so much economic hardship, would be chastised and treated poorly.

Trying to ignore the conversation, Terry sped up as they came down the hill past the Motor Works. Liam had been parked in the upper lot by the storage, and he slowly turned down the hill after them towards Echo Lake and the grab point. The stone gate at the entrance to Lovejoy Shores was the three-minute mark. Liam picked up the small radio he had under his hat on the passenger seat and spoke the words, "Three minutes out."

All of the men were dressed in the same Cabela's tree-bark camouflage pants, shirts, and hats. Mac thought they looked like Boy Scouts, but Jackson had insisted on it. They had also all dyed their hair black, head and facial.

The Escalade proceeded past the Fayette Country Store and around the corner towards the Echo Lake road and the camp that King had rented for the weekend. Terry was to stay with them. Roscoe felt very comfortable with the pilot, even though he knew that he was screwing his wife. Terry had become more useful to him now that he carried a firearm and had taken some personal-protection courses in jujutsu. The 9 mm Glock was under the seat on the driver's side. Terry was relaxed. He did not plan to use it today—hell, they were in the woods of Maine. Who would he have to protect them from, a moose?

Jackson had planned on him having a gun, and he looked forward to taking it from him, as well as giving him a pistol whipping on the side of the head.

Terry spotted the Volvo in his lane on the side of the road near a wooded area. He saw the tall woman with the do-rag on her head and a large pair of Jackie Onassis-style sunglasses on. She kneeled, flashing her tightly fitting shorts and red thong at the approaching vehicle. Roscoe motioned for Terry to pull over and smiled at his pilot. "Let's help the poor lady—maybe she needs some companionship for the weekend." He paused, "I was thinking of me, Dowd, don't get alarmed."

Both doors opened on the SUV, and Gloria flipped her husband the middle finger from the back seat. The men started walking towards Hannah and the trap.

"Liam—" Jackson's long-anticipated command came through, "secure the woman, while we deal with the two men." Liam had the booklets for Terry and Gloria, explaining their schedules for the next two days—schedules to be adhered to by the minute in order to save their precious lives from these fortune hunters.

"Do you need a hand?" Terrance Dowd asked, as he and King approached the Volvo.

"Yeah, I could really use some help." Hannah was careful not to look them in the face, and she turned towards her car.

Jackson and Mac sprang from the bushes and kicked the legs out from under both men. Hannah tossed Jackson his shotgun, and he had it under Roscoe King's nose in seconds with both knees on the man's chest. King played dead, like an animal brought down.

Dowd had got away from Mac, in flight for the Escalade. Mac tackled him to the road. A wrestling match began.

Liam pulled up behind the Escalade with the Suburban and touched the bumper solidly. He jumped out, put his foot on Dowd's neck. Mac drew a gun for the first time against a human being and rested the barrel of the PPK purposefully into soft flesh under the chin bone. Dowd stiffened into silent resistance as they bound him hand and foot with tie-straps.

Liam withdrew to duct-tape Mrs. King's mouth and bind her likewise. "Come on lady, you're riding in the front seat with me now."

She recognized a New York accent in the tall, bearded man with the dark hair.

Hannah had thrown the spare tire into the back of the Volvo and shut the hatch. She was sitting in the driver's seat with her hand underneath her purse on the passenger's seat, holding a 9 mm Glock.

Jackson was getting too rough with King, she thought, looking back. There was a black drawstring bag over the captive's head, and Jackson was hitting him with the butt end of the shotgun.

Dowd was now in the front passenger seat of the Suburban. With a glimmer of pleasure, he watched the valuable waste of time being absorbed by his boss. Jackson finally dragged the trophy round to the back-seat floor, feet and hands bound.

He then collected himself and strolled into view by the front of the car. Theatrically, he withdrew an apple from his pocket and placed it on the hood. Next, he had Dowd by the ear. He pushed the pilot's head onto the dashboard: "Watch asshole!"

Through the windshield, Dowd was just a few feet from the apple. Jackson slammed a fist onto the outside of the glass and gave a thumbs-up. Buckshot took a short breath and touched off a round from the .223 Winchester. There was a small crack, and the apple exploded from one of the green-tipped bullets.

"Dowd, you're a sailor," said Mac softly, as Jackson got into the back seat and pulled out a gun in the same way he had the apple. Mac put his pistol away and continued. "The man behind that rifle is two hundred yards in the woods. He's not a pilot—he's a sniper. He will be watching you all weekend—and as long as he has to, into the future. You can choose whether you live or die in the next forty-eight hours. We will be back here Monday morning with your employer. All of your instructions are written explicitly in notebooks. Mrs. King has them now—with instructions to be followed to the letter. Just be a good boy, and it will all turn out okay for you."

Buckshot had broken down his rifle and was on his way to meet Hannah on foot at the end of the snowmobile trail as it crossed Route 17. He ran like a deer through the woods. It had taken years of therapy and practice, but the prosthetic leg did not slow him down one step.

Liam drove away down the Echo Lake road with Mrs. King helpless, minus the duct tape, removed so as not to catch the eye of anyone on the road. The suburban was close behind.

They came to the end of the camp road at Brown's Point and pulled into a swimming area, which had been trashed beyond recognition. Now it was posted with "No Trespassing" signs. A woman's voice came over the radio, "ETA twenty-eight minutes KAUG." It translated to Jackson and Mac that the Pierce jet would be touching down in less than half an hour at Augusta State Airport.

The kidnappers pulled their captives from the vehicles. Jackson addressed them as they stood in shock: "We are going to let you go now, Terry. You and Gloria are going to get back in that Cadillac and drive to the camp you have rented on Windless Cove. You will do all of your schedule together. I am sure you have a little love-time in there. You tell Naomi that her daddy had a last-minute business emergency. We will meet you Monday morning at a spot near this lake that will be delivered to you over the weekend. If you do the work we have put down on paper for you, then on Monday afternoon you will all be landing in Teterboro, and you will still be richer than ninety-nine percent of the rest of the world. If you don't, you will all be dead, including Naomi. If it is announced that you all perished in some accident over the weekend, not one person will shed a tear for you. You know that, right?" He brought the last remark home with a gloved fist to King's ribs. Mac was sure he heard a crack from the blow. "Do we understand each other, Terry? By the way, we know where your kids are today. That daughter is getting hot—she's sixteen now, right?" Jackson grabbed, pulled and twisted the pilot's nose, releasing a stream of blood, and let go.

Terry made eye contact with Gloria, who stared petrified. "We will do exactly what you say, I promise. Please don't kill us." Terry's voice was quivering, and he was feeling a lot of pain.

"You are a pilot, remember that, Dowd. You do your killing from ten thousand feet above the earth. You know who we are. We do our killing up close and personal—Terrance. Don't fuck this up. You can live a long, healthy life. Where is your piece?"

He suspected they were some rogue Navy Seals—at least that's what Jackson wanted him to think. He nodded and said, "Under the driver's seat."

Liam took the gun and left the holster. He remembered Jackson's edict: "Every weapon that is not in our hands is to be unloaded and in our possession." He removed the clip and jacked the remaining shell onto the ground, then quickly stooped and retrieve the bullet.

Mac was watching Gloria closely and spoke solemnly. "Do you understand us, Gloria? We know that you hate that prick husband of yours, but we will kill Naomi. Easy shot—we will take her out on one of her little nature walks. You will never be able to protect her. Are we clear with you, Gloria?" Then he raised his voice: "Your lives will be normal Monday morning—if you just follow directions. If you don't, you all will be dead and at the bottom of a very deep lake."

Gloria nodded, a hint of tears in the corner of her eyes, the remains of her two-hundred-dollar-a-tube Chanel lipstick was smeared grotesquely.

"Say it, Gloria!" Mac was in her face. She could smell bug repellent and sweat.

"Yes, sir! We understand you clearly." She had not called a man sir in twenty years.

Jackson pulled out a very wide knife and cut the ties from Terry's and Gloria's wrists and ankles. Mac held the shotgun on them. Liam felled Roscoe King to the ground and kneeled on his back. The journalist had lost a lot of weight, but with 215 pounds remaining, the billionaire was having a hard time breathing.

Jackson walked up to Terry and put the shotgun barrel on the end of his bleeding nose. "Be cool, jet jockey. Think about everything you are doing, and you will live a long, sad, Irish life. Try to be a hero for that scumbag, and you will regret it to your last breath." Jackson turned the shotgun end over end and gave him a quick jab in the guts. "Don't fuck with us, commander—do your job."

Terry and Gloria were pushed back into their seats in the Escalade. *They know my rank in the Navy*, he thought. He feared these men had done their homework, and he looked over at Gloria. She broke down, sobbing hysterically—big tears and hyperventilating.

"We need to move. They are waiting for us to move, Gloria!" He backed the large SUV around and started towards the peaceful cottage in the cove on Echo Lake.

"What do we do?" Gloria half whispered, half cried.

"Roscoe has a security tracker implanted in his right rear thigh. The security people will come looking for him if they detect something unusual." She grabbed for Terry's arm, as if she needed his hero mode to engage.

"Gloria, did you see the apple that was shot off the hood of the other vehicle? We do exactly what those schedules say in the booklets. That sniper will be following us all weekend." He was not willing to give up his life to save his asshole boss.

She was disheartened that the bold fighter pilot who had turned her on sexually at the airport two years earlier was going coward on her now. "What! We do nothing all weekend? How can you let them take my husband and do who-knows-what to him?"

"Really Gloria? Think about what you are saying and who you are talking about. We're going to play it by their booklets all weekend." He was already starting a plan for after his boss had been killed. These guys would take about ten minutes of King's shit before they stuck one of those PPKs in his ear.

At the deserted swimming hole, Jackson had traded places with Liam kneeling on the boss. He pulled the black drawstring hood off the man and got very close to his face. Jackson always had a wad of chaw in the corner of his mouth while on mission. Buckshot had given him a can that morning. He leaned down very close to King's wide-open eyes. He spat a wad of tobacco into the left eye and grabbed a handful of thinning hair. He brought out the knife again. "You have an implant on you Mr. King, and I will cut you until I find it. I will start behind both ears, as that is a common place. Where you are going, those tracking devices aren't allowed. So I need to cut it out—right now."

King shook his head emphatically and lied to Jackson, "No, I don't have a tracking device. I swear to you, I don't have one." He knew that it was his only hope with these men. Those former Seals would burst into this Mickey Mouse operation, rescue him, and kill them all.

"We're starting off all wrong, Roscoe." Jackson still had a fistful of hair. He started banging King's head on the ground until Mac told him to stop. The good-cop-bad-cop routine had begun, as planned.

Mac read out the date of the implant surgery, the company name and contact. "Every time you lie to us in the next forty-eight hours will lessen your chances of living by one percentage point, you poor fuck. You understand percentage points in your business? We have read every email you have sent for five months and monitored your phone calls. We have notes from every contact you've made. We've even hired your hooker for an evening! LRA is not loyal to you, asshole."

King tried to marshal his thoughts as Jackson took over: "You can't buy a friend, Mr. King, not even a high-priced hooker. Tell me where the implant is, or I start cutting in thirty seconds—twenty-nine, twenty-eight, twenty-seven—" He placed the knife behind King's right ear.

His eye still stinging from the tobacco juice, he relented. "It's under my right buttock, just below the crease."

"Hand me the antiseptic—and the scalpel!" Jackson smirked. This was too easy.

Mac passed the small kit to his brother-in-law.

Jackson flipped the billionaire onto his stomach and pulled his pants and underwear down as if he were preparing to gut a deer. He had no more compassion for this slab of flesh lying beneath him now than for a fresh kill in the woods. In fact, he would have had more compassion for a wild beautiful buck deer that he had shot to sustain his family and friends. This man did not deserve that respect and treatment, as far as Jackson was concerned. "Hand me your headlamp, Chief?"

Jackson lit the area below King's ass-cheek and saw the small surgical scar. He had Mac put a knee on the neck and started a slow slice across the scar. The tracking device was immediately visible just below the skin. With the forceps he slowly tore it out and swabbed the area with disinfectant. Three pieces of medical gauze and tape patched the wound.

Jackson stuffed plugs in into King's ears and added a pair of ear protectors over his head, all wrapped with duct tape tightly round. He pulled the black bag with the draw string back over the head and flung the whole catch back onto the floor of the SUV. He cut the leather watch band. The Breitling Chronograph and the implant were placed in a Ziploc bag and handed to Liam. They pulled out of the forbidden beauty spot, Liam at the wheel.

Jackson again made physical contact with the captured victim; as his voice rose, there was a connection between the brain and the body; he had perfected the technique in Afghanistan. He squeezed King's neck hard with both gloved hands, causing him to cough. King could just barely hear Jackson yelling: "Is there anything else, Roscoe? We will examine you completely in a few minutes, but it will be easier on you if you come clean. Apart from the watch and the implant, is there anything that will let people know your location? If we find anything you don't tell us about, I will just maybe have to slit your throat, and you will bleed out in about three minutes. Gloria and Terrance will be fucking in the French Riviera by fall, and you will still be dead."

Mac was enjoying the spin of a little deadly humor into the act.

"No! nothing, I swear it, I swear it!"

The Suburban continued slowly around the head of the lake to intercept the Pierce Mercedes that was just being loaded for the weekend at the airport in Augusta. The grab point was two miles from the Chimney boat launch on the Mount Vernon road out of Kent's Hill.

Mac leaned round from the front seat and yelled up close: "You don't have to swear it, Roscoe, my boy. You have already lied to us. Because we have just told you the rules, the rules about the percentages, we assume that every answer you give us from here on out is the truth!"

King nodded his head under the black hood. He lay still, as the transport rounded the corner by the dam at the boat launch. It was 11:45 a.m., and so far the day had gone as planned.

The seat belts and seats had been removed from the back of the Suburban. Jackson had customized it to suit his needs of the day. He had set up ratchet straps to hard-bind his prisoners. He was cinching down King's body above the knees and around his chest. His wrists were tightly held together with the tie straps.

King was breathing but very shallowly, and he was trying to remember his breathing exercises from his yoga instructor. He hoped to be alive at the end of this day. *Why are these guys so angry?* he wondered. *What have I ever done to them?*

Liam drove to the top of the hill and turned around at the Methodist church parking lot in Readfield. Jackson saw a Sheriff's SUV heading in the wrong direction, pulled out an old flip cell phone and hit the send button. On the south end of Lovejoy Pond an explosion went off, and the front wall of the camp belonging to the former principle of Livermore Falls High School blew out. Jackson checked his watch. Three minutes later, four police cruisers and a fire truck passed at high speed heading for the fire. One minute later the same Sheriff's cruiser sped by. Now Jackson could focus on Pierce. He removed the memory card and threw the flip phone out the window.

As soon as William Pierce was grabbed, both captives would get a shot to put them to sleep. Buckshot had brought Jackson some Sodium Pentothal in a vial with a syringe that he had gotten from a nurse at the VA in Atlanta. It had cost him ten Vicodin; he would have given twenty.

There were just two people in the Mercedes SUV—Pierce and his new bride. They were giddy and laughing at the houses along the road to the cabin the camp had secured for them on the opposite side of Echo Lake from the King's spot.

The summer camp tuition for eight weeks was $20,000. The place was top notch, with educators, athletes, and guest lecturers. The sons and daughters of rock stars, movie actors, and politicians were there— and five full-time security men throughout the summer. One of the guards was to meet the Pierce family, to unlock the cabin and show them around. He was a young man from Chesterville, who was a part-time firefighter and reserve police officer in New Sharon. His phone was buzzing with the need for firefighters to go to the camp explosion on Lovejoy near the Wayne dam. He was itching to go—he wanted to turn on that red light and race down the highway. His email vibrated. The source looked strange, but it had the camp logo on the header. It said to go ahead to the fire; someone would meet the Pierce family. It was signed from the camp director.

With fire hat and boots behind the seat of his Ford Ranger, that's all he needed. He was gone like a flash. Hannah smiled as she got the return email: "Thanks, I'm on my way to Wayne."

Buckshot was in the woods with the rifle. It was the same routine as before. He had sprinted through the woods on a GPS heading to the cabin on the lake. He was back in action, he had no idea why Jackson was doing this, and it didn't matter. He would do anything for Jackson and Hannah. They were his family. He liked Mac. He didn't know the third guy, but that didn't matter either. If Jackson had said *kill* to protect Mac or Liam or to take them out, Buckshot would have done the chore and never given it a second thought.

William Pierce was freewheeling down Route 17 and looking forward to a weekend skinny dipping with his new bride and visiting with his son and friends at camp. They turned off 17 and passed the Alpine Ski Training Center. The waiting, dark-blue Suburban gave them a three-count—one thousand, two thousand, three thousand— and turned right to follow. They passed the security guy going 75 mph toward the fire.

Jackson smiled; neither Liam nor Mac had a clue what he had just pulled off. Jackson was back in his high school days in a flash.

24

In the first minor setback of the day, their timing was off, and the lovers got to the cabin about two minutes ahead of the Suburban. Buckshot knew what to do. He removed the silencer and slung the rifle over his shoulder. He looked for security cameras around the camp. He walked quietly behind the cabin and round to the side, choosing his steps like the make-believe Indian warrior he had dreamt to be.

The lovers opened the doors to the Mercedes and got out. They both had cell phones with a panic button attached. Buckshot took the rifle off his shoulder and checked his 9 mm to make sure that a round was in the chamber. Pierce passed the key to his wife. She fumbled, and they laughed at one another. Buckshot jumped from behind the wall and struck Pierce in the ribs with the rifle butt. He looked like a cast member from Duck Dynasty and had the Southern accent t' boot: "Down on the ground, both of you! Lemme see your hands, now!"

They were in shock. Pierce was in pain. Buckshot moved them to the front of their vehicle, knowing there was a camera in the rearview mirror. He put his prosthetic leg on the woman and pushed the barrel of the rifle onto the man's head. It was hard and forceful. Both Buckshot and Jackson knew that feeling a little pain now would give the captured an indicator of the bullet entering the brain just before death, painlessly, execution style.

Neither person flinched. Buckshot gathered the phones, wallet, purse, and watch. Pierce hoped that this would just be a redneck robbery of his possessions, and the man would leave them in peace.

The Suburban pulled into the driveway. The three men jumped out, not displeased to see that half of their work had already been done by the man from Georgia.

"Check the trees and the utility poles for game cams, B. These camp owners have them everywhere," Mac suggested. Sure enough, Buckshot found two and knocked them out of their placements with a canoe paddle. He hoped there were no more. He pressed the review button for the video display. There he was in living color, jabbing the man in the ribs and putting the couple on the ground. He hated technology sometimes.

"Mr. and Mrs. Pierce, we are your hosts for the weekend." Jackson was taking the lead again. Mac and Liam prepared Pierce for the back end of the Suburban.

Jackson turned to the new wife and began by consoling her. "Alexis, isn't it? We know you're scared. You just need to listen, and you'll be fine. These are instructions for you to follow for the remainder of the weekend." He handed her the booklet and added simply, "If you vary from this schedule, you will be killed. Mr. Pierce will be killed and his little boy. My friend here is a trained military sniper. He will be watching you all weekend. If you both do as you're told, Mr. Pierce here—" Then Jackson grabbed Pierce's throat with one hand and lifted him off the ground a little. He wished his hands were as big as Liam's so he could strangle the man—just like that. "As I was saying, Mr. Pierce here—and you—will live a long, happy life aboard your sailboat in the Bahamas and play your sick little sex games. But if you do one thing off this script, I will cut your husband's throat from one ear to the other." He pulled the knife from his chest sheath, cut off Pierce's sports watch, and handed it to the woman.

Her knees were shaking and her lips were trembling. How did they know about the sex games and the boat in the Bahamas? How did these horrible men know about their personal love life? *Moralistic scumbags!* But she said with a quivering voice, "I will do everything that you ask. I give you my word."

Jackson responded, "Your word is no good, Mrs. Pierce. The biggest decision of your life—and you choose a lowlife, asshole, scumsucker for a husband. So how can we depend on you keeping your word? We will not. My friend here that was your welcoming committee will verify every move that you make. Remember that!" He pointed to Buckshot, dressed head to toe in camouflage. Mr. Peller tipped his hat to the lady from the Upper West Side.

The Suburban, now loaded with their new cargo, backed up and proceeded out of the camp driveway. They were back on the Mount Vernon road, on their way to Mac's floatplane dock.

"Do you want to depart from Lovejoy?" Jackson had to ask. It would save them a full step of the exercise.

Mac thought a minute and then saw the flag at the Kent's Hill school blowing out of the southeast—a summer thunderstorm wind. Mac knew it like a bad penny coming up tails when he called heads. "No way, Jackson. We will have to go off the boat launch at the Chimney. We have to go out to the south, and we will be overloaded by about three hundred pounds still. Love to help you with this one, brother, but no can do."

Jackson had never heard his brother-in-law call him brother. Maybe they really would be brothers now, in some sort of way.

When they dropped Mac off from the Suburban and drove away, the emergency vehicles were still racing by his home. He wondered what the hell had happened. He jogged down through the woods and onto his dock. He could smell his sweat coming up through the outdoor camo wear. Kelley would not like that smell on him. She would throw a bath towel at him and yell, "Get that stink out of my house!"

He wished he had given her a longer kiss that morning and a tighter squeeze for little Jackie. He untied the ropes of the airplane and made sure the three bags were in the extended baggage compartment. He sat in the pilot's seat, hit the fuel pump, and listened for the fuel to be pumped up into the cylinders. He had pumped the floats early that morning. This ship was ready for Canada, for the Saint Lawrence, the big dam lakes, and a night arrival at the most special trout pond Mac ever knew. Why was he bringing all of this badness to his special place? *What was I thinking?* He shook his head, checked his gauges, snatched two notches of flaps, and powered up the three hundred horsepower Continental motor. *No turning back now.*

It was a three-minute flight to the end of Echo Lake, where the boys were eating Granola bars on the dock. Liam had his gear, and he would back the Suburban into the water and up to the strut of the airplane. Jackson would hold up a tarp just in case someone might be looking a little too close. The plane idled down and water-taxied to the boat-launch dock without power. Mac was a master on the water at maneuvering an airplane. The Suburban had its backup lights on; Liam was eager to unload. Jackson was still showing aggression and manhandled King and Pierce out of the Suburban, almost indistinguishable with Pierce now wearing ear plugs and a bag over his head. Their bodies were moving and they were still alive. *That's good*, Liam thought.

They flopped on the floor in the back of the airplane. The rear seat had been taken out, and the ratchet straps were transferred to the 185 Cessna. There was almost no conversation. King was trying to pick up on something that could be used when these criminals were arrested. He could smell the odor of aviation fuel and the inside of an aircraft. The big man with the New York accent pulled his hood off and offered him a drink of water from a military canteen. He took it and noticed for the first time that he was not alone in the black-drawstring-bag seating section of this flight.

Mac hit the fuel pump, then the starter three seconds after, and the engine came to life. He was grateful—they usually started miserably when they were hot. He made one turn in the cove and double-checked Liam's shoulder harness and seat belt. He started to power up and caught a Maine warden service green truck entering the boat-launch area. But they were as good as gone. The power came up, and the plane went on the step.

Still, it was not ready to fly and kept using more and more valuable lake as it sped toward the south. He hated the thought of rolling one of the big 3000 PK floats with this heavy load inside. He decided to fly it straight off the water and added another notch of flaps. It was a tricky maneuver to take off with an overloaded airplane. He raced passed the children's camps and by the island, and he still was not airborne. The electrical wires that crossed the lake were coming up fast. Would this plan end in a crash at the end of Echo?

A breeze stiffened out of the south, and the seaplane broke water and started to climb. The engine had been redlined for almost four minutes, and the temperature gauge had jumped a hundred degrees. The rate of climb was slow, as they passed over the Fayette Central School, where Jackie read aloud to her classmates.

Liam Mitchell had squeezed the support brace in the airplane so hard that his Yale class ring had marked the paint. But the plane was climbing, and Mac made a slow turn to the east to put them on course. He would connect with the Kennebec River in four minutes and activate the GPS system with his special low-altitude route. The tailwind was nice and indicating fifteen knots blowing straight on the tail; that would make their flight time to the Québec camp four hours and thirty-five minutes. Unfortunately, the visibility was lower than hoped for, and thunder clouds were building in the air around west central Maine.

Mac activated his new GPS unit— The latest technology on terrain avoidance and course deviation, it would flash a red terrain warning two miles ahead of any mountains, towers, or obstructions. The device would purple warn the pilot if the aircraft was more than a hundred feet off the charted course. It was the best available technology.

The passengers were getting a little restless and were kicking at their straps and the two pilot seats. Liam made a motion to Mac in the form of a syringe plunger and Mac nodded. The two passengers were about to take a long nap. Liam loaded the syringe with the sleepy-time drug. Mac hoped that it was the right dosage and cringed at the thought of landing in Canada with two corpses from an overdose. Both men were about the same size and Liam gave them the same dose.

The flight was bumpy with turbulence from the midday heat over the land. Mac flew low and fast with the Cessna 185—it was a real hot-rod compared to what he was accustomed to. The Cessna had a high-compression engine that was like a finely tuned racecar. The noise was a high-pitched whine that took some getting used to. The Beaver was a low-compression radial engine made by Pratt & Whitney. P&W made the engines for the war bombers and other classic flying machines from the '40s and '50s.

Mac had crossed the Harris Station dam in the Forks and was turning up the big lake called Moosehead. His airplane was on the deck, forty feet off the water. The ground speed was 140 knots; he was running the engine at 23 inches of manifold pressure and 2,350 rpm; the fuel burn and the speed were better than planned. The team had three hours and forty-two minutes left to fly.

He felt like Harrison Ford flying the *Millennium Falcon* and Tom Cruise buzzing the tower in an F-14. Mac felt like a kid with all of the excitement of his first solo flight more than thirty years ago. He was going over people in canoes on the West Branch of the Penobscot out of Lobster Lake. They were dropping their paddles and pointing up at Mac and Liam. The prop was in flat pitch, loud and screaming. The airplane came roaring up these wilderness areas like an air assault. In all of the years of guiding canoeists, summer Maine guides had never seen a floatplane flying so fast and so low up the lakes and rivers. One party of twelve teenage girls from the Chewonki camps could feel the breeze from the propeller and smell the engine when it passed over them on Chamberlain Lake. They flashed the single hand "rock on" sign to the airplane.

Liam looked at Mac and pointed to the MP3 player jack in the airplane's panel. The passengers were deep in dreamland, thanks to the needles. Mac looked at Liam, and they both gave giant shark smiles to each other. Liam gave thumbs-up and plugged his iPod into the panel with Stevie Ray Vaughan blasting through the headsets— "The House Is Rockin'" from one of the greatest guitar players who ever lived. These two men were alive, and they had not felt so alive in their entire lives. All of this could go bad at any minute, but for right now, for this moment, there seemed no place better in the world for either one to be.

Mac knew he did not have the reflexes of his earlier years as a pilot, and he was taking longer to react. Tall pines that held eagle nests came up quicker and did not appear on the terrain indicator screen.

He bobbed his head with the beat of the music a while longer and then turned his side of the headsets off. There was no one to talk with all the way to Canada—no control towers, no customs people. This flight was illegal from the start, and he would not be caught.

The flight was getting smoother as the air cooled and any thunder clouds were mostly left behind. With the clear air could come a change in wind direction. They were one third of the way into the flight, and so far the tailwind continued to save time. He checked the weather on his satellite system for Baie-Comeau—the wind was ten knots out of the northwest. It looked like he would be fighting a headwind for the last one-and-a-half hours of the flight.

The good news was that the 185 had not appeared on one radar screen, as of yet. He flew over the Jalbert sporting camps, just missing the water tower placed among the large pine trees. There were canoes in the front, and Mac wondered if the girls were in camp. He rocked the wings as he flew over, hoping that the hot tub was full of the Jalbert sisters, naked. A buzz job with this 185 Cessna would wake them up, he dreamed.

He had flown this route over a hundred times at higher altitude. This time he followed the Allagash River close into the town of Allagash and turned a hard left up the Saint John and crossed over the town of Dickey, low and fast. The weather was clear. He made a slow banking turn and headed out above the mountain tree line for the first time during the two-hour flight. They were ten minutes from the border crossing at Estcourt Station. The border was manned, and there would be no chances taken flying over the checkpoint. He stayed west of the course by a mile and saw the waters of the Little Black River below him. The coldest recorded temperature in the United States had been on the Little Black—fifty-seven degrees below zero Fahrenheit on a nippy little morning in February. Today there were very few people near the river, but one party of canoeists had their swimsuits on. Mac hoped that they were happy and enjoying this day that he was so much alive in.

The airplane had crossed the border; the GPS told him so. Bold letters flashed, and the display said, "You are now in Canadian airspace. Please notify all federal authorities." Mac read the display, cleared it, and tipped his hat to the land, *Hello Canada! the shit will be goin' down soon—*

25

Jackson was detained at the boat launch by the local game warden when he got back into the Suburban. The locals knew Jackson as a war hero, but the game wardens put him in a different category. He was one of those overly successful hunters and fishermen. They automatically thought he was a lawbreaker and used illegal methods to bag his game. He had been trained by his father and grandfather and his freezer was never empty. In fact, most of the time it was overflowing, and he shared his game with his neighbors, family, and friends.

The warden at the Chimney boat launch had been trying to catch Jackson for years, driving deer or taking one too many brook trout out of Echo. He knew that Jackson was a tough customer and was known to have killed many men during his war service. "What are you up to, Jackson?"

Jackson did not like the fact that the warden was seeing him with a beard and hair dyed black. "Not one thing concerning the taking of fish and game in the state of Maine." He looked at his feet, kicked a rock and thought he better tone it down a little. "Just out checking out the boat launch. I'm bringing the kids over here next week fishing."

"New Chevy, Jackson?" The man only had questions.

"Not hardly. It has 250 thousand on it. I'm borrowing it for a couple of hours—to move some furniture for my mother."

"Who you borrowing it from?"

Jackson spat a wad of chew on the ground at the warden's feet. "It's July, warden. Is there any time of the year when you are not a total prick to everyone you meet?"

The warden was wondering if this man would go hostile on him; he could have PTSD from the war. "No. I'm sorry. You are not fishing or doing anything wrong that I can see. Whose airplane just took off out of here?"

"Don't know. They were looking for directions to Twitchell's seaplane base."

"Boy, they were loaded heavy getting out of Echo, don't ya think?"

"Look man, I don't know anything about loading airplanes or flying—that would be my brother-in-law. You know him, right?"

"Yeah, we know him. Did you hear about the explosion down on Lovejoy at the old principal's camp? What a blowout!"

Jackson just shook his head.

"I guess the old geezer was walking up from the lake to take a leak in the cabin and the front wall blew out knocking him right on his ass. Probably a propane leak—the camp burned flat."

The two ceased the conversation just looking at one another. Who would move first? It would not be Jackson, that was for sure. He would stand there until the sun went down before he would let this guy know what direction he was headed. The warden finally got into his pickup and drove off. In the woods across from the boat launch, Buckshot put the safety back on his rifle and lowered it. For the first time in twenty minutes the warden's head was not in his crosshairs. He didn't sigh, he didn't feel relieved. It was just one thing that he didn't do that he would have done for his friend, his brother-in-arms, in Buckshot's exclusive world.

Jackson pulled out and tapped the horn twice. His buddy came running out of the woods and jumped into the Suburban.

"Lucky day for Mr. Greensuit," Jackson commented, looked Buckshot in the eye and winked. They would be meeting Hannah at the car-crushing transport at Mac's cousin's place in one hour. This day was going exactly as planned.

Jackson knew Buckshot would want to go to Québec. He could not take him, and it was killing him. Jackson leaned over to give him some weekend instructions. "Tomorrow, drop off the implant they dug out of Bad Boy One, and his watch, to the wife and pilot at the cove camp; let them know you are in the area."

"This watch is worth sixty grand, at least. You sure you want to give it back?" Buckshot asked.

"Yeah, I am sure of that, my friend. I am not going to tell you what we are up to, Buckshot. You need to *not* know, if you get my drift." Jackson smiled to himself. He knew how much Buckshot would love being in on the whole plan. "When this is all over, you will know all of it, every bit of it. For now, you have helped more than you know. You need to sit for our kids over the weekend. On two of the check-offs for these wives, you'll be able to take the kids with you. Saturday afternoon at Barnes & Noble they will be at the high seats near the checkout in Augusta. One will be there at 2:00; the other will be there at 4:00. Take photos of them with your phone and send them to Hannah. The other connect is Sunday morning at the public beach in Readfield. They will each have a child with them, a twelve-year-old girl named Naomi and an eight-year-old boy named William. Take photos of both. The pilot that is screwing King's wife will be with the woman and the girl." He handed Buckshot a copy of the itinerary and instructions. "It's all here, to be destroyed, of course.

"Hannah and I will be leaving tonight for Québec and the rendezvous cabin in the woods. It could get rough up there." This was code that someone may very well die. "We will be back on Monday morning around 10:00. The floatplane will be arriving at the same time. If we are delayed, take the AR-15 to both of the instructed spots in camo. Don't take the bolt-action; it's way to slow for the job. As you know, the AR is dead-on at two hundred yards, and the forward switch is full auto.

"Drop the kids off at my mother's at 8:00, and get set up early. Any activity gathering, you text this number and say 'L2 DO.' That means location two for the drop off. Otherwise, you will see a plane and a door open near the shore, and a swimmer will be in the water, swimming towards an awaiting SUV. The only reason you should fire is if they are firing at the aircraft to stop it. Then you have to kill them all, including the SUV occupants. Too bad, but we want no one remembering any of this. Within twenty minutes the cavalry will be here with dogs—plan your escape."

Buckshot already knew the back road to Auburn through Livermore from Fayette and the Maine turnpike exit to enter southbound. He would not be leaving Maine until his friend was bouncing his namesake off his knee safely at the Gunther's humble abode.

26

The 185 was crossing the tops of oil transports bound for Montreal on the Saint Lawrence Seaway. Pods of whales broke the surface of the water twenty feet below the bottoms of the seaplane's pontoons. It was a fifty-mile diagonal crossing, and it was happening right on schedule. The two men in the back were stirring; the drugs were wearing off. It looked to Liam as if one man was having convulsions.

He slid his seat back and undid his seat belt. Pierce was airsick and vomiting all over inside the hood. Liam was careful not to get his fingers near the mouth as he wiped vomit up and put as much of it as he could into a sick-sack tucked behind the pilot seat. Pierce looked at him with great fear. His eyes were filled with tears from vomiting. Liam offered him some water from a Poland Spring bottle. He took the water and tried to drink it all. Liam pulled it away, wiped off more vomit and replaced the black drawstring bag.

The dams began in Baie-Comeau and went two hundred miles north near the Labrador border. It was the largest waterpower project in the world. Hydro Québec was the builder and operator of the dams. Mac flew west of the town of Baie-Comeau, still flying low and fast. There was a radar facility and a seaplane base there. He wanted nothing to do with either of them. The seaplane base operated by Labrador Air Safari was where Mac had cleared Canadian customs for twenty years; they knew him and his Beaver.

The country was magnificent. It was cut from steep rock showing lots of granite. The bodies of water went on for miles and miles. It was cold, clean water filled with fish that would live their lives without ever encountering a lure or a hook. Mac had taken fishermen on trails along the tundra on top of the lichen that few men had ever walked. They would stand in wonder with their fly rods in hand, wondering if this was real, this place they would visit once and never return. The big, powerful rivers were holders of strong, healthy, well-fed fish. To catch one on a fly rod and land it was a feat in itself. They were not the lazy stocked trout of southern Maine or the weak strain of northern lake trout that could be reeled in like a dead branch. The salmon would break water, the trout would go deep, and the togue would shake their teeth across your leader madly trying to saw the line off.

The land had also claimed some of Mac's closest friends. It was a pilot's dream for locating backcountry wilderness opportunities, and it was a pilot's nightmare and killer when the weather went down and the wind blew hard. He had learned to sit it out and wait. Even if they were out of food and supplies, he would await the fair winds and clear sky. Three of his friends had flown into a mountain trying to get home from fish camp for Father's Day. Mac never got over it. He would see his friends' faces at night in bad dreams; they were waving to him to come to the river and fish. He never had the dream interpreted and never would. He had a feeling he knew what it meant. This country in Québec and Labrador was truly wild and free to a bush pilot with a full tank of fuel. Mac would always come here no matter what; it made him feel alive.

He had not seen one airplane in or around him for the four-hundred-mile flight; in the last ten miles, fifty miles south of his destination, he had seen four. Two Beavers and the larger Otter model northbound on his route of flight and at a higher altitude. He also saw a Bell Jet Ranger patrolling the power lines. Three had tried to contact him on the radio; all had French accents and yelled for the U.S. 185. It was unusual to hear them asking for a U.S. aircraft so far north of any airport. Mac played dumb and kept his heading and altitude, thirty feet off the water.

They would be at the cabin in thirty minutes. The two bound men on the floor were getting increasingly restless. Mac wondered what was going through their minds. He had to be the tough guy now, and Liam was the man-handler. They had discussed this in full. Jackson and Hannah would not be there until morning.

Mac buzzed the cabin and saw no activity. He was tired. It had been a very intense flight at low levels and high speed. He felt accomplished in his day of piloting the new aircraft he had borrowed from Rocky. He had had to do things slowly and use his checklist to make it all happen without incident. He slid Liam's seat back two notches. He did not want those big feet screwing up his landing and getting in the way. All of Liam's features were big, all of them—feet hands, face, back, and he knew from camping with the man he was hung well. Mac looked at Liam, smiled and laughed—"North America's newest criminal mastermind."

Liam elbowed him and smiled back.

He landed the plane easily on the lake in front of his cabin, lowered the water rudders and taxied to the dock on Liam's side. He motioned Liam to remove his Yale class ring, an overlooked clue they did not want seen.

The plane was secured, and the pilot and his partner removed the bags of supplies and coolers through the rear baggage compartment door. Mac signaled that he would unlock the cabin and prepare the holding room. He had lag-bolted livestock rings to the floor during his previous trip in June. There was twenty feet of chain with carabineers and padlocks ready for the captives.

Liam brought both men up from the airplane and into the cabin with their black hoods on. He spoke very little, saying, "Move, step, straight ahead, and walk slowly." Every time one of the men spoke or uttered a grunt, Liam would hit him with a small billy club on the shins.

Jackson was adamant while training Mac and Liam. "These men are your prisoners. Show them no compassion or emotion. Handle them firmly. Let them feel your power over them. Grab them firmly whenever you touch them. Yell if they are questioning. Let them feel your breath in their ear. Let them hear the dry firing of a pistol or the action of an automatic shotgun or rifle. This is the time where they decide whether you can take their lives at any moment, and there should never be any doubt. Only let them see with their eyes when you want to invoke fear into their brains." Jackson Gunther had had some of the world's worst terrorists kneeling at his feet begging for their lives and soiling their pants. Liam and Mac just had to hold the fear in these two until he arrived. It would be a long night in the Canadian woods.

The loons began to call their long, lonely howl into the crisp night air. It was 8:00 p.m. and the sun was still up in the western sky. It would be another half-hour before it set. Roscoe King and William

Pierce would be offered "lying" or "sitting" for the night's captivity. They both chose lying on the floor. Liam made sure their ears were completely covered and plugged with industrial hearing protection, which would largely dampen but not block all sound. Mac ground up four sleeping pills and mixed them into the captives' water bottles.

Mac would take the first shift guarding them. They were not to be left alone for any amount of time, and no talking would be allowed. The two men drank their water, and Liam helped them both urinate into the bait bucket. No food—it was Jackson's demand. They drifted off to sleep.

Mac opened his copy of *Selected Poems* by William Butler Yeats. He read it every first night at the Canada camp. He believed Yeats could set you free in verse.

27

Hannah was behind the wheel of the Toyota Sequoia—Jackson hated renting or driving a Japanese car or any vehicle that didn't have Ford, Chevrolet, or even Dodge branded on the rear panel. She pulled up to the checkpoint at the border crossing at Coburn Gore. It was a small, limited-period crossing point on the U.S.-Canadian border. She stepped out of the rented SUV and took a long stretch. A female customs officer came out of the gatehouse on the Québécois side and said, "Please remain in the vehicle at all times."

"Oh, I'm sorry—did I do something wrong?" Hannah was stunned and a little spacey from her long day of work and planning as she returned to her seat. Jackson was asleep, and the Sequoia was loaded with coolers and gear with a seventeen-foot Old Town canoe strapped to the roof rack.

"Please present your passports for entry into Canada." The woman was all business, and she looked as if she was alone in the gatehouse. Hannah took the passports from the visor and handed them out the window. "Do you have any tobacco or alcohol to declare? Do you have any firearms in your possession?"

"No, no, and no. We are on a fishing second honeymoon and intend to buy all of our romantic drinks from the great province of Québec." She was trying to lighten up the mood. Jackson was awake now and nodded to the guard.

The woman took the passports inside and looked at a computer screen for a few minutes, but it seemed like an hour to Hannah.

The officer returned with the documents. "Mr. and Mrs. Gunther, I have a trained dog in the back of my guard shack. Should I search your vehicle, I will not find any firearms, ammunition, alcohol or drugs, is that correct?" She held her hand on her service weapon.

Jackson leaned towards the driver's window, "Feel free to search this from top to bottom; we have nothing to hide. I spent four years hiding from the Afghans. I am completely open to you searching every nook and cranny of this automobile."

Taken aback by Jackson's openness and realizing he was a veteran with a 101st Airborne tattoo on his forearm, she said, "Please proceed and welcome to Canada. Enjoy your stay, both of you." She paused. "And sir, thank you for your service. We Canadians are appreciative of what your military does around the world."

With a sigh of relief, they drove off from the checkpoint. It was 8:00 p.m., and they still had a ten-hour drive ahead of them.

Jackson was awake now, and had just put the second hour of Johnny Cash music from his iPod on the stereo system.

"Could we listen to Sheryl Crow, please?" Hannah had heard enough from the man in black. "Matter of fact, why don't we just talk for a while, honey?"

He shook his head and took a drink of water from the canteen. "What's up, baby?"

"I know that I wasn't supposed to be a part of this plan. I think Mac is still a little sore about it. I know that we'll pull this off. You will scare the life out of those two tomorrow, and they will let us have it all. Mac has a good idea of not touching the money for two years. But I think his idea for the health-care thing is crazy, a waste of billions. If this was a good idea, don't you think Warren Buffett would have tried it a long time ago? I'm not supportive of that part of the scheme. Ten billion dollars? The connection I've made in the islands could help change our lives forever, honey. I think that we can make a fortune doing this work for Ortiz legally. I really think so, Jackson."

Jackson wasn't hearing any of it. "Listen baby, this is Mac's plan and we're along for the ride. Liam doesn't like the single-payer health-care thing, either. Mac is, like, going through his midlife crisis, and he ain't buying a Porsche or banging strippers and teenagers. He thinks that a man or a woman should do one good thing in their God-given life. This is what he thinks is his "one good thing." We'll all be rich after Monday. We'll leave these guys with $500 million and take a $100 million each for the three of us. I'd never be a part of this if these guys hadn't closed the mill and screwed all of these people for life."

He was getting fired up now. "I'm tired of people in power taking the rest of us to our knees financially. Mac is right about these men. They are worthless human beings. If I killed them both tomorrow, not one person would mourn for them, not even their own mothers. We will humiliate them, beat them if we have to, rob them for sure, and return them to their jets, their perversions, and half a billion dollars. If they try to find us or get their money back, I will kill them both. Buckshot and I would make a day of it, and they would disappear forever. We both have killed men with more courage and honor; this is just a final chapter in a book for me, Hannah. I love you and our children more than you know. I'm taking their money, and I will not look back, even if I have to take their lives."

Hannah had never heard her husband speak like this. She was now a little afraid of the man she had married—something was missing in his words, but they were not empty. She knew from his bad dreams and gazing off into space that there was something buried deep within him, and now she was seeing that dirt uncovered and exposed. She had an idea when Buckshot showed up that the we-ain't-fuckin'-around club was back in business. It occurred to her that Mac and Liam were just along for the ride. Jackson was driving and had been from the start.

"What do you think of Ortiz and Lana and what I am doing with them for work?" She knew he had a strong opinion about this and had been holding back for a long time. "They are really nice to me," she pressed, "and see me as a part of their future business. They both want to get out of banking in the next five years, at least that is what they told me. They are so wealthy, Jackson, and such good people. Do you know he goes home to the Dominican Republic three times a year and helps the poor and sick?"

Jackson waited for a minute. He knew that Hannah was somewhat enamored with these people and all of their wealth and power. "You're one of the most talented people I've ever met, baby. You can figure things out that teams of men and women can't do after years of work. Ortiz and his Russian squeeze are at the top of their game in the world they live in. They see you as a connection in the cyber-world and all its potential. I think you should stay with 'em for a while and learn what they have to offer. They may move on to another phase, and maybe that's why they want you to be involved with them now. The reason they employ people is to help bring more wealth—to them. I think we'll do this deed this weekend and be successful. But it's my last in this type of work, I swear it. I know that money is not happiness in any form. From all that I have seen, it ruins people and their children. We will never let that happen, so help me God!"

Hannah reached over and took hold of his hand. "What if we said to hell with it right now, baby?" Jackson knew this was the hook to this conversation. "We can take our chances with Ortiz and Lana. You know, I'm getting a $150,000 retainer for a year of work. That is more than we've ever made in a year of work, even with your good job in the mill. What if we are caught? What if we go to jail and we couldn't see our babies for years? We could never take it, Jackson. Let's not do this, please!"

"You were the last person that I thought would want out, Hannah. Hell, I've been counting on Mitchell going south on us for two months! He's working like a dog. The man lost fifty pounds! We are not leaving my brother-in-law with his dick swinging in the breeze. Now you've put us in a bad position, because of your demand to be included, and we cannot do this without you. You need to stop the doubting and engage in the successful completion of this mission. If you do not or cannot perform, I'll propose that we take these jerks and leave them on the Canadian border tomorrow morning. No harm no foul. What the hell, Hannah? Are you in or not?"

She glanced over and saw the lie in his demeanor and took the bait. "Sure baby, they'll never come after us—not like we are going to get them!"

Jackson reeled her in with one of the oldest tricks of his training, and the glistening side of a fish leapt in his mind's eye. "You've found me out," he sighed. "You're right. They'd sense weakness if we let 'em go, and all our plans built on fear would be useless. Yep, Buckshot an' me, we'd kill 'em both."

"OK, OK, baby. I'm in. Still, I hope all my technology works. I hope I can keep my end up."

Hannah was not satisfied with the conversation. She felt guilty and threatened by something obscure. She wanted to nap and turned over the driving to Jackson, but she couldn't sleep. Her mind was reeling. As they passed by the Basilica of Sainte-Anne-de-Beaupré, renowned for miracles, Jackson asked, "Do you want to stop here and pray for a miracle, honey?" He was making good time.

Hannah replied quietly, "I don't think praying to God to successfully commit a crime is going to work for us, or for God."

He reached over and touched her leg. His touch broke her trance. She unbuckled her seat belt and leaned over to kiss him on the cheek. She extended her long leg over Jackson's and started to loosen his belt while he was driving. "What the hell are you doing?" he asked playfully.

"When is the last time we drove down the road without two sets of eyes watching our every move from the back seat?" She smiled, pulled down her tube-top, hit the automatic seat adjustment and slid the driver's seat back. She brought up her knees, slid off her Daisy Dukes, and slowly re-extended her leg across the console to straddle the man at the wheel.

"That's what I'm talking' about—" He reached for the sound system and cranked up Sam Smith's love song, "Stay with Me."

The SUV sped up and then slowed down. It swerved side to side and then sped up and slowed down again. The two lovers in the driver's seat sped up and slowed down in unison. The sound system at seventy-five percent volume moved two minutes into Smith's "I'm Not the Only One," and they were done. Both man and woman were climaxing at the same time just outside the entrance road to Mount Saint Anne in the Province of Québec. They had changed lanes six times in eight miles.

Hannah climbed off her husband, and he could see the road clearly. "I'm with you baby right to the end," she said and smiled at him, buttoned her shorts and pulled up her top, like she had just won the shootout at the OK Corral.

28

Mac had completed his shift on guard duty. The two captives were stirring, kicking at their bondage straps and groaning. King yelled, "Where the hell am I? What is going on? Who are you people? Do you know who I am!"

Mac gave him a jab in the ribs with his rifle butt and leaned close to his head. He reached up inside the black hood and moved one of his ear muffs to the side. "We really do know who you are, Mr. Roscoe King. We also know that you can choose your own fate in the next few hours. Not only yours but the fate of your family. You have no friends; we are pretty certain of that. Now if you need to take a piss or would like a sip of water, I can assist you. Otherwise I do not want to hear another sound out of that ugly puss of yours."

Liam stepped inside the holding room. "All good here, chief?" He avoided names, as agreed. Outside, the sun was on the water and not a breath of air. It was a rarity to see this place so calm and serene. Trout were rising on the pond. Some were breaking water, snatching the hatch of mayflies. Mac stood looking out the window and loved what was happening out there. His June guests had left a five-weight fly rod on the rod holders, on the side of the cabin—it was a caddis hair fly, ready to cast. Mac thought about it and said, "Fresh trout for breakfast, cap." Liam gave him the thumbs-up.

He hauled the canoe out from under the front deck to the water's edge and put the rod and a small box of flies under the thwarts. He grabbed a paddle from the end of the dock and pushed off into the mass of trout rings surfacing all around him. It was a magical moment on the small lake, and Mac wanted to seize this moment and catch some of these beautiful creatures.

The cast to a rise of a feeding trout in the early morning or twilight is a fisherman's delight. A fly fisher can set the fly in the middle of a rise and await the trout to encircle from below and take whatever flying or floating insect has landed in his ring. The trick for Mac or any fisherman is to match the hatch, put the right fly on the end of your leader that will attract a fish with colors patterns and flotation. Mac had matched the hatch this calm morning in the Canadian wilderness. He had no thoughts of the two men being held captive in the cabin, as he cast to rises and caught and landed four bright red-bellied brook trout, all between twelve and fourteen inches.

Now he had food for him and Liam. Two eggs over easy, some juice, a can of baked beans, and two fresh trout each would be a breakfast. There was a part of him—the civil, human part—that wanted to feed King and Pierce from his catch. He had flown men like them to this spot and cooked and guided for them. Then he remembered the collection jars set up at the Fayette Country Store for the unemployed workers at Paul Bunyan Paper. "Fuck 'em!" He spoke the words out loud and pulled the canoe up the bank.

Not far away, Jackson was still behind the wheel of the Sequoia. He knew these Toyotas were tough; he had shot several of them through the engine block in Afghanistan. Many of them kept running until the oil drained from the pan and the pistons seized up. He was going to test this SUV now. He reset the GPS unit in the direction of Mac's cabin. It was a trail at best. Mac had purposely let the road deteriorate to keep the locals out, and the thaw had been wet in the woods of Northern Québec. There were four rough miles to go. The lovers crept slowly in four-wheel-drive low range. It took them over two hours of gathering scratches and branch marks on the paint, plowing through the alders and small black spruce. Jackson looked at his wife as she grimaced to the fingernails-on-a-chalkboard. "I haven't got a nickel in it," he commented and smiled, stepping on the gas to mow over more trees.

Mac heard the low-range whine of the motor come through the woods. He sighed a heavy breath of relief. They needed to get this job done and get out of here. Once Hannah set up her satellite Wi-Fi, he could keep track of any weather moving between his flying party and Echo Lake, over six hundred miles away. He saw the front of the Toyota plowing through the mud and trees and waved like a wild man.

"Any coffee?" The first words out of Jackson's mouth, asking for some of Mac's strong camp java.

"We have coffee and fresh trout."

"Get me a cup, man. I think Hannah could use one as well. Gather Liam, and we will go through the schedule for the day. You may want to fly out Sunday instead of Monday morning. There's some weather moving up the east coast and it could be sopped in solid in Maine on Monday morning. You don't want to be stuck here with these assholes for a week, I'm guessing." Mac nodded and waved at Liam to come down to the vehicle.

The mannequin was buried under gear bags in the passenger bench seat in the Toyota. It had been used to train medics in CPR, until they had stolen it. "Mr. CPR," as they sometimes referred to him, was all dressed and ready for his fake murder. "Hannah has the tapes to play with our friend here," Jackson hit the dummy in the chest. "Liam, this has got to look real, man. If it doesn't, they will make fools of us and know that we'll never kill 'em. Then we'll have to." He made a bang-bang motion with his fingers at the dummy's head. "This will be their wake-up call, the fake bastards. We'll let them both shit their pants, get hungry and thirsty—then we will kill Mr. Dummy here. They will break pretty easily, unless they see any humanity in us. King will be the tough guy. Pierce wants to see his little boy and his new wife with the big, fake tits. King has nothing to go home for, other than his pot of gold and the misery he can create for anyone he comes in contact with. It keeps him going. Liam, I want him to feel one big hand round his scrawny little neck at least three or four times today." Jackson had thought this through to every detail. Hannah was wide-eyed and scared—she was realizing increasingly that she did not know everything about her husband.

All four went into the cabin, ate and drank coffee. The two men in the back room could smell the food and drink. They were hungry, but more pressing to them was whether they would live through the day.

Hannah carved out a space in the cabin for three people to sit and set up her computers and two large screens. Jackson climbed onto the roof and took an angle for the mini satellite dish that they had brought. He had a small Honda generator to run the battery packs and power the operation. They worked like elves, climbing around the cabin, running wires, and changing seating arrangements. Hannah was ready for a test run in less than half an hour. She had powered up her primary computer and had a backup running.

Liam set the dummy up in a chair on the deck of the woodshed forty feet from the main cabin. Anyone looking out the window would see a man looking out over the lake, a man with a hat on, bound to a chair and chained to the cabin. Liam and Mac would drag the dummy to the lake, one holding each arm. They would load him into a rowboat and motor him off the shoreline, shoot him in the head, and dump him overboard. They would spray a plastic bottle of beet juice all over his hands and face to show King and Pierce the grisly results of a point-blank execution.

Mac had asked Liam to get a crazed look of satisfaction when he reentered the cabin, as though he had cut up his victims with a buck knife. Liam had been practicing the look in his bathroom mirror for two months.

Jackson had the schedule in his shirt pocket. It was time to take King and Pierce for a walk in the woods, along the narrow path that took fishermen around the lake to a couple of streams, where trout could be caught swimming in and out. Mac cut the ties loose on their legs, and Jackson brought them to their feet. King did not like the manly grip. Pierce, who had been training for his karate advancement, was looking for possible weaknesses. He felt the power in Jackson's hands as he was grabbed up and shaken like a rag doll. Pierce weighed 160 pounds and had very little body fat. Jackson was now 185 pounds of lean muscle and quickness.

"We are going for a walk, boys. I will remove your hoods in a moment, and you can enjoy what's left of this beautiful day we have brought you." Jackson and Mac walked them out the front door. It was 10:30 in the morning when Jackson got the two round-point shovels hanging in the woodshed. He tied the two men together, their hands still bound behind their backs from the day before. He was carrying a PPK pistol and Buckshot's Remington automatic shotgun with a short barrel. Their feet untied and hoods removed, they felt new blood circulating through their bodies and the warm sun out of the southeast on their faces. They recognized each other but tried not to show it. And saw the shovels. "Yeh, you know who you are, but it doesn't matter any more does it!" Jackson marched them up the path. Were they going to be executed in cold blood by some lunatics? Just for kicks? Revenge?

"You're the leader, Mr. King. There is a little clearing about a hundred yards up this trail. Keep walking and don't look back or talk. Would you care for some water?"

King nodded yes, even though the sarcasm made his blood run cold. He turned a little bit sideways to look at his kidnapper and spotted the man in the chair tied to the woodshed. Jackson slapped his head quickly with an open hand and said, "Don't look back—keep your eyes on the trail!" The slap stung. It was forceful and blunt, the man had strong forearms and quick wrists. King weighed these against his own training.

They walked for a while, until Jackson stopped them at a clearing in the woods and paced like a football referee. With some sticks he had gathered, he marked two plots on the ground, three feet by six and handed them the shovels. "Dig, assholes! Stay within the sticks and go four feet deep. Your belt will be the mark where you will stop. For all of those movies where you saw the digger swing the shovel and hit the man and get away—" Jackson lowered the barrel of the shotgun and fired, cutting a small, black-spruce tree in half. King looked on in horror and Pierce went to his knees. "This shotgun has killed over sixty men, and they were all more honorable men than the both of you combined. It has a hair trigger, and the safety is off. There will be no escaping or overtaking me today. If you try to attack or escape, I will end up digging your holes for you, and you will spend the rest of eternity here. This shotgun will completely blow your head off."

Buckshot had killed those men in wartime. He had insisted that Jackson take it, as it was good luck and had brought them both home alive from Afghanistan. Buckshot had sacrificed his leg, but they had the gun—sometimes that said it all.

Hannah, Mac and Liam knew there would be a gunshot; it was part of the plan—to the minute, just as Jackson had done a hundred times before, but in theater of war.

Hannah tested her email. Svetlana had assigned a special projects banker to handle the funds transfer that would occur later that day. Hannah would Skype him at 12:30. The technology was being tested and it was working.

The captive billionaires had dug for thirty minutes, and King felt he might be getting blisters for the first time in his life. His grave was poorly dug; roots and rocks had prevented him from squaring the corners. He thought it weird and creepy that the lack of professionalism bothered him. Jackson picked up on the strange dismay. "You will be placed in the ugliest of graves in the northern hemisphere, Mr. King. You should both have a little hard labor, digging trenches before your pathetic little lives end."

King mentally rolled his eyes. *This guy has it bad*, he thought. *Humor him and maybe survive.*

Standing quietly for a moment round the empty graves, all three men began to look a sorry scene. Jackson snapped out of the mood and showed fear for the first time that day, fear of being on the defensive, fear of indiscipline, fear losing an aging grip. "Let me tell you both where you are," he countered, though no one was asking anymore. "First off, you are no longer in the United States of America. You are both north of a band of land more than halfway between the equator and the North Pole. There are no hedge fund managers here. You are under the laws of Native tribes; in many of their eyes your execution would be just—not a crime. There are no *Forbes* editors or *Money* magazines to hail your wealth and greed."

Or wipe my ass, thought Pierce, anger rising.

But Jackson felt the old power coming back and warmed to his theme. "There's me and a team of sharpened people who intend to rob you. Whether we rob you and you live out your greedy little lives is a decision you'll have to make in the next several hours. Whether we rob you and you are shot in these pathetic little graves—well, that will be your choice, too. We have done complete and detailed analysis of both of you and your funds and investments. We will never be tried for anyone's murder here, and you know that you are outside the Manhattan district attorney's territory." He laughed out loud, emptily. "You are deliberate, intelligent men. Think carefully about all that I have just said to you."

King and Pierce recognized their man right away and almost laughed too; the motive was clear; they could relate. Pierce tried not to like him. They would play along and lose some money; it would be a dip in the market, not a grave. They would of course respect Jackson's military skill. But it was all for show.

The poor fuck, Pierce thought, trained to try and empathize with your enemy. *Obviously got a screw loose in some foreign war.* Pierce hated billionaires, too.

King stood in the kidney-shaped hole in the middle of the woods overlooking the beautiful wilderness lake. He was beginning to think it was a good setting for a movie, while Jackson replaced the hand ties.

The black fly were getting intense, forming indiscriminate clouds around each man. King choked on one, coughing, and Jackson gave him a small sip of water, resisting all the while the reality of a more threatening undercurrent of camaraderie, honor among thieves, something twisted from "comrades-in-arms."

He had a can of deep-woods bug spray in his cargo pocket. He would not spray either of the men, he had decided. The flies feasted. Just one bite would raise a red pimple of itching skin for endless days. "I have an allergy from childhood," Pierce spoke up. He would soon choke and not be able to breathe.

Jackson looked at him and pushed him to his knees: "Shut up!" He leaned his shotgun against the tree and pulled out the can of bug spray. As he sprayed around Pierce's face and neck, he continued, "I know you are thinking of some karate move, my friend." He leaned down and removed the PPK from his armpit holster. He placed it so hard against Pierce's forehead that it left a clear round mark of the barrel on the pale-white skin. Pierce shook his head as if to aggressively disagree with Jackson's last remark. "Dig it?—my weasel-eared friend. Now shut up! We have a schedule to keep, and we are behind."

Pierce distractedly wondered if his ears looked like weasel ears. He'd had surgery on them as a boy because his mother thought they stuck out too far. He could feel them swell from the black-fly bites, and his nose and throat started to itch.

Mac had begun the process of transferring the fuel from the large storage tank in the back of the rented Toyota SUV to the tanks of the 185 moored at the dock. He grabbed two one-hundred-foot sections of garden hose under the cabin and screwed them together. He tied the hose to the wing strut of the airplane and looked through the bags to find the twelve-volt transfer pump to run off the battery of the Toyota.

He found a loose pack of Camel straights that his mechanic had placed in there at the last annual inspection. He smiled and looked for the Bic lighter that was always in the bag and tucked the cigarettes in his shirt pocket. He would burn one of these when this task was done. Well away from the flammable one-hundred-octane aviation fuel, he would suck it down like he was Humphrey Bogart. Kelley would kill him if she knew, but he looked forward to lighting up.

The pump and the hose did their jobs, and the aircraft was ready for departure at the turn of the starter key and the buzz of the fuel pump.

Mac checked the oil, and the engine had not consumed a quart in the four hours of intense low-level, high-speed flight that had occurred the day before.

Jackson had found some road-kill on the way from Baie-Comeau. Liam had placed the dead porcupine in a trash bag behind the dummy to draw flies to the future murder victim.

"On your knees, King! I will spray you with the bug dope." Jackson had buckled to the strange, emotional undercurrent, when he could see the welts of bites gathering behind King's ears and on his neck. He put the shotgun up against the tree again. He grabbed a handful of King's hair, pulled his head back, and started to spray the head and neck area like he cared. The bugs looked to him as bad as he had ever seen them.

Pierce idly glanced at the shotgun. Jackson stopped spraying and stood up. He grabbed Buckshot's gun, walked towards Pierce, and with his boot—a thick-soled logger's twelve-inch boot with a hard rubber heel—he kicked Pierce down and into his grave.

Feeling much better, he yelled, "You had to stop and look at my weapon! Do you know why it is my weapon? That's because it is not your weapon! For a second your mind thought you could have my weapon!" He jumped into the hole and raised the shotgun over his head, as if to strike. "You will die here before this day is done! If you think escape, you will die! If you think revenge, you will die! If you let your mind wander to that place now—or anytime in the future—you will die. Sure, I may die, if you decide to take revenge. But because I have friends, who are much more capable than anyone you can hire, you will also die—for sure. Do you understand what I am saying? Do you hear me?" No one answered, as if the question were not for them.

Jackson dragged Pierce from the hole and took them both by the neck and shook them together. All three shook like trees in a squall. Pierce thought he saw the wild in his captor's eyes and face. Jackson released them and finished spraying King, offered him a drink from his canteen.

King took it and muttered, "Thank you," softly under his breath.

Jackson hit him solidly in the ribs but not hard enough to distinguish it from a slap on the back, so he yelled in his ear, "Do not speak!"

The trio marched back to the cabin like hunters, until the billionaire hoods went back on, and they were walked into the main room.

29

They started with William Pierce just after 2:00. The flies were buzzing around the mannequin. It looked like a black cloud around a living man.

Pierce was shown the computer monitors with the accounts and told to memorize them and remember any others accounts, if he could. The goal was for him to catch sight of the "man in the cloud" and identify as a co-captive. Liam had monofilament line attached to the dummy's head and legs to provide some movement. It was theater; Mac would be puppet master.

Pierce claimed that those were all the accounts he had. Hannah had left two off deliberately to catch him in the deceptive act. These were energy stocks of over $700 million. The scene of threats was about to begin, when Mac heard the distant sound of an aircraft engine. He motioned for Jackson and then Liam to meet him outside. It was one problem they had not thought of. The noise got louder. The airplane flew around the lake and then the cabin.

Mac was emphatic: "They must not see me. We must create a diversion and get them to leave immediately. Liam will be the only face they see. Liam, pull your hat down tight and put on your sunglasses."

Liam nodded.

Jackson looked at Mac: "I will be in the woods with the AR on them at every minute. If they step off the dock, I know that we must consider, well, you know what I mean—"

Mac hesitated and nodded. Liam followed suit.

The unwanted airplane turned into the light breeze on the lake and began its final approach to land on the water. Mac recognized the PA 12 Super Cruiser. It belonged to a pilot who was also from Maine, who had a cabin on another lake nearby in Québec. The airplane pulled up to the dock on the opposite side of the 185. The pilot did not recognize the airplane. He saw the registration but no familiar markings. He had a retired game warden in the back seat of the two-seater. They were fishermen looking for big trout. They shut down the engine and floated to the dock. The pilot jumped out and grabbed a line. Liam approached the dock, not getting too close, hoping to be rude enough that they would depart without a visit.

"Is Mac around?" The pilot reached to secure the aircraft through a metal ring.

"No, he is not here and is not planning to come. It is a private rental for the week, *very* private!"

The pilot thought it wasn't Mac's usual happy welcome to newcomers to the lake. The man in the back seat started to undo his shoulder harness, and Liam said in a thick New York accent, "Boys, I was just about to go fishing and really would like to get at it."

At that moment the door to the cabin opened, and Hannah stepped out. She was wearing only thong underwear and a low-cut Victoria's Secret push-up bra. She looked spectacular on the deck in black lace. Her skin was tan from the recent visit to the Caymans and taking her children to the Readfield beach.

She yelled to Liam, "Everything okay, baby? I thought you told me we would be totally alone here in the woods!" She swung a little on the support post of the deck, like in a pole dance.

Jackson was going back and forth with his scope on the AR-15 from one man's head to the other. He looked to his left and saw his wife on the deck of the cabin in the crosshairs. "She is a fucking genius," he said to himself.

The bugs were finding a new victim in the black thong. She reached to swat a few away and hoped the trespassers would leave soon. King could hear something, but it was unintelligible. They had replaced the muffs and had them both chained in the holding room. Pierce was having a hard time breathing; the poison from the black flies was rushing through his veins.

Jackson flipped the safety to the off position on his fully automatic weapon. He was trained to give no quarter to his targets—they were either friend or foe. The two chained to the floor in the holding room were a challenge; they had broken his stride. The crosshairs went back and forth between the two intruders.

The pilot pointed to the woman on the cabin deck. The passenger looked out as if peeking from under a rock. In all his years patrolling the backwoods of Maine as a game warden, he had seen a lot of sights, but never anything quite like that. From his vantage point, Hannah looked like Aphrodite emerging from the Canadian waters. She had an L.L.Bean Stetson hat pulled down over her face with large round sunglasses on. Her efforts to hide her face also created a look of desire and adventure. *If Calvin Klein could capture this image in the pages of* Vogue, Jackson thought, *they would double their sales overnight.*

The pilot put one foot on the dock and one on the pontoon of the aircraft. He untied the rope and pushed off. "Sorry to bother you, man. You have a great week fishing here—didn't mean to interrupt anything. Looks like you will have some fun!"

Liam gave them a very unenthusiastic wave and never took his eye off the plane as it taxied into position and took off out of the lake.

Jackson double-checked the action of the AR, as he had with every gun he had ever handled. There was still the brass color of a bullet ahead of the fully loaded clip in the chamber. Mac had watched it all from the small window in the woodshed, where the mannequin was in temporary hiding. The dead porcupine was starting to smell badly. *What a team!* he thought. He had never seen Hannah look like that. He could do anything with these people—they were good!

The plane made a distant hum from the Piper's small Lycoming engine. It disappeared as a dot on the horizon, flying westerly from the hostage-occupied cabin on the beautiful little trout lake.

Jackson came out of the woods near the lake and waved at all to gather by the dock and regroup. Hannah put her camo outfit back on to match the others. They huddled around the canoes. Mac had lit a Camel, and Liam had a childlike smile, as if he had spotted the presents under the tree on Christmas morning.

"How are the bug bites, girl?" Jackson kissed his wife on the cheek and smiled with a double fisted thumbs-up to her. "Nice to know someone in this crowd can think on their feet," he joked and put his arms around both men standing next to him, shaking them to and fro. "Well, we didn't think of that, did we Mac?"

Mac did not respond. He stared down at his boots and kicked some gravel into the lake. "My feeling right now is that we should speed this entire operation up by eighteen hours." He looked at his military-style chronograph and then to the others around him.

Hannah said, "My guys in the islands are good to go now. I believe we can do all of the transfers in less than two hours, with cooperation. You know that Pierce did not purposely reveal two accounts, so there may be more."

She looked at Jackson, who responded, "I will deal with him— write down the account names and the amounts." Someone was going to get a beating.

Mac said he would like to check the weather one more time. "If the Monday morning forecast is bad, we should leave at 4:00 tomorrow afternoon for a twilight arrival on Echo Sunday evening. We will not have any wiggle room. The plane is fueled and ready. Has anyone been in touch with Buckshot? He was to pay a visit this morning to Gloria, Alexis and the pilot."

Hannah had emailed him. "He will be sending photos of both families this afternoon and let us know if they've been keeping their schedules."

"OK," Jackson said, "so that's it. We had a time-cushion in the plan, but we don't need it. We'll move things up by eighteen hours. All agreed?" Everyone nodded. "Bring them both out front in the room, and we will murder the dummy after they have both gotten a good view of him in the chair. Mac, you move the monofilament while they have the hoods off. Liam, you have got to make this look as real as possible. I am thinking you should use the shotgun to make the noise impact. The PPKs are too quiet. If I had my .44 magnum, it would have a much better effect on our friends."

Liam nodded. They were all eager to please Jackson and make it all work perfectly.

They heard choking and coughing from the holding room, where Pierce had been returned. Hannah opened the wooden door to find Pierce in convulsions on the floor. Mac took the hood off and was shocked to see Pierce's face swollen beyond recognition. He was choking as if someone had hands around his throat.

Jackson took charge. "Get the epi pen, Liam. He is having an allergic reaction to the black-fly bites. Worse than we thought. There is a bottle of Benadryl there as well. Let's feed him directly out of the bottle now."

Liam was into the first-aid kit in a matter of seconds and had the pen, the Benadryl, and a bottle of water in front of Pierce. Jackson picked him up and laid him on the long dining table, pushing Hannah's equipment aside quickly and gently into the corner. Pierce had so far avoided his beating. "Clear his airways, and if he doesn't react to the pen or the Benadryl, we will cut him for a tracheotomy." Pierce's feet were jerking wildly as he lay on the table, and he was foaming at the mouth. His face was pie-shaped, and he could not fully open his eyes.

Jackson poured some water into him and turned him on his side and cut the ties that bound his hands and arms.

Mac called out directions from his first-aid manual: "Hold his arms over his head, create an airway clear to his lungs." The releasing of his hands increased his ability to get air.

Jackson was making eye contact with Pierce, who was blinking but unable to speak because his tongue had swollen up. Hannah, who had used an epi pen on her brother as a child for a bee allergy, pulled the top and jabbed him quickly in the groin area. They grabbed a pillow off the bunk and put it carefully under his head. Five minutes had passed but seemed like hours to the group.

Pierce was coming back slowly and was able to drink water. The man sat up and breathed while looking around. He spotted the mannequin on the porch with a cloud of black flies around him so thick it looked as though someone were shooting at him with a can of spray paint. Pierce pointed in horror, hand shaking. Jackson seized him and looked him in the eye. "You can't save that guy, Mr. Pierce. Save yourself! That man would rather die than give us a penny of his billions. That isn't you though—is it, Mr. Pierce? I'm afraid he won't be able to spend it where he is going this afternoon—"

Pierce's eyes opened wide. They had saved his life and now they might kill him? He took a deep breath and considered the contradiction. They hadn't killed him in the woods. That was to scare him. Now they were doing it again. He looked around and saw a bunch of amateurs from central Maine, trying to go pro. Should he ask to speak to the guy about to be murdered? His head reeled, but he was recovering. *Don't push them*, was his next thought. They are newbies—with this whack-job Jackson here, who probably has no experience either—off the battlefield. After a few more quick, shrewd calculations, he decided to go for a small risk to confirm his suspicions, the sort of thinking that had made him lots of money cheating a bunch of creeps like these. "Look, guys, let me have just a last word with the guy out there; I think

I can convince him—it's been my stock-in-trade. I can sell anything to anyone. Give me a minute with him, and you will have another billion dollars to take home. What d'ya say?" He took a grateful breath.

King could hear this discussion. He was coming down from a very real level of fear and had to go to the bathroom. He needed to have a bowel movement; it was cramping him badly.

There was silence in the room, a silence the criminals knew had to be broken fast.

Pierce saw the dummy's head twitch and his leg move. *Poor bastard, if he's for real,* he thought. He wondered what the dummy might be worth; was he on the Forbes list? He stopped himself from laughing. He reminded himself to be especially careful. He had a family. He would give these wannabes all the money they wanted. He hoped his wife and his little boy were all right. He really loved them. He had found love and wanted to keep it—way more than the money.

In silence Pierce was removed from the table, and his hands were now bound in the front of his body for the first time in twenty-four hours. He sat in a stuffed chair in the corner. Mac connected a small rope from his ankle straps to his wrists so that he could not raise his arms up beyond his chest. Hannah gave him some water that he could give to himself in a bottle and fed him two granola bars.

King still needed to go to the bathroom and was almost ready to release his bowels in his pants. Liam walked in and smelled the gas coming from the man on the floor. He lifted him to his feet and unclipped his chains. Mac showed up and unhooked the leg ties and walked him past Pierce, out the door. The trip to the outhouse went without incident, and Liam assisted him with the baby wipes and paper towels. King wondered—if he could just speak to one of these crooks, he might convince one to abandon the others for a bribe. Or maybe he could encourage them to listen to Pierce. "Every man has a price" was King's religion. There was no way he would give them all of his money; he would surpass his worst rivals in the next three years— maybe someday the British royal family or even Vlad Putin, he had dreamed. He just had to survive this nightmare. Besides, the nightmare was sordid, pathetic, disgusting. They just wanted money—like him, no different. He would call their bluff—but wait to see what happened to Pierce first. These assholes would all wipe his ass in the end!

When King reentered the cabin, Jackson had a seat for him next to Hannah and Pierce. They would all be looking quietly at the computer screen. Mac and Liam were out the door to murder the dummy. They could all see out to the woodshed, out to the small boat and the lake. It reminded Pierce of a play they had put on at camp. He relaxed and decided to enjoy. The ticket would be pricey, but where else could he get an adventure weekend like this?

King's paranoid disposition had his eyes darting around the room and at the computer screen. He glanced meaningfully at Pierce and was not reassured by the other's careless demeanor, which was being taken by the gang as exhaustion.

Mac and Liam cut the ties from the dummy and started to drag him towards the water. They acted as though there was great weight to the man they were pulling. Mac had placed a seat with small bungee straps in the boat to have the dummy appear to be sitting upright with his hands bound. His hat was safety pinned to a wig Liam had borrowed from a cancer victim at the new MaineGeneral hospital. Pierce thought it looked as though it could have been worn by Tom Jones, the Welsh singer with tight pants from the seventies.

Hannah, the first to speak since Pierce's request, directed him coldly to the screen and his accounts. But she wanted him to see past the computer and out the window, where Liam and Mac were about to execute the fake billionaire. That would be his answer.

Jackson cuffed Pierce softly, unusually softly for a change. "Pay attention! Watch this screen and cooperate—not out the window!"

Yeah, right! Pierce thought. *Like we're not going to watch the billionaire-blasting fantasy show we're payin' to see.* He took a chance and winked at King. But everyone was looking out the window. They could not help themselves, even Hannah and Jackson wanted to watch the dummy go for a boat ride out into the lake. It was their plan in action, their fantasy enactment, at last.

Mac would drive the boat while Liam kept the shotgun under the mannequin's chin. The little outboard motor started with the first pull, as Mac poled them away from the shallows with a paddle. Hannah made an effort to look down and pretend to point out the line items she had prepared on the spreadsheet. The two captives could not take their eyes off the scene going on out the window. A hundred feet from the shore the players in the small boat turned to pass in front of the camp.

Mac, who knew Liam was nervous about his performance with this fake murder, leaned forward to him and said, "Don't fuck this up, buddy. Make sure that shotgun goes off pointing away from your foot, the side of the boat, and more importantly, the boat's driver!"

It was all Liam could do to keep himself from laughing. He turned his head away from the cabin and almost belly laughed right out loud. "You asshole, McCabe. How the hell did you get me into this mess?"

"Liam! Voices travel on water—"

They tried to collect themselves. Liam checked the hat and the wig. A gesture that from afar looked like a pat on the head. The sound of voices had reached the audience with a sense of backstage levity. But then Liam began to slap the dummy's face from side to side and grabbed it by the jacket lapels. He put his nose next to the dummy's nose. Almost cracking up laughing again, he yelled, "You won't give us your money! So this is what you get!" The powerful voice reached the audience clearly through the open window.

Pierce tried not to give himself away with a grin. King's eyes narrowed. Liam reached across the seat of the boat and grabbed the shotgun. He tried to make himself believe he was playing Shakespeare and put the barrel of the gun on the face of his fellow actor, the dummy, and was about to squeeze the trigger. He saw Mac about to jump overboard and realigned Buckshot's gun for the heavens. Mac sat back down as the shot rang out.

Unbeknownst to them, Jackson had injected the head of the dummy with sixteen ounces of strawberry syrup, and it exploded everywhere, rained down on them. The billionaire was partially headless now, faceless. Mac yelled at Liam, "Put 'im over, quick! That goddamn Jackson just got us good!"

Pierce was killing himself inside. They had all heard every word, including the name of one of their captors.

Hannah put her face in her hands and said, "Oh no—" She turned and looked at her husband and yelled, "Did you order this? Did you know this was going to happen?"

Is this about the syrup? Jackson wondered briefly, with a smile that looked to King incredibly evil. Hannah continued ad libbing, but the ambiguity was about to overcome her with contagious laughter. She composed herself and redirected a pokerfaced Pierce to the screen.

Jackson took both captives by the back of the neck forcefully. "That dumbass billionaire's last name began with an S—for Shithead—we will deal with the letter P now, Mr. Pierce. And then the letter K, Mr. King. We all agreed it would happen in reverse alphabetical order, nothing personal. Shithead didn't want to cooperate with us. His body is weighted down. It will be eaten by toothy northern pike before the ice forms on this lake. To be completely eaten off the bottom, by bottom feeders like the two of you!"

Liam and Mac came in the door after spraying the beet juice on Liam's face and clothes, added to the strawberry syrup. Mac gave Jackson a dirty look and wiped a sticky hand on his brother-in-law's shirt. Liam stared down at King and Pierce with his perfected "Charles Manson." It was at that moment that King decided he wouldn't give them a penny.

Pierce was squirming with restrained hilarity. He couldn't hold it anymore. He exploded into paroxysms that the players took for a resurgence of his reaction to the black flies, combined with stress and exhaustion. Was Pierce having a breakdown? What was happening?

Liam put the hood back on King and pulled him, chair and all, into the holding room, dumped him out of the chair and smacked him with a fist to the ribs and face. You could hear bone connecting with bone at the kitchen table. "Keep your mouth shut, asshole! Not one word. You will have your chance, either at the table or in the boat!" Liam had stepped into Jackson's role, and the latter looked at Mac and Hannah and nodded approvingly.

Pierce came round from his fit and stared blankly into the monitor. Hannah was in motion. She did retinal scans with his eyes and got entry into his accounts. Four funds were transferred. Her new best banking buddy confirmed deposit activations and balances as she proceeded. The islands were gaining hundreds of millions in new deposits from the little fishing cabin in Northern Québec, while Pierce watched.

Jackson interrupted, "If any of this banking activity triggers some emergency rescue attempt, Mr. Pierce, let me assure you that we will shoot you first. We will hold your friend in the back room hostage. We only need one hostage. Any friends coming for you?"

"No, I had complete control over my money. Anything you want to leave me, that's fine. This has been the experience of a lifetime." *Some reverse psychology might help*, he opined.

Hannah figured he had lost more than his money and felt a little sorry when she got the email from Svetlana with a one-word message: "Impressive." Six billion, seven hundred million dollars in assets, gone in minutes.

Jackson pulled him down to the end of the table. The men

assembled there. They formed a half circle of chairs around him. Jackson reloaded the shotgun and said, "We have all your money, Mr. Pierce, every penny. You have some real estate and a jet left. What is it worth to you to save your life and the lives of your wife and child?"

"I don't understand," Pierce responded.

Jackson pulled his chair a little closer. His wife looked on with great admiration.

"We are going to pay you now, Mr. Pierce. We are going to pay you with our money that we have just robbed from you." Jackson touched him on the nose with the barrel of the shotgun. "I am going to pay you half a billion dollars to not try and track us down. You will still be in that one-percent crowd you run with. If you want the lifestyle that you had, you will have to do what you have already done—screw people over and build another billion-dollar fortune. My friend here with the computers has a printed contract that you will sign. We will mail it to you every six months reminding you of our agreement. If you try to find us or hunt us down, we will still kill you. We are paying you for our protection and yours. Now do you understand?"

"I understand, but why are you giving me my money back?"

"I just told you why. Are you dense! Would you like to negotiate or counter our offer? We will give you half a billion dollars back. We own it now and will give it back to you. Now tell the woman which account you would like it restored to."

Hannah piped up, "Would you like it in the energy account that you did not tell us about, Mr. Pierce?"

"There is no honesty in you, not one ounce of it!" Jackson had him again by the neck and dragged him back down to the computer screens. There were photos of his wife and son at the beach in Readfield, at the bookstore in Augusta, at the ice cream shop in Manchester, and in front of the rented cabin.

Hannah scrolled down and there were pictures of him at his office and at restaurants in New York City. Each photo of his child and wife, as well as the shots of him in New York, had the image of the crosshairs of a rifle scope placed directly on each one's head. "We are professionals. There are none like us in the world, I can assure you of that. None with our skills combined as a unit." Jackson whipped around and yelled toward the holding room, "Can you hear me, King? Grunt if you can hear me. Don't speak!"

King grunted like someone had let air out of him.

"We are all willing to die for each other and this thing we have planned," Jackson's tirade continued. "Our former captive was willing to die rather than give us a penny of his hard-stolen money. Don't be that man; life is too precious. Reinvent yourself! And there is time for you to do some good in your life—" Jackson got a hold of himself mentally, leaned close to Pierce and whispered, "Now, what account do you want the money in?"

"Any one will do."

30

Mac took Pierce aside and fed him jerky and trail mix; he drank a quart of water. Mac was applying After Bite to his black-fly bites—it stung sharply but soon eased the pain of the hundreds of red welts on his skin. Pierce thought to himself, *This man has compassion. Time to make my move.* "Hey, Mac!" he said intuitively and got lucky.

Mac stood up with alarm, itch-eraser stick in hand.

"Don't sweat it, man. Here's the thing—"

Jackson heard him and was instantly on the spot. Pierce had everyone's attention, as Liam and Hannah looked up with surprise.

"Let him talk," said Mac, realizing the name could be a coincidence, but they had all been caught off guard.

"Here's the thing—King's goin' t' take it to the wall. I know the guy. He can't help it. I'd bet my life that he has decided not to give an inch, *nada*, nothing. He had you guys figured, like I do. Thing is, him and me, we are opposites. I'm in love. He's a fuckin' psychopath."

Silence.

"But I've dealt with him, so here's what we do."

"We—" said Liam sarcastically.

"It's up to you, of course." And Pierce looked round the room. He lowered his voice, so King couldn't hear, and the captors had to gather round to hear him. He gave them a plan, and they returned him to the holding room.

CB   BD

It was now evening, shadows lengthening, and it was the letter K's turn to sit at the computer screen. Roscoe Edward King was hauled out of the holding room. Jackson was looking forward to this. They all were eager to get on with the plan. Hannah had the palm screen technology set up. King recognized it immediately. She emailed her banker that more activity would begin and last for several hours, including the complexities of changing accounts.

"Unfortunately, Mr. King, your wealth is much more difficult to deal with but just as important to us." Jackson was getting slowly closer to King's face. "The problem we have is that we just lost a fortune at the bottom of that lake." He pointed out the window and moved even closer.

"Your problem is different. You have already created a permanent trust for Naomi, and you have a prenuptial that gives your wife everything. If we had our man contact her now, cuddled up with Dowd on Echo Lake, do you think she would pay us for your permanent disappearance?"

King stared at the floor. He was replaying the gory end of the man in the boat in his mind: "Not one red cent!"

Jackson froze, nose to nose.

"Not from me, not to no one! Take it or leave it—" he added under his breath.

Hannah brought up on screen the photo taken that morning of Gloria and Terry. They were smiling, sitting at the Starbucks café inside the Barnes and Noble in Augusta. "Look at their faces, King. They are so happy you're not with them. They don't care whether you live or die." The two men looked at the image together.

Hannah scrolled to the next set of photos. These were of Gloria and Terry leaving the cabin on Echo Lake, smiling. "Our bugging device has them having sex for three hours straight last night. Did you know that Gloria and Terry were into S&M? They both hate you, and Gloria gets everything when we take you out in the boat. We can have them killed in the next few seconds, just need to send a quick email. Just like that. Isn't technology wonderful, Mr. King? Do you want us to kill them?"

He shook his head no.

"Well, here is the quandary before us." Jackson was tired. He wanted to quit now and go home. He had been exhausted like this before in places further from home than Québec. "We have a goal, and because we had to murder Mr. Uncooperative out there, we have to make a new deal with you. How much do you have in total wealth at this time? Please show him what we know." He nodded to Hannah.

Jackson cut the ties behind King's back and rebound him in the front, tying his legs and arms together. He put an open bottle of water in his hands.

King smelled something sweet and syrupy in the room. *Strawberries! like Pierce said.* They had been left together in the holding room just long enough. King quivered with delight and spoke with determination. "The market moved at the end of last week to my benefit. I think all told it is around $7.8 billion, as of Friday morning." That was a full billion more than Hannah had on record, and now she understood there must be more money hidden in Switzerland, on the islands.

But King repeated: "Not one red cent!"

Jackson gave the high sign, and Liam disappeared into the holding room.

"You can live, Mr. King, but you have to change," said Jackson. "You, yourself, one man, have hammered hundreds of thousands of men and woman and families across the United States. Abused them. Crushed them. Ruined them. If I called those men and women now and asked them to spare your life, what would they all say to me and my partners? You know what they would say—" He jabbed King in the chest with pointed knuckles. "What would your wife say if I told her she had the option of you returning or disappearing, never to be seen again? You know that hole you dug this morning is still open. Would Gloria let you live? Terry? Naomi?

"This is your moment, my greedy, sex fiend of a friend. We are going to rob every penny of your worth. Did you hear the deal we offered your friend in the other room? We will open all of your accounts now and scan your eyes and take your palm prints and drain every cent you own. Are there any triggers for you moving any amount of your money that will alert a security team? You need to tell us now. Mr. Roommate in there just bought himself a happy life with his new wife with the big tits and a son, that, believe it or not, actually loves him. You, on the other hand, have an open hole of a grave through the woods, and a tall friend with a New York accent that would love to take you for a boat ride. I will ask you again, are there any triggers that might send people looking for you?"

This one's got to be Jackson, King thought, *and she's his wife. Syrup sex must be their thing.* But he remained silent, unsure how crazy Jackson might be. *These moralistic whack-jobs are known for their pathetic lectures while they get out their implements.* And he was waiting to discover what would happen to Pierce, who had advised him to follow his example and hang tough. He was still in the back room.

"Triggers?" King asked, stalling.

Liam returned with Pierce and pulled off the hood to reveal an expression of failing confidence. "Did someone say triggers?" Liam asked. "Allow me to introduce Mr. Triggers! The man who said he had none. But hey, Mr. Triggers had triggers. So now we go to the lake. Maybe we will find some there!" Liam looked hard at King with the attempted "Manson Look." The fact that the Look failed again was this time deeply unsettling to behold.

Pierce was frog-marched—and King was dragged—down to the water's edge. Jackson made Pierce kneel and took him by the hair and neck. He forced his face deep into the mud. Pierce's hands were still tied in front, but his legs were free to flail and kick up mud, sand and rocks. They repeated the performance twice more. Jackson paused to explain, but shouted in spite of himself, as though hurt, enraged: "Mr. Triggers, here, has ruined the show!" Jackson looked almost in tears and laughed horribly. "Triggers saw through us and our entertainment! He found us out! We all got egg on our faces! We got the rotten tomatoes! Sappy syrup shit-faced!" He held up Pierce's face, and it was a gruesome expression.

"Now let's wash our faces, folks!" Pierce was dragged to the water's edge, where he was dunked repeatedly and convincingly, gasping for air at intervals with cries from Jackson, Mac and Hannah: "Not dead yet! Nope, not yet, not dead yet—" while Liam grinned with the failing, silent Look.

Pierce had said it would be an act of faith if they let him live, that he could hold his breath for almost three minutes. He liked to practice a little free-diving as a hobby in the Caribbean. He and Jackson played it up expertly, and the last dunk was especially convincing—the minutes were long, as far as King or anyone was concerned. In the expectant quiet of the drowning, Roscoe King changed his mind. This was not going to happen to him. And anyway they might give him back a fortune once they had stolen it, as unsettling as that was to his way of thinking. *Definitely out of their minds. Still,* he thought, *let's wait and see if Pierce lives, if he's really dead—yet.*

Jackson had let go of the body and let it loose in the water for another long moment. Then Liam leaned in to help dredge Pierce up and disguise a giant, desperate intake of air, flopping and hauling him in the mud and water. Hannah got up from an Adirondack chair, where she had displayed open pleasure at the scene. "Is he really dead?" she asked with excitement. King's blood ran cold.

The murderers all huddled round like crazed children, while Liam kept practicing the Look, glancing back at King who cowered on the edge of the mud. "Is he dead? Is he dead?" they repeated in turn. "Did he really drown 'im, Mac?" Hannah asked earnestly.

"Can't always be sure." Jackson intoned. "We better string 'im up just to be sure."

"Maybe cut him up would be better," Liam recommended. "For the fish," he explained defensively.

"And get more syrup on us all!" Hannah, laughed, and they joined in gleefully, hissing and slurping with suppressed hilarity.

King felt something rise in this throat.

Jackson put a stop to the fun with raised hand and commanded: "Get a rope! We'll use the same ol' hangin' tree we use for game!"

They each took a limb of Pierce's body and dropped him by the tree. There was a rope a little too conveniently nearby. But it was thrown over the game-hanging limb in cowboy-movie fashion. A knot was tied with flair, and Pierce was strung up convincingly. Jackson all the while boasted of a buck he had taken the year before. Then they dragged King back into the cabin and set him up again in front of the computer. Pierce's body was hanging in the shadows outside the window beyond the monitor, a continuous reminder.

"Now we must impose a nice, rip-off wealth tax on your assets, Mr. King," said Hannah, laughing a bit too easily, it seemed; she was finally really enjoying the adventure. She was so relaxed, and King needed no further convincing.

"Two of my accounts are on twenty-four-hour alert with the managers," he said. I need to have a face-to-face electronic communication with them for any funds to be moved, even one dollar. It can be done by Skype or face-to-face text. They will, however, be suspicious of anything but Skype."

"There are several funds doing this these days, for board of director adjustments for large fund transfers," she assured Jackson who was looking dubious.

"So let's clean him up, give him a solid-white backdrop, shave him, and put some makeup on his face!" Jackson barked.

"The show must go on!" chimed in Liam threateningly.

They were all on it. Hannah started transferring funds as directed with King's cooperation. Liam shaved the stubble off the billionaire's face with a cutthroat razor he had brought, "just in case"—with a touch of pancake makeup added so softly that King was creeped out entirely. Was he being had, after all? But Pierce's body hung limp, as though it had been there for days. And King noted that they had cut free the hands and feet. That thought was the clincher. *They would only let a dead man go free.* It had been a condition, a deal breaker in the plan, the act of faith, and they were to carry Pierce hand and foot splayed out, for King to see.

They combed King's hair, and Jackson gave him instructions, "Most of what they will be doing is verifying you are of sound mind and not under any form of duress, correct?"

King nodded ruefully and looked from one to the other.

"Our favorite boat-tour guide here will be sitting across the table from you with this shotgun loaded and aimed at your head. If you double-blink, move your mouth the wrong way, or attempt to give the people on the other end a sign that you are being held at gunpoint, I nod to the lady, she disconnects the feed, and Charles Manson here blows your brains out. Shooting the dummy was work—this will be easier and more fun. I will have to clean up your brain matter all over the walls or maybe I just put the airplane gas all through this place and set it on fire with your headless body inside. That will save us a lot of cleaning and DNA nonsense, won't it boys? Won't it Hannah!

"No syrup!" she said and winked disconcertingly.

"Now give her your contacts. You have already set us back three hours. We are not happy having to do a rerun, dummy! But third time's a charm."

More weird shit from this Jackson and his ol' lady, thought King.

They brought the feed up, and he was there with a nice, clean t-shirt on, with a fresh shave, hair combed. He hoped that it did not look too phony to his fund manager. He hoped that he did not blink too much.

He smiled when Shamus Fitzmaurice came up at what looked like a Saturday night out on the town in Manhattan. "What's going on, RK? What can I do for you?"

"How far are you from your office, kid? I need some money moved pronto."

"I'm in Midtown; can it wait until tomorrow?"

"You get your scrawny little ass into your office in the next ten minutes and bring my fund up. What part of 24/7 don't you understand with my contract. I will call you back, and you better not have any of your little fuck buddies in the background when we speak again."

"How much are we talking about, Mr. King?"

"All of it. Now, shit-face!" The screen went blank. Hannah started to replay the entire feed with Mac watching over her shoulder.

"Now that's the man we all love so well. Give me ten minutes exactly," Jackson said. He nodded toward his geek goddess. "Then reconnect with our friend. If he's not there, we will take what we have already and end this shit-bag right now."

In short order, Shamus was back. But losing a two-billion-dollar account on his watch could cost him his job and set off bells throughout the financial community. He hoped this really was Roscoe King on the other end of the internet. "I have to move money now. Ever hear the phrase, 'money never sleeps?' You tell your boss that there are seven more billion where that came from, and if he ever wants to see a penny of it, keep this quiet. I will be in my office on Monday if he wants to discuss how you would not move my money as requested."

"Ready to fire, sir. Send the account information. I will complete your request, as asked."

King twitched from the bug bites, and Liam raised the shotgun. Hannah was ready to disconnect. He did his best to recover and smiled at the screen, an uncommon smile.

And just like that, it was done. All of his money, his life's work, had been stolen by this band of Robin Hoods. Now—would they kill him anyway? He looked out the window.

Jackson was getting up-close and personal again. King's chair was dragged over. "I am going to pay you a billion dollars, Mr. King, to not pursue us or your money or anything connected to this little trip. We have all of your money, and we are willing to pay you to agree to our terms. A billion dollars, and you get to work for us for the next five years moving the money that we stole from you. The only thing that you have to gain from doing this is your life." Jackson paused, letting the offer sink in, then lectured on: "You could go back and take your payment that we are giving you and hire several mercenaries.

Maybe they would find us, but we would kill half of them, because we are much better than anyone you can hire. We might die or you might go to prison for hiring a hit man for a crime that happened in another country under Native Indian jurisdiction. A rich guy got robbed at gunpoint, wah wah," Jackson twisted his hands like he was crying tears.

Creepy, King reflected once more on Jackson's little ways.

"Plus, Mr. King, the first sign of that kind of activity and you would be killed immediately. You might be hiding in a bunker when all of the shit goes down, but when that pointed little bug-eaten head of yours came to the light of day, you would be executed immediately. Do you believe what I am saying, Mr. King?"

"Yes."

"Good. Now you sign that contract for the lady, and you will hear from us in thirty days. You will know it is us." Jackson dropped the contract in front of him.

"We are everywhere, all the time, Mr. King. If one of us dies another will step in to take our place within the day. We have honest-to-goodness friends and people that love us in the true sense of the word, unlike your sorry ass—"

It was 8:30 p.m., the sun was beginning to set in the western sky.

"You believe me, don't you? You understand our agreement?"

King signed and looked up at some movement in the window. Pierce had been given the signal and was working up his Irishman's hanging dance. It began with air-bicycling, the feet pedaling slowly at first, sending a shock wave through King's body. But as the cycling gained speed, the arms spread out and flapped like a bird on a unicycle, trying to gain altitude, headed for heaven.

It wasn't long before King was on his feet shouting expletives. He would not give in! He would take it to the wall. But he couldn't, and Jackson knocked him down with the shotgun butt. He and Mac threw him into the holding room with a warning to shut up.

Pierce had tucked his wrists into his armpits and gone for the funky chicken, head free to move in both directions, while the rope turned him like a merry-go-round to an old Irish ballad, sung at full-throated lung power.

When Mac got his breath from hauling King, he called out, "for God's sake someone please put him out of his misery! Liam went out the door and pistol-whipped the dancer. Mac stared in silence at the floor. "My great grandfather danced when the British strung him up. Old family story."

They all got quiet, and Mac, with Liam's help, went to get Pierce down from his Jackson-improvised harness. The two returned to an awkward atmosphere in the room, dragging Pierce, who regained consciousness, hands and feet tied once again. *Double-crossed!* was his first thought, as he looked round the room. Taking the continued silence for a yes, he added, "So who's your banker in the islands, assholes?" He grinned knowingly.

Hannah couldn't resist the name-drop, "Ricardo Ortiz."

Pierce chuckled to himself.

"What's so funny?" asked Liam.

"Well, well, so Ricardo Ortiz finally has an interest in my business. I've been trying to get the ol' boy on board for years, now. I think I owe you folks a debt of gratitude, the more I think on it," and he rubbed the bump on his head.

"How so?" asked Jackson.

"Your accounts are with Ortiz—nobody told you. An account with Ortiz is Ortiz's account—get it? Come to think on it a little more, I definitely think you will be needing all the help from King and me you can get to have any leverage at all on ol' Ricardo Ortiz." A grim smile took over his face.

Someone chuckled. It was Liam. He had suspected the rotten ol' boy connection all along, ever since they were introduced by Wilmot "Willie Boy" Dixon. But what could he do? Everyone was so gung-ho. Anyway, he had lost a lot of weight and never felt better. Maybe he wasn't even a thief! He had just facilitated a transfer and got into a new business with another bunch of mobsters. He could live with that. He felt like a drink to celebrate. But first they'd have to toss Pierce back into the holding room with the other ol' boy—and chain them down.

A confirmation email arrived on cue from Svetlana: "Bravo to you and your team, your money is safe."

31

Jackson stopped smiling and drove and looked straight ahead, on the road back to Maine. "Money ruins people; it ruins people and makes assholes out of the ones that it does not ruin. Hundreds of millions of people bought lottery tickets last night so they could become like the rich and famous of the world. I did not take part in this to become rich; I did it because these men deserved a good beating and a robbery. Where the money is and what becomes of it, I don't care. What Mac wants to do with the money is foolish in my mind, but that's what we agreed to. I always keep my word, Hannah—and so will you!"

She was getting angry. "D'you know how much good we could do with the extra billion dollars that these two men had? We could reopen the mill; we could educate children beyond their wildest expectations; we could build a green-energy company, support start-ups for a diverse economy, instead of a one-company-dependent mill town! We have all of the skills and now we have the money. We could be rich for generations and give to so many charities. I could move the money now at seven o'clock this morning in thirty minutes—today!"

08   80

The sun was up and Mac was up. He'd had a hard time sleeping for the past few months; he was taking melatonin substitutes. The natural supplement had done nothing for him. He started brewing his rugged camp coffee. The aroma woke all in the cabin who had been sleeping;

it was 5:15. Liam came into the kitchen and said, "Morning Mac!"

Mac looked at him with disdain and thought *You dumb Yale jerk*. He wrote down on a piece of paper, "Call me Billy three times by accident before we load them into the airplane!"

Mitchell knew immediately that he had screwed up. But he didn't really care. He covered his mouth in mock shame. Mac ignored it.

Mac was a fishermen first and a pilot and guide second and third. He had caught fish on light fly rods from the age of twelve. It was the unknown, under the surface, that made him giggle and smile as a middle-aged man. Sometimes the fight in a small trout amazed him as they came to the surface, worn out from the diving and darting on a barbless hook. Before he knew it, he was out in a canoe, fishing one more time before departure from this particular Canadian paradise. The fish was weighty, he thought, and played it slowly and with purpose. He held the rod tip high and watched as the movement of the line slowed after four minutes.

The trout was a good one, and it saw the boat and Mac's hand reach into the water and made a strong dive for its life to the bottom of the lake. The drag made another clicking whirr, as the fish went under the canoe. That was the only sound on the lake, as a light breeze began to pick up. The sun was over the hills, and Mac thought this day needed to start moving. But he had this issue on the end of a five-weight line to deal with. "Ah, you little bastard!" He was getting angry at this trout and remembered to keep his temperament harnessed. No angry, jerking-pole fisherman ever landed a good trout. He moved the rod to the front of the boat, tip still held high, and the trout swam out to the right side of the canoe. He could handle this fish on the right side, he thought. He took a series of reels and brought it up to the surface where it was played out and exhausted. He reached under the belly of the two-foot fish and hoisted it into the canoe.

The fish was beautiful with the bright reds and greens of these native trout in Québec waters. He held it into the sun and then away from the sun, admiring the wild artistry that had been a gift to him this morning. He knew he could have it in his mother's fry pan by tomorrow morning or maybe even eat it now with his friend, Liam, who he had just skunk-eyed. He nodded to the morning sun for giving him such a glorious look at this fish, which he gently lowered into the light-reflecting water to swim away.

Mac paddled the canoe back to the dock in front of the camp.

Then he checked the lines on the airplane and walked to the cabin. His day had been completed with the fish; now he just had the work of a pilot and criminal ahead of him.

Liam had watched the entire catch-and-release through binoculars from the window. He hugged his friend as Mac came through the door; Liam was not the hugging kind of man. He had made a friend for life and admired his skill and qualities with this small gesture. It was just after 7:00 a.m., and they had to prepare the passengers for flight. Mac motioned for Liam to go outside of the cabin. There had to be some discussions about the day's events and how the men were to be treated and what the procedures would be.

"We have to remember what Jackson said—that these pricks are to never get a break while they are in captivity. If we soften up, they may try to escape or overtake us. We'll slip them some sleeping meds, when they take a drink before the flight. Handle them firmly and rough. Jackson will get in touch with Buckshot to let the wives know about the early pickup." Liam nodded and then said, "Whatever you say, Sam!" Mac scowled at him.

Liam helped Pierce to his feet. He was a weakened man; the poison of the black-fly bites had taken a lot out of him. The rough treatment, the cold double-cross and lack of food mixed with the medication had made him a walking vegetable. He struggled to follow, as Liam led him to the outhouse and gave him a small tube of hand cleaner.

"Next I am going to give you some fruit. Don't speak, nod if you can eat apples, bananas, or oranges." Pierce nodded at all three menu items and Liam released him into the outhouse.

When they returned to the cabin, Liam placed several peeled orange slices, apples slices and a peeled banana on a paper plate and held it up so Pierce could feed himself. The black fly welts covered his face, neck and arms. His face was swollen again beyond recognition.

Liam fed him all of the fruit with two granola bars; the captive was famished. Liam believed that they had made a mistake about the starving of the prisoners for two and a half days. He shook his head at Mac in concern; it would be awful if Pierce died. Jackson had been clear that if anyone was dead or close to death, that the person would not be brought back to the States. The plan was to kill them and drop them in the big lake, weighted with the weapons in five hundred feet of water. Liam shuddered at the thought that this was premeditated, for sure. Where was the famous honor among thieves? he wondered.

He covered William Pierce with more After Bite and aloe; the man sighed with relief; his breathing had less panting, got more balance. Liam gave him a bottle of water and another tablet of meds. He had become the caregiver for this broke-ass billionaire, weakened and desperate to breathe. The clothing was beginning to stink from urine and poor outhouse cleanups. Liam wanted to clean him up, but Mac shook his head no. He was chained back down in the holding room. He began to tremble and shiver when the chains were jangled.

Both Mac and Liam grabbed King and started along the same procedure. They held him firmly and jerked him along the path to the outhouse. King could not help himself; he had to make a deal with his kidnappers. "I know you two are alone now, and I want to make a deal with you both. I have other monies, and you can be rich beyond your wildest dreams—if you join me. Leave the other guy here; I don't think he'll make it anyway. He was breathing very hard last night. He will die, and then your little robbery becomes murder. It's not too late for you two to make this all OK. You played that sucker like pros last night. Now you're with Ortiz, but out of your depth. You think your money is safe with the master banker. Try moving something from your accounts. You'll need Ricardo's say-so. You'll need me to leverage your wealth. Oh, he'll be polite with his conditions. But you're worth nothing where you stand. I'd bet my life on it—"

Liam tripped King to the ground and stomped on his chest.

⋈

The airplane had enough fuel for five hours of flight, and the flight was four and a half without any headwind. If the wind blew over twenty miles an hour on the nose of the airplane, Mac would find he and his passengers seventy-five miles short of their destination and out of fuel. When they crossed the border, they could climb to altitude and text Jackson to meet them in Greenville with cans of fuel. They had discussed this briefly before Hannah and Jackson's departure. It would be another chance for trouble, and Mac was hopeful that it need not be done.

Meanwhile, Buckshot moved slowly through the woods, quietly, smoothly. Without crossing a road or driveway, he came upon the camp that King had rented for the weekend. He had his sniper rifle with the silencer, a small pistol in his boot, and a 9 mm pistol in a shoulder holster. He was delivering the updated message of the pickup time and place.

Dowd was sitting on the picnic table outside the camp with a cup of coffee and a flying magazine. Mrs. King was still in bed after a night of rough sex play. They both were tired. They had spent a minimum amount of time with Naomi and most of the time twisting the sheets up in the rented cabin. He had a plan should King still be alive and a preferred plan if the prick were dead.

Crack! his coffee cup shattered, and he jumped up reaching for the automatic tucked behind his blue-jean belt.

"The next one goes straight through your ear." It was definitely a Southern accent, Dowd thought, a deep Southern country accent he had heard in the Navy. He placed the gun on the table and put his hands in the air. Buckshot stepped from his position on the edge of the wood line and tossed King's watch, bloody tracking device, cell phone, and wallet onto the table. "There has been a change in schedule, Mr. Buddy-Fucker. You and your friend upstairs are to pick up Mr. King at the end of the Echo Lake road at a spot that is marked with florescent orange paint on a large pine tree. He will be dropped off, and you are to take him straight to the airport and fly out of here tonight. No calls to anyone but flight service to file your flight plan and complete the fueling. We will be watching every minute; King has his instructions as well. Nod so that I know you understand me. While ya'll been getting your little stinger wet in that cabin, Mr. King has decided to return alive. I'll bet you're pretty happy about that, jet jockey."

Dowd nodded and waved off at the same time.

Buckshot had seen Navy Seals use the same sign, chuckled to himself, and backed slowly into the woods. He made his way across the lake and through the woods to the other camp rented by William Pierce and wife, Alexis. He spotted the Mercedes SUV parked in the driveway. There were no signs of other vehicles. She had followed her prepared schedule to the minute. She had spent time with her stepson and apologized for Pierce's absence. Buckshot texted her to come to the door with her hands in the air and walk to the front of the SUV. She obeyed.

"Hold it right there, missy—don't move, you have a gun pointing at your head. Now nice and slowly come toward my voice."

She was trembling. She'd had no idea she would become a target by marrying William Pierce. "I will do whatever you tell me. I have, and I promise I will."

Buckshot could smell her fear. "Your man is alive and coming back to you. Do you remember where the Chimney on Echo Lake is?"

She nodded her head emphatically.

"You go there to pick him up at 8:15 tonight. Do not get out of your Mercedes or call anyone. You take him to see his son for fifteen minutes, then call your pilot and get that plane loaded and out of here by 9:30 tonight. You understand me, girly?"

She nodded again forcefully up and down.

"Your man has done a good job these past few days. He is a little sick and will need some help. You convince him to stay with the plan, not just for tonight but forever, and you and he will be just fine. Now, you do hear me, missy?" Buckshot's voice echoed a tone of Southern threat that hit the woman to the core. He started backtracking and made no noise with his prosthetic leg. He was gone. The woman put her face in her hands and began to cry again. She cried for joy as she had learned that Pierce was alive.

೮೪   ೦ೂ

Mac was moving in his pilot mode, looking everything over twice. It was his nature only when it came to airplanes and flight to double-check. He pumped all of the floats dry. He checked the fuel for any water contamination. The oil and the belts were all part of Mac's pre-flight procedure. The airplane looked pretty ratty, but it was sound; the floats were tight, the engine strong, and the propeller new. He would take this airplane any day of the week, if he couldn't have a Beaver. The Beaver was gone, far away, but not gone from Mac's dreams yet.

Liam appeared in the door of the cabin holding King by the neck under a hood and by his bound hands behind his back. The captive was amazed at the size of the invisible hand that completely encircled his neck. Liam gave a painful lift to the arms, and they started to move slowly. Liam had mixed a sleepy-time cocktail for King and asked if he wanted a drink of water. King nodded, Liam turned him towards the cabin and lifted the hood. King drank most of the twelve-ounce bottle quickly. Liam moved him onto the dock and lifted him into the airplane. The man was light like a woman, he thought. He completed his binding and ratchet straps. He returned for Pierce, who was being handled with care.

"Mr. Pierce, if you do as we say today, you will live a long, healthy life; if not, you will be dead at the bottom of a very deep lake in another country. We want you to live; your traveling companion apparently does not. Are you OK? Would you like any more medicine? Water? Any food?"

Liam was caring much more than Jackson would want him to for this captive. He lifted the hood off Pierce, who nodded and said softly, "I am better, please don't kill me, I need to see my son, I will be a better man, just some water, and maybe another pill." The swelling in his face had gone down considerably.

Liam's dyed black beard was beginning to show grey roots. His hat was pulled low, covering most of his face and sunglasses, more out of guilt than caution, with the memory of abruptly ending the Irishman's jig. *A treacherous act*, he thought, *no better than an imperial thug*. But he walked the captive to the aircraft and cinched him into position. King was sound asleep. The plane was secure and loaded.

Mac knew this takeoff would test all of his piloting skills; they were 1,600 feet above sea level and overloaded by at least 250 pounds. The wind was good and facing the departure off the lake. Mac hit the fuel pump and the starter key; the propeller sprang to life. The airplane surged forward in the water, taxiing into position.

He steered with his feet mechanically connected to the floats' water rudders. The rear spreader bar was slightly underwater, indicating a heavy load on board. He wished that Liam weighed fifty pounds less. He went into the weeds, where he knew he would be able to use the entire lake for a takeoff run. The weeds grabbed at the floats and rudders.

He pulled the lever to raised the rudders and advanced the throttle to the wide-open position. He tried to push it another half inch, but the throttle was at the end of the stop—the plane was moving way too slowly out of the weedy end of the lake. He had eyeballed a tree at the three-quarter distance down the lake and promised himself that if he was not off the water by then, he would shut down, back-taxi, and try it again. The 185 was just coming up to the step and planing out when he passed the tree. He pulled the throttle back to idle and hauled the stick back into his lap. His palms sweat wet, he wiped them on his pants. The takeoff had failed.

"Liam, I want you to slide your seat back, reach way back, and pull all that weighs anything out of the baggage and put it on top of those men. We need to change the center of gravity for this airplane in order to make it fly. Then you pull your seat up as far as you can—and keep those gomey size-fourteens out of my rudder pedals!"

Mac laughed and nodded at his friend. Motoring back for take-off, Mac knew that the airplane would create some ripples, and therefore the suction of the water to the floats would break easier.

The weeds had cleared from the first try; the plane got on the step earlier. Mac was watching his airspeed indicator: 35 knots, 40 knots, 50 knots—the plane was almost ready to fly, but the trees and the shoreline were approaching fast. Mac pulled on another notch of flaps and rolled the windward side float out of the water. The plane arose slowly like a fat goose that had overeaten in the morning feed. It was climbing slowly, and Mac picked a spot between two trees to climb out through. The airplane and its passengers, baggage, and fuel had just made it out of the small Canadian lake. Mac's hatband was soaked. Liam was frozen in astonishment. Mac looked straight ahead, scared and relieved to be airborne.

The engine had been redlined, and the temperature gauge was climbing. The propeller was supersonic and making a whining noise that had caused all the loons to dive deep. The water had rushed off the floats, as the boat became an airplane. Mac quickly adjusted his trim, raised the flaps, and set the craft up to cruise low and fast. He had avoided his first potential disaster of the day; the flight home had begun.

The party flew west over Lac Manicouagan and south down that giant water body in northern Québec. Mac lowered the airplane and reduced the power setting. He added two notches of flaps and continued to come closer to the water, as if to land. Liam had grabbed the bag full of weapons and electronics. Mac had GPS'd the location, and they were now over the deepest part of the lake. Liam pushed the door open as he had practiced and threw the bag over the side of the floats. There wasn't a boat within fifty miles of the plane. The black bag went to the bottom of the lake. Mac added the power back in and climbed a little. He was glad that it hadn't been a weighted body that had just gone out the door. They had practiced that as well.

His route coming from Maine had been low and fast, following the rivers, lakes and seaways to avoid any radar surveillance. Now he had to make up some time by flying GPS direct. If he followed the route home that he had flown coming up, he would run out of fuel. The visibility was good, and he chose to follow a direct route to the Saint

Lawrence Seaway. It could save him twenty minutes, he calculated. He adjusted the throttle and the propeller to the fastest cruise and lowest fuel consumption. He needed to save another twenty minutes between New Brunswick and Echo Lake, in order to make it home. There were over five hundred miles of flying distance in the problem now facing the pilot of the 185 Cessna. Mac was figuring fast on a calculator.

He began a list of places he knew, where they could camp out for the night in the North Woods. Places where no one would be around and where the plane could land and depart safely. Liam held the plane level in flight with the yoke and felt more needed and important than he had in years. These were real friends that he had made, even the man from the South, in the bushes, would fight for him. He was happy, confident and at the controls of the aircraft. Mac had a large map of northern Maine laid out on his lap. He was making notes with a pencil and planning; he was a man always planning, dreaming.

It was all coming to a head now. They had crossed the Saint Lawrence and the passengers were resting quietly. Mac hoped that Jackson had gotten his text about Pierce seeing his son. He hoped that his horoscope was good today; he hoped that three things would not go wrong and that Nora O'Donnell was wearing a Kelley green dress on the CBS Morning News. He reached into his pocket and felt the Saint Christopher medal and remembered the smile on his older daughter's face when she had given it to him in Saint Peter's square at the Vatican. He hoped that she would call him more. He leaned the fuel right to the edge, keeping the rpms at their best performance setting. The flight was up and down, hills and valleys, but exactly straight on the compass heading. He would intercept the Saint John River in twenty-six minutes, according to the GPS. He hoped that the fuel gauges were correct in this new aircraft that he had not much flown. He hoped that the fish he had released this morning would double its weight and he could catch it and bring it to his mother next year. If he wasn't in prison, he would have so many hopes and dreams to make real. *Just get through this day*, he thought, and gave Saint Chris another rub.

It was four in the afternoon, and they had entered the United States of America. The visibility was still good. Liam was indicating he had to pee. Mac reached for the Johnny pee bottle behind his seat and Liam relieved himself at 125 knots, engine screaming south over the Allagash River.

Then Liam texted Jackson, who was pulling into his driveway in Fayette. Hannah was checking her emails and posted a picture on Facebook of Jackson reading the Kennebec Journal on the deck of their porch. Jackson had alibis for all.

Buckshot looked both ways and crossed Route 17 in front of Jackson's home. He had been on foot for the last two hours covering thirteen miles through the woods as a silent stalker. He busted into the kitchen. "Do any of you Yankee bastards carry any cold beer in this place called Ma-aine?"

Jackson and Hannah both hugged him, and Hannah pulled the top off a Shipyard summer ale from the refrigerator. Both men had mission stink on them that caused Hannah to wave her hands in the air and point them towards the outdoor shower that Jackson had built. "Don't come back in this kitchen stinking like BO and bug dope." They went to the shower, one man sitting outside handing the other the cold brew.

Later, Jackson and Buckshot in fresh clothing loaded gas cans into the pickup truck they had to take it to the Chimney and fuel the plane directly after it landed. Mac would have to move the plane to Lovejoy and hide it in the cove, away from his dock.

Now at the head of Moosehead Lake, heading due south towards Kineo Rock, the plane was an hour from home. And the fuel gauges indicated exactly one hour of fuel remaining. Mac shook his head and tapped them to see if they might be off a little. They were not. Cessna fuel gauges had lied to pilots for seventy-five years.

King was stirring. Liam reached back and loosened his ratchet and helped him sit up. "I have to piss, really bad. I may be sick, too."

Liam handed him the portable pee bottle that was not full and loosened his ratchets some more. King relieved himself with the hood still on. Liam had been taking Maalox pills on this trip; he reached into his cargo pants and put one into King's mouth and retightened the black hood.

The sky was becoming darker, and the clouds were coming in as the ceiling lowered. Mac had crossed over the town of Greenville with Squaw Mountain to the west obscured by cloud cover. He would have to fly to the Kennebec in Skowhegan and follow it to Augusta on the deck, "scud running," the old bush pilots called it. He was forty minutes from Echo Lake, according to the GPS. It looked as if the cloud layer would not go below one thousand feet, and he could make that flight in his sleep. He wondered if Rocky heard his airplane fly over. The radio was turned off.

Mac was never so glad to see Lovejoy Pond. He had to fly over it to land on Echo. He spotted the black Escalade parked in the right position on the Echo Lake Road. He was running on the left fuel tank which indicated the most fuel remaining. He banked the aircraft over the ridge line behind the girl's summer camp and pulled the power back. He raised the nose of the aircraft; the airspeed indicated under 80 knots, and he pulled on two notches of flaps. He nodded to Liam to prepare to dump King into the lake.

Liam released the ratchet straps. King's feet and hands were still tied. Liam reached down and cut the leg ties. "Can you swim?" he yelled at King.

"Yes!"

"You will be swimming fifty yards to shore. Do not look back. The only thing that you will see looking back is my rifle aimed at your head, and that will be the last thing you will see. If you need a life jacket we will put one on for you."

Unsure of the altitude of the plane, King called out, "Please! Please don't kill me—let me live!"

Liam had lied; the rifle was at the bottom of a lake five hundred miles north, but he enjoyed King's sudden fear. It felt like a fraternity prank.

The plane landed on the water. It was slightly behind the trees and out of view from the Escalade and its two occupants. It was a smooth landing, and Mac was pleased the engine was still running. Liam stepped over his seat and freed King's hands. The airplane was taxiing slowly away from the shore. Liam kicked the door open and took King by the belt. With an unconscious show of strength, in a weight-lifter's jerk, he threw the hooded man into Echo Lake, tossed him like a bag of trash. Mac confirmed that King had removed the hood and was swimming. It was a slow stroke with his head just barely above the water. Neither Mac or Liam would return to save him; they had discussed it; an accidental drowning happens once a year in the lakes of Western Kennebec county. They did not wait to see if he made it. Mac advanced the throttle and broke water quickly. He was low on fuel and light one passenger. He had to fly the two miles up the lake to drop Pierce. Fuel and friends would be waiting. He gave Liam the thumbs up. The sky was darkening.

The tired pilot makes the mistakes. Mac forgot the two power lines strung from the summer camp to the island. They were stretched tightly with two small balls secured for pilots in seaplanes. He was flying the plane just off the water at high speed. The wires appeared in the windscreen. Dead ahead. He grabbed the yoke with both hands and hauled it back into his lap. They lurched skyward—just missed catastrophe, sure death for all inside the airplane. Mac had his reaction time back as if he were sixteen again. The float bottoms had brushed the power lines. The hat band had another sweat soaking. This was surely some sign, Mac thought, and swore to change his life after this deed. Liam was shaking like a dog pissing on an electric fence.

They flew straight in, so as to land at the Chimney boat launch site. Mac would not land into the wind as was customary, but downwind. They spotted the Mercedes SUV and its lone occupant. Mac wondered if there were law enforcement people in the woods awaiting him. He wondered if Kelley and Jackie were worried about him.

Liam prepared William Pierce for his swim at the north end of Echo Lake. "You can swim, can't you?" Liam knew the answer to the question. "You will have to swim thirty yards—can you do it?"

Pierce nodded. Liam removed the hood, so Pierce could gauge their altitude. They would drop him closer to shore than they needed. He and his wife were to depart immediately.

The airplane needed fuel; they were running on fumes now. Mac made a thirty degree bank turning over the northwestern end of the Echo Lake. The engine coughed and sputtered as the fuel was starved from the injection system. This had happened to Mac before with Cessnas and unreliable fuel gauges. He leveled the wings quickly, and the engine roared back to life. He talked out loud, "No steep turns, you stupid bastard! You have come this far—no steep turns."

They taxied toward the boat launch and cut the engine short of the dock. Liam opened the door, cut Pierce's ties hand and foot, and gently helped him step onto the floats. "Don't look back, Mr. Pierce. Do what you agreed to do. Your life will be long. You will be all right." Liam raised a heavy boot and kicked Pierce into the water. The latter began swimming like an Olympian toward the shore. His wife saw the drop and stayed as instructed in the vehicle. Buckshot turned his night vision on and watched through his scope. Jackson was watching through binoculars, proud of the way Liam had kicked the man into the lake.

Pierce hurried up the boat-launch ramp. His wife unlocked the door and he got in. He smiled at her and motioned for her to leave immediately. The SUV drove towards the summer camp. There was no conversation. He was glad to be alive; he didn't know if he would ever feel safe again. He was so glad to be alive. Why was he picked, of all the billionaires coming to Parents' Weekend? Why was he picked? Would he ever really know? he wondered, and all the dollars and cents, before or since, would never help him shake the lingering fear.

Buckshot and Jackson came out of the woods with headlamps on to fuel the airplane. Each man climbed atop the wing and dumped the fuel in the main tanks in less than five minutes. Liam watched for boats or traffic on the road. The caps were put back on the tanks, and Mac started the engine. He had a three-minute flight to his hiding spot on Lovejoy Pond, and he would be in his home in twenty minutes. He saw the prosthetic leg of Buckshot Peller, while the man fueled the pilot's side wing. He marveled and wondered if he would ever have such a friend. Buckshot and Jackson were closer than brothers; each would die for the other. What would he say to his wife?

Liam shook Mac's hand tightly and left with Buckshot and Jackson. The deed was done. The 185 roared into the sky to the south, home to Lovejoy Pond and his loving women. He watched for the wires this time.

In the Escalade, Gloria was acting shocked and concerned for her husband and kept asking, "What did they do to you, Roscoe!" She was working towards an Academy Award with her tearful concern. What she really wanted to know was if Roscoe had lost any of her shared fortune. That was it—not a speck of real concerned emotion.

King had no reply. He needed to leave this place now and return to the city. He would deal with her and Dowd later. He had no one to call, no one to speak with. He was still scared for his life. He smelled like urine and human stench. He told Dowd to get that plane in the air, pronto. "I want to be on the ground in Westchester County—in an hour."

Dowd thought he could shoot the bastard right now and blame it on the kidnappers. But there was no trace of the criminals. So Dowd handed the boss the watch, wallet, and personal locator bloodied two days ago. King grabbed them along with his mobile device in the center console. He looked up the number for the FBI. But as they drove by the Fayette Country Store, he spotted two men dressed in camouflage getting out of a pickup truck. He kept his eyes on them, and Dowd drove by slowly. The boss threw the phone back in the cup holder. He too was glad to be alive, and he wanted to stay that way—alive.

Mac walked into his kitchen. His wife and daughter were reading to each other, each playing the role in the Mo Willems book about the pigeon. "Hey Daddy! I missed you—did you catch any fish?" It was the voice he wanted to hear so badly.

"Hi honey, Good trip? I heard you fly over. The weather is getting bad, huh?"

Mac hugged them both and gave each an extra squeeze. He had shaved on the banks of the pond and washed the dye out of his hair in the lake. "I got an extra good tip today." He smiled.

His wife returned the smile and said, "That is great, honey; I'm going to put the baby to bed now." She got up and walked away. Mac was glad she did. He did not want to answer any questions tonight. He texted Jackson with an OK and a question mark. The response came in seconds. "B on the way to Ga. All quiet here. Kids and Hannah sound asleep."

32

Next morning in the kitchen, Mac grabbed a bottle of Clorox from under the sink. Kelley, glowing, watched him while she drank a cup of coffee. "Projectile or seat-puker?" She had seen him do this a hundred times with the Beaver, cleaning up the vomit from some unsettled flyer.

He laughed and said, "Both!"

King had urinated on the carpet in the airplane as he slept from the medication. Mac spent a half-hour wiping the airplane down with the doors and windows open to air it out. He needed to move the plane early, so no one would see it on the Lovejoy. He did not need anyone to say to a cop, "Yeah! That is the plane I saw on Echo." He needed this 185 stripped and painted and on its way to Sweden in the next few weeks. This is exactly what Rocky had planned and the sale fit in perfectly with the crime.

Mac cranked the three hundred horsepower motor up and slow taxied out of the shallow cove. He came around the corner in the lake and through a narrow passage onto the much bigger part of Lovejoy Pond. He advanced the throttle, and the 185 popped into the morning air. So different from the takeoff the previous day. He turned to the northeast and headed for Greenville. He buzzed over his friend's home and saw Liam come out onto the lakeside deck and wave his long arms and big hands at the machine that had taken him so far. Mac felt pride in Liam's performance throughout, including his ability to function with Jackson and Hannah.

Mac McCabe had to have his game face on. He was headed to

negotiate with one of the worst Yankee traders he had ever encountered—on the preparation and purchase of his new airplane. The airplane that soon would be put into service for Allagash Air. Rocky had his feet on his desk, awaiting his next victim.

Hannah was up early piling up all the clothing and personal items she and Jackson had worn over the weekend into the family's backyard fire pit. Even the full-faced Jackie Onassis sunglasses and hat were getting burned. She grabbed her phone and texted Mac—"We all need to meet here tonight."

Mac got the text, flying over the Kennebec River above Skowhegan and wondered why she would be calling a meeting. She had never called a meeting, and this was a little brazen, he thought. He texted her back, "Not now."

By the time he had flown from Skowhegan to Greenville, his phone had lit up twice. Jackson had heard from his wife and was calling his brother-in-law. Mac ignored the calls and landed the plane on Moosehead Lake. He would get back to Jackson and not Hannah. Right now he had to do some horse trading with a shark.

Mac the dreamer who worked off lists and maps had a list of things he wanted in the new airplane. It currently had a fancy leather interior that would be trashed within a year with his clients and their fishhooks and tent poles. He wanted a utility interior installed with a removable fourth seat. He had given up so much weight and space with the selling of the Beaver. He had now become a two- maybe three-person flying outfitter and guide. It was a sad reality setting in for him to face. He so badly had seller's remorse, and now he had to deal with Rocky. He would rather be receiving a root canal.

Rocky looked at his target for the day, Mac McCabe, sitting in his office at the floatplane base in Greenville. "Whatever you need, Mac, for this plane, excluding a new Garmin avionics package, is fine with me."

Mac looked at him with a twisted glare, as if Rocky had been smoking an illegal substance.

"I would like those Wipline amphibious floats and will give you a great set of PK straight floats that are just like new.

"Sure Rocky, plus fifteen grand in cash to me. Are you going to be an asshole all day long? Should I come back after you have had some lunch? Or maybe tomorrow after you've screwed a few more people?"

Rocky broke out laughing and said that he would give him ten grand in trade for the amphibious wheel pontoons.

"OK," Mac retorted. "This is painful to me. I need this deal done today and that airplane in service next weekend. I want a fifty-hour warranty on that new motor; they have been having a lot of problems with the Continental cylinders. Rocky had already negotiated a hundred-hour guaranty with the factory. Mac was leaving fifty hours of operations on the table.

"The PKs are at the airport, and you can see them today. Whatever else you want, write it down and send it to me in an email." The meeting was tilting toward Mac; at least he felt that way. He did not feel $100 million richer. He felt he was still scraping pennies off the floor of Rocky's maintenance hangar. It felt familiar. And familiar was good.

The deal was done. It was noon and Mac would pick up his reconditioned 1978 Cessna 185 the following week for the sum of $175,000 cash. He still had a fund from the sale of the Beaver that Kelley had no knowledge of. It was the operations money for the kidnapping and robbery; he had not spent it all. He wondered if he would need a lawyer soon.

Rocky filled up the airplane he had loaned Mac for the weekend and muttered "What a dumb bastard" under his breath as Mac came out of the port-a-potty. He flew Mac back to Lovejoy Pond and his dock. There would be no airplane moored there that night.

Mac pushed the redial button on his phone. "What's up, Jackson? Any problem? Why all the phone calls?"

He could hear his brother-in-law stammer a little on the other end. "Look Mac, you are the leader of our little criminal escapade that went on over the past few months. Hannah thinks that she should get an equal cut and that maybe not all of the money should go for your idea—"

Mac stopped him in mid sentence. "If you want to change the rules now, Jackson, I'm not buying it one damn bit. We should get together right now, if you both want—" He took a breath. *Hold that temper,* he thought. "I'll get in touch with Liam, and we'll be at your place at seven tonight. I do not want to talk about any of this on a goddamn cell phone, copy Jackson?"

Jackson was a little embarrassed; he agreed to the time and place.

When Mac drove to their house, he had a small chip on his shoulder that he hoped would not grow larger with this meeting. Liam was already there, and Mac parked round the corner.

"Thanks, guys, for coming. I know you must be really tired." Hannah was running the meeting. The children were watching clips from Moosey Moose and Z on Apple TV. "I know that you brought me into this because of my demands, when I found you all out. It worked, just as planned. It was successful, and I think it was because of my work that it became successful."

Mac was beginning to steam, as he started to speak, even as Liam grabbed his arm. "Hannah you were an important cog in a wheel that went round. So were you, Jackson and Liam. We agreed on our endgame before we started. Hannah, you said that you would be happy with Jackson's share. You might think that the game has changed as well as the rules—it hasn't."

Hannah leaned forward. "Will you let me finish my thought before you interrupt me, Mac?" She was showing her own fiery spirit. Jackson was not good with these situations. He sprang up and pulled a six-pack of beer out of the refrigerator. He set it in the middle of his kitchen table. All grabbed one, save Mac. His arms were folded, and he was staring at his sister-in-law with disdain.

"Go ahead, honey, tell him your idea," said Jackson and popped open his brew.

"We got into this because of the paper mill and this town and Jackson's job. We have all learned so much more since our first meeting at the Chimney. We found more money than we expected with King's accounts. Hell Mac, you decided to give him an extra $500 million from the original plan."

Mac nodded. He was cooling down.

"What I would like is the same cooling-off period for our portions of this, but to allocate the difference in King's money to a fund, maybe a buyback for the paper mill, with a new ownership team. We'd spend that money in addition to Mac's health-care plan, of which you know, Mac, we don't all agree with."

Mac looked around the room. She had all the votes—that he could tell. Liam out of the blue said, "I think that Hannah should have an equal share, just like the rest of us."

Mac realized that like the bandits in the history of world crime, they were now haggling over the split of stolen money. It was the worst case that he could imagine and knew that nothing good would come of a bad fight within the group. In addition, he knew that Jackson was firmly in Hannah's court. "I am OK with Hannah's cut being fully equal. She earned it and will continue to earn it with her monitoring of those two pricks in New York. Your mill fund may be throwing good money after bad. Look at Lincoln, Millinocket, Madison, Jay and Livermore Falls, fer Chrissake. I think that Hannah should create her account out of King's extra money. I'll sign electronically tomorrow. We are not moving the money to the health-care fund until this fall. Let's not see each other at all for a month, maybe longer. What we have just done is a change of our original agreement and the rules. Money does not do good things for people, except pay their larger bills that they create. I heard a Stephen King quote the other day: 'Rich people are boring like dried-up dead dog shit.' Let's not be these people. Keep your thoughts to yourself and don't write them down. We will lay them out at the picnic table when the leaves begin to turn."

Encouraged by a little buzz, Liam was quick to philosophize in his own Yale style. "This piece of American history will go down as the Greed Age. Great creators of wealth will be destroyed by continued unchecked lust for more, more, more. We have been given a gift of our own design, and we should think of a long-term goal for this money and our work. We could create the new paradigm for wealth in America. I think Mac's idea of a Wall Street, single-payer system for New England and America is folly and will turn us into insurance financiers. Single payer has to be government run, like in Canada and other countries, or not at all. It's like the military—defense against disease. We're not mercenaries, making money off the sick and the elderly. Mac does have passion, however, and that is what caused us to rob these men. Passion, and vengeance. America needs passion, and we have some—the four of us together, all of us! Let's never turn on one another, and let us all think with the power of a God-given, creative mind." *Wherever the money may be*— He kept the thought to himself, including a quick paraphrase from Orwell's *Animal Farm*, as he looked at his coconspirators: *"They looked from pig to man and man to pig . . . it was impossible to say which was which—"*

The four thieves looked at one another and nodded in agreement. Mac was surprised and proud of what his friend had just said. But he wished that Liam had spoken to him about Hannah's cut in advance. He knew that the moment had to cool down, and heads of a lower temperature would prevail, especially his.

The group opened more beer, and Jackson complimented the team and said it was a great performance and execution of the plan. They toasted in unison, "In memory of Mr. B, departed Dummy of the Lake!" Liam yelled out nervously.

Mac would not look at Hannah. The tension had diminished but was still swirling lightly in the air. They were cleaned and shaven. The hair was grey, brown and blonde; the eyes were blue and green; the meeting was good; the air was clearing. Mac would meet with Hannah in the morning to sign and create her own account. He would resolve their differences with a night's rest behind them. The children were giggling in the living room.

33

J oe Dieter had not received the text that he had been looking for. He was a new man with a new mission. He had gotten some new Wall Street-type glasses and colored his graying hair. His office had new furniture and had been painted. There was a new Keurig coffee system, and his office space had a sparkle to it. There were interns from Bowdoin and Bates, along with business majors from USM and medical professors from UNE holding constant meetings and think sessions. A new life had come to this old liberal icon of health-care policy. It was late August, and he had been awaiting a phone call from an old friend. He was getting nervous. Had McCabe started drinking and was just leading him on with false hope? The Irish were known for being filled with empty unending hope; he had studied the history of Ireland at Harvard. If you added alcohol it became the unending centuries-long strife and revolution, so the British said, according to conventional wisdom.

It was Monday August 17, and the late summer air would soon begin to cool. Joe had been arriving at work early with his newfound mission. He walked up Congress Street as usual, and there on the step was the man leaning against the building with the same old oil-stained flight jacket and a cup of Dunkin Donuts coffee in hand.

Joe knew he was here to tell him that it was all a hoax; he looked the same, run down and beaten. Joe had a crisp, white shirt and on with a new Brooks Brothers tie and jacket. "Spiffy Mr. Joe! I have something for you—" Mac even had aviator sunglasses on.

Joe unlocked the office. Mac smelled as if he had been under the

Beaver changing the oil and filters. "Do you have the money, Mac? I've done it all. Everything we discussed back in that dingy Bath pub. Every stone's been laid. Do you have it?"

Mac looked at him and the office and the motivational posters on the wall. "I like what you've done with the place." He wasn't dressed for business, but business was what he'd brought. "I have $400 million for you and will deposit it on Wednesday of this week. Let's go over what your plan is and talk about the infusion of cash, when you will need it, and how it will be managed." Mac swirled his coffee cup idly. No dollar in it this time.

℃ ℅

Hannah begged Mac to go to the islands; he would love that Ortiz was sending his Gulfstream to the Augusta State Airport. Mac said it was too soon to meet with him. He needed money moved to Patriot Healthcare tomorrow, and he would go to the islands after Columbus Day in October. After they had the foliage meeting of the partners at the picnic table by the Chimney on Echo Lake, Mac would consider talking to the man holding the money in the islands. Mac thought that Hannah did not understand one thing about him. And the fact that Ortiz would send a Gulfstream to Augusta, Maine, to pick him up— actually turned him off more than she could ever imagine. He was getting on well with her now, but she would never understand him. He didn't want to be "rich"—she did—she was showing it now, and it was distasteful to Mac. She figured he was just turning out to be an inverse snob.

Jackson was going along to snoop and find out why Ortiz and Svetlana really wanted his wife to work so closely for them. He was distrusting to the core when it came to Hannah. He thought she had very poor radar as to the things people wanted from her. He suspected this from seventh grade when she began developing breasts and grew to five foot nine. Boys, he believed, were impure, and they grew into bad sniffing dogs around beauty and brains. He had proven unconditional devotion and love to her for over thirty years now. She knew why he wanted to go to the islands.

Mac took Jackson aside the day before they left. "You know that the pilot of the jet will have to make out a manifest, and your names will be on it. Ortiz is watched by every financial regulating entity in the

Free World. I cannot restrict what you and Hannah do with him and his friend. I really wish that you would both lay low for at least a year before you start some mission with him. You will call the government hounds just by being associated with him. Talk to Hannah about this, Jackson. Convince her to work from home, and watch her cyber-games. Have you seen all of that NSA stuff?"

Jackson looked at his brother-in-law, who was already trying to move hundreds of millions of dollars. Who did he think he was? "Have you told Kelley, yet?" Jackson's sister had many of his deepest secrets, from boyhood to his war years. He hated keeping her in the dark.

"I have not told her and will not until I know that we are free and clear of all of this criminal activity—probably in a year and a half."

Jackson snorted in disparagement.

"If I am arrested," Mac continued defensively, "I want to make sure that she can say without equivocation that she had no knowledge of this entire crime. You and Hannah will raise your profile in a very bad way by traveling on that jet. We have already shown up on some radar screens from our past visits with Ortiz, I'm sure of it."

Jackson hated taking advice from Mac, but he knew Mac was right with this particular bit, if only hypocritically.

"Three trips in one year to the Cayman Islands—you must really like the place." Mac watched himself turn sarcastic. "This is what I would do. You and Hannah cancel the jet today, make commercial flight plans. Have Hannah email a realtor near the low-rent area of the island and set up showings for you. You have now fallen in love with the place so deeply that you are going to own a small vacation home there, put a small amount of money down and have a thirty-year mortgage. The home will be a throwaway in a few years. Create some cover for yourself. Take the kids, travel to Cuba. Hell, you're a war hero! Don't screw this up, Jackson! Don't put a bull's-eye on your back. I'm sure there's been one there before—" Mac stopped himself.

Jackson looked at his in-law partner-in-crime and let it pass. He had accepted that Mac was correct in his assessment of the situation, even though the pilot couldn't see his own folly. "OK, I will call Hannah now."

She was not happy; she had looked forward to walking up that air-stair on that $30 million jet. Maybe one of her friends from high school would see her boarding like Angelina Jolie. She thought that Mac was

a son-of-a-bitch—hadn't they worked out their differences together!
But she did exactly what Jackson said. She called Lana and booked
flights out of Boston. First-class seating only. She imagined herself
on the Gulfstream. After she put down the phone, an unwelcome
question crept into her cunning mind: Why would the maestro Ortiz
expose them in such high-profile fashion? Was it an oversight? Were
they being suckered as newbies with the idea of routine jet-setting?
Was Ortiz setting the hook with the Mainers as bait? With a smile, she
cursed Mac for his smarts. *Or is he just a superstitious paranoid bush pilot?*
She was more determined than ever to enjoy the trip.

෫   ෮

Kelley was a chatterbox and full of questions, when she picked up
Jackson and Hannah, back from the Caymans. She could have easily
been a detective in a different career choice. She had wonderful instinct
for human nature. Especially regarding wandering-eyed men, she had a
sixth sense. There was something up with Mac. Even after he sold the
Beaver, he just could not stop rolling in bed and talking in his sleep.
She believed the uneasiness was caused by guilt and that the two birds
sitting in her SUV this day both knew what was wrong with the man
she loved. Hannah had always dished the girl-talk, complaining about
men, their bad habits and behavior. In the past few months she had
been shelled up like an oyster, not saying a word about Jackson, Mac
or any man.

"So how is your business going in the island, Hannah? Who are you
working for? What are you doing? Do ya like it there, brother?" She
banged on the steering wheel as if to say, *I want answers now, goddamnit!*

"Well we have bought a little house there, Kelley. It is super cute
and has two bedrooms and a foldout couch, and all furnished to the
nines."

Kelly looked at her sister-in-law in amazement. "You what! Hell,
Mac and I were worried about you making your mortgage payments
on your home last summer. Jackson, did you get a new job? What are
you people up to?"

They assumed she included Mac. "Well you have heard about
that VRBO, haven't you, honey? When you rent your own vacation
property out on the internet?" Hannah was backtracking fast with Ms.
True Detective sitting in the driver's seat. "We bought this place to rent

out and visit a couple of times a year. Jackson loves the beaches and the snorkeling. You and Mac will love it too."

Kelley glanced over at Hannah, who was poised in semi-high-fashion attire. "Yeah right—"

Jackie put down her iPad long enough to chime in, "I like to snuckle, Aunt Hannah!"

They arrived in Fayette all bottled up in the SUV. Kelly still did not have the answers she was looking for. She would continue to probe her husband; he was bound to crack. She knew if she wore the Lucky jeans she had just bought and that tight tan Ralph Lauren sweater and the thin-heeled, four-inch Cole Haan boots, she just might get enough information out of Mac to piece this puzzle together. He would be like putty in her hands. These two she was dropping off were like a dry well, all hole and no water.

Mac was gathering firewood among the trees around his property. The local wood cutters were dropping off five cords of tree length to be cut, split and stacked. The winter of 2014–15 had been the worst in decades. His family had run out of firewood for the second year in a row. Five cords would get them through the '15–16 winter for sure. Mac liked the exercise. He would use a splitting maul for some of the logs, and he envisioned ancient Celtic war games and the beheading of foes as he swung the heavy, weighted axe. The routine of the swing felt familiar. It felt good.

There were a few more trips for the flying service this fall. Mainers liked the late September river-and-lake fishing. Fish colored for the fall spawning were beautiful in Mac's eyes. He never killed a fish in the fall, male or female. They all went to place the thousands of their eggs to compete in nature's lottery for life—fish life. The Cessna 185 had proven to be what Mac could use adequately for the smaller numbers of sports he was carrying. He would of course long for the Beaver, the smell of the puff of smoke, the size, the performance. No matter what airplane he was flying, he would always be the same Beaver pilot he had been for two and a half decades.

His head was full of the future now. It was full of proposed meetings and spreadsheets and projections about health-care costs and negotiations with doctors, hospitals, and testing labs—things way outside his area of expertise. He had a plan, as always, a dream of the amount of time he would spend with this "one good thing." Five years for the startup in New England, three years to the initial public offering to shareholders on Wall Street, and ten to see his dream go nationwide.

It had been about two months since Parents' Weekend, and no one was at his door or his brother-in-law's. He saw Liam once a week for coffee and quiet, small, laughing conversations about their deeds of the past summer. Neither of them would ever do anything like this again, they assured each other, ever so often, even as they remained impassioned about injustice and inequality. They both had settled into the patient wait for two years to pass, for the money to cool, with the exception of immediate transfers of wealth to start up the health-care company, somehow exempt, unchallenged in dreamland.

Mac saw Jackie playing with a toy airplane on the steps. It was a model of an old Beaver on wheels that he had been given as a present twenty Christmases past. He sat on his deck and looked at the woodpile. It looked like a lot of work on this bright sunny day. He took a short nap and was awakened by his daughter making airplane noises around his head with the toy plane.

He grabbed her and hugged her and kissed her ten times on each cheek. She giggled from being tickled. "Do you know what is wrong with your airplane sweetie?"

"No Daddy, what?"

"Your airplane does not have floats on it." He pointed to Jack Weston's Super Cub tied up ahead of the 185. "That one does—do you want to go fly it?"

"Yes Daddy," she said, "I want to go cloud busting!" She pointed to the puffy clouds hanging in the fall air. Mac had taken her through the clouds on sunny days when she was in kindergarten. Now she was a first grader and wanted to do it again. She would yell through his headsets. "Do it again Daddy!"

Mac peeked around the corner to make sure that her mother had gone grocery shopping and placed the little girl atop his shoulders. They headed for the Super Cub tied to the dock, awaiting a pilot and his passenger, a father and his devoted daughter.

Mac put a life preserver cushion in the pilot's seat and realized that he would need two for his daughter to see out over the instrument panel. He would fly the tandem-seat Cub from the back seat, and give his daughter the best view out the window. The airplane came to life on the first crank of the starter. *Jack has such a fine airplane*, Mac thought. He was a true friend who would have loved this adventure and crime of the past summer. The cub was in the air with the two occupants in less than six seconds of water run. Jackie would reach down and move the stick as she saw her father move it around from the back seat.

They climbed through 2,500 feet above sea level and started to spot some puffy white clouds at their altitude. "There's one daddy— bust it up!"

Mac was in a wonderful place. He had true happiness and the wonder of his first own flights through the eyes of his daughter. He could see her reflection in the windscreen, the smile, the eyes so wide and full of joy. They flew all over western Kennebec County that afternoon, for an hour and a half. He landed with his daughter holding the controls as he guided it in for a smooth landing on the water by their home. So smooth was the landing, without the slightest bump.

He taxied toward his dock and saw his wife standing there with her hands on her hips. She was building up an attitude as only she could; he had taken Jackie flying without telling her mother. That was cause for trouble in itself. Maybe she was angry about something else. The closer he got the more he could see she was wearing new jeans and the tan Lauren sweater that he loved, with the high-heeled Cole Haan boots. She could never be mad at him in that outfit. As he got closer, the red from her hair color was shining in the sun, and a smile appeared on her face. She was a beauty standing on his own dock next to his own floatplane. This was going to be a good Saturday night.

Kelley scowled at Mac for a second and helped her daughter from the pilot's seat. "You two have been cloud busting, haven't you?"

Jackie was so proud of herself. "Yes Mommy, and I am a pilot now. Daddy let me bust the clouds myself, all by myself."

All three walked hand-in-hand up the dock to the home on the Pond. The evening was filled with freshly harvested food, wine, and spirited talk about the school year to come and the neighbor's daughter's wedding coming up. There were no questions or inquisitions from Kelley. To Mac it was fine evening in the country, in the fall air in Maine. The night ended early. The sky was clear.

Mac thought about a meeting he'd had that afternoon with his coconspirators and all that they had done together. This paper mill restart would be good, if it all fell together. He was happy with his brother- and sister-in-law. He had come to know them so differently as individuals. Jackson had had that one additional item he wanted to bring up at the meeting; he'd raised his hand as if to make a parliamentary motion: "This is way off the charts, but I need to say it. Liam never even met him, but my friend Buckshot was here covering our bases while we were in Quebec. He has no idea what we did; he just did his job without asking any questions. I plan on giving him a million dollars of my money when the two-year cooling period is over. Would any of you others like to kick in? He would never want a penny, and he will pick up and help us if I called him tomorrow. He is the best friend that I could ever have, and he is the godfather to our son." He nodded to Hannah.

Mac had spoken up. "His help was invaluable. The shot off the hood of that vehicle was a game changer. The apple exploded like a man's skull. We will all gain five percent interest in the interim, according to our banker." He nodded with a hint of swagger towards Hannah. "I'll kick in a cool million."

Liam was feeling so jolly and welcome in this successful group of billionaires. "Me too." The commitment of a crime had left all of their heads.

The group had laughed and enjoyed the venison burgers and cheap wine and good Maine beer. They had their lists and things to do for the hopeless mill deal, rebuilding the dependency of a town, instead of a community of small businesses, farms, some street life. But just like before, they were in sync with one another, an inner circle, now forever changed, warped, enlivened and empowered, all at once by the miracle of boundless wealth hard-won. Mac thought that the Chimney table might have some magic. Kelly had stopped her house chores and wondered where he was and with whom.

The fall sky gave color to the western sunset. Brilliant color, he thought, so much more than the other seasons and past equinoxes that had been the comings and goings of seasons without any significance in the painted sky. Kelley was still wearing the red shade in her hair; she knew that Mac loved the red-haired beauty that he slept with every night. She would at least do this for the man who had sold his most beloved earthly possession, the de Havilland Beaver, to someone three thousand miles away. It seemed to Mac she would always give away more than she took.

He fell into bed that evening and went straight to sleep without a word to his wife lying unclothed next to him. She looked at the ceiling and the light coming off the lake in the full moon. She still did not know about the kidnapping and robbery. She thought happily of life without debt and new school clothes for Jackie. Mac rolled to his side facing her and felt her next to him in the most intimate of places. He was dreaming deeply. He was now banking around the mountain, flying his old Beaver over the small pond. The sun was shining, and a dream smile appeared on his face. He was peaceful and loving, and the plane was in flight, and he was the flyer; he flew on through the night.

———————————

Patrick K. McGowan was born in Bangor, Maine, and raised in Somerset County. He learned to fly at the age of sixteen and began a lifetime of adventure and backcountry bush flying. Inspired by his home state, a place of magnificent beauty, he began a public service career, which included being a legislator, presidential appointee, and member of a governor's cabinet. He has owned and operated many small businesses over four decades.

His drive for continued adventure included ten years as a skydiver, forty years as a floatplane and backcountry airplane pilot and multiple Maine canoe trips. *One Good Thing* brings his public service, floatplane adventures, and love of storytelling to the public in this first novel. He campaigned for single-payer health coverage in a congressional race in 1990 and has never given up on this bold idea for America. McGowan is an accomplished conservationist.

The father of four lives in central Maine with his wife Kirsten and daughter Amelia. His alma mater is the University of Maine at Farmington. He is currently the president of PK Floats, Inc., an aircraft float manufacturing company in Maine.